Critical Acclai[...]
A[...]

TIME FOR ETERNITY

"The he[...] Squires'[...] story of[...] revolutio[...] across ti[...]

"A roma[...] combines time travel, vampirism, and a bygone era into a compelling and original tale…Squires has created one of the most mysterious and appealing vampires since Lestat."
—*Romantic Times*

ONE WITH THE DARKNESS

"Superb writing, vivid narrative combined with complex plotting, and intricate characterization make each novel by Ms. Squires an absolute winner. Don't miss this exciting chapter in this unique and captivating vampire series."
—*Romantic Times BOOKreviews*

ONE WITH THE SHADOWS

"Full of colorful characters, romantic locales and vivid details of 1820s life, [*One with the Shadows*] has a delicious pace and plenty of thrills, and her vampire mythos is both mannered—almost Victorian—and intriguingly offbeat. Bound to net a wide audience of paranormal fans, this one may even convert devotees of traditional historicals."
—*Publishers Weekly* (A Best Book of the Year)

ONE WITH THE NIGHT

"Superb...captivating...With her usual skill and creativity, Ms. Squires has crafted a novel that is passionate, heart-breaking, suspenseful, and completely riveting."

—*Romance Reviews Today*

"Few writers combine a sensual romance within a supernatural thriller as well as Susan Squires consistently does. Her latest is a terrific Regency vampire romantic suspense starring two courageous heroes battling one hell of a meanie."

—*Midwest Book Review*

"This is an incredibly unusual take on historical vampire stories. Susan Squires delivers an exciting story."

—*Fallen Angel Reviews*

THE BURNING

"A terrific tale...the story line is action-packed."

—*Midwest Book Review*

"Blazingly hot and erotic." —*Romantic Times BOOKreviews*

"Marvelously rich, emotionally charged, imaginative, and beautifully written."

—*BookLoons*

"A fantastic erotic vampire thriller." —*Fresh Fiction*

THE COMPANION

"A darkly compelling vampire romance...the plot keeps the reader turning the pages long into the night."

—*Affaire de Coeur*

THE MISTS OF TIME

Susan Squires

St. Martin's Paperbacks

This is a work of fiction. All of the characters, organizations, and events portrayed in this novel are either products of the author's imagination or are used fictitiously.

THE MISTS OF TIME

Copyright © 2010 by Susan Squires.

Cover photographs:
Stonehenge prehistoric stone © Harald Sund/Getty Images
Golden Gate Bridge in fog © Richard T. Nowitz/Corbis
Man and woman © Shirley Green
Cover illustration © Don Sipley

For information address St. Martin's Press, 175 Fifth Avenue, New York, NY 10010.

ISBN: 978-0-312-94355-4

Printed in the United States of America

St. Martin's Paperbacks edition / September 2010

St. Martin's Paperbacks are published by St. Martin's Press, 175 Fifth Avenue, New York, NY 10010.

10 9 8 7 6 5 4 3 2 1

Prologue

Jails were always either too hot or too cold. This one was too cold. Jenna Armstrong pulled her sweater around her. The barred door clanked open, sending echoes through the gray hallway, and Kracken pushed out. The shrink looked disgusted.

"She's all yours," he muttered, holding a handkerchief to his forearm. Long bloody scratches disappeared under the handkerchief.

"Diagnosis?" Jenna called after him.

"Homicidal maniac," he threw back over his shoulder.

"That's not a diagnosis." How a child psychologist could be so bad with kids she'd never know. She gave an apologetic smile to the matron who waved her in. As a social worker from Child Protective Services, she was a frequent visitor to the juvie lockup.

"Good luck with this one, honey," the uniformed woman said, shaking her head. Her iron hair matched the surroundings.

Jenna flipped open the arresting officer's report again and once more tried to make heads or tails of it as she walked, her steps and those of the matron echoing down the corridor of cells. Shouts and cries and mutterings from the occupants of the other cells reverberated, making it almost impossible to think. Witnesses said the girl "fell off a roof onto the street" in front of a convenience store. There was no ladder and no one knew how she got onto the roof. She kept everyone who tried to help her away by waving a big knife. The convenience store owner called the police. Three officers got the knife away from her only when she passed out. Both officers and patient made a detour through the ER over at Cook County. They tranq'ed the girl to examine her. No broken bones. Hadn't been sexually assaulted. She was released with a mild concussion and stitches. But there was nowhere to take her. She didn't respond to any questions about who she was or where she lived. The officer said the little girl spoke a language he called gargley. But no one had yet identified it. Unless she was tranq'ed, she was so violent the only place they could take her was back to the juvenile lockup until they could get an order to get her into a mental hospital. Jenna was sure Kracken was on his way to do just that.

Great. One of those. Glancing up, Jenna found herself in front of the "homicidal maniac."

Jenna had never seen anyone so frightened in her life.

The report said the girl was thirteen or so. Maybe. She was skinny, with big blue-gray eyes, translucent, pale skin and light brown hair in a long braid. Escaping wisps gave her a halo of sorts. She was dressed in a long-sleeved straight dress to her ankles of some rough fabric with a kind of a long, straight jumper pulled over it. She wore soft leather boots that looked homemade. Maybe she was from one of those crazy families who lived in the wild, expecting Armageddon. She sat on the bunk, pushed up against the wall, her hands behind her.

"Thanks, Mabel," Jenna said as the matron unlocked the cell door. "Why don't you leave it open? We'll probably be heading over to the children's interview room."

The matron raised skeptical brows, but she shrugged

and left. Jenna headed into the cell. "Wait! Mabel?" The matron stuck her head back into view. "She handcuffed?"

"You're darned right," Mabel said fervently. "Did you see Kracken's arm?"

"Leave me the key to her cuffs." Jenna held out a hand. At Mabel's doubtful look, she said, "My responsibility."

"Your funeral more likely." But Mabel handed over the keys. The girl pushed herself even farther into the corner. Jenna crouched in front of her.

"Hey," Jenna said. "I'm the social worker." That didn't make an impression, though it wouldn't if the girl really didn't speak English. Maybe she was not connected to reality at all and the language she spoke was entirely made up. It happened. It had been almost twenty-four hours since she'd been arrested. Dark circles hung under her eyes. She was exhausted, and ready to shatter into a thousand pieces from stress.

Jenna didn't touch her. That might set her off. Jenna held out the hand with the key in it and raised her brows. A thousand thoughts raced through the girl's eyes as she considered the offer. Her breathing started to come fast and shallow. "It's okay," Jenna soothed. "It's okay."

At last the girl nodded once in decision and scooted out a little so Jenna could unlock the cuffs. The girl's wrists were chafed. These weren't the first cuffs she'd had on. "Poor thing," Jenna muttered. She tossed the cuffs aside and sat back on her haunches. She smiled and touched her chest. "Jenna." Then she nodded encouragement and gestured to the girl.

After a long pause, the girl whispered, "Diana." Then the walls she'd built around herself shattered. She cried hard, racking sobs. Jenna took her in her arms and rocked her.

Diana sat in the white visitors' room. It had been nearly a month since Jenna had first seen her in that cell. She was dressed in conventional clothes now, her braid fresh and neat. She'd been living in the temporary holding facility for runaways. Jenna couldn't bear to send her into the foster-care system, fragile as she was, when she *must* have parents out there somewhere. Jenna had combed the missing-persons reports, going back six months and a year, to find families who might have lost her. Her first name seemed to be the only thing the girl could remember, or the only thing she'd say aloud. Her fierce rebellion had slowly disappeared. Violence had been replaced by withdrawal. She was afraid of even common things such as toilets and television. It seemed to take all her courage just to face new situations. Jenna had come to care for her, more even than she usually cared for the runaways or children taken from their parents for neglect or abuse who came through the system. Maybe it was because Diana kept mustering the courage.

"Some people are coming to see you."

Diana understood the language. It had taken a week or two for Jenna to be sure of it, because the girl didn't speak. Not ever. She sure understood about families coming to look at her. Now she held herself still, as usual. But Jenna could see the tiny flame of hope there in her eyes. Jenna knew what she was thinking. Maybe the people would know her this time. Maybe they had lost her and she would be found. Maybe she had a home, familiar and safe, somewhere.

Jenna motioned the couple in. The woman who came through the door had been crying. The husband loomed behind the woman. Jenna found herself hoping nearly as much as Diana must hope that recognition would light their faces. It was the husband's expression that shut down first. It took the woman longer. But finally, the woman collapsed in tears of disappointment. Her husband held her in his arms.

Jenna ushered them out. "It's okay. I'm sure you'll find your little girl."

Jenna turned back into the sterile visiting room and saw Diana's hope flicker out. Jenna took a breath and managed a smile. Time to stop putting the little girl through this. It had been going on too long already. Jenna sat beside her. "I thought sure the piece in the newspaper would help us find your family." She sighed. "But I know there's someone out there who doesn't have a little girl who is just waiting to love you." Jenna put an arm around Diana and squeezed.

Diana was now officially an orphan. And she was about to go out of Jenna's life forever.

Chapter One

The machine that lowered the casket into the ground made a grinding noise. They really ought to oil the mechanism. Fog rolled in as the light faded. Diana pulled her black wool cape tighter around her shoulders. Spring in San Francisco still seemed far away in March. A guy waited in a small tractor-thing to scoop dirt back into the fresh grave over by the huge camellia bush, maybe fifty feet away from her parents' grave. Indoor-outdoor carpet was draped over the excavated pile, as if that would camouflage the finality of dirt.

She looked down at her parents' brass plaque, now three years old. They were together finally, but she was entirely alone. Would she ever find for herself the love they'd shared? *The fact that you adopted me is the reason I can write romances. I knew two people who found love.*

Diana heaved in a breath and pulled her eyes away from the simple plaque. She turned and sloshed down the slope. Her car looked lonely in the visitors' parking lot. Fitting. She'd always felt . . . separate. Maybe it was because she didn't know where she really belonged, since she didn't remember anything before she was thirteen. Or maybe it was because she had . . . well, to be kind she'd call them quirks. Like being able to find things that were lost and hearing what people would say just before they said it—not what they were thinking, just what they would say. What use was that? It was like living inside a constant round-robin song. And she couldn't reveal it or people would think she was crazy. She'd never told anyone, not even her parents. The secret as much as the noise built a wall between her and the rest of the world.

Sliding into the driver's seat, she closed her eyes, hugging her shoulder bag. Her life was getting beyond her control. She couldn't even write anymore. She had only twenty-five pages done on the novel that was due next month. The whole thing made her want to rip her hair out. Much as she loved the setting of Camelot and her hero, Gawain, the romance just wouldn't come to life. She'd give back the advance and call it a day, but the money was already gone. She was still paying off the last year of nursing-home care for her father. Happy endings seemed to be in short supply right now, fictional or not.

She put her shoulder bag on the passenger's seat beside her. The priceless book inside had been taking up more and more of her thoughts. It was by Leonardo da Vinci.

Yeah. *That* da Vinci. She'd be set her for life if she sold it, but her horror at even the *thought* of selling the book made the word "obsession" seem inadequate. She carried it around constantly, unable to bear even leaving it at the apartment. Okay. As long as she was admitting things, she slept with it. But sometimes it seemed that book was the only thing that was real to her anymore.

Whoa. Obsession over a book, writer's block. She had to admit she'd been depressed. All on top of her little natural proclivities . . . she needed a therapist. As if she could afford one. Unless she sold the book. But she probably couldn't sell the book without some serious therapy. Well, *that* was circular.

She took two deep breaths and started the car. Okay.

Time to go home to her little apartment just east of the Mission District. Unable to help herself, she reached over to touch the book. The way it had come into her life was a little surreal. . . .

Diana had been coming out of the office at the Explor-atorium, the children's science museum where she super-vised docents, when she practically ran into the family. The woman had very green eyes and very red hair and that translucent, perfect skin that goes with them. Her baby bump was just beginning to show. The little girl was a paler version of her mother. The father was a looker. Anything in range with a female hormone was casting surreptitious looks at him. He ought to be standing at the prow of a Viking ship, preferably stripped to the waist.

"Closing time," Diana announced.

The Viking's next words echoed in her mind: "We'll just stop at the restrooms before I take my two girls home." He gathered the little girl into one big arm and took his wife's elbow protectively.

The woman took one look at Diana, gasped, and slumped against her husband.

"Lucy, are you all right?" The Viking hauled her in against his free hip.

Diana guided them to a bench beside the door marked with a large sign that read: Danger. Keep out.

The little girl was worried. "What's wrong with Mommy?" she asked in a small voice.

"Nothing, honey," the woman called Lucy managed as she eased down on the bench. "Mommy didn't eat enough at lunchtime." She clutched a large shoulder bag to her chest.

The Viking's gaze swept the area. "Can you look after Pony?" he asked Diana, setting the little girl on her feet. "I'll buy a mug at the gift shop and bring some water."

Diana grabbed Pony's hand, and the Viking strode away. Pony. Odd name, but cute.

The woman examined Diana's face. "Have . . . have you been a docent long?"

A connection sparked between them. Did Diana know her? "I'm actually a supervisor. It pays the bills while I wait for my ship to come in."

"And what exactly would your ship look like?"

Diana mustered a smile "Well . . . I write books." She looked up to see the woman's expression of sympathy. Everybody and their brother was a failed writer these days. "Oh, I'm published," she assured the woman. "But it doesn't come with health insurance or a four-oh-one (k). City of San Francisco provides those."

"What do you write?"

Now she'd see the flash of derision or the uneasy shifting of the eyes. "Romances." Did she sound defensive? "I write historicals."

Not even a hint of eye rolling. Emboldened, Diana continued. "Right now I'm researching Camelot. I think it was the origin of courtly love." She sighed. "That was the time to live." She couldn't help the longing that drenched her voice.

Lucy gave a sharp intake of breath. She looked as though she'd just had a revelation. The Viking strode toward them with his cup of water, a worried frown creasing his brow. The woman smiled, first at him, and then at Diana. A look Diana could only describe as sureness suffused her expression. "I have a gift for you." She hauled a very large leather-bound book from her bag and handed it to Diana.

"This . . . this is old. I . . . I couldn't take this." The tooled leather binding was beautiful.

"Of course you can. I'm giving it to you just as it was given to me." The woman glanced to her husband and

*stilled what Diana was sure was an incipient protest with
a look.*

*Diana opened the book gingerly, scanning the pages.
"It's written backward."*

"Yes. It's in archaic Italian and Latin."

*Diana frowned. "I have some Latin, but I'm afraid I
don't read Italian."*

*"You can get a translation from Dr. Dent over at
Berkeley. He'll authenticate it." The woman rose, looking strangely serene. "I'm feeling fine. We can go." Diana caught her husband's pointed look at the* Danger
*door. "I've done what I came to do," his wife assured
him. The woman pressed Diana's hands. "Use the book.
It will change your life. And when you're ready . . ." She
leaned forward to whisper in Diana's ear. "Look behind
the door."*

*Diana drew back in shock, then glanced to the door
marked:* Danger.

*"Yes. That one." The woman smiled. And then she
and her family strolled out into the San Francisco fog.
The whole scene looked like the fade-out happy ending to
a movie.*

Diana jerked her head around as a car honked and sped
by on her left. Once she'd read Dr. Dent's translation, Diana knew what Lucy thought was behind that door. The
very fact that Diana could half-believe it must be a sign
that she was going around the bend. The book was a hoax,
even if it was a hoax by Leonardo da Vinci.

The manuscript recorded Leonardo's effort to build a
time machine. It said he succeeded.

There was a picture on the last pages, after all the dia-
grams and calculations and all the scientific stuff she
didn't have any hope of understanding. In the illustration the machine seemed to be just a bunch of gears.

Appropriate for 1508 when the book was written, but not exactly the kind of thing that could manipulate the time/space continuum.

It would be easy to check it out. As a supervisor of the docents she had a set of master keys. But in the five months she'd had the book she'd never used them on the door. Opening it, thinking there might be a time machine behind it, seemed like crossing some line toward insanity.

Like it wasn't crazy to carry the book around all the time. Or to sleep with it.

Okay. A little crazy. But it was like the book was shouting at her now, where before it had only whispered. That made it harder to think clearly. Still she wouldn't believe a time machine was hidden in a children's museum.

Oh, hell. If she didn't believe there might be a time machine might behind that door, why had she brushed up on Latin? Because that was what they spoke in Camelot as a second language to Brythonic Proto-Celtic? Because she *wanted* there to be a time machine behind that door and she wanted it to take her back to Camelot, to a time when things were simpler, when anything could happen and people believed in love and magic and honor. As she researched her newest novel she'd grown to feel like she belonged there, and she, who had no childhood, wanted so *much* to know where she belonged.

Her chest heaved and she couldn't seem to get air. She glanced over at the book. It exuded hope. It seemed to push at her, like maybe it could make her happy, like the red-haired Lucy said it could, like maybe deadlines and obsession and loneliness were what was unreal and there was some new and wonderful reality just waiting for her.

That was dangerous. Sanity was knowing reality for what it was, no matter how stark, and learning to cope with it. If there were no machine that could change your life behind that door, then she'd be able to go home to her empty apartment, make an appointment with a therapist at some free clinic, and face her future.

So she knew what she had to do.

She was going to the Exploratorium tonight and look behind that door marked: *Danger.*

Diana parked in the front lot, close to the museum entrance. The fog was a blanket down here near the bay. The ornate colonnades that lined the path to the Rotunda of the Palace of Fine Arts loomed to her left, the angels on the capitals looking more like gargoyles in the mist. The Palace had been restored a couple of years ago for the umpteenth time, on this occasion to make it earthquake proof. Originally built for the Panama-Pacific International Exhibition of 1915 as a temporary building, it had never been meant to stand the test of time. Excavations to install the reinforcing struts had revealed a basement of sorts, a secret room now buried again to protect the earthquake infrastructure. Diana pulled out her keys and unlocked one of the front doors. The beam of Clancy's flashlight caromed over the cavernous ceiling. He was about to call out to her.

"Hey!" he called. "You're here late."

She managed a nervous grin. "Forgot to post this week's docent schedule."

Clancy had a gut on him, but his perpetual frown, lurking among his jowls, hid a kind heart. "Can't have that." He grinned. "But, Ms. Dearborn, you got to get a life."

Wasn't *that* the truth? Her face fell. If only she knew how.

She heard his words, of course, before he said them. How kind he was about to be.

"Well, you don't have to get one right this minute. You

take your time." He must have seen her expression. "I'm due to take a turn around the outside. I'll escort you to your car when I get back."

"Thanks, Clancy."

He turned out toward the rank of double glass doors. "Don't you open these doors until I get back," he warned.

She gave a little nod. Clancy would be gone for half an hour at least. She checked her watch. Three minutes past seven. Standing in the entryway to the exhibits, she watched him push through the doors and cast his flashlight through the wall of fog. She spun on her heel. The exhibits were silent now. The machine that mimicked waves was still. The simulated geysers were cold. Work lights in the back cast a harsh glow that barely illuminated the shapes of the exhibits that marched off into the darkness. The mezzanine that housed the aural and biology exhibits loomed over her.

Best get this over with. She made her step purposeful as she strode past the gift shop, its dark recesses crammed with souvenirs. She clutched her bag with the book in it to her chest. She didn't have to read the personal instructions to someone named Donnatella in the front pages. She knew the translation by heart. The note said . . . that time was a vortex. That you could think of another time and the machine would . . . would take you there. *Oh, right, and how was that?* And that the machine couldn't stay in the new time forever. It would slip back to its point of origin. There was the little slip of paper, almost like a bookmark, that gave the sequence of the switches to flip on the power source. There was a dire note from someone named "Frankie" that said you shouldn't ever meet a former version of yourself because you couldn't both exist at once. Both of these were recent and in English.

The door loomed before her. *Danger. Keep out.*

Danger, all right. She took a breath. Best get it over

with. She glanced back to the entrance. Clancy was no-where in sight. This door was on the side of the museum next to the Palace of Fine Arts. Maybe something to do with the construction?

She pulled out her key ring and sorted through the keys. *Damn*. Her hands were shaking. She held up her ring by the master key, the rest of the keys clinking for attention. Then she descended on the lock. The book almost hummed with excitement inside her bag. The very air around her seemed to vibrate with expectation.

The door was heavy but silent on its hinges. Diana peered into the dark passage that sloped slightly down-ward. She flicked on the little LED light attached to her key chain. The corridor was lined with unfinished dry-wall. The floor turned from cement to rough boards. She stepped inside, her steps echoing. The boards gave way almost immediately to packed earth.

The door behind her slammed shut. She swallowed, trying to push her heart out of her throat and back down where it belonged. That door better have a handle on the inside. But she wasn't going back to check now. If she stopped now, she might lose her nerve.

Her eyes got used to the illumination cast from her tiny light. A black gap yawned at the end of the corridor. She stood on the edge of that gap and held her light out. Several metal girders set at angles loomed out of the darkness.

Earthquake reinforcements for the Rotunda. She must be directly below it in that basement they'd discovered. She cast her light around. Other struts jutted at crazy angles out of concrete roots. She ducked under one and around an-other. It was like a maze, smelling of metal and damp from the lake beyond the Rotunda. She was so absorbed in mak-ing her way through the forest of metal girders she was surprised when she emerged into an open space.

Something gleamed dully in the darkness. She held her little light above her head.

Her lungs grabbed for air.

The gears were bronze or brass or something, a thousand of them, big and smaller and really tiny. And they were set with jewels. Some were really, really big jewels. Red and blue and green and . . . and diamonds. They coruscated under her tiny light. The machine must be fourteen, sixteen feet tall. It disappeared in the darkness above her. Stabbing out from the center was the control lever she'd seen in the illustrations, ending in a diamond bigger than her fist.

Leonardo's machine was real.

And she just knew. She *knew* that the Viking-looking guy was really a Viking from long ago and the woman, Lucy, had gone back to get him and changed her life with this machine. You could make these gears and jewels take you through the vortex of time just by thinking about a destination. The book inside her shoulder bag seemed almost jubilant.

Diana put out a hand to the nearest girder to steady herself and took some deep breaths. Then she examined the machine more carefully. A modern steel box about the size of a lunch box sat at the bottom with several switches and lights on it and a big steel button like the kind you pushed with your palm at traffic lights. That hadn't been in the illustration. But the instructions on the bookmark mentioned switches. She hauled the book out of her bag and took the slip of paper out, shining her light on the spidery handwriting: "Blue, then the two whites from left to right, twice, and then the red. Push the big button. Then pull the lever down."

This was the moment. She could see Arthur and Guinevere. She could see Gawain, the hero who wouldn't come to life in her current work in progress. She could be infused with that "one brief shining moment" and come back with a tale to tell. She might be renewed.

It felt right. Very, frighteningly, *right*.

Her parents were dead. She had no friends. In the end what did she have to lose? Nothing.

She knelt beside the metal lunch box with the lights and switches. Her hand had stopped shaking. She flipped the blue switch and a blue light came on. *In for a penny, in for a pound*. She flipped the switches in sequence and palmed the round metal button. The machine stood silent.

Wait . . . was that a hum from the lunch box? The hum accelerated rapidly. It screamed up the scale until it disappeared. She scrambled over to stand in front of the three-foot brass rod topped by the diamond.

"Okay," she muttered. "This is it." She grabbed the diamond and pulled. It moved about a foot. Nothing happened. She put her weight into it. It slowly descended. The big gear in roughly the center of the machine began to turn slowly. Smaller wheels spun into action. The machine came alive. The diamond vibrated under her hands. Power hung in the air like a coiled spring waiting to be released. The tension grew almost unbearable in her chest. Whirring gears assaulted her eardrums.

Don't faint. Don't faint. Think of the time you want to go to. Suddenly the myriad jewels seemed to light from within, sending colored beams careening around the ceiling. The machine leaped into brilliant focus. *Okay. Okay.* She tried to calm herself. *Camelot. Back to the time when everything was possible.*

The machine slowed until all was still, as though even time had stopped. Disappointment drenched her. How stupid had she been to believe this was all true?

A scream of power tore through the room. She couldn't breathe. The gears all spun into action almost instantly and she had a feeling of being flung forward, like a slingshot, as her body tore into a million pieces under the stress.

Or maybe it was her mind. The past was dark . . . black even . . . then nothing.

Chapter Two

Diana heard herself choking before she was fully conscious. She waded her way up through eddies of fog, the kind that only came to San Francisco in January. But when she opened her eyes, no fog enveloped her. She was lying in the middle of . . . where? She sat up slowly and her head ached. . . . A ragged circle of standing stones marched around her. The machine loomed above her, quiescent. Stars blinked in the black velvet sky she associated with deserts or mountains, away from city lights. More stars than she had ever seen were dusted across the creamy swaths of organza that were the Milky Way. The only light was a sort of orange glow off to her left.

My God. Where am I? She surely wasn't in the basement of the Rotunda anymore. She gasped for air and scrambled to her knees, looking around frantically.

Smoke filled her lungs. Coughing, she turned toward the glow. She and the machine were in the open at the crest of a hill crowned with the huge circle of stones.

What have I done? How could she have been so rash as to just take a time machine back to God knew where? *Get hold of yourself,* she thought sternly. *Just get back. Start the machine up. . . .* But what if this was actually Camelot? Shouldn't she just take a look?

She glanced around but didn't see anybody threatening, so she took a couple of tentative steps toward the edge of the circle of stones in the direction of the glow. The slopes of the hill were covered by woods. In the valley below, across a broad river, buildings surrounded by wooden palisades were burning. Tiny figures clashed in the meadow in front of the gates. Horses reared. Swords gleamed red in the light from the flames. People staggering under packs of their belongings streamed through a cluster of huts toward the river, dodging swords and hooves.

She clapped her hand over her mouth in excitement. This wasn't a reenactment. This was actually a city from a really long time ago. She was a time traveler! Maybe it wasn't magic, but it was close. Even as she watched, wind swept showers of sparks like a swarm of hellish insects to the near side of the river. The fire flickered and took hold in the grass. It swept toward the woods on her hill. *Uh-oh*.

But this palisade and its few poor wooden turrets couldn't be the legendary Camelot. She knew not to expect the crenellated towers of the Medieval drawings. But this? Maybe the Camelot that provided the proverbial shining moment was yet to be completed and this was some primitive precursor, long before Arthur and Guinevere were born.

Her visit might be short, no matter where she'd landed. The fire was gaining momentum as it hit the brush of the forest. Flames chewed their way up the hill, leaping from treetop to treetop. She had to get out of here.

She knelt and began to power up the switches again, but before she could complete the sequence a man and a boy ran up through the standing stones.

Diana jerked back, her eyes widening.

They were dressed in jerkins and leather leggings. The man, maybe a little past middle age and clean shaven, was big and rugged, with dark hair. He could be called handsome, with those cheekbones. She could see little more in the dark. The boy was gangly, all elbows and knees, at the age when his joints still seemed put together with rubber bands. One couldn't miss the resemblance between the two.

Both had eyes only for the machine. As they came closer, the father held up a hand. Glowing sparkles danced in the air and formed themselves into a ball that cast brilliant light over both people and machine. Diana gasped. The man's eyes were piercing blue or maybe green, proof that there had already been some Nordic stock intermixed in the local population. Still, light eyes would be really unusual in this time. The color of the older man's eyes seemed to shift and change as he fixed her with a gaze so powerful, it shook her right down to her ankles. She tried to calm her breathing. *Okay.* Sparkles and changing eye color. Magic *was* possible here.

The boy tore his own light eyes from the machine to ask his father, "Is it magic then?"

"Mayhaps," his father muttered, studying the machine. "Or it may be the work of men."

"Not any men we know," the boy snorted, his eyes still wide with wonder.

Diana understood it, at least pieces of it. And they weren't speaking Latin. Assuming she had actually come back to Dark Age Britain, it must be . . . Brythonic Proto-Celtic. How could she understand even a word? She blinked at them, her mind frozen.

"Is she a goddess, or a witch?" the boy asked. "Her clothes are not like ours."

She swallowed and said slowly, "I am neither," picking the words from her memory. Her breath came fast and shallowly. This was the language she'd spoken after they found her wandering in Chicago, before she'd learned English. Her eyes filled. What did this mean?

"She speaks our language, Father!" the lad said in the same tongue. He was brave in the face of what must look like sorcery to him.

Her brain clicked into gear as she stood there blinking. No surprise the social workers in Chicago hadn't recognized Proto-Celtic. How had she not known? But it wasn't a language you just happened on, like the Old English of *Beowulf.* She'd never seen anything written in it, never heard anyone speak it. While it sounded vaguely Welsh or Gaelic or something, it . . . it wasn't.

She spoke *Proto-Celtic?*

"Who are you?" the father asked her. She hadn't known what he would say. The boy, either, come to think of it.

"I am Diana Dearborn," she said carefully. The words came easier now, as if the language had been lurking inside her, waiting to flow. "I come from the future time."

"And these metal wheels brought you here?" the man said, putting out a reverent hand to touch the nearest gear. He set the sparkling ball of light free and it floated near his shoulder.

"It looks like a mill, Father, only more finely wrought, in metal."

"I, of anyone, should know that time is not linear. Space, either," the man murmured, caressing the jewels. She didn't catch all of that. He glanced back over his shoulder at her. "I have seen you in my scrying pool. Not in the full flower of womanhood, but as an untried girl."

"You . . . you know me?"

He smiled, and it was as though the clouds that foretold rain raced across his eyes, making them a swirling gray. "I do not. I only know you are important."

Her? Important? The man was mad.

"Is . . . is this Camelot?"

"Oh, aye. Or was." Those two words held all the sorrow in the world. He shook himself. "But we must face the future without it now." He turned toward the woods and waited.

A crashing sounded in the underbrush and a man stumbled into the clearing between the standing stones. He had a fierce face, with a jutting nose and sharp angles. He was dressed for battle, with linked chain mail over a leather jerkin and greaves of hardened leather on shins and forearms. He carried a sword almost as tall as he was, and he'd been using it, to judge by the blood on it and on him. Some of it was his, leaking from a slash on his upper arm just below the short sleeve of his chain mail. His dark hair was plastered to his head with sweat.

"I've been waiting for you," the man with the strange-colored eyes said.

"You know why I'm here," the newcomer panted, his palms braced on his thighs. Diana was shocked to find she couldn't predict what he would say, either. Had her curse entirely disappeared in this time? "With your support I can hold against the Saxon hordes. . . ." He trailed off as he seemed to notice the great machine for the first time. He was too exhausted to react violently, but he fell silent as he tried to understand what it might be.

"Yours?" the warrior asked slowly.

"Hers." The man with the many-colored eyes nodded to Diana. "It moves through time."

The warrior turned on Diana. He had paid her no more attention than the boy until now. His expression grew covetous. "To whom do you owe allegiance?" he asked sharply.

"Uh . . . nobody. I guess maybe to God." She'd never been particularly religious, but she'd tried to live her life by a moral code that a just God might create. You had to make a choice and do the best you could. So, she did owe allegiance to God, if there was one.

"A priestess of the gods," the warrior declared. "That is good."

The man with the shifting eyes just smiled. His eyes were swirling gold now, bearing no resemblance to human eyes at all. The boy, his brows drawn together, looked up at his father.

The roar and snap of fire was growing louder. Actual tongues of flame could be seen as drafts swept them up the hill. Wind created tendrils of hair around Diana's face. Somewhere, men shouted. Bodies crashed through the brush.

"Not much time," the warrior said to the man with swirling eyes. "Do you stand with me?"

"You threaten me with your troops? Not wise."

A flicker of fear flashed across the hard face of the warrior and was suppressed. "I am the future of Camelot, old man, if it is to have a future."

"That may be, but not by my hand." The man's eyes went to brown and his voice was kind.

The warrior frowned while the crash of bodies grew closer.

"He's here somewhere!" a voice shouted.

"He'll be in the circle of stones!" another called.

Voices came from two directions.

The warrior turned to Diana. "If he will not stand by me, you will have to do."

"Do what?" Diana trembled.

"Go back the way you came, young woman. You court disaster by staying." The father's eyes roiled with burgundy and orange now. Was that just the reflection of the fire?

"We've all got to get out of here," Diana cried. "If the soldiers don't get us, the flames will." She pointed. Fire had circled two sides of the hill. The clearing wouldn't save them.

"Well, then, your choice is clear," the man with the swirling eyes said.

Okaaaay. She wasn't going to argue. She knelt beside

the machine and, though her hands shook, she finished the power sequence. She couldn't hear the machine hum, but she could feel the heaviness of power in her lungs. She pulled the lever. The gears began to spin.

The warrior let out an amazed hiss. "Magic!"

A handful of soldiers crashed in a body through the edge of the forest, yelling, "We've got you now! Come with us!" The jewels began to send their sweeping beams of colored light in all directions. The soldiers fell to their knees, yelling in fear. The man with the swirling eyes hugged his son to his body. More warriors stumbled up from the left.

The hard-looking warrior yelled to the newcomers, "See what power I wield!"

The gears slowed. In the silence, Diana thought about March 10, 2010, San Francisco. She imagined the basement of the Rotunda. Behind her, soldiers staggered to their feet. Eyes rolled at the sight of the machine. But their attention turned back to the warrior, fierce and focused.

"You are a dead man," one said. Warriors from each camp surged forward. The fierce-faced warrior had a sword, but they had a dozen.

"Come on!" she yelled to the warrior. "If you want to live." What else could she do? She looked to the man with the many-colored eyes and his son, but the man shook his head. They weren't coming, and didn't seem concerned. Maybe the man's magic could protect him and his son from the army. Even the warrior who was the soldiers' target hesitated. She felt the gears begin to whir. The slingshot was pulling back. If he didn't come soon, his fate was his own fault. They'd kill him for sure.

At the last possible moment, he lunged toward her. His arm grasped her waist.

His shriek blended with hers as they catapulted forward into the future.

* * *

Diana hit the ground with a thud. After a horrible, wrenching attempt to breathe, she finally managed to gasp a lungful of air. This time the feeling of dislocation was not unexpected. She managed to keep conscious. She breathed in the smell of damp and metal and dirt. Relief washed through her along with the familiar smells. She was back in a place and a time she knew. Had she dreamed the burning fort and the circle of stones, the strange-eyed man and his son, the fire about to engulf them, the bloodthirsty soldiers? It all seemed so impossible.

She opened her eyes on blackness, wishing for even the feeble LED light now. She felt around in her immediate vicinity, but no light materialized. Instead she encountered the soft leather of her shoulder bag around Leonardo's large folio book.

Someone groaned.

Oh my God. What was she thinking to bring back a guy from Dark Age Britain? Bring him back or condemn him to death, those were her choices. All those thoughts about a moral code and what a just God would require had fueled her foolish impulse. What if she'd changed history?

Was that really Camelot? If so, who was the man with his son? Who was the man she'd saved? Could it be Arthur? He'd said he would unite the Britons against the Saxons. Who else could do that but Arthur? But in that case, what soldiers would be bent on his death? Maybe Mordred's. Her brain reeled. She pushed her confusion aside. They had to get out of here.

"Are you all right?" she asked, then realized she had spoken in modern English. She spoke again in the older language. The fact that she knew Brythonic Proto-Celtic was absolutely frightening. She couldn't fit that fact into any kind of coherent whole at all.

She heard him push himself up with a grunt. "My head

thunders." It was so strange that she didn't know what he would say. Welcome, but strange.

"We will get you to a healer." She reached toward the groan. Her hands encountered metal links. "Can you stand?"

"I am a warrior, woman. I can stand." The voice was clipped and gruff. "Where are we?"

She settled for the location. Any other explanation would have to wait. "In a cave by a lake. My home is near." She felt him getting his knees under himself. He rose gingerly.

She felt behind her and encountered the slick metal teeth of the time machine's gears. *Okay.* She turned. The corridor must be straight ahead. She felt her way carefully forward. Her companion settled for following in her footsteps. Metal clanged on metal.

"You brought your sword?" she whispered.

"How not, woman?"

Great. She couldn't get him the medical help he would need if he was carrying a great big sword around. What they'd both get was arrested. "Best leave it here."

He stopped following abruptly. "I will bring it."

She blew out a breath. He was in a strange place where he probably felt embattled. Okay, they could put it in her trunk. "Bring it. But quietly!"

There was a slither as he sheathed it. Now she'd find out whether there was a way to open the door to the Exploratorium from this side. She extended her hand but felt nothing. That was actually good. She waved it from side to side and slapped the wall of the corridor. Halfway home. They were out of the maze. "This way," she said.

The cool metal of the door met her hand. Carefully, she felt for a bar release. Nothing. Okay, a lock. What she encountered she didn't understand at first. It was a narrow metal rod with a flat pad at the end. It took her a moment to realize it was like the release on the inside of a walk-in freezer. She pushed at the pad and the door popped open.

After the utter darkness of the cave under the Rotunda, even the work lights of the Exploratorium were shocking. She squinted and held up her hand, peering around. No sign of Clancy. She checked her watch. Seven twenty-four. She'd left Clancy at three minutes after the hour. What with the time it took to start the machine, she'd probably disappeared at seven-twenty or so. The machine had come back to the second after it had left. She glanced back to her companion. He was a handsome man, she supposed. His nose was a sharp blade, his eyes the dark of a Celt. His hair was cropped short in the Roman style, reminding her that in the days of Camelot the Romans had only recently abandoned their outpost in Britannia. But her fifth-century guy didn't look healthy. His complexion was sallow. Dark shadows hung under his eyes. He needed a doctor. He was staring around him with a furrowed brow.

"I'll explain everything." She shut the door and locked it with her master key. "But we have to go before the guard comes back." She led the way past the gift shop and the information desk toward the glass doors. Her key in the box to the right silenced the alarm.

He touched the panes tentatively, running his palms over the glass. "What is this?" Glazed windows were unheard of in his time. He would have seen glass only in small bottles like the Romans made. There were wonders far more difficult ahead of him.

"Think of it as sorcery."

His eyes widened, then gleamed for an instant. "Magic, then."

She pushed open the doors and pulled her charge into the glare of the security lights over the parking lot. She glanced around for Clancy. Was that his shadow making its way down the colonnade toward them? *Uh-oh.* The shadow didn't have Clancy's paunch. As she watched, the figure emerged into the light.

Her stomach fell. She knew this guy, at least by sight.

Dark hair, fair skin, bulky shoulders. She might have been mistaken when she'd seen him across the lake as she came out these very doors the other day. He could just have been someone who looked like the guy who had pushed past her in the corner liquor store near her apartment.

But this time there was no doubt. It was the same guy all right. If he got closer, she'd see the gray eyes (or maybe green?) and classic features she'd glimpsed in the liquor store. Was he stalking her? *You can't stalk somebody if you look like the cover model for a romance novel!* she wanted to shout. *People notice a guy like you!* Women anyway. And while she might not be someone guys ever noticed, she was still a woman. In the liquor store, as his whatever-colored eyes had met hers, she'd experienced some thrill of . . . well, of the sort she only wrote about. Spooky, really. You couldn't be attracted to a man you didn't even know. Not like *that.* But it meant you'd recognize him when you saw him again.

A thrill of fear found its way into her stomach as she stood, frozen, in the parking lot. Why would any man be stalking someone like her? Romance writers occasionally acquired stalkers. The guys who wrote all those fan letters from prison sometimes got out. But she wasn't a big name or anything. She wasn't rich, and she wasn't beautiful. He just stood there at the entrance to the colonnade, the huge columns and the angels who crowned them dwarfing him. He looked . . . well, he looked as shocked as she did—even more than he did at the liquor store.

And he looked . . . familiar, somehow. She couldn't know him . . . and yet . . . it felt like she knew him more intimately than three sightings would suggest.

Get hold of yourself, she thought, panic layering on top of panic. *And get out of here.*

"Now is the time to show your courage," she said to her warrior as she tugged him toward the car. "This . . . This wagon is powerful magic I control." No word for "car" in Proto-Celtic. She fumbled for her keys and opened the door. "Inside." She glanced to the colonnade, but her stalker had disappeared. Had she imagined him? She raced around to the driver's side and jerked open the door. Scooting behind the wheel, she pulled the door shut and stabbed the key into the ignition. "An enemy is coming. In!" she ordered.

He examined her face for one long instant before he folded himself into the passenger seat and tucked his sword beside his feet. Its hilt was jammed against the roof of the car. The engine roared to life. He pressed himself back against the seat in fear and she thought he was going to dive out the door again. "Hold on," she said through gritted teeth. "We go." She threw the transmission into reverse and the Honda shot backward out of the parking space. The door banged open. Her passenger grabbed for the dash.

"Stop!" he yelled. She spun the wheel and gave it gas. The passenger door slammed shut. She swung left onto Bay and took two rights to get out to the light at Richardson. Luck was with them; the light was green. Glancing to her passenger, she saw him hanging on to the door with one hand and the dash with the other, his teeth gritted. But he wasn't yelling anymore. She checked the rearview mirror every few seconds, expecting to see flashing lights. A car honked as she changed lanes and cut him off. *Get a grip, Diana.* She forced herself to slow as Richardson turned into Lombard Street going through Cow Hollow. This part of Lombard was actually Route 101 through the city. There was too much traffic to be reckless. She scanned her rearview mirror again. No pursuit she could see. She turned right off Lombard onto Laguna, a much smaller street. Easier to see anyone following them. It climbed the steep hill up into the gracious houses of Pacific Heights.

She calmed her breathing and peered over at her passenger in the light of the street lamps. His eyes were big as he stared out at the brick houses, the apartments with bay windows that overlooked the Golden Gate behind them, the stoplights and the storefronts. What must this be like for him? He looked like he might faint, in spite of the grim set of his mouth that indicated his determination not to do so. Or possibly he was trying not to throw up in her car.

He *was* bleeding all over it. She could see the slick dark ooze over his chain mail.

Damn. He might die bleeding to death in the twenty-first century rather than be hacked to death in the fifth. She looked around her, trying to remember where the nearest hospital was. Pacific Heights. She was just passing Broadway. Pacific Medical Center was only a block over and a few blocks down. She hung a left on Washington, right on Buchanan. The hospital took up a couple of square blocks, if you included parking. A green sign signaled the emergency room, but she turned into a multistory parking structure across the street instead. Her guest couldn't show up in bloody chain mail. She parked at the back where the lights were dim. Her fifth-century companion sighed in relief as the car stopped.

She pulled her bag over her shoulder, popped the trunk, and got out. She ran around to the passenger door and opened it. He swung to face her. "You cannot look like a

warrior," she said as she began to unbuckle his greaves.
"You need a healer." She grabbed his wrist and unfastened
the hardened leather from around his forearms each in
turn and tossed all the pieces into the trunk.

"You stitch me." It was a command.

She glanced to his arm. The slice went right through
his chain mail over his deltoid muscle to his biceps. "Too
much wound for me." After being cut with some filthy
sword he needed antibiotics, too. She pulled him out and
he leaned against the car, blinking and looking around in
wonder. She unbuckled his scabbard and tossed the huge
sword in the trunk. He didn't even protest. He was looking stunned, as though he just had absorbed that everything had changed.

"No mailcoat." That's what they called chain mail.
This was going to hurt, but he had to lift his arms. She bit
her lip, surveying him.

He grabbed the hem of the chain tunic and pulled it
over his head with a grunt of pain.

"You are a brave man," she murmured. He was wearing
a leather tunic that laced up the front over a billowy shirt
probably made of flax or something. Right now it was
crusted with blood and sweat. He had on leather breeches
with a pouch on a belt and soft leather boots. He'd look
like some homeless guy with a fetish for leather to the ER
staff, or maybe a down-on-his-luck rock and roller. She
heaped the heavy mail into the trunk in a cascade of
shushing metal.

"What is your name?" she asked.

"Medraut," he said. So much for the idea that he was
Arthur.

"Is that a first name or a last name?"

"Medraut of Orkney."

"We will call you Jim Medraut. Can you remember
that?"

He nodded but raised his brows in question.

"No one can know you do not belong here," she explained, thinking of all the questions he would raise, and questions about her sanity. Worse yet, would she be forced to tell the police or the army or anybody at all about Leonardo's machine? That machine was dangerous. Very dangerous. She had to have time to think what to do. "You tell them you live on the street, yes?"

"Will they speak my language, then, as you do?"

Uh-oh. Forgot about that. Why *did* she speak his language? "No. I must speak for you."

A gleam came into his eyes. "For a while." She didn't like that gleam. It suddenly occurred to her that she didn't know anything about this guy, other than that he had been about to get killed. What if . . . what if he wasn't one of the good guys? The morals of the fifth century might not be honor and justice at all. Maybe that was just a dream, like a shining city of Camelot.

He must have seen her misgivings. "I need you," he said, looking straight into her eyes. "I will not harm you. I will not harm anyone."

She heaved a breath and felt better. That was just what she wanted him to say. She pointed to the brightly lit entrance to the ER. "We will go there for a healer."

Chapter Three

Diana took Medraut by the arm and guided him out the doors of the ER and across the street to the parking structure. Instead of delivering him to Social Services on the second floor, as the doctor had recommended, she filled his prescriptions for Keflex and Vicodin in the pharmacy and they left. Through it all, Medraut had been watchful. He thought the televisions in the various waiting rooms were scrying pools. Now *that* been difficult to explain.

The thought of her little apartment had never seemed so good. It was only midnight, but it seemed like she'd been up for days. She had no choice but to take Medraut home with her. Was that stupid? But he'd seemed so sincere in his promise not to harm her. At the least he knew he needed her. She'd be okay. Maybe she needed him, too. It occurred to her that her stalker might be waiting for her at her building. It might not be so bad to have a guy around right now. Medraut might be wounded, but the stalker wouldn't know that. And Medraut sure looked fierce.

As they headed down Laguna again, Diana realized that giving him a place to sleep for the night was the least of her problems. He was a fifth-century guy now stuck in a century he couldn't possibly understand. The folly of bringing him here washed over her. Even if she hadn't changed history, she still had a guy who didn't speak the language, thought television was a scrying pool, and made his living with a sword.

Could she send him back in time again after his arm was healed? To when? Before she had appeared? That was condemning him to death. After? Yeah, after would be better. Maybe. Maybe he was meant to be in this time. . . . *How are we screwed? Let me count the ways.*

She turned on Twenty-second Street and cut over to San Jose. Her apartment building was made of brick with clapboard bays and fire escapes zigzagging down the front. It was a tad run-down, but since it had been built in the thirties, the apartments had arched doorways and coffered ceilings. More personality than those sterile concrete boxes they built these days. She drove through the wrought-iron gates to the left of the building and around to the back. Somehow she coaxed Medraut into the creaky little elevator with his sword, since he wouldn't leave it in the car.

He followed her in, looking around as she snapped on the light.

What would he see? A cramped one bedroom with a little kitchen visible through the bar and little dining area. She had a fold-out couch, thank goodness, in slightly sagging brown tweed. The bright autumn shades of the quilt her mother helped her make when she was fifteen brightened it up a bit. A potted ariaca palm and a huge philodendron made the place look alive. Books occupied three floor-to-ceiling shelves she'd gotten at one of those stores that specialized in cheap oak furniture. Her desk sat under the big bay window that looked into the street. Simple, but hers.

"Is this your abode?" Medraut asked.

"Yes. You can sleep here." She pointed to the couch. "Until . . ." *Until what?*

He nodded. "Thank you." The warm light of the apartment should have softened his bold features, but they didn't. Women would think he was a handsome man. Strange, but he held no attraction for her. She gave a mental shrug. Just as well, since he was going to be here until she could decide what to do about him. And when would that be?

She eased her bag off her shoulder and realized with a shock that the book inside no longer held its strange attraction for her. She pulled it out and put it on her desk. Once she would have felt anxious about putting it down. She looked inside herself. Now . . . nothing. She ran her hands over the tooled leather. A wonderful book, to be sure, but not an obsession. Was that because she had used the machine it described?

She certainly hadn't gotten what she wanted. Far from seeing Camelot in its shining moment, she'd seen its downfall, and in the few minutes she had been back there she'd seen some magic, sure, but no honor, no love, only fierce and bloodthirsty warriors, a man with eyes that changed color, and a gawky boy. She hadn't been transformed. The experience wasn't going to help her work in progress. She *had* learned she spoke Proto-Celtic. What did that mean? She was too tired to think. She should just get Medraut's bedding and fall in bed herself.

Instead, she felt drawn to the window. She pulled aside the filmy curtain. The street was quiet. It was still Sunday night. Cars lined the streets. As she watched, the door on some kind of SUV opened and a big man got out. He must have been waiting there.

Her heart skipped. She swallowed. Was it the stalker?

He wandered over to the pool of light from a street lamp and stood there. Brazen. Dark hair. Fair skin. Six three or four if he was an inch. Heavily muscled. Bulkier than the older man who wandered through the apartment behind her, exploring. She couldn't tell the color of his eyes from here, but she could imagine them from that time at the liquor store. Gray-green. Why had her stalker been shocked when he looked at her, even in the liquor store? She was sure shocked. He'd had an immediate and unwelcome effect on her. The very effect he was having now even from outside in the street. She shook herself. Of course, a man like that would have an effect on women. He was probably used to that. Arrogant bastard. He stood in the light now just to see her afraid. That's what stalkers did. It gave them a feeling of power.

Did he have power over her? Why was she so attracted to him? Was it because of the danger? But she wasn't attracted to the dangerous guy in her apartment. Not at all.

The stalker . . . reminded her of someone, actually. She just couldn't think who it might be. Again the feeling that she knew him washed over her. She twitched the heavy drapes together, the rings hissing over the metal poles. She wouldn't be afraid. She wouldn't. Let him stay out there in the cold all night if he wanted. He couldn't get in here. There was a security keypad downstairs and a dead bolt on her door. The fire escapes didn't pass her apartment. And if push came to shove, there was Medraut's big sword.

"Do you have food here, witch?"

She blinked. Medraut must be famished. She was hungry, too, now that he brought it up. "Yes. Yes of course. Sit here while I prepare some." She pointed to the comfortable leather chair next to the desk. He eased himself down into it. She could tell he was in pain. First things first. She poured a glass of water from the tap and ripped open the bag from the pharmacy. She shook out some pills. His eyes were big as she handed them to him.

"Where does the water come from?" he asked.

"A lake outside the city. Pumps bring it to each house."

Did she get the word for "pumps" right? "Do you know pumps?"

He nodded, thoughtful, and downed the pills. "Tell me where I am." His voice was a command. "To what world have you taken me, witch?"

Well, he had to know sometime. "The name is Diana. And I'm not a witch." He might need a drink for this. She opened a Ruston Syrah from the little wine rack she kept at the end of the counter and poured him a glass. He took the wineglass she'd gotten from Cost Plus because you could put them in the dishwasher as if it were a chalice encrusted with jewels. Yeah, glass was precious back then. He brought it to his lips but hesitated.

"It isn't poison," she said. Though with the Vicodin, it might send him a little loopy. "Why would I save your life, just to kill you?"

He grimaced in acknowledgment and sipped. He looked surprised. "This is good."

Better than the wine they had back then. Everything would have had to be shipped in from the vines the Romans planted in France. (Best gift from an invading army ever, better even than roads and bridges and aqueducts.)

He looked up in speculation. "You must be wealthy, witch."

She took a breath. "You are in the future. More than fifteen centuries in the future. The metal machine . . . the machine you saw travels through time. I live here. This place is not magic to me. And I am not a witch."

"Can this be true?" He spoke more to himself than her.

"Yup." Let him chew on that for a minute. What was she going to feed him? She didn't think he'd be wild about the Lean Cuisine that filled the freezer. Or the Kraft Macaroni & Cheese she kept on hand for comfort-food emergencies. She opened the fridge. Chicken breasts. She had a package of those. And she always had pasta and salad stuff. She clipped some sage from the little pot in her kitchen window. Sage pasta, a broiled chicken breast, and a salad. Not exactly Julia Child, but . . . nourishing.

"I would know more of your world," Medraut said as they sat to eat. And all the questions he had been hoarding silently came rushing out. He marveled at the salt and savored every taste. When she brought out some Sara Lee chocolate cake, she realized someone enjoyed her guilty pleasure as much as she did.

"What weapons do you have in this time? No one wears swords."

"Uh . . . swords have been . . . uh . . . replaced."

"By something which deals death more quickly?" he asked, his expression sharpening.

"Yes. Unfortunately. We call them guns. They . . . fling a small piece of metal called a bullet through the air." She had no word for "shoot." "It does great damage to a body."

"I would like such a weapon."

"That is not a good idea."

"I would study everything about your time," he said, changing the subject. She was willing to bet he wasn't giving up on guns. Warrior and all. "My time can learn much from it. Then you will come back with me. My knowledge and your magic will make me the greatest king."

"I do not wish to go back there." Still . . . there were things she wanted to know. "Was the Camelot I saw in Arthur's time? Do you know that name?"

He grew wary. "Arthur is dead."

"Oh." Her last bit of hope whispered away like ash on the wind. She put down her fork. "Well, I guess if there was a shining moment, it was over," she muttered to herself in English. Maybe there was no possibility for happy endings.

"The Saxons wait to pounce on the kingdom if we cannot unite behind a successor. I am the only one who can hold it. I will marry his queen. I'll give her what she didn't get from him." His expression was self-satisfied.

Marry Guinevere? This man? Perhaps he was some king of a smaller kingdom. Orkney? "Perhaps she will mourn too much for Arthur to marry. Or perhaps she would go to Lancelot."

"Who? I know not this man." He was wolfing down the pasta.

She thought so. Lancelot had been made up in Medieval times. She heaved a sigh. "It is not important." Camelot wafted away like the dream it was. It had been literary dream, not a real one. She should be used to that. Wasn't her specialty making up stories about finding true love in unusual places? She liked to think she wasn't writing fantasy, that's all.

She answered his questions patiently, as well as she could, as she did the dishes. Then she showed him how to use the bathroom to wash and relieve himself. She felt obligated to explain that in this time men were expected to bathe daily. That was a shock to him. When he finally emerged from the bathroom with the towel around his waist, she had the pullout bed made up. She glanced up to see that he had a lean body with ropy muscles. Not her type.

He sat on the bed. His gaze roved over her. "It is customary for a warrior to take a comely woman to his bed on the eve of a victory," he said. How could he have the energy to even think about that? But he was thinking it all right. The bulge in his towel said so. Revulsion washed over her on some elemental level she couldn't explain.

"Hold on. I didn't see a victory," she protested, backing toward her bedroom.

"I lived." He held out a hand. "Come. With your powers and mine, the world is ours."

"I do not have power," she hissed. "I have told you that.

And I will not be a marker of your victory." Indeed, the whole thought of bedding him made her just go *ewwwe,* inside. Her gaze darted to the great sword leaning against the desk. "Keep your hands to yourself or leave."

He held up his hands, palms out. "Forgive me, my lady. Our ways are different. I shall not touch you. My honor is my promise."

She chewed her lip. She couldn't throw him out. (A) it was cruel to abandon him in a world he didn't understand, and (B) she wasn't sure she shouldn't be bundling him back to the fifth century. Oh, this was bad on so many levels. She had no idea what to do. "You will sleep there." She pointed to the fold-out bed. "I will sleep in my bedroom." *With the door locked.*

She was bone tired, but still she was drawn to the front window again. She drew back the drapery. Her stalker moved into the pool of light and there was something infinitely attractive about him, Most horrifying of all was that she wasn't horrified at that.

Maybe tomorrow it was time to buy a gun.

The man with her was dressed in fifth-century chain mail and had a sword. He'd seen them at the museum and entering the apartment, not up close, but you couldn't mistake chain mail. He could hardly swallow. His mouth was dry. Where had she gotten him? How?

Or maybe this man had come to keep her from fulfilling her destiny, whatever that was. Was she in danger? It took all his restraint not to burst into her apartment and strike down the man. But if he burst in now, without preparing her, she'd be even more frightened of him. She might call the police. He knew where that would lead for someone like him. Then he would have failed his father once again.

Still, he had to know if she was in danger.

He slid across the street in the darkness. He stood in front of the door to the apartment building, ignoring the keypad. He laid his palms flat on the glass and willed his center to stillness. His eyes went unfocused and his breathing slowed.

Mist. I am mist and darkness, he sang to himself. *I am fog.*

He felt himself dissipating. His center would not hold. His molecules fanned out in infinitesimal thinness. He slid between the door and the jamb, the lock irrelevant.

Inside, he gathered himself, molecule by molecule, in a whirling mist that grew more solid by the second. Warmth caressed his coalescing body like heat lightning.

He was in. The experience of dissipating always left him a little weak and breathless. He took a moment to gather himself before he slid silently up the stairs and down her corridor to hover outside the door. He listened. They were talking and eating. Everyday. Ordinary.

"You can sleep there. I will sleep in my bedroom."

That was a relief. She was not taking this stranger to her bed. The very thought had a green monster choking his throat and then, as he imagined her lying in her bed, the quilt pulled up over her breasts, her beautiful hair splayed over the white linen of her pillow, his body reacted almost violently, just as it had the first time he saw her.

He flushed. *How pure are you?* he taunted himself, willing the painful reaction to subside. Not effective. Inside the apartment, he heard the man agreeing to the sleeping arrangements. Well, whoever this man was, she was in no immediate danger. But he would stay near, in the street, in case something went wrong and she cried out. That also left him near enough to enter her dreams and prepare her to trust him. He trotted silently down the stairs.

Why hadn't she recognized him? Surely she would

trust him once she knew who he was. But in several en-
counters she hadn't.

No need for dissipation this time. He simply walked
out the front door.

He stood under the streetlight and saw her come and
stand, silhouetted, against the light in her window. She
looked down at him. Her gaze locked with his. *It is I!* he
wanted to shout. But she twitched the draperies shut. Did
she know him and yet push him out of her life?

It didn't matter. He leaned against the lamppost. He
was here for the duration.

*She was walking down the colonnade of the Palace of
Fine Arts next to the Exploratorium. Fog drifted in among
the giant columns until she could hardly see the huge angels that hovered at the capitals. Dusk was deepening into
night and she was alone. Maybe. Or maybe someone or
something was lurking in the fog. It swirled around her
feet, coming in fast off the bay in a way that hardly seemed
natural. She glanced behind her, but the columns disappeared into a wall of gray. She hurried forward, passing
columns in the mist. They seemed to go on and on.*

*What was that noise? A scraping sound . . . a chink.
She looked down. There was a golden bracelet on her
hand, covered with what looked like primitive runes.
From the bracelet hung a delicate golden chain that disappeared into the fog behind her. Where had that bracelet come from? It was rather like a handcuff, what with
the chain. The chain scraped across the asphalt of the
path. She pulled and it puddled at her feet. She tugged
again but met resistance. It was fastened to something.*

*She wanted to run through the fog to her car, but she
couldn't because of the chain. Fear circled around her,
though she felt it from somewhere far away. What she*

refused to do was walk back into the fog toward whatever was at the other end of the chain.

She heard a step behind her. The fog magnified all sound. It was a solid wall of swirling night gray that circled her. The chain went slack. More steps. Something was coming toward her down the path between the columns.

Damn it all. *She wasn't going to be afraid. Not everything you couldn't understand was bad. Maybe what was at the end of the chain was her parents, still tied to their earthly existence. Wouldn't she welcome the chance to see them one more time? The steps came closer.*

"Dad!" *she called. Tears mingled with the damp of fog on her cheeks.* "Mom?"

Out of the wall of mist stepped the man who had been following her. She couldn't help the squeak of surprise. He was wearing a leather jacket, and his dark hair hung over the collar, damp from the mist. His eyes were the color of the fog and serious, his brows knit in a frown. He was one of the most handsome men she'd ever seen. The bulk of him, his strong hands, the way he filled his jeans, all washed over her and made her acutely aware of her nipples. The figure put out a hand. Was it in threat or solace?

He wore a bracelet connected to the other end of her chain. She wanted to run from him. But part of her wanted to run toward him, to bury her face in his chest and let him soothe her.

Soothe her? He was more likely to strangle her.

"You!" *She tried to catch her breath. There had been a monster in the mist after all. She felt the pull of his body on hers. She'd been reading too many romances. She must resist that pull.*

"Why are you following me?" *she practically wailed.*

"To protect you. Trust me." *His voice was a baritone growl, intensely seductive.*

Too creepy! He was the one she needed protection from. *She turned and ran as the chain played out behind her. Columns loomed out of the mist and faded behind her. How long was the colonnade? How long was the chain? She could just make out the open area beyond the corner pieces that marked the entrance to the colonnade. The parking lot was just beyond that. She was going to make it. She'd get the tire iron from her trunk and pry off the bracelet or the chain.*

The chain pulled her up short. No! *She turned to face her nemesis. There was no escaping him; she knew that now . . .*

Diana sat up with a gasp. What kind of a dream was that? It felt both real and unreal and she couldn't seem to sort out which was which. She was handcuffed to the stalker? They were connected somehow? It had been so clear—every detail of his face, the sound of his voice. He'd said he was protecting her. Right. All stalkers probably said that.

Okay. She had a good imagination. That was all. He was haunting her daytime, why wouldn't he haunt her dreams?

She was definitely buying a gun.

Chapter Four

The next morning was Monday, which meant ten to five at the Exploratorium. She felt like warmed-over seafood—definitely past its prime. Not enough sleep. How could she sleep when her dreams had been invaded? It felt like a violation.

She realized, when she saw Medraut dressed once more in leathers and his bloody shirt, that she'd been so preoccupied with her stalker she hadn't thought about what to do about her houseguest. He'd seemed so sincere when he promised not to touch her. Maybe his advances last night were just a cultural misunderstanding. . . . God, she didn't know *what* to do.

She scrambled Medraut some eggs and showed him how to work the television. She loaned him one of her oversized sweatshirts and helped him get it on over his bandages, told him to take more pills at noon. Then she got her shoulder bag and keys. The weight of Leonardo's book was comforting but not essential. That was both a relief and a disappointment. In some ways, her obsession with the book had given her life purpose. She had always had the possibility of looking behind the door marked: *Danger.* Now she'd looked, and acted, and everything was worse.

"Don't leave this house for *any* reason," she warned. "I'll be back at dusk."

"You are not happy I am here," he said, carefully. "I can pay you for my care."

"There is no need," she said, feeling small.

He got his pouch from beside the bed and dumped a considerable pile of coins on the table. They glinted gold and silver, sharply cast, almost like new. She spotted a man with a hook nose and a laurel wreath, and some had a ship with a Viking prow and . . .

"These . . . these are worth a fortune."

"You may take as much as you need for caring for me."

Was this a test? "I will take nothing." He didn't know he couldn't just use these in a grocery store. But they *were* a way to his independence if he was going to stay in this time. "We use paper money now, but you can trade them for paper money if we can find a dealer."

"Excellent," he said with great self-satisfaction. "You will help me do so."

"When I get back from work." Those coins would keep him in venison and chain mail for quite a while. Maybe she'd get him a room at a boardinghouse, sign him up for English as a second language . . . She shook her head. Or maybe she should get him back to the fifth century. To certain death? She wanted to scream. How were you supposed to know what to *do*?

She had to get to work. That's what she had to do. No stalker skulked in the back parking lot or on the street. No SUV lurked ominously. Even stalkers needed to sleep, apparently, if they spent all night invading your dreams. Of course he hadn't really invaded her dreams. The whole situation was just getting to her, and she was having dreams about it.

It was hard to work that day, knowing the time machine waited behind the door marked: *Danger.* Knowing it really worked and that she'd brought back a guy from Camelot weighed on her. And she couldn't even consult anyone.

She hurried back to her apartment after work, having used the computer in the office to find a reputable dealer in antique coins on Angie's List. No one sat in the cars on San Jose Street. It was empty of pedestrians, except for Mrs. Gable unloading her three kids from day care at the house squished between apartment buildings down the street.

Medraut greeted her at the door, opening it before she could use her key. "Don't do that," she scolded. "I might have been anyone. This time is dangerous."

"I knew it was you by your step. I watched your automobile turn into the drive."

She froze. She'd spoken in English and he had answered back in kind. She gaped at him.

He gave a sly grin. "It is my gift. The languages are close. I studied by watching the glass scrying pool."

"You learned a new language in one day from the television?"

"And by listening last night in the healing place. And I scanned some books. You have many books. They are common now, and not just for monks or kings, yes?"

"The languages aren't close at all. English is based on Anglo-Saxon, and you speak early Celtic." Learning a language in twenty-four hours was not natural. Yet . . . hadn't she herself learned English quickly once? The social workers thought what she spoke when she was found was a made-up language, brought on by some sort of trauma. But it wasn't. It was Proto-Celtic. And she'd learned English just like Medraut, by listening, though not in twenty-four hours.

Medraut shrugged, as if to say, *Don't believe me then.*

She glanced at her watch. "Yikes. We have to go if we're

going to get to the coin shop before closing time. Bring one coin only, one of the Roman ones." Guilt stabbed her. "I forgot to ask, are you feeling better?"

"Yes. The wound heals, and the tablets take away the pain. Thank you, my lady."

Let's see, he'd had one at noon. She grabbed the bottle and dispensed another one. That would hold him.

She pulled out of the parking lot onto the sidewalk, peering into the oncoming traffic to her left for a break. So she wasn't looking for pedestrians coming from the right. Her stalker practically ran into the passenger side of the car as he strode down the sidewalk.

She gasped and Medraught snapped his head around to look at the man. *Here? In front of my apartment building, in broad daylight?* The stalker was getting bolder. This was *so* not a good sign. But as the stalker's gaze fell on Medraut, her nemesis was the one who gasped.

"What are you doing here?" he accused Medraut. The stalker looked stunned. His stare flicked beyond Medraut to Diana. "What have you done?" There was a horrible, frozen moment. Medraut looked confused, Diana probably looked as stunned as the stalker had a moment ago, and the stalker's stunned look turned ashen. Then he vaulted over the hood of her Honda and loped off down San Jose and turned the corner, heading toward Mission.

"Who was that?" Medraut said, his eyes narrowing. "He seemed to know me."

"I don't know," she said, and put the Honda in drive. "And I don't want to know."

They got two thousand dollars for the coin, which turned out to be a commemorative piece issued by Tiberius for Augustus Caesar's death. That meant the dealer thought he could get twice that from a buyer. It was in the best condition the dealer had ever seen. Two thousand would allow Medraut to do a little clothes shopping and get settled. But she'd have to find an auction house to get him top dollar next time. His collection would bring more as a unit than if each coin was sold individually.

"We have to make another stop." She'd been busy on Angie's List. "We need a gun."

"A gun?" Medraut's eyes lit. "I would like to have such a weapon."

"Cool down, buddy. It takes ten days to buy a gun in California, and *you* won't be able to get one at all, because you don't have any identification."

His face fell. Then his eyes slid sideways to her. "But you can buy one."

She checked her purse to make sure she had the ID she'd need and nodded absently. "Yeah. I hate guns. Never wanted one around. But that guy hanging around unnerves me. I guess I'd feel better with some protection."

"But yes. You must buy a gun."

The gun shop attached to a pistol range over in the warehouse district on the west side of the city was open until nine.

"I'd go with a shotgun for home defense." The guy helping them didn't have a brush cut. That was a relief. And he wasn't a crotchety geezer. He'd been in the military, though. He had that clean-cut look and biceps that had been through boot camp. "Anyone can use them, and you don't have to aim. Light gauge so you don't take out the neighbor's kids through the walls. A Benelli with a Surefire Responder sight would be my choice for someone like you. But if you want defense in your purse, a shotgun's no use."

"So . . . so what would you recommend if I wanted a gun for my purse?"

"I'd go with a Kahr M40. Tiny, goes anywhere, and packs a wallop."

"Well . . . uh . . . that sounds good." It actually sounded all very technical and much harder to shoot than it looked on television. Her uncertainty must have shown on her face.

"Why don't you try one of each out on the shooting range? That way you can tell whether they'll fit your needs. I'll get you started. Then you can play on your own." He winked at Medraut, automatically assuming that the man was silent because he was trying to let his girlfriend feel in control of a "scary, gun-buying situation."

To her amazement, Medraut winked back. "I saw that, you two," she grumped. "Okay. I'll try them out." She wondered how long after the clerk left them on their own it would be before Medraut wanted to try the guns.

Not long. He had been startled by the noise when the clerk first demonstrated, even though he'd been fitted with those earmuff-looking sound blockers. But when he realized that the holes in the target had been made by the gun, his excitement was palpable. The clerk showed her how to sight and how to hold the gun with two hands. That entailed his big body surrounding hers and steadying the gun. He must love his job. The kick was not bad—according to him. To her it felt bone jarring. But she got better at it. Her shots hit the target more often than not, and he reassured her that soon she'd be reliably within the outline of a human form.

He left her with ammunition and a word of praise. He knew how to sell guns.

She wasn't loath, however, to cede the gun to Medraut's excitement. He got better faster than she did. When he had placed five shots inside the outline, he raised the gun and smiled. It was a little, interior smile of pure ecstasy.

"Better than a sword?" she asked.

He nodded, pleasure and amazement darting alternately across his face. "One can kill from a distance.

How I would have liked to have this weapon in my own time."

"Yeah, they're great when you're the only one who's got one. When everybody has them, it gets pretty bloody." Maybe not bloodier than hacking each other to death with swords, though.

"We must wait ten days to get these?" He frowned. "By then this man who follows you and who says he knows me may have attacked you."

"Yeah, that reminds me, how would he know you?"

"He wouldn't. He has mistaken me for someone else, or he is what you call 'crazy.' I suspect crazy." Medraut was fondling the gun. Caressing the grip and the barrel. "So how can we buy guns before ten days have passed?"

She shrugged. "Short of buying something illegal from the gangs over in the Mission District, we can't." She saw the look in his eyes. "Don't even *think* about it. They would kill you, or if they didn't, the police would put you in jail for having a gun like that."

"Ahhh." He handed the gun to her ruefully. "I understand."

Diana bought the two guns and plenty of ammunition and filled out all the paperwork. She paid with a credit card, and the clerk let her take the ammunition home with her. Boy, having a stalker was an expensive proposition. How long would it take her to pay off that card? On the other hand, she might not even get to pay the card down if her stalker got her. She pushed down the fear that had been making her stomach tight ever since they ran into her stalker. Maybe she should file a police report. Not that they'd do anything, but at least his description would be on record. If he killed her, they might be able to get him. After the fact.

She trudged out to the parking lot, Medraut in tow. Far from being alone as she had been since her father died, she had both a stalker and an unwanted houseguest. How could things get worse? She couldn't stomach sending Medraut back to his death. But how could he live in the twenty-first century? How would he get a driver's license? A Social Security number? She was probably going to have to find someone to make him an identity before she could get rid of him. She had a feeling that service would not be on Angie's List.

She'd parked right under a security light. Medraut went automatically to the passenger's side door and opened it. "Give me the ammunition. . . ." He leaned over the hood.

The glass of the passenger's side window shattered, followed by a cracking sound.

"Get down!" Diana yelled, and sank to her knees.

Medraut fell to the pavement. Something scraped the hood where he had just been leaning. The windshield collapsed. Another crack sounded. He crawled around the back of the car to where she crouched by the driver's door. Several men burst from the gun store and strode out, keeping to the cover of the large cypress trees on either side, swinging their weapons, stiff-armed, just like on television.

"What's going on here?" an older man barked.

"Someone shot at us!" Diana called, from her knees.

"Call the police," the older man said. The guy who'd waited on them backed into the building.

Oh, shit, Diana thought. *How will I explain Medraut?*

The young officer had tattoos. Green snaking lines just peeked from under his short-sleeved blue uniform shirt. Diana was shivering, even in her jacket, but he seemed impervious to cold. Probably a point of police pride not to wear long sleeves or a jacket even in March in San Francisco. The parking lot of the gun store seemed filled with people. The employees were strutting around offering theories, though an officer had them corralled near the front door. A female officer crawled around Diana's car with a flashlight. Two other men in plainclothes hiked back from the far side of the parking lot.

The shooter had to be her stalker, and she had told the police that.

"So, no idea why this man is stalking you, Ms. Dearborn?" the tattooed officer asked.

"No, Officer. I mean, sometimes people think they know you when they've read your books. I get letters from prisons and people in skilled-nursing facilities and hospitals. They write really personal letters, as if I'm a friend. I know a couple other authors who've had stalkers."

He made a few notes. "No ID, Mr. Medraut?" the officer asked in a stony voice.

"I . . . I was driving, so he left his wallet at home."

The officer looked up under his brows from his notebook. He didn't say anything. He didn't need to. They'd want her and Medraut down in the station house tomorrow with full ID, if he just left it at home. And they all knew that wasn't going to happen. Medraut watched her warily, letting her take the lead. If only she could. How would she write this in one of her novels? She'd take three days to think up a story first of all. But if her heroine had no time to think . . .

She heaved a sigh. "All right, Officer Larrabee. He doesn't have any ID. He's here illegally. We didn't want to tell you that, but you'll find out anyway."

"Not Hispanic. Didn't come over the border. Accent sounds a little Germanic."

Okay, okay. If he'd come on a plane, he'd have had to have a passport. "Just because he's not Hispanic doesn't mean he can't come over the border. He came through Canada."

"Then he's got a Canadian driver's license, and before

you tell me he doesn't drive, then he'd have a government-issue ID for health care . . ." The threat implied was clear. If he didn't have any ID at all, then he might be an escaped prisoner or a terrorist or someone hiding out.

The guys in plainclothes arrived, interrupting this unpleasant conversation.

"What have you got?" the officer asked.

"Guy was behind a car on the far side of the parking lot, near the entrance from Richardson. He made the shots and then peeled out the back way onto Bay. Left some rubber and two casings from a 9 millimeter. Would have been quite a shot from over there."

"I got bullets," their female compatriot announced. She still held the knife she'd used to pry them out of the Honda, and she raised the plastic Baggie she'd put them in for evidence.

"So why did this guy want you dead, Ms. Dearborn? You said he'd been stalking you?"

"Oh, she wasn't the intended victim, Officer," the woman said, surprised. "She's short. She was behind the car on the driver's side, entirely protected. This gentleman was the target." She nodded to Medraut. "Only leaning over at the last second saved you the first time. When you dropped to the ground you dodged the second bullet. Then you scrambled around the back and he didn't have another clear shot. But those first two should have got you dead to rights. You're a lucky man."

"Two shots. From that distance. With a handgun. Guy knows his way around guns," one of the other guys noted.

Medraut and Officer Larrabee looked as nonplussed as she felt. "Why . . . Why would he want to kill . . . uh . . . Jim?"

"You got a past that followed you here?" Larrabee asked.

"No, sir. I left my past behind."

Way behind, Diana thought. But would the police believe him?

"Well, if he's fixated on you, Ms. Dearborn, maybe he isn't exactly going to like you hanging out with another man." Larrabee was proud of his psychological insight.

"I . . . we're not . . ." Diana wondered if they could see her blush in the bright white security lights. The whole thought of her and Medraut being a couple made her queasy.

"He doesn't know that. Which brings us back to what Mr. Medraut is doing here."

"I came looking for work," Medraut said, shrugging apologetically. "The recession isn't limited to your country."

How did he know about the recession?

"Not likely to get work without an ID," one of the plainclothes guys said.

"Diana told the truth. It may be a Canadian driver's license, but I do have one. I left it at her apartment. We met online, and she told me she'd help me after my company closed. I'll bring it down to the station tomorrow. Canadians can stay six months without a green card. . . . Then if you send me home, well . . . you send me home. I don't want trouble for her."

Diana hoped her expression didn't show her shock. How did he know to say all that?

"Now, is it possible for us to go? It's very late."

The cop would never let them go. Diana just knew he'd take Medraut in for being illegal. But he didn't.

"Okay. Your car isn't drivable with no windshield, Ms. Dearborn. I'll have a squad car take you home. I'll keep your driver's license. You can pick it up tomorrow at the station when you two come in."

"Thank you, Officer," Medraught said, and smiled. He was very sure of himself.

"We should be done with the car tomorrow, too. If you

have roadside service, they'll pick it up at the precinct and tow it to a repair shop of your choice to get the windshield replaced."

"Thanks. . . . Thanks, Officer." Diana wanted nothing more than to get out of there. It had been a long night.

"Go home, and lock the doors, and stay there, Ms. Dearborn. This guy isn't done. Maybe Mr. Medraut should think about going home just to get this guy off your back."

Diana shuddered. Medraut couldn't go home because he wasn't from Canada. And the stalker had been fixated on her before Medraut arrived.

"I'll be in after work tomorrow," she promised Officer Larrabee. "I get off at three." Medraut still wouldn't have an ID. There was no story that could cover that. She wasn't quite sure how Medraut had talked the guy into letting them go at all.

"Call us if you see the stalker hanging around outside your apartment again."

Chapter Five

But she didn't see her handsome stalker outside her apartment when they got back. She ordered delivery pizza because she was too tired to cook. They sat down in her little dining area with a bottle of Smoking Loon Merlot. "Where did you get that stuff you said about the recession, and meeting online? How did you know all that?" That had been bothering her all the way home.

"While you were working today, I watched the news and a program called *Law and Order* and several others. I went out and walked among the people to hear them talk."

"You *what*? You left the apartment?"

He took a gulp of wine as she dished him up a slice of pizza. "I met many interesting people, many of them these Hispanics who are illegal."

"You must have walked over to Mission."

"I had a taco. Very good. More spicy than the food I know. Spices seem very common here. And I had ale. No . . . beer."

"Medraut, you . . . you can't walk around in this century without . . ." *Without what? A chaperone?* Oh, this was *such* a disaster. Her mind did a little cycle around the "take him back, help him live here" dilemma. If he stayed how did she keep him out of jail or an asylum?

He set down his slice of pizza. "Diana, I have changed my mind about going back to my time. I like your time. It has many possibilities. . . ." He smiled. It was a strange, inward kind of look, and his brown eyes gleamed.

He wouldn't go back. Well, that kind of settled it. She couldn't *make* him go back. "You can't tell anyone you're from another time. They won't believe you."

"I know. I thought at first that your time was magic, that everyone was a sorcerer. But this is not true. The people are just people. They gamble and argue and strut in front of the opposite sex. The passage of time has made things so different they only seem like magic."

"Speaking of magic, how is it that you learned the language in so short a time? And don't tell me it was from listening to the television." She wanted to know this for a couple of reasons.

"But it was. I told you. That is my gift."

Diana narrowed her eyes. "Gift? No one has *that* good an ear for languages."

"My mother was a witch. That is the magic I have from her, to hear a language and understand it. To understand the way of a people and mimic it."

His mother was a witch. Right. Well, he was from the fifth century, and they believed stuff like that back then. Diana had learned the language quickly, too, but that was just a child's natural facility. It didn't explain Medraut.

They finished the meal in silence as she tried to think. In some ways his belief in magic was what she had gone back in time to find. She smiled ruefully to herself. It hadn't worked. Medraut believed in magic, but she still didn't.

As she was cleaning up the kitchen, suddenly the whole situation got too much and she found herself crying, for the fact that the stalker had shot at someone tonight, if not at her, and for the fact that she had brought a man back from the fifth century out of a kind heart and that seemed so foolhardy she wondered if someone else had done it. *And let's not forget the creepy dreams I'm having.* More fun waited in her dreams tonight, no doubt. She could hardly wait.

Medraut came and put his good arm around her. "Shhussh. It will be well. I will thrive here; you will see. And then"—here he held her away from him—"because you are alone, you will need a man. I will be your man."

Revulsion washed over her. He wasn't coming on to her. He kept his promise. But that didn't seem to change her reaction. "No," she said, and slipped out of an embrace that was only meant to be comforting.

Anger flashed across his face. "You reject my offer of protection?" Then his face rearranged itself into sympathy, as if he had made a conscious effort. "I understand. You are not ready. I will be here when you become ready."

She would never be ready. She ran into her room and shut the door. In the living room, the television came on. It was tuned to another crime show. She locked her bedroom door.

"Get out of my dreams!" she shouted. He pulled her to him with the little chain, which apparently was a lot stronger than it looked, because twist and try as she might, she couldn't break it. His eyes were gray like the fog, or maybe green, or maybe both. They glowed through the fog like he was some otherworldly beast.

"You're just a man," she breathed, more to herself than him, when he had drawn her close enough to clamp her upper arms in a grip that would probably leave bruises. The most horrible part of all was that half of her craved his touch. The bottom half, apparently. Her hands moved over his forearms of their own accord. He wore the sleeves of his flannel shirt rolled up. Her palms

*scraped the crisp dark hair. The corded muscles felt more
masculine than she had ever imagined a man's forearms
could. And she'd imagined how forearms felt. She was a
romance writer after all.*

*Of course this was just a dream. And the fact that she
knew it was a dream meant that it would soon be ending.*

*"Don't you know me?" he asked as he searched her
face "Don't you remember?"*

*She shook her head convulsively. "Remember what?"
But he did remind her of someone. Someone she had seen
just recently . . . She couldn't think. It wouldn't come.*

"I am here to protect you."

"You . . . you frighten me."

*His face took on a hard resolve. "You must talk to me.
You must believe me. And then you must trust me. Trust
me. Remember that." And with that he began to dissolve
into the fog like the Cheshire Cat in* Alice in Wonderland, *
until only his eyes were left, glowing green and swirling
with gray, and she felt like she was dissolving, too. Her
knees gave way.*

"Remember . . . talk to me. Trust me."

She was kneeling in front of the window, crying and
gasping. The wood floor hurt her bare knees. And the window was open. The chill wind off the bay rippled the draperies now thrown back, though she had closed them before
she went to bed. Had she been sleepwalking? Oh, this was
bad. She hadn't done that for years. She couldn't quite remember her dream. Even as she tried, it slipped away. It
had been about her stalker, though. And she had found him
both frightening and infinitely attractive. And familiar.
The fact that she had gotten out of bed and opened the window while she was dreaming about her stalker seemed
ominous. Did he have some kind of hold on her through
her dreams?

She pushed herself up and shook herself mentally. *You're losing your mind.* She snorted. *Like someone could enter a person's dreams.* She closed the window, peering out to see if anyone lurked in the street. The fog had lifted sometime in the night. The pools of light from the street lamp showed only wet pavement. The grinding of an early garbage truck echoed in the quiet.

Actually, she felt a little ashamed. She was attracted to a stalker, for pity's sake. What did that say about her? Was she so desperate for a man to pay attention to her that she would enjoy some guy stalking her? She'd gotten used to the fact that she was invisible to men a long time ago. And in fact, she *wanted* to be invisible in a way, to everyone, because she was invisible to herself on a very basic, elemental level. She was the ultimate imposter, walking around in society pretending to be somebody she probably wasn't. She had no origin, no childhood. She had been abandoned by her real parents, obviously. She didn't make friends, because she never really shared herself with them. What was hers to share? Not her secret quirks like hearing what people would say. That would only make people think she was crazy. So she was a courteous acquaintance of Mrs. Kim at the doughnut shop or whatever clerk was currently employed at the liquor store or the docents she supervised. But that was it. No deeper, no closer.

If only she were invisible to her stalker. He was sick, sick, *sick* for following her. And she might be sick for being attracted to that. Was it because he was the only man who ever noticed her? She'd heard about women who made up men following them just for the attention.

She glanced to the clock. Five A.M. There was no way she'd get back to sleep. She turned on the light and blinked against the glare. Her bedroom was done in blues and greens, and in March she could still use the big quilt from her grandmother (well, not *really* her grandmother).

It matched the Chinese wool rug from her father's old house, now laid in front of the bed.

What to do? She couldn't leave the apartment to go to the doughnut shop for a coffee, not with her stalker somewhere out there. If she did, she'd wake Medraut, and she didn't want to deal with him, either. Her laptop was out in the living room. But there was no way she could muster the focus to write, anyway. Her mandolin made too much noise. That would be inconsiderate. She grabbed a manuscript from a stack by the desk. Publishers sent them when they asked her to give a quote for the cover. She crawled back under the quilt.

In the first ten pages she knew it wasn't going to work as a distraction. The book was clearly overplotted. Too many coincidences and connections between the characters, and they didn't seem organic and natural at all. She could predict every turn it would take on the way to the happy ending. Was she getting bored with romance? Or was it just that she was a writer and she couldn't just *feel* the romance anymore but had to analyze how the story was written?

She set the manuscript carefully aside. It was, after all, someone's life's work and should be treated with respect. Her movements were almost overly controlled. A bad sign. Inside, her thoughts and feelings caromed around in chaos.

She had to get out of here. Stalker or no.

She dressed in jeans and a bulky brown turtleneck sweater and put on her Ariat boots and a slicker. She was going for coffee, damn it. And then maybe she'd walk up to Powell and Market and take the cable car over the hill to the wharf and watch the fishing boats come in and eat crab from the steaming pots on the sidewalk for breakfast. Stalkers weren't out at five in the morning. Her stalker would expect her to be safely asleep. If she didn't take back control of her life, she really would end in an asylum.

Diana slid in through the door of Moon Donuts, from the dark into bright fluorescent light. The bell over the door jangled. No stalker. She left a note for Medraut, relieved he hadn't wakened as she tiptoed past the sofa bed. Voilà, her life was hers again. She felt like a weight had been lifted from her shoulders.

The shop was owned by a very nice Korean couple. He made the doughnuts in the back, starting about midnight, and she manned the cash register. Their daughters, nieces, and nephews took turns helping during the busy hours, and ran the place when Mr. and Mrs. Kim went back to Korea for three weeks every year. The shop had a small counter and a couple of booths. The smell of grease and sugar and coffee was heaven. The place was empty, of course. People on their way to work wouldn't start descending on it until six or six thirty. Mrs. Kim poked her head out from the back.

"Hey, Mrs. Kim, how are you?" Diana slid onto the stool at the far end of the counter, against the wall. Mrs. Kim would remark on how early she was here.

"You are up early," the tiny woman said, going to the coffeepot. She spoke English well but still had an accent. She poured a large automatically.

"Couldn't sleep." Mrs. Kim was about to ask her if she wanted her usual maple bars.

"The usual?"

"Crumb, I think, if you have them." This was a day for breaking out. "Two." Diana was shocked at what Mrs. Kim would say next.

Mrs. Kim raised her brows. "Is the writing not going well?"

Did she order two doughnuts for comfort only when she

was stuck? Apparently. "Not going at all." She wouldn't mention time travelers or stalkers or the fact that she could speak Proto-Celtic, and her dreams. . . .

A terrible thought occurred. What if this whole thing was some elaborate psychosis? They always said that creative people were only a step away from madness, and she'd begun to think that she was going mad anyway. . . . Maybe . . . Maybe none of it was real at all.

The bell over the door tinkled. Diana jerked her head around with a dreadful premonition.

He wore a quilted vest and a plaid flannel shirt. His wide belt was rough leather and his jeans fit him like they were custom-made. His boots looked lived in. His black hair was tousled, like maybe he had just gotten up and run his hands through it. Or like he'd never been to bed at all. This close, his eyes were gray. Her heart pounded around randomly in her chest. He didn't look like a psychotic apparition.

He didn't even glance at her but stood perusing the case of doughnuts. If she tried to squeeze past him, he could grab her. Would he do that, right in front of Mrs. Kim?

"What can I get for you?" Mrs. Kim asked politely.

"Two crumb doughnuts and a large coffee," he said.

His voice was just like it was in her dream, a baritone rumble. Had she ever heard him speak? On the sidewalk when he'd recognized Medraut. That was it. He seemed so familiar! The dark comma of hair flopped over his forehead, the lips . . . Was he ordering what she had ordered just to let her know he knew everything about her? If he was trying to intimidate her, he was doing a bang-up job. She realized she was staring at him, and looked down at her doughnuts.

"Here or to go?" Mrs. Kim asked.

To go. To go. To go.

"Here, I think."

She felt paralyzed. She hadn't known what he would say. When had that ever happened? Back in the fifth century . . . And with Medraut. He turned to the counter. He wasn't going to sit at a booth. *Why* had she taken the stool next to the wall? The narrow space between the stools and the windows meant that if he sat at any of the stools, he'd be blocking her path to the door.

He slid onto the stool beside her, pinning her against the wall. "Mind if I sit down?"

She just stared at him. She'd been wrong. His eyes were blue. Not a bright, clear blue but more a steely blue-gray. At least Mrs. Kim was still here. Diana wasn't alone with him. What could he do here? Talk dirty? Mrs. Kim wouldn't like that. And Mr. Kim could come and throw him out. Better not call Mr. Kim. This guy was twice Mr. Kim's size and had fifty or seventy pounds' advantage at least. Okay, but Mr. Kim could call the police.

Her stalker plunked down the plate with his doughnuts and his Styrofoam cup of coffee on the counter. He was so much bigger than Diana, just his presence was intimidating. And there was something else. He was very male. It was having an effect on her, just like in her dreams.

No big deal. She'd read all about pheromones and how there was an immediate effect on the opposite sex, stronger if their genetic makeup was such that they would make a good mating pair. But she'd never felt that effect before. Good. This was good. A writer should experience what she wrote about. But did it have to be with him?

Great to know what it was, too. Just pheromones. Because otherwise she'd have thought it was plain old lust taking over when she should be frightened for her life. Which she was. But the feelings of lust and fear were all mixed up and making her confused. She felt like she knew this guy, that she'd always known him. Like . . .

Like she'd always longed for him in just this desperate, pitiful way. He felt . . . familiar.

"Just call if you need anything." Mrs. Kim waved as she went into the back to help her husband produce the many dozen doughnuts they'd need to make it through the rush.

Oh, boy. They were pretty much alone. But clearly visible through the glass walls of the shop from the street outside. And Mr. and Mrs. Kim were a shout away. *Not a dangerous situation,* she told herself. Why was he *doing* this?

"What do you want?" She was ashamed that her voice wasn't stronger.

"Just to talk to you." He reached for cream to put in his coffee. And Equal. She thought she was the only one who bothered to use Equal at a doughnut shop.

He just wanted to talk to her? Right. All stalkers probably said that. And maybe it started out that way. But it ended with knives, and scars. If you lived.

"I don't want to talk to you." She reached for her coffee and realized her hand was shaking, so she grabbed her doughnut instead and took a bite.

"Yes, you do. Remember?" He looked at her then. How had she thought his eyes were blue-gray? They were definitely pure gray and very resolved.

She *did* want to talk to him. The need to talk to him was so basic it seemed like she'd been born with it. Okay. She'd talk to him.

"What is a guy who looks like you doing stalking a girl like me?" There it was. That was the niggling problem she'd had with all of this all along. This guy could get anybody he wanted just by asking. Why would he bother to stalk her?

"I realized that might be how it seemed. I had some

time to think about it out under the streetlight. I'm not stalking you."

Great. He was going to deny everything. "If this isn't stalking, I don't know what it is."

"I . . . I was supposed to protect you." His lovely mouth was rueful.

That made her mad. "Did you or did you not try to shoot me last night?" It had to be him.

"I would never shoot you." He sounded outraged.

Oh. Right. He'd been shooting at Medraut. And if the officer was right and it was due to jealous rage, this guy was far along in the "stalking obsession" business. She could just ask him why he'd shot at Medraut, but why get bad news? She bit her lip, wondering what to say.

"You brought him back, didn't you?"

"What?"

"You went back to the fifth century somehow and brought him back. I thought maybe my father sent him forward. But he wouldn't have done it, not for him."

Diana tried to get her breath. He *knew.* He knew about the machine. But no. He couldn't. Because he didn't know *how* she'd gone back, just that she had. She mustn't admit there was such a thing as a time machine to a guy who was crazy. That seemed like a bad idea all around.

"Maybe he forced my father to do it." The guy looked pensive. "But my father would have died rather than loose him on an unsuspecting century."

Oh, this guy was a loon all right. But something about what he said was tickling her brain. She couldn't quite . . .

He had decided something. "You don't have to admit it, but I know you brought him here somehow. And there's no getting him to go back once he's seen the glories of this century. That leaves one choice."

Oh, this was great. He'd keep trying to kill Medraut.

But wait a minute. This guy from the twenty-first century thought he *knew* Medraut. How could he? Maybe her stalker was creating a fantasy out of his obvious mental illness. Maybe they were both crazy as bedbugs.

"And who . . . who do you think the man I was with last night really is?"

Her stalker glared at her. "Don't use that patronizing tone with me. You, of anyone, know he's from another time." Then his face softened right before her eyes. "I'm sorry. I know this must be hard for you. You never knew him, but he's why you went back, isn't he?"

"Look." His sympathy annoyed her. "His name is Jim Medraut. That's all I know."

"Well, the Jim part you probably made up together. But one of his names *is* Medraut of Orkney." He examined her face. "You really don't know, do you?" He paused and took a breath. "Medraut is called Mordred in the history books."

Mordred? Her gaze flitted over his face. The killer of Arthur? The man who ended the dream of Camelot and single-handedly brought on the Dark Ages? It took almost a thousand years for England to claw its way up to the Renaissance. This guy knew that Medraut called himself Medraut of Orkney. Did that mean he was right about him being Mordred, too?

He blew out his breath. "Yeah, that Mordred," he muttered. "So you didn't know."

She shook her head. Her throat had such a big lump in it she couldn't say anything for a long moment. After pressing her so hard, now he gave her space to think. He sipped his steaming coffee and took a hefty bite of his doughnut. She watched the muscles in his throat work.

"How . . . how do you know him?" she finally asked. And then, like a series of falling dominoes, it all fell into place. "Wait." She turned to him. "Look at me." As he glanced up from his doughnut, a lock of hair flopped over onto his forehead. "You're the boy I saw back there." She could hardly get her breath. "You were with your father. And your father's eyes . . ."

Changed color.

His eyes, now riveted on her, swirled for a moment and went a light, clear brown. He frowned. "I don't remember seeing you when you came back. Were you in a crowd perhaps?"

She snorted. "Not unless you count a bunch of soldiers. I was the only woman there. And . . ." But she shut her mouth. He would have noticed a fourteen-foot machine of bronze interlocking gears and giant jewels. He wouldn't have forgotten that. What did it mean that he didn't remember seeing her?

He shook himself. "It doesn't matter. Our problem is Mordred. He must be eliminated."

"I'd say we could send him back, but he doesn't want to go back and, anyway, that would be condemning him to death. He was about to be killed."

"That is his destiny." The stalker's voice was soft. "Arthur and Mordred slew each other at the Battle of Camlan. So it doesn't matter if I kill him now. We cannot risk a man like Mordred in this time." He looked at her quizzically. "He's already learned the language, hasn't he? And he works the modern appliances and seems to understand the culture?"

"How did you know? He says it's his gift."

"He's an Adapter." He looked at her expectantly, as if waiting for her to say something.

"He said his mother was a witch." Her eyes widened. "Morgan le Fey?"

Her stalker nodded. "Arthur's half sister. In that time they called her Morgause. So if you think he can make no trouble in this time you're wrong. He can make very big trouble."

"By adapting quickly?" Diana kept her voice low. "That hardly seems sinister."

"He wants power at any cost." The guy's eyes were hard. "His gift just makes it easier for him to get it. He adapts himself to what men want to hear in their souls and they follow him. He raised an army against the best king Britain had ever seen in just that way." His eyes searched hers and must have seen she didn't believe him. "How else did he get you to take him home? Don't tell me you were afraid at first and then suddenly you weren't."

Oh my God. He was right. Medraut said exactly the right thing at the right time to earn her trust, even when he almost lost it by making a pass at her. The bell on the shop door tinkled as a man in a suit pushed inside. Mrs. Kim came out from the back. The customer began ordering as he surveyed the neat racks of sugared treats.

She saw her stalker's chest heave as he sucked in air and turned back to her. "I have to kill him, Diana," he said, his voice low, his eyes now a very serious, clear blue. "I am the only one who knows what he is. So I must do it. Or die in the effort."

He was obviously insane, with his wild theories about what Medraut could do. He was contemplating murder, for God's sake, and all she could think about was the riddles that surrounded him. He was the boy she had seen in the fifth century. "How did you get here?"

"My father sent me."

"The man with the eyes who changed color?" *Like yours.*

"You know him as Merlin." He rose, looming over her.

The bottom dropped out of Diana's stomach. Had she seen *Merlin*? But of course—the sparkling light. A thousand thoughts ran through her head, caroming off belief and doubt. Whatever the truth, asking how his father sent him forward in time when he insisted his father was

Merlin seemed foolish. But there was something else. . . .
"*Why?* Why did he send you?"

"To protect you," her stalker said simply. "Poor job
that I've done of it." He chewed a lip and looked out the
glass windows at the street. His gaze grew distant, as
though he were already gone. "If I don't come for you in
an hour, leave town. Go to a big city. Get a new name and
lose yourself in the crowds."

"Wait a minute!" she called. "I didn't know Merlin had
children. What's your name?"

He heaved a breath. "Gawain. My name is Gawain."

He pronounced it "Gah-wen"—like as in the hero of
the book she couldn't write? The Gawain said to be pure
of heart and with the strength of ten? She felt her mouth
hanging open and snapped it shut. "*That* Gawain?"

He gave that rueful smile. "Sorry. Yeah." Then he
turned and left her sitting on the stool in Moon Donuts as
he walked out into the dawn. Camelot and Mordred and
Merlin and Gawain swirled in her head like a carousel
with too many lights and too much music. She couldn't
think clearly. What should she do about the fact that a
murder was about to be committed?

Chapter Six

Too stunned to know what to do, Diana watched people line up for Mr. and Mrs. Kim's fresh doughnuts. Slowly her brain began to function again.

You couldn't just kill a person in cold blood without . . . without a trial or something. No matter who he was. What if Medraut (Mordred?) had rebelled against Arthur justifiably? Maybe the history books were wrong about Mordred and Arthur and Camelot. It sure hadn't looked like any place you could have a shining moment. What if everything she knew about Arthur was as fictitious as the made-up, perfect knight Lancelot? And even if Medraut *were* ambitious and treacherous in the past, maybe he would use this change to turn over a new leaf. They had to at least give him that chance, didn't they? They couldn't play God.

She'd already played God. Deus ex machina. That was she. Why had she gotten herself into this mess? She'd taken the time machine back to the past and plucked Medraut out of his awful situation and brought him to the twenty-first century. And now she was just sitting by while her stalker killed him? She only had her stalker's word that he was Gawain, honorable knight par excellence. What did she really know about him, other than the feeling of familiarity and . . . longing? Longing or not, standing by while someone was killed was as good as doing it yourself.

She pushed herself up from the stool.

She'd talk Gawain out of it. She'd ask Medraugt to go back, maybe. To a different moment when he wouldn't be killed by the soldiers. She could get out of this mess yet.

She slapped a twenty on the counter to cover both their breakfasts and pushed out past the tubby office workers here to grab a fresh dozen for the break room. She ran the three blocks to her apartment building, fumbled, panting, at the keypad that let her in. The stalker hadn't asked for the combination to get into her apartment building to confront Medraut. Or a key to her apartment. Frightening thought.

Hope to God I'm not too late. The stairs were at the end of the hall. Too far. She raced into the creaky little elevator, punched *4,* and then hit the *CLOSE DOOR* button about twenty times. *Come on. Come on. Come on.* From the elevator lobby she could see her apartment door standing open. She thundered down the hall and then wavered to a halt just outside. It was too quiet. Somebody was probably already dead, either Medraut—Mordred?— or the stalker.

"Hello?" she called softly as she pushed the door open to reveal the entire room. Mordred's quilt was strewn over the carpet. No sign of a body. No blood. The sword still leaned against the desk. She moved silently to the bedroom. A channel of light leaked from the door ajar. She pushed it open with her fingertips.

Gawain, or whoever he was, was sitting on the bed, head in hands. As she entered he looked up. "He's gone." His expression was bleak. His eyes were gray again in the light from the lamp by her bed.

She breathed a sigh of relief. No murders today. "He was asleep when I left."

Gawain scooted forward on the bed. The quilt shifted to reveal a very disturbing knife. It looked like something Rambo might have come up with, or Crocodile Dundee. She stiffened.

He picked up the knife as he stood and slid it into a kind of a shoulder holster under his quilted vest. She could hardly get her breath. He'd been wearing that horrible knife all the time they were eating doughnuts. Was this it? Would he kill her?

"A warrior doesn't sleep through anyone moving around him. He was playing possum." Strange colloquialism for someone from the fifth century. His deep voice held no expression. But as he glanced up, he saw the look on her face. His gaze strayed briefly to the knife and back to her with no apology. "I've got a gun, too. Or had one. You already know that." He examined her face. "But I'm not a danger to you. I'm here to protect you."

"Yeah. So you said." And what else would a stalker say?

"While you're deciding about me, look around. See if anything is missing."

That seemed sensible. One way or another, they had to find Medraut. Mordred. But she had no idea what she was looking for. The room seemed just as she had left it except for a very large guy with . . . blue—they were definitely blue eyes right now. *Oh, shit.*

He sighed. "You had your purse with you?"

She nodded.

"Any other money in the house?"

"He had a bag of coins on him when he got here. I can check around for it. . . ."

"He wouldn't leave them behind. But it's not like they're spendable cash."

She sighed. "I took him to a dealer yesterday and traded one for two thousand in cash."

He pressed his unfortunately delectable lips together in chagrin, then forced a smile. "Well, that's one place to look for him later today."

He pushed past her into the little living room. Diana trailed after him. She looked around. "Oh no." She went to the desk and slid some papers around as though her computer and the power cord could be hiding under them. "He's got my computer." All her books, all her research, was on that computer. Thank goodness she'd saved her work to a thumb drive, or she'd have lost everything. What could Mordred do with a computer?

"Okay." Gawain looked grim.

"Why wouldn't he take his sword?" It leaned against the desk, dried blood on the steel.

"Too difficult to conceal. Besides, he'll move on to better weapons. You showed him how guns work." A stab of guilt struck through her. Gawain's gaze fell on her mandolin. He smiled. "Do you still play?"

"Yes." *Still* play? What did that imply? She frowned. How long had he been stalking her?

He closed down. "Yes, well, never mind." He stalked into the kitchen and bore down immediately on the wooden knife holder. Two slots were empty, the one for the big kitchen knife and a paring knife. "In the dishwasher?" he asked.

She shook her head. Unlike swords, knives could be concealed.

"Doesn't matter." This guy was really a glass-half-full kind of person.

"He . . . he can't be far away," she said. "I wasn't gone more than half an hour."

"He could be anywhere. Buses run this early. BART trains. Or he could have stolen a car."

"He wouldn't know about any of those."

"He would if he saw them on television, or heard people talking about them. He saw you driving when you took him around yesterday."

Oh yeah. Adapter. What an unusual "special power." Not exactly the kind of powers X-Men had. She gave her stalker a rueful look. "I really botched this up, didn't I?"

"You didn't know," he said, and his voice was surprisingly soft. "I didn't realize that. I thought. . . ." But he apparently thought better of what he was going to say and trailed off. He felt more familiar, more real, to her in that moment than anyone else she had ever met. That was dangerous. And he was looking at her . . . like she was some kind of lifeline and he was a drowning man. That didn't make her feel scared or anything.

He broke the mood and took a breath. "If anyone botched it, it was me, right from the first." He looked around, checked the kitchen window locking mechanism. "So, we'll go to my place and I'll get some things. I'm moving in."

Diana felt her jaw drop. "What? You are *not* moving in here."

"Or you could move in with me. That's better. Mordred doesn't know where I live. It was never any good trying to protect you from afar."

"I don't need protection from anybody but you." She was actually standing with her hands on her hips. If she wrote that in a novel it would seem trite. But apparently people really did stand that way when they were angry.

"You know who Mordred is. He'll return and make sure you don't tell anybody."

"You mean *kill* me?" She shook her head impatiently. "All I ever did was help him."

"Doesn't matter. The man is evil, Diana."

"And you aren't? I don't even know you, and you want to move in."

"Oh." That took him aback. "But you know my name from the legends."

"That means nothing. All those were written about a thousand years after you were . . . you should have been dead."

"Yeah." He shrugged again apologetically. "And they did exaggerate. Mostly."

"The part about the strength of ten men?"

"Yeah. Not ten." He looked abashed.

Oh, *that* made her feel better. "The honor?"

A fleeting look of regret or shame crossed his face and was gone. "Not that honorable."

She remembered the tale of the Green Knight. In that story Sir Gawain vowed to give the Green Knight anything he got from his wife and then neglected to mention the magic girdle she gave him. He did tell the Green Knight about the kisses she bestowed on him. That was honorable. Unless . . . "Your relationship with the Green Knight's wife was a little more than kisses, right? Anyway, you lost your strength in some versions of the legend, for that transgression."

He looked away. "I didn't actually lose my strength. The Christians told that version to make it a better lesson about why you shouldn't lie. Even lies of omission."

He didn't deny he'd taken more than kisses from the Green Knight's wife. He was *so* not staying in her apartment. *Wait a minute.*

"Gawain was Mordred's half-brother, along with Gareth, Geheris, and Agravain." This guy might be as evil as Mordred. If Mordred was really evil.

"Nope." He was matter-of-fact. "Not sure why I got tagged with that. By the time anybody wrote the stories down, maybe they just assumed I belonged with the others because my name started with 'G.' Poetic license, I guess."

"But you *were* a knight of the Round Table." This man really *knew* Arthur and Guinevere. If that shining moment existed, he'd experienced it. But when she'd seen him . . .

He shook his head. Got that wrong too. "I was too young. Legends get time frames mixed up."

Yeah. She'd seen him at ten or eleven, on the day Arthur probably died. That made him pretty young to be Mondred's half-brother too. "Then when did you do all those deeds in the legends, if the Saxons overran Camelot?"

He glanced away. "Didn't happen right away. My father and a few knights held out for a time. After the Saxons finally prevailed we formed a resistance of sorts. We punished those Saxon lords who abused the people. We raided their lands, killed their cattle, that sort of thing. The Saxons started the legends you read."

Resisting the Saxons must have been a hard life. But still, he'd know something about how it really was in Camelot . . . even if he was young when it all happened. He could tell her. And *how* she wanted to know, to believe in Merlin, in Arthur and . . . She wanted to believe this man was Gawain, the semiperfect knight, sent by Merlin to protect her. Who wouldn't?

And that was a problem. "Why me?"

He held his face very still. But he couldn't hold the color of his eyes still. They roiled with swirling color. "Why not you?" he said after a moment. "You're a damsel in distress, aren't you? Code of a knight and all." He shrugged as though to conceal the fact that he was lying. He didn't lie very well. Maybe a "parfait knight," as he was called in the Medieval texts, wouldn't. "Get your purse." He glanced toward the window as the first spatter hit the pane. "And a raincoat. I'll come back for your things."

"I am *not* going anywhere with you." He just assumed she'd follow orders. How fifth century of him.

His face turned hard. "You're coming with me or I'm staying here. I'm not leaving you alone where Mordred can find you."

"I'll . . . I'll call the police." Would she? "Home invasion."

He stalked up to her, exasperated. She didn't even come to his shoulder. Weren't people supposed to be smaller back then? She swallowed. "You are my responsibility," he practically growled. The police can't protect you from Mordred. I can. So don't make me tie you up and throw your pretty little iPhone in the toilet."

He knew a lot about her. From stalking her. And that was exactly the kind of threat a stalker would make. Her fear must have shone in her eyes. He looked embarrassed.

"I don't mean to frighten you," he said grudgingly. "But don't be stupid. I'll . . . I'll tell you about Camelot. You'd like that. I'll find Mordred. I'll kill him, and then you'll be free of me. Mordred must be what I was supposed to protect you from."

"You mean you don't know?"

"My father didn't tell me . . . exactly." He looked uncomfortable.

"Oh, great." But he had her. She wanted to know about Camelot more than anything. Enough to take a chance on a stranger? A stranger from the fifth century . . . yeah. How often did an opportunity like that come along? To her, apparently, twice.

Gawain lived in one of those Oakwood corporate apartments over on Dolores, furnished with everything, down to the silverware. Which was too bad. You could usually tell a lot about people by where they lived. Diana always used home settings in her books to reveal telling details about her hero and heroine. All she could tell from this place was that Gawain didn't think of it as home.

"We've got a few hours," he said as he shut the door. "The coin dealer probably doesn't open until ten or eleven. And if he wants a gun or an identity card, the action on the streets doesn't start until late afternoon. *If* he's still in San Francisco." He gestured around the living room. It was done in burgundy, hunter green, and navy blue to appeal to Oakwood's masculine residents. Did they have a feminine version? "It won't be a hardship on you to stay here. See? All the amenities. Flat-screen TV with TiVo. Home theater system."

He moved to the kitchen through the little dining area. "Microwave. Basic small appliances. We can cook here pretty comfortably."

She followed him, hoisting her bag, heavy with Leonardo's book, up over her shoulder. Actually, Gawain had a top-of-the-line KitchenAid mixer, and an industrial-strength blender. Would Oakwood provide that kind of stuff to transient corporate types? She noticed a well-thumbed copy of a Sheila Lukens cookbook and some computer printouts with the Food Network logo on them scattered over the counter.

"Do you cook here?"

"Uh. Yeah." He gathered up the recipes and stuffed them in a random drawer as though they were pornography. Where had a fifth-century guy learned to cook? Except haunches of venison over an open fire. Women did all the cooking back then, what cooking there was.

"How long have you been here?"

"A month or so." He pushed past her and led the way into the back. "My bedroom." He waved to an open door. Boy, Oakwood liked plaid. He pushed open a door across the narrow hall. "Bathroom. Uh, there's a tub if you like baths better than showers."

Did he know she liked baths? Scary . . . It was really quite amazing that she had no idea what he would say

before he said it. Why *was* that? Because he was from the
fifth century like Medraught and Merlin, whom she also
couldn't hear? Was it a time thing?

"And in here's your bedroom. I . . . uh, use it as an office. It's only a full-size bed, but . . ." He trailed off. He'd
make a really bad real estate agent. The room was tidy.
The desk had the newest version of the MacBook Pro
laptop open on it. She practically drooled. She'd wanted
to replace her old iMac for forever. He looked back at her.
"A little institutional, but not sinister. Just make yourself
at home. I've been up all night, so I could use a . . . uh . . .
well, a shower, and then you can tell me what you need
from your apartment."

She nodded thoughtfully. She'd rather be in her own
place, but he might have a point about Medraught. Mordred. *If* Mordred was looking for her. *If* he was Mordred.
What a mess!

She sat in the big green squishy leather couch with the
striped and plaid throw pillows while he went into the
bathroom. She heard the thunk of boots on the floor and
the rush of water.

This whole thing was as strange as it got. An honest-
to-god knight? To protect *her*?

Nope. This was all some hoax by a very sick man and
she'd better get out of here pronto.

But he knew Medraught of Orkney was Medraught's
full name. He looked just like that boy she'd seen in the
fifth century. And then there were the eyes . . .

What could be stranger than the fact that she'd gone
back in time using a machine made by Leonardo da
Vinci? Maybe he *was* Gawain. She was definitely not in
Kansas anymore.

She looked around the living room. Nothing personal
here. Okay. A book. She scooted over to the little side
table and turned it around. *The Missing Manual* for Mac-

Book Pro. He'd been studying how to work his new computer. Not revealing.

The shower still hissed from the bathroom. She took a breath and decided. She refused to tiptoe, but she did walk very quietly back to his bedroom and slipped through the half-open door. *Ahhh.* Bookshelves. Lots of them. Crammed with books. This was more like it. Books always told you something about their owner. She went over to peer at the titles. *Wow.* Eclectic. Modern mechanics, Proust, Kurt Vonnegut, some manga, lots of history . . . And an entire set of romance novels by Diana Dearborn.

Oh my. They weren't pristine, either. The spines were bent. Someone had read them. Unless he bought them used, *he* had read them. She felt a blush rising as she straightened.

"Of course I'd want to read them."

She jumped out of her skin and whirled around. He was standing there with only a towel draped around his hips and tucked in precariously on one side. He held his boots and an armful of his discarded clothes. She noted all that, even as the heat rose in her chest and neck and face. What was making her blink was all that expanse of chest dusted with dark hair, and how broad and muscled his shoulders were. And then there were the nipples tightened from the cool air after the warmth of his shower and the bulge of his biceps where he held his clothes. And let's not forget the corrugated abs and the narrow hips. The feeling between her legs was almost pain. Really different reaction than she'd had to Mordred in the same state of dress. Gawain smelled like soap. An image of him washing himself all over in the shower with a bar of soap floated around in her mind and wouldn't dissipate. His hair was wet, and though he'd toweled it dry, a drip of water coursed down his chest. . . .

What was *that*? A tattoo. Her eyes raced over his body

with slightly different awareness. He had several others, all intricate, fancy knots of some kind. Celtic. They were Celtic. But they weren't expertly done like other tattoos she'd seen.

More like prison tats. *No, no, no.* She didn't want them to be prison tats. They were just primitive tattoos done in the fifth century. That was all.

He followed her gaze. She realized he'd been letting her look her fill.

"Is that how they did tattoos back then?" That's what he'd tell her, no matter where he got them. And she'd never be able to prove he was lying.

"No."

That was surprising. And she was *never* surprised at what people said. He looked sad, just for a minute, or maybe ashamed. Then he turned to a large wicker basket in the corner and lifted the lid to toss in his dirty clothes. "I got them in prison. In this century." His broad back had muscles and more tattoos. She registered scars and realized she'd seen some on his chest and shoulder as well. He opened a drawer in the dresser.

"I thought you said you'd only been here a month."

"At this apartment a month. I've been in this time for twelve years, maybe a little more." He had a fist full of socks and some boxers. He pulled open the closet to reveal hangers with jeans and shirts and a single suit that she could see.

"Oh," she said in a small voice. *Prison.* "What . . . what were you in for?"

"Killing a couple of men."

"Oh." *Maybe he didn't do it. Wasn't that what they all said?*

"And I wasn't innocent. But it was a fair fight." He'd surprised her again. He glanced back to her as he pulled out a hanger with jeans on it. "Well, pretty fair. There were about eight of them. Some of them had guns, but I had my sword. I expect I had a slight advantage."

He was so matter-of-fact. He didn't make excuses, or say it was wrong to have put him in prison. And he took his prowess for granted.

"You know, sooner or later, you're going to have to decide whether you trust me." He turned around, and his eyes were that clear green again. He looked so serious. Then suddenly he looked away, chuckling and shaking his head. When he turned his face back up his eyes were still laughing. He shrugged helplessly. "I know it all sounds crazy. But you went back in time. What's crazier than that? We're in this together, whether you want that or not. So trust me."

That echoed somewhere deep down inside her. As she took a long breath, she knew she believed him, whether that was smart or not. She exhaled. Her lips curved into a small smile.

"That's better," he said. "Now. Tell me what you need from your apartment."

"Have you ever known any woman who could do that? I'm coming with you." She'd made her decision. She wanted to know this man, and know what he knew. Besides, she still had to talk him out of killing Mordred.

Mordred opened the computer on the park bench under the big gazebo in the gray morning light. It was drizzling, but here the air was cool and he was dry. Shabby men slept on benches. Others played some board game set between them. The button to turn the machine on was self-evident. While it powered up with a hum, he opened the book he'd stolen from the girl and scanned it quickly, learning about touch pads and clicking. It had taken him some time to learn to read the modern language yesterday and he still wasn't entirely proficient, but he got the gist. He spent some time clicking on pictures. *Interesting.* This little window on his new world would tell him everything he needed to know. Including another place to sell his coins for the paper that passed for money in this time. One the girl wouldn't know he knew about. He typed in "coins" and "San Francisco." His new home. He smiled to himself. Soon it would belong to him. He clicked on various names of dealers. They had addresses, hours, even maps. *Perfect.*

What could one not do with machines that let you look into other places? This time was venal, too. That would suit his purpose. And the leaders were soft. He had seen them on the television. He would be another Caesar, with tribute paid to him from many lands.

First he needed an army. Some might think that difficult, but it was easy to find an army. You looked for disaffected men with much rage and little leadership, already organized, but bickering and impotent. Then you offered them what they most craved: people to blame for what they feared and a leader to give them direction. And they were yours. He'd thought about using the brown men he saw lounging on street corners yesterday. They fit the bill. But they might not accept him. They were too different. He must find a group who could see themselves reflected in his countenance. He would find them. And they would be his.

In the same way, he had known that the girl with the magic machine in the circle of stones was so tender-hearted she'd keep him from being killed if she could. She'd been almost too easy. Too bad he'd not been able to have sex with her while he slept in her apartment. But he couldn't ravish her while he needed her goodwill. Then she'd gone to the man who seemed to know him, and Mordred had been forced to move on quickly. They both would know him now.

Inconvenient. But he knew how to take care of that.

Chapter Seven

Gawain sat in his Range Rover outside the coin dealer's shop over on Polk trying not to look at Diana, asleep in the passenger's seat. The dealer said he hadn't seen Mordred. So they were on a stakeout, hoping Mordred would show up.

Not comfortable for Diana. Women always had to go to the bathroom. But there was a McDonalds' at the corner where he could watch her all the way into the Ladies through the glass. He wasn't letting her out of his sight. Not now that he'd tracked her down after all these years. She'd had to make the trek a couple of times already in the steady rain. The last time she'd brought back big cheeseburgers and Diet Cokes. Between the doughnuts and McDonald's, he was going to have to run a few extra miles tomorrow. If he got the chance. He might be dead tomorrow if he found Mordred. He was strong, but Mordred had better magic.

It was cool in the car because they had to leave the windows open to keep them from steaming up. Gawain was the one steaming, in spite of the brisk air. He glanced to Diana. The bulky sweater was nothing if not chaste. Jeans and boots? Hardly provocative. But the swell of her breast under the sweater did things to him. The curve of her bottom in the jeans . . .

His own jeans were getting uncomfortable. You weren't supposed to think of the one you were sworn to protect like that, no matter how long it had been since you'd had a woman. That was a failure of honor. Not surprising, from him.

He'd even failed at protecting her, for more than twelve years at least. He'd been too late to prevent her going back in time, too late to prevent her bringing Mordred forward, a disaster he would now have to correct. To spare her pain he must ensure she remain ignorant of some things.

Since he'd found her, he'd studied her movements, read her books. He felt he knew her soul now. Her books were packed with her sensuality and her intelligence—emotional as well as intellectual. They were fierce forays into other lives, other times. She was courageous, of course. The only glaring weakness in her writing was her heroes. They talked about their feelings. What man did that? Yet, all in all, he liked the woman who wrote those books. Not surprising. He only hoped that who she was would let her accept . . . well, who she really was.

He glanced away from the coin dealer's shop to take in her sleeping form. You had to see her eyes to really appreciate her. Oh, she had lovely fair skin and silky brown hair. Her heart-shaped face was quintessentially feminine. But her eyes grabbed your soul and shook it. They said she knew sorrow, that she *understood* things. Except maybe men. The way her eyes shifted from gray to green in the light almost made him think she had eyes like his own. But no one had those anymore.

Lucky for them. He had a hard time controlling his eyes changing color these days. Which was why he didn't look at anybody directly. He mostly glanced up from under his brows and let people's inclination to call the color change a trick of the light do the rest.

He'd had to let Diana see his eyes in the liquor store. That was the only way into her dreams. He needed her to trust him, and the way to get her trust was through her dreams. He wasn't sure she did trust him even now. He'd botched even so little a task.

She stretched and opened weary eyes. She probably hadn't been sleeping well lately, he thought with some guilt. The stretch was . . . unfortunate. Her breasts swelled under the sweater.

"Good afternoon," he said, clearing his throat and willing his thoughts into other channels.

"Nothing?" she asked.

"Nada." He spoke Spanish now as well as Latin, Celtic, and English. Thank prison for that. It was easier to get by if you spoke everyone's language. And if you were good with your fists.

She fell silent. Not a good sign. He could practically hear her thinking. Her curiosity was his worst enemy. True answers to her questions would only frighten her. The only thing to do was put her on the defensive. "So how did you go back in time to get him?"

He saw her thinking about lying, or refusing to tell him. In the end, she just sighed. "I warn you, it's hard to believe."

He shot her a look under his brows.

"Okay. I see your point." She shrugged apologetically. "Well . . . a woman I didn't know gave me a very valuable book, out of the blue." Her glance stole to her shoulder bag on the floor at her feet. "She insisted I use it to make myself happy, that it was my destiny. And she told me to look behind a door that's always locked at the Exploratorium."

"What was this book?"

"It was by Leonardo da Vinci. Do you know about him?"

"Of course I know about him. There *are* history books in prison."

"Don't be so sensitive. I'm just trying to be polite and not make assumptions."

"Okay. You're polite." He didn't mean his voice to be so gruff. She was right. He was sensitive. Being Merlin's son was a curse. Everyone either feared him because they thought he might have his father's magic or pitied him because he didn't. He'd kept quiet about what small powers he came into at puberty. Better his father think the magic skipped him altogether than that he was only a fraction of the heir his father wanted. His disappointment had been a ghost that haunted Gawain. Instead, he trained. He poured his frustration and his disappointment in himself into becoming a warrior. Muscles you could get through force of will alone. Magic you couldn't. His father discounted his achievements, of course. And he failed at being a truly perfect knight at every turn. But he wouldn't blow this chance to prove himself. His father had given him a task. He might be late in executing it, but he could still protect Diana. "And what did Leonardo have to do with time?"

"The book said he made a time machine." She glanced again to the bag at her feet. "I didn't believe it of course."

"But he did. Mordred is certain proof. So the machine was hidden in the Exploratorium?"

"Yeah." She seemed a little amazed. God, when she looked at him with those clear, gray-green eyes, he could feel it right through to his soul. Or . . . maybe right straight down to his . . .

He shifted uncomfortably, and felt a flush rising to his face. "So show me."

"What?"

"Well, you've got the book in your bag, haven't you?"

She looked like she'd been caught robbing a bank.

"Don't be ridiculous. I won't take it."

She unfroze herself and, after some hesitation, reached for her shoulder bag, hefted it onto her lap, and pulled out a large book bound in beautifully tooled leather. A scene of angels swirling up toward heaven decorated the front cover. Clearly Renaissance. She ran her fingertips over it reverently. "It's miraculous, really, that he could have built a time machine in 1508. And yet, if anyone could do it, wouldn't it have been Leonardo da Vinci?"

"He was a magician, you know." Gawain knew about magicians.

She laughed. He hadn't heard her laugh before. It shot straight to his heart. It sounded like the Diana he knew from her books. "Artist, emphatically yes. Scientist, of course. The best of his time. But magician?"

"What do you think a magician is but someone who understands the beauty inherent in the way the world works on such an elemental level that the way he uses those rules seems miraculous to us?"

Her mouth parted. Her lips formed a soft, "Oh." She blinked twice. "I . . . I guess I never thought of it that way." And then the way she looked at him . . . changed. Her head cocked and she examined him with a new curiosity. Was there . . . was there a little heat in that gaze? God preserve him from a look like that. His treacherous body was already urging him to abandon the sanctity of his role as protector.

"Who would know a magician better than I do?" He stared out the windshield into the rain. "I was born of one."

"I guess you're right." She held out the book, hesitant. "Do you want to see it?"

He turned his head only. She offered her most prized

possession to him. If that wasn't a gesture of trust, he didn't know what was. He nodded, and opened the book carefully.

Only one day since he'd been on his own and he had money, a roof over his head, and a plan. Medraught of Orkney threw his duffle onto the couch. Through huge sheets of glass he could see the harbor on one side and a street that cut straight up a steep hill on the other. The man who had rented it to him said it wasn't finished yet. But Medraut didn't care. One could have gatherings of many men here. And because the other lofts were not yet inhabited, there would be no one to report those gatherings to the king as long as they occurred at night, after the workers had departed. *Wait*. In a city the ruler was now called a mayor, though he seemed relatively powerless, according to the online edition of the *Examiner*. He couldn't even rule his own council, who might be called Supervisors but appeared to supervise nothing.

This time was perfect. It needed someone willing to take power and use it. This teeming city would be his. Its wealth, the ships in its harbor (made of metal!), the cars that hummed everywhere—all would bend to his will. He had even seen his first airplane today. How they could make a metal tube fly through the sky like a bird he didn't yet know. But he would.

He put his palms on the glass of the huge windows, his forehead pressed against the pane, giddy with the possibilities of it. It seemed that he was falling through space and that only magic kept him afloat above the city. He was charmed with the danger of it, the wonder.

He shut the door on the old time and for the first time in his forty years he felt some measure of peace. He'd done what he'd had to do to take his birthright in Camelot. He'd killed the man who kept it from him. Arthur. His father, though not in name or fatherly concern. Mordred had come face-to-face with the man who had no other heir of his loins and yet refused Mordred the kingdom, who thought he wasn't good enough to steward Arthur's life's work, and he had run him through and watched him topple, life's blood leaking into the soil he so loved.

Now who was the better man?

Mordred's arm throbbed. He would take some of the tablets the girl had given him in a moment. He had come away with naught but a scratch, and though uncomfortable, it did not seem to be festering. He would live while Arthur died.

More important, he had been swept away to a world that was truly worth his talents. The poor wooden palisades, men hacking at each other on horseback with swords—was this enough for a man like him? No. He no longer cared what happened to Camelot. It would fall to the Saxons. He laughed. *Had* fallen to the Saxons no doubt, fifteen hundred years ago. He ran his hands over his beard, listening to the wonder in his own laugh.

The girl had been his savior in some ways. But she would have to die. She and the man who recognized him. That was the one who had shot at him. It was him the girl had gone to meet when she sneaked away this morning. They were plotting against him. He couldn't let them reveal his true identity. So now they had to die.

The man looked familiar, but Mordred couldn't place him. Was he, too, from the past? Had he used the machine to come searching for Mordred? Sent by the remnants of Arthur's army?

Or Merlin? Merlin had never been his friend.

It hit him like a stone. The man looked like Merlin and Merlin had a brat, got off the witch Nimue. So. Merlin had sent his son to track Mordred down, even unto this century. But this one was not the great magician his father was. Mordred snorted in derision. This one would be easy to defeat. Mordred would find and kill them both.

But first, to start upon the path to an army. Time to get busy, as they said here.

He went to the couch, delivered today, and plugged his computer into the outlet in the floor next to it. The couch and two big stuffed chairs sat around a finely woven rug in many colors over the bare stone floor. A bed crouched in the corner with clear bags of quilts and pillows strewn across it. A dining table and chairs of some dark wood he didn't recognize occupied the center of another rug, like islands in the vast sea of open floor.

Now to find like minds he could bend into an army. White, like himself. Manly men, familiar with weapons, self-reliant. And angry. He needed to find angry.

He found Google as the boy this morning at the large gazebo had shown him. . . .

Chapter Eight

.

"Well, that was time we'll never get back," Diana said as she shook raindrops off her slicker in the hall just outside Gawain's apartment.

Gawain wiped his feet on the doormat as he turned the key in the lock and pushed it open, holding it for her to enter. What guy did that for a woman these days? She furled her umbrella. He hung her slicker on a coatrack to drip, then shrugged out of his leather jacket and hung it on an adjacent peg. Her huge roller bag sat under the coatrack from their trip to her apartment this morning. He'd insisted she bring her mandolin. He'd set the tiny instrument case carefully against the wall. All that was missing was her computer bag. No computer anymore. She touched her sweater and felt for the thumb drive that hung around her neck. There it was, under the thick knit, hanging between her breasts. That was all she had left of the book she'd been writing. Twenty-five pages and an awful synopsis. It felt tiny and vulnerable there, like the wispy flame of a candle guttering against the darkness.

"There's always tomorrow," Gawain said. But he was frowning. His hair dripped on his red flannel shirt. Why couldn't guys use umbrellas? Three buttons were open at his neck. That meant you could see dark, curling hair.

And *that* meant that you couldn't stop thinking about how his chest had looked just out of the shower this morning. At least she couldn't.

She cleared her throat. "Uh . . . I'm not sure we can count on him showing up there tomorrow, either. He's a smart guy. He must know we'd look for him at places familiar to him."

"Then he could be anywhere." There was a note of desperation in Gawain's voice as he flopped onto the green leather couch.

She put down her precious shoulder bag and sat in the plaid wing chair across from him. A nice safe distance away. "We'll find him."

Gawain gave her a look under his brows. His eyes were dark, dark blue. He looked disgusted with himself. Sure enough, he said, "My father *must* have meant to protect you from Mordred. And now I cannot find him to kill him."

"Well, I'm still okay. All's not lost yet." She wanted to touch his arm, his shoulder, to steady him, but she was pretty sure the effect on her would be a disaster, and she didn't want to seem like she was coming on to him. He'd think she was pathetic, a girl who looked like she did coming on to a guy like him. She'd been startled this afternoon at how intelligent he was. All that talk about what made a magician . . . Was it fair for a guy who looked like that to be smart, too? "You're just hungry. Do you want to order out? Or I could forage in your kitchen and see what I can come up with."

He cracked a smile. *My, my.* White teeth, crinkles at the edges of his eyes—could a guy get more gorgeous? The smile made him look much younger. That smile actually seemed . . . familiar, comforting, as though she had waited for it before. "Let me do the foraging," he said. "I shall provide." He was up and striding over to the little kitchen. "Haven't had time to buy much lately." He opened the freezer.

"Too busy stalking me." She wandered after him and leaned on the bar between the kitchen and the living room.

He rooted around in the freezer until he came up with a freezer bag filled with something brown. "How about some leftover brisket?"

"Sure." Wasn't brisket about the toughest and cheapest cut of meat there was? And she'd get to eat it left over. *Yummy.*

He rummaged around in the refrigerator and came up, to her surprise, with a head of cauliflower. Her least favorite vegetable besides kale or chard or something else weird like that. "No salad stuff, I'm afraid. But I can make something out of this."

He seemed cheerful about it. Brisket and cauliflower. He continued to rummage. His fridge actually had things in it, unlike hers. He took out a white wine bottle and examined the label. Another smile. "Here's a Ferrari-Carano chard. Bet you'd like that." He glanced over to her. "Cooking goes better with wine."

Well, that at least sounded good after a day like today. "Let me open it. That's probably how you got all those scars. Drinking with knives around." She took the bottle. He spun around and pulled a corkscrew from a drawer.

"Nope. Got them all stone-cold sober. I never drink and fight."

She didn't know what to say to that. She'd never had to fight in her life. She opened the wine as she watched him set the freezer bag with the brisket in it in a sink filled with warm water and turn on the oven. She took two glasses from the cupboard over the dishwasher where everyone kept their glasses. Oakwood was no exception. She poured two glasses of wine and put one on the counter next to where he was chopping up the cauliflower. What guy had cauliflower in his refrigerator, by the way? Oh, cauliflower had been around for forever, and it kept a long time. Of course they would have eaten it in the fifth century. Wasn't it related to cabbage? *Great.* Another least favorite vegetable.

She eased past him, thinking the kitchen was way too small for both of them. She was very aware of his body. *Concentrate,* she told herself. She sat on a stool where she could watch him work. He was good with a knife. Probably not surprising.

"I learned to cook in prison," he remarked as he got out a big, straight-sided Calphalon pan.

"You're kidding."

He didn't seem inclined to elaborate. *Guys.* But after a minute of silent chopping he cleared his throat and said, "I got assigned to the kitchen. The food mostly sucked. But the cons in Cell Block B tended a garden, and there was a chef in for knifing the sous chef who'd been, uh. . . . having relations with his wife. The meat wasn't high quality, but he made it palatable."

"So you learned from him?" She was about to get prison food for dinner.

"Yeah. The kitchen was a good assignment. It gave you a trade when you got out. And I guess I was interested in eating. We didn't do it real regularly back in the Resistance. I wouldn't have been in line for the kitchen except they had to get me out of the laundry."

"Why was that?"

"It was that or enlarge the infirmary." He shot her a glance as he gathered the florets and threw them into the big pan. "I didn't play well with others." She stared at him. "I never started it," he assured her.

But he finished it. "I've heard gangs in prison are really bad."

He rummaged in the fridge again and came up with

some butter. "Bullies are everywhere. I tried to keep to myself. But I didn't speak modern English when I first got there. Guess they thought I was an easy mark."

So that's how he got the scars. At least some of them.

When he spoke again, his tone was deliberately light. "The literacy program was pretty good in the joint. Better than the one at the mental hospital. I'm not an Adapter like Mordred."

"Mental hospital?" She realized with a start that she thought this guy was saner than most people she knew. To know that he had been in a mental hospital shocked her. Was she wrong?

He saw her look, and his expression clearly registered his "oops." He turned to confront her: "I'm not a serial killer, I swear. When I first landed in this time, dressed in crazy clothes, speaking a language no one recognized, having just killed two guys in an alley, they . . . they thought I was . . . uh . . . a little off." He shrugged and stared out the window over the kitchen sink into the wet and shiny black of the San Francisco night. "They couldn't even interview me. There was no doubt I did it. There were eyewitnesses. And I . . . uh . . . tended to struggle when they tried to put the shackles on." That rang a bell with Diana. He'd been scared. "So, mental hospital it was. And lots of drugs." Here he broke his reverie and pulled the freezer bag with the brisket in it out of the sink full of water. "So I acted sedate and palmed the drugs. I realized one of the doctors was using Latin words. I spoke Latin." He glanced up at her and shrugged. "He didn't want to think about why I spoke only a dead language like Latin. He just wanted me out of there. He got me transferred to prison. That was lucky."

"Lucky?" *Right*. She was suddenly glad she'd avoided a mental hospital when she'd been scared like that. This guy didn't have a Jenna Armstrong to help him.

He tossed the butter into the pan and sprinkled in some salt. "Prison was way better. Fierce and coldhearted I understand. Crazy I don't. I got twenty to life for multiple manslaughters, once the shrink told them that my language 'problem' was post-traumatic stress syndrome. Time off for good behavior after I got kitchen duty—I only served about twelve years."

Didn't the eyewitnesses tell anybody that he'd been attacked first? They sent him to a mental hospital where they drugged him and to prison, where he had to fight for his life. That was lucky? He *was* a glass-half-full person.

"The worst part," he continued, "was not knowing if you needed my protection when I wasn't there to give it."

Again with the protection thing. "So, you going to tell me why it's me? Or not?"

He grabbed his glass of wine and took a sip, buying time. What would he say? She wanted to know in the worst way, and the only way she could find out was to wait for him to tell her. Finally, he gave a shrug and poured some of the white wine into the pan with the cauliflower. "My father just said you were important."

Merlin. Merlin, who lived fifteen hundred years ago, thought she was important and needed protection. A girl in twenty-first-century San Francisco. She watched Gawain put the brisket in a pan with some orangish sauce from the plastic Baggie it had been in and slide it into the oven.

She sighed. If he knew more, he wasn't going to tell her. "You don't make it easy."

He was back to stirring his cauliflower. "Whatever the reason, we're going to find Mordred and I'm going to kill him and then you'll be safe."

Diana looked up into eyes that were a swirling mass of color again. Now why exactly did she think this guy was sane?

* * *

"So, was Guinevere really having an affair with . . . with someone? We all say it was Lancelot, but apparently he's fictional."

Gawain chuffed a laugh and shook his head. "She loved Arthur, hard as he was to love."

The brisket was so tender it flaked into little strings spiced in a kind of New Orleans style. Gawain said you got it that way by putting it in the oven overnight on low. The cauliflower was braised with butter and wine. She'd never tasted better cauliflower. Prison food? It was a nearly perfect meal. It served her right to be so wrong about him. He was a complicated guy. Masculine to the nth degree, and yet able to turn simple ingredients into a fabulous meal.

"Arthur was hard to love? We idolize him." Maybe she didn't want to really know the truth if all her dreams were to be dashed.

"Oh, he was idolized back then too." Gawain sat back in his chair at the little dining table. "Brave in battle. A superb strategist. His men would follow him into the nether realm itself. He cared for the common people. You've no idea how rare that was in those days. And he was building a city out of stone where there was only mud before." He lifted his wineglass and drained the last. They'd switched to red. "But that doesn't make him easy for a woman to love."

A perfect hero. How not? And yet . . .

Gawain sighed. He must have seen her expression. "Exactly. Always thinking of other things. Away at war. He didn't treasure her as he should have."

Diana couldn't help the fact that her eyes widened. "You loved her."

He flushed and made a deprecating gesture with his

mouth. "Calf-love. I was ten when it fell. Remember? We all loved her, even the least of us."

"What happened to her, after . . . after Camelot fell?"

"She went to a nunnery. But of course, Cerdic couldn't leave it at that. She was too much an icon. Men would follow her, even with Arthur gone."

"So Cerdic was . . . ?"

The leader of the Saxons. When Camelot fell, he burned the abbey with her in it." Gawain's voice was flat, as though that could conceal the emotion behind the words. A terrible look crossed his face, devastation, anger . . . self-loathing? His eyes went an angry, churning brown.

"Not your fault."

"We should have sent a force to defend her. My . . . my father wouldn't countenance it. He said . . . he said it had to happen. He'd seen it in the future."

Whoa. How hard to live with was that? *Your father essentially condemning the woman you loved to death? Refusing to let you protect her?* No wonder he was so obsessive about protecting people. "It must have been hard to be Merlin's son."

"Sometimes." His expression said, *All the time.* But he wasn't going to elaborate. He took a breath. "Her death created the Resistance. We punished those who committed atrocities like that. We lived in caves, in swamps." He managed a smile.

"Until your father sent you forward in time . . ."

"Yes." He stood and began taking dishes to the sink. "He gave me a job to do."

His expression was closed but also telling. She saw it all. He clung to that job. After a life of learning to live with unconscionable loss, it was all he had. He'd not only lost the woman he loved, but he'd also lost his whole world, his father—difficult as his relationship with his father was—everything he knew until he came forward in time. All gone. He had only the honor of fulfilling his job. His eyes turned steel blue.

And that job was . . . her? To protect *her*? For God's sake, *why*?

She wasn't worth that kind of effort. So what if Mordred killed her? She was a person no one even noticed. Gawain was mistaken. He might have been sent to protect this century from Mordred. Mordred had consequence. He'd brought down Camelot. He'd changed the course of history. He even had magic powers. Gawain had been sent for him.

So maybe, hard as it was to stomach, Gawain was meant to kill him.

But what could Mordred actually *do* here in this time? He could be a serial killer. Would it change history? This century spawned serial killers right and left. Maybe he was going to kill someone important like the president or something.

"What is the saying now? A penny for your thoughts."

Diana started and looked up. "Sorry. Just thinking about what a mess we're in. How will we ever find Mordred if he doesn't want to be found?"

While she'd been lost in thought, Gawain had taken dishes into the kitchen. She couldn't help but watch how his big body moved under his shirt. "I'd say we could bribe someone to trace his credit cards, but we don't know whose cards he's using," Gawain said over his shoulder.

"Let me clean up at least." She rose and pushed him out to the little dining room. "Unless you have some hidden source of income, we don't have the money for a bribe." *Hmmmm.* Oakwood apartments cost an arm and a leg, because mostly corporations footed the bill. How could he afford to live here when he was just out of prison? "Besides, he's using the cash from the coin I sold for him, not credit cards."

Gawain gave her a look out from under raised brows. "He'll have stolen credit cards by now. Maybe even killed for them. Easier and quicker than selling coins."

"If he killed for them, the police will be after him. *They* can trace his use of the cards." She put the rinsed plates into the dishwasher.

Gawain's brows drew together. "They'd put him in prison. That would be bad. Not only could I not get in to kill him, but he would have a ready-made army of hardened soldiers in there. He'd have them converted into fanatic followers in no time."

No help there, then. "Oh my God! I was supposed to go down to the police station with him today." She moaned and tossed the sponge into the sink. "They have my driver's license, and my car. How could I have forgotten? Oh, I am in so much trouble."

"We'll go in tomorrow," he soothed. "You'll say he disappeared, that you spent the day looking for him. All true, by the way. Not a big deal. I'll go with you."

"So I show up with another guy with no identity? That'll be just great."

"I've got an identity. Driver's license. I've even got a prison record. I'm a real citizen." He poured soap in the dispenser, shut the door, and pushed the button to start the dishwasher. It gurgled to life. Where had he gotten a driver's license? Maybe she didn't want to know.

Straightening, he said, "Really, don't worry about this."

Yeah. They did have bigger fish to fry. "So how are we going to find him?"

Gawain plopped back down in his chair and sighed. His eyes were gray. He ran his hand through his hair. Diana gave a little gasp. The gesture was so familiar, it sent an electric jolt of . . . of longing straight down to . . .

"What is it?"

She shook her head convulsively. "Nothing. Nothing.

This is just all so strange." A sense of *tristesse* washed over her. Something was missing and she'd lost it, and it was something she wanted more than anything in the world.

He reached across the table as though to take her hand, then snatched his back. He sucked in a breath and his eyes changed from shifting gray to a steel-hard blue-gray. His face shut down. He took two ragged breaths and shoved himself up from the table. "Well, I'll just take your bag into your bedroom. I'm sure . . . Well, it's been a long day. You . . . you probably have writing to do."

Writing?

"You're close to a deadline, aren't you? You can use my computer. All set up on the desk in that bedroom and everything."

She blinked twice. "How did you know I was close to a deadline?" Almost past, in truth, and not a book in sight. But how would he know that? A chill ran down her spine.

He looked confused. "Uh. Well, the clerk at the liquor store says you let your milk go sour when you're on deadline and you buy more at the liquor store instead of going over to Ralphs. He's really proud of you and your books, you know."

"Uh . . . yeah." This man knew more about her than . . . than anyone had a right to know.

It hit her. This guy was the closest thing she had to a friend in the world. That was pathetic. She'd known him one day, and yesterday she'd been sure he was stalking her. She'd taken a time machine and brought back the baddest of bad guys, and now they couldn't find him or tell anyone and tomorrow she had to go to the police station, for goodness' sake. Her head bent of its own accord and she stood there, wavering, trying to get a grip.

A strong arm slid around her shoulders. Heat radiated through her body. "You just go to bed and get some sleep," Gawain murmured.

She looked up to find that his eyes had gone a soft, clear green. The color of his eyes was like a new language, one she wanted to learn. The weight on her chest began to melt a little. Her eyes filled, though. She couldn't help that.

He gathered her into his arms and hugged her to his chest. Hard muscle surrounded her. He laid her head against his chest. "Don't worry. I'll take care of you now." And that was so tempting. The masculine smell of him, his warmth of his breath on her head as he bent over her, the beating of his heart, all assuaged a longing she hadn't even known she had until now.

Then the melting feeling grew hotter. The weight seemed to move from her chest to pool between her legs. She looked up at him, acutely aware that her body was pressed along the length of his. Her eyes would reflect the heat. He would know she lusted after him. She pushed herself away. How embarrassing! Throwing herself at him like that.

"I'm so sorry. I . . . I don't mean to be a burden. . . ." His hands hovered at her shoulders. "It's just . . . it all seemed so much. I . . . You're right. I need to get some sleep." She ducked away and backed toward the hallway.

He looked acutely embarrassed, too. How would he not be embarrassed that she'd turned a comforting gesture into something it was never meant to be? "I'll just get your things." He reached down for her roller bag with a pained expression.

She turned and ran for the second bedroom.

Chapter Nine

Damn. How could he have ruined everything by getting an erection when he had meant only to comfort her? She'd felt it. She must have. He'd heard her lock herself into the guest bedroom after he delivered her suitcase. Who could blame her? Some honorable knight he was. It was one thing to bed willing women and quite another to frighten a woman dependent on you for her protection. Around Diana his control evaporated like water on a griddle.

She couldn't know that he would never force himself on her. And his body betrayed him at every turn. He used the bathroom quickly and splashed cold water on his face. That didn't help. He went into his own room and shut the door firmly, so she could hear. Not that it would make her feel secure. His own discomfort only seemed to be growing as he thought about her. He threw himself down on his bed.

But he could hear her unpacking, moving around in her room, perhaps getting ready for bed . . . taking off her clothes. . . . What would her body be like? Soft, lush, pale. Was she innocent?

How dare he have such thoughts? *He* was not innocent. That was what mattered. Another failure. Even now, his cock strained at his jeans. He got up and stripped off his clothes. He opened the window. Chill sea air from the bay swept in. He would sleep naked in the cold. That would take care of his erection.

But it didn't. He tossed and turned, refusing to relieve his torment himself. He was not that small a soul. He had descended to jerking at himself sometimes during the long years in prison. It had given his body some relief. But this was more than just a weakness of his body. It was a sickness in his heart that allowed him to lust after and frighten the woman he was sworn to protect. He was unlucky that she had turned into a delectable woman. Or maybe he was lucky. No. He couldn't think like that. He would enter her dreams again tonight, let her know she could still trust him. He waited until he saw the tiny glow of her light disappear from the crack under his door. He could practically feel it when she finally fell asleep. He might not have his father's powers, but he was good with dreams.

Diana couldn't believe she'd embarrassed herself by letting him know that she . . . she . . . was attracted to him. Like a guy who looked like he did would spare a glance for a girl like her.

Was that why she wrote romances—to work out a happy ending where a guy like Gawain loved and treasured a girl like her? And had sex with her? Because she did write sex in her romances. How could you not include sex when it was such an important part of the relationship between a man and a woman?

Maybe that was why she wasn't a bestselling author. Maybe everyone knew that she'd never truly experienced what she was writing about. They always said write what you know. And instead she wrote about what she'd read in other books, something she'd never experienced firsthand. Not that she hadn't had sex. She'd made sure she had. But that one rushed time with a drunk college guy on the dark floor of his bedroom in the frat house didn't seem to bear any relationship to the kind of sex other romance writers wrote about.

And she knew how to pleasure herself. You could buy books that told you just how to do it at that store over on Mission Street that specialized in sex toys and a female-friendly atmosphere. But it wasn't the same, and everyone who read her books probably knew exactly how much experience she'd had.

She finished unpacking the few clothes she'd brought and put her mandolin case in the closet. She wasn't going to intrude on Gawain's insistent hospitality long, regardless of the situation. It was just too demeaning. Her attraction to him was pathetic. How could she even face him tomorrow?

She needed a distraction. She'd just check that her thumb drive was okay. She powered up Gawain's MacBook Pro and pulled the cord with the thumb drive from around her neck. She stuck it in the UBS port. Clicking on the icon, she held her breath.

The list came up. All her books were there, including the latest. She sighed and opened the document. It was still there, all twenty-five pages of it. She glanced over the first pages. First sentence not evocative enough. First page wordy. Too much thinking going on and not enough action for today's market. Why did she even bother to save it? The heroine was an overconfident bitch who'd be more at home on *Melrose Place* or *Desperate Housewives*. The hero—well, her Gawain seemed made of cardboard, not a real man at all. Not, at least, compared to the man in the next room, who was annoyingly protective, and no doubt knew how to use that big knife he carried, and yet also knew how to cook, at least guy-things like brisket. The real man had issues. He was . . . difficult. And nothing could mask the fact that he still mourned Guinevere.

She put her head in her hands. She'd come on to a guy who was in love with *Guinevere.* Guinevere was in a league even movie stars couldn't be in, let alone a mousy-looking romance writer. No one could remember what color her eyes were two minutes after she left them.

Write what you know. Like she would know anything about love. Or men.

She scrolled down to where she introduced the hero. What he needed was a few scars. Gawain was a fighter after all. And there had to be a lot more dirt in Camelot than she'd put in. More soot from the fires. The place would be drafty at night. And maybe it wasn't completed. It still had sections of wooden palisades in the outer wall.

Sometime later she realized she was writing because she didn't want to think. She didn't want to think about how she felt about the man in the other bedroom, since it was going to go nowhere, and she didn't want to think about how she had totally embarrassed herself tonight. She sat back in the desk chair. If only she could just leave right now, run away.

But she couldn't. He might be right. If Mordred wasn't wild about the fact that she knew who he was, she might need that big, protective guy around.

She'd probably embarrass herself again tomorrow, making calf eyes at him or something. She got up and put on her sleep shirt and got into the double bed. Depressing. And yet she couldn't stop thinking about him, lying in his own bed in a room with all that Oakwood plaid. Did he sleep in the buff?

Oh, she shouldn't have thought about that.

How she fell asleep that night she never knew. Or why. But she did. And woke up strangely rested, dreams dissipating in the morning light.

It would be okay. Somehow she could trust Gawain to make it okay.

She heard him moving around in the kitchen. *Very well then*. She couldn't avoid him, if she was stuck here. She'd just have to have more self-control today. She gathered her clothing, slipped into the bathroom, showered, and washed her hair. There was a hair dryer under the sink. The very concept of a man from the fifth century owning a hair dryer, even if Oakwood provided it, made her chuckle. That chuckle further relieved her tension. Maybe today he'd come forth with confidences about his love for Guinevere. She could use those in her novel.

That was what he was to her. Research. She'd never known a man up close other than her father, and you never ascribed real emotions and reactions to your father. Fathers were another animal altogether from a man your own age. Or Gawain's age.

She brushed her hair ruthlessly straight, despairing for the millionth time that it wasn't chestnut or auburn or endowed with natural honey-blond highlights. It was brown. A particularly undistinguished brown. Of course, these days you could highlight and lowlight, or make it vibrant red if you dared. But she deserved plain brown hair. She was a plain-brown-hair kind of girl.

That was just what she needed to anchor her. That's who she was. Someone a man like Gawain would never notice. A person who wrote about other people's love stories. So today she'd just apologize to him about getting the wrong idea about his kindness, and that would clear the air. She might be mousy looking, but she wasn't a mouse.

She pulled the white turtleneck tee she'd ordered from Lands' End a couple of weeks ago down over her jeans firmly and opened the bathroom door.

* * *

Gawain started scrambling her some eggs when he heard her drying her hair. He always had bacon, and he made some coffee. He'd better get to the store if they wanted to eat tonight.

He'd not only had access to her dreams last night, but he'd also decided just how to address the . . . the . . . issue. He'd just pretend it never happened. She'd take her cue from him and it would be as though it really *hadn't* happened. That would be good.

God, but you're an idiot. Couldn't you control yourself? You scared her. No. He wouldn't think about that. He'd fixed it up by entering her dreams.

She came out from the back looking like . . . the Christian version of an angel. Her soft hair framed her face. You thought her skin was luminous until you saw her eyes. Then you revised your definition of "luminous."

"Hey, your eggs are just ready." He took down a plain white cup and poured it full of coffee. "Sorry—no Equal, and no cream. Can you do black?"

She looked around, a little dazed. Then she blushed. "Yeah. About last night . . ."

"Did you sleep well?" He scraped the eggs onto a plate.

She took the plate he thrust at her. "Thanks." She looked around. "I did sleep well. But . . ."

"Sit, sit." He shushed her over to the little table. "Eat hearty. We have a lot to do today."

"Gawain, I want you to know . . . about last night. . . ."

By the Grail! Women could *never* take a hint. They had to talk over every detail of a failure until it was fixed in everyone's minds forever. He took a breath. "What about it?" He tried to look expectant. He couldn't help that his eyes slid to the side.

She blinked. "I'm sorry I reacted badly. . . ."

Just push on through. "If you mean having you here is some kind of imposition, it isn't. Oakwood apartments are awash with loneliness. All those transient corporate types, you know." *Why* had he mentioned loneliness? He rushed on. "It's good to have a roommate for a while." He gestured toward her eggs. "They aren't any better cold."

She blinked again, confused. She remembered all too clearly what she'd felt against her belly last night, and she wanted to *talk* about it, for God's sake. After a little silence when her eyes bored in on his expression, she turned to her food. He watched her delicate bowlike mouth slip the eggs from her fork. He couldn't help but smile a little. He'd provided for her. And he'd distracted her from her need to discuss things that should not be discussed. He turned back to the bowl of eggs and splashed some more into the pan. "I was up early." Or late, as you would have it. Or all night long, if truth be told. "And I checked on some other coin dealers. I think that's our best shot."

This Internet was really a marvelous tool. Mordred sat back in the leather couch and sipped a glass of red wine better made than any from the vines the Romans had left in Gaul. The lamp next to him cast a golden cone of light that kept back the dark spaces of his loft. Out the wall of windows, the lights of the city were winking on as dusk settled in. He'd been on the Internet all day, using the girl's computer.

One could talk to people far away as though they were in this very room, just by entering the words and letters of this new language he had learned. For once he thanked Arthur's diligence in making him wield a pen as well as a sword when he was a young man. Now, because he was literate, he could find people. And they could find him. What better for his purpose?

It didn't take him long to learn the secret code to attract the ones he wanted. "White," "pure," "American," "liberty," "taxes," "big government," "Jew," "nigger," "fag." Who they were was in their words, and he fed it back to the Internet, and the responses came pouring in.

These were the disaffected ones, the angry ones. The ones that could be fooled into fighting for him. They would fight for a cause and never know that he had assumed the mantle of that cause until the cause was he and he was the cause. They would put him in power.

They were his.

Now to bring them to his side.

"You speak brave words," he typed. "But where are the deeds that make the words live?"

Immediately a chorus of responses cascaded onto the "post" he'd made. They talked of gatherings of protest. Mere shouting, of course. They talked of pamphlets written. To a small audience of believers only, of course.

He searched the Web sites he had found for evidence of deeds. Long ago some leaders whose words spoke for the side of right and justice had been killed. Nothing recent but a couple of doctors who performed some surgery they didn't like, and some isolated instances of suspected homosexuals. Nothing large scale since that government building in Oklahoma years ago. That meant they craved someone to take them to the next step. On several Web sites he saw a single saying, often available on T-shirts or banners:

The tree of liberty must occasionally be watered by the blood of patriots.

That would do nicely. Add something from the Bible as sauce. He entered several keywords in a concordance of the Bible. Many phrases came up. He scanned them. The Lord's Prayer. Excellent. Religion was always like oil to a fire of ignorance.

He returned to his posting, scanned the replies. Time to put a red-hot poker up their anuses:

> The tree of liberty must occasionally be watered by the blood of those who have trespassed against it. Anything less sends a message of weakness.

Mordred sat back and reached for his goblet of wine. He watched the replies roll in.

Gawain fumbled in the hall for the keys to his apartment, arms full of grocery bags. They'd stopped at Ralphs after a very silent trip home. It shouldn't have surprised Diana that he wouldn't let her help carry any.

"Did I leave the keys in the car?" he muttered, balancing his load and shoving a hand in his front jeans pocket. "I always put them . . ."

"Right jacket pocket," she murmured absently. It had been a depressing day.

"You're right," Gawain said, startled, coming up with his keys. He unlocked the door, looking at her strangely. "I never put them there. Too easy to lose."

Oops. Shouldn't do that. It only draws attention. I should know that by now.

Another little "quirk" she had—finding lost things. She always knew where they were. But she'd learned to camouflage that little knack by asking a few questions of people before she told them where to look for whatever they'd lost. She threw her coat on the couch and pushed herself up onto one of the stools at the bar as Gawain put away the groceries.

"At least we'll have Equal tomorrow," he remarked. His light tone masked a disappointment that matched hers. "I know oxtails don't sound great, but cheap cuts are all I learned to cook in prison."

Had he seen her expression at the meat counter? "If they're as good as the brisket, I'm a lucky woman." She put her chin in her cupped hands, propped up by her elbows.

"At least you've got your car and your license back."

They'd reported Jim Medraught missing. Diana had gotten a lecture about taking in illegal immigrants. The detective had liked Gawain for the shooting until Diana swore he was just a neighbor dragged into taxi service. Of course no one really believed a guy like Gawain would be obsessed with Diana, so they let it drop. Cheery all the way around. And the police thought Mordred had just headed back to Canada. They wouldn't be lifting a finger to look for him. "Yeah. But no Mordred."

He popped open some more white wine. This one was a Sauvignon Blanc from Chile called Caliterra. "We got closer. Here, this will make you feel better."

She sipped. It was great. "I'm not sure we're closer." They'd found the coin dealer Mordred had visited but no information on Mordred himself. That was depressing enough, but all day, in and out of the coin shops from as far away as Saratoga to downtown Marin, she'd been hyperaware of Gawain's body moving inside his clothing, all muscle and sinew, just as she'd seen it after his shower yesterday. She'd never really felt the physicality of a man before. Maybe she'd never been around men. Boys in her classes at college didn't count. Gawain had a mature man's bulk of muscle. His face had lines around his mouth and at the corners of his eyes born of experience and hardship. And she was aware of him with parts of her body that she'd never realized knew how to recognize a man. More than recognize. If she weren't careful, she would embarrass herself again. He hadn't let her apologize for her sad lapse when she'd turned a simple act of comfort into something more . . . or less. Maybe his way was best.

She sipped her wine in silence.

"So, my writer friend," he said finally, as he dumped the oxtails into a big iron pot. "If you were writing this in a novel, what would our heroes do to pry Mordred's location out of the coin dealer?"

That made her smile a little. His eyes glinted in return. "Uh . . . well . . . First of all, only one of them would have accosted him the first time, so he wouldn't recognize the second one."

"Oh." His voice fell. "And why is that?"

"So the one he didn't recognize could pose as some kind of federal agent looking for stolen coins without proper provenance." She lifted her brows at him. Did he know provenance?

"Every antique must have documentation saying where it comes from, so the dealer knows it isn't stolen. I'm not *that* ignorant." He looked at her reproachfully. "So you would imply that this man accepted these coins to sell without provenance."

"Which he did, because Mordred doesn't have any documentation."

"And the second one would frighten him into telling how to reach Mordred."

"All this assumes he knows where to contact Mordred at all."

Gawain sighed. "Yeah. And Mordred would be cleverer than that."

"We don't even know if he'll return to the dealer or when." This thing was all hopeless.

"He may not need to sell them if he's stealing credit cards." They both knew that left them nowhere. Gawain put some butter in to brown the oxtails. A lovely sizzle rose from the pan.

"Give me something to do," she said, sliding off her chair.

"You want to cut up some garlic?" He handed her a knife.

"Yeah. I want to cut up *something*."

He grinned at her.

God, that grin.

"You'd be ruthless with a sword."

She laughed. "You could teach me. Why shouldn't girls know how to use a sword?"

"I might have known you'd want lessons in swordplay." He sounded disgusted.

She looked at him quizzically. "Why?"

He paused. "I know you better than you think."

"Which is not at all," she harrumphed as she peeled mango.

"I've read your books," he reminded her.

Yeah. He'd read her books. Including the sex scenes. She felt herself coloring.

"That's not bad. They're good books. I enjoyed them," he insisted. "Mostly."

"What *mostly*? What didn't you like?"

There was a long pause. He busied himself with chopping some onion.

"Come on. You can tell me. Lord knows I'm used to hearing it. I used to read all those comments on Amazon even." She didn't anymore. But what would he say? She had no idea.

His knife stilled. He took a breath. Then he looked at her.

Uh-oh.

"First let me say that the women in your books—well, they're wonderful. Complicated, smart, courageous . . . But, well, the . . . the men are like the men on the covers. They're not quite real. Too . . . tidy. They talk about things too much."

She felt another flush creep up her cheeks. In her heart she knew he was right.

"Either that or they are, what is the modern word? Scum."

She burst out laughing. "Scum?"

His eyes laughed with her. "Yes. Selfish users, villains."

"Well, you have to have villains," she protested.

"Have you never known men who were honorable? But yet . . . manly?"

She leaned her butt against the counter and thought about that. "I haven't known too many men. My father, of course. He was a good man. He and my mother didn't have to take in some difficult case like me. And I try to remember him when he was strong, not weak and sick." She sighed, breathing out her loss. It was still fresh, even after three years. "But you never think of your father as manly. He's just your father."

"I'm glad he was a good man."

She couldn't do anything but nod. She missed her father—mother, too, but since her mother's death when she was sixteen she'd spent six years with her father as her only family.

"Women are more open about their desires in your time," Gawain observed after a moment. It was kind of him to change the subject.

"It's your time, too, now," she reminded him. "And yes, they are. Thank goodness for that."

"That was hard to get used to. And how little clothing they wear sometimes. Like when sea-bathing at the beach." He stuck some potatoes in the oven to bake. He stole a glance to her, but she couldn't read his expression. Or maybe she could. Was that heat in his eyes? Had she seen that look before? Like maybe last night?

No, definitely not. But she bet he loved women being more open about their desires. Women on every street corner just drooling to get into the bed of a guy like Gawain. He'd cut a swath through women like a mower through a field of grain. After he got out of prison. And between finding and stalking her. Still, how much time did it take for a man like that?

"The most difficult thing is that sex is no longer a sacred bond meant for getting children and becoming life partners. I miss that part."

Absolutely surprising. True? "Come on. You had women outside a sacred bond. Admit it."

It was his turn to flush. He bent his head over his work. "A man struggles. Sometimes he's weak," he muttered. "It *should* be a sacred bond. I . . . I was not always honorable. I lost my honor with the Green Knight."

"You told the Green Knight about her kisses." She wanted to remind him that he'd been honorable about that part at least.

"She gave me a magic girdle, too, that made the wearer invisible." He doused the oxtails with red wine and clapped the cover on the pot a little too hard. "I didn't tell him about that. A sin of omission." His head jerked away.

She wanted to tell him that the tale of Gawain and the Green Knight was famous for its moral ambiguity. The woman had seduced Gawain. And why did the Green Knight send him to his wife but that he knew she would do just that? He may have been guilty, but he wasn't the only one. The jury had been out on the moral of the tale for sixteen hundred–odd years. It probably always would be. But she didn't try to tell him. This was obviously a painful subject. It wasn't that she didn't know him well enough to continue. Sometimes she felt that she knew him well indeed. It was more that she didn't want to cause him any more pain.

Gawain got up and went to the little pantry. He hoped she'd liked the oxtails. She said she did. Several times. And she cleaned her plate. But she had seemed distracted, not concentrating on her food. Perhaps it wasn't to her liking and she told a white lie to spare his feelings. He liked providing for her. He wanted to keep her safe, protect her even from the fear of Mordred. That's why he had talked so much through dinner. When had he talked so much? Not in many years. Not ever. And he wouldn't let his other feelings get the better of him, no matter what.

He wouldn't even think about that. He poured her a tiny glass of Grand Marnier.

"How did you know I like Grand Marnier?" she asked, her brows drawing together.

"That's what you were buying at the liquor store the first time you saw me," he said simply. "Grand Marnier and milk."

She looked shocked. *Damn!* He'd reminded her that she'd thought he was a stalker. But he saw her get control of herself. "Sorry I was a washout about how to track down Mordred."

He handed her the glass. "His actions will reveal him in time."

She shuddered. Gawain couldn't seem to stop frightening her. He poured himself a glass of Scotch whiskey and motioned her into the living room.

"What if he damages this century with his actions? We *have* to find him first."

Gawain shook his head. He wouldn't tell her that was exactly what he was worried about. Or that he had no idea how to find a man who was, by his very nature, adept at blending into his surroundings. "I'll think of something." She sat in the wing chair, so he took the corner seat in the couch. It felt so natural sitting here with her after dinner. It felt right on some fundamental level that he hadn't experienced in many years.

And why not? He *should* feel comfortable with her. Well, almost comfortable. There was the physical discomfort she raised in him. He felt it rise now, brought on by the soft light on her gleaming hair, her cheeks flushed from the wine at dinner, the almost imperceptible rise and fall of her breasts beneath the light sweater she wore. It was pale gray-green, just like her eyes. The urge to claim her for his own came over him like a rushing charger.

Best take his mind off that by focusing hers. She'd been so busy going back in time, searching for Mordred, and getting used to Gawain's own guardianship of her, she hadn't been reflecting on what all this might mean about her. It was time she did. He had to bring her round to it slowly. "You said your parents took you in? Were they not your real parents?" He tried to ask it like he didn't know the answer.

"No. They adopted me. I was rather a lost cause at the time."

He merely lifted his brows.

"Well, the social services agency didn't quite know what to do with me."

"Because . . . ," he prompted when she fell silent and sipped her brandy.

"Because I was found wandering around a suburb of Chicago with no memory, except my name. I spoke a foreign language they didn't recognize." Her eyes got big. "Brythonic Proto-Celtic." And then the dam broke.

"I'm . . . I'm from the past."

Chapter Ten

"That's why I could understand Mordred." Now she was unable to contain the flood of words. "And how I could speak to you and your father when I went back in time. . . . Oh my God. That's why no one came forward to claim me. And I just dropped out of the air like I came out of nowhere. And I . . . I did, didn't I?"

Gawain nodded and kept silent. Best let her sort through this revelation herself. He saw her eyes focusing inward. "But I can't remember any of it," she said. "Not coming through time, not anything before. All I remember is the fear, of everything and everyone. . . ."

He tried not to look disappointed. He'd thought when she realized, she'd remember it all. That she'd recognize him. "Not unexpected. The experience was probably pretty traumatic." *Damn right it was.* He'd been disoriented and wandering aimlessly himself before he was set on by that black gang on the South Side of Chicago.

"But the time machine wasn't built in the fifth century. So . . ." Her gray-green eyes shot up to his. "Did Merlin send me like he sent you?"

He took a breath, and nodded.

"But why? Why me?"

He couldn't answer that. He didn't know why this girl

was so important that she must needs be protected at such great cost to his father. It had taken all Merlin's power to send them forward. Even as the haze of magic had enveloped them, Gawain had seen the power draining from his father's eyes. He was most afraid the act of sending them forward had left his father a broken man. If he lived at all.

And for what? The Resistance lost its strongest arm, all so a gawky thirteen-year-old could be protected? And this girl? His father should have hated her. But he hadn't.

She saw Gawain's thoughts in his face, and her expression shut down. "You really don't know, do you?"

He shook his head. "I'm sorry."

"Why didn't I realize this before?"

"You were on overload from going back in time. You had a stalker and a very difficult houseguest. You thought I shot at you. You were under stress."

Her eyes narrowed. "What prison were you in?"

"Joliet." The other shoe was about to drop, as they said.

"That's in Illinois." She sat back in the chair. "You were in Chicago when you killed those gang members. We came together." She said it like an accusation.

He nodded. "We came together. But we were separated. Even in prison, I looked for you. I went to the prison library, combed the newspapers around the time we came through. I saw the notice that you'd been found. That was at least a relief. You'd made it. After I got out it took some doing to find you. You had a new name and a new family. The records of the adoption were sealed."

"How did you do it?" she asked.

"There was a girl who worked in the hall of records. She . . . she desired me."

"You . . . you made love to a woman to get her to do something illegal?" Diana's voice was an outraged squeak.

"No," he protested. "I . . . I never went that far."

"Oh, Mr. Honorable, excuse me. You just let her think

you might, and that was enough for her to just roll over and do whatever you wanted." Diana sounded so disgusted.

"That wasn't how it was. I just told her we'd been separated and asked her, very nicely, if she would help me." He cleared his throat. No sins of omission, so he had to tell Diana all. "She might have thought you were my sister." He'd let the girl think that, in itself a sin of omission. He felt his blush rising. He was not honorable, no matter how he struggled.

"And you are so used to women falling all over to do things for you when they desire you that you just knew you could get what you wanted that way."

"You make it sound like . . ."

"And did you ever think about how the girl felt about it? She wasn't pretty, was she?"

How had he become the villain of the piece? "No, but . . ."

"And when you walked into her office . . . was it her office?"

"No! I met her in the deli next to the hall of records."

"Oh, devious! Where they all went to lunch. You were bound to run into one of them. Like flies to your web . . ." She had a head of steam up now. "And then you just look so handsome, and vulnerable with that comma of hair that goes over your forehead like that. And she says she'll help you."

"It was all to find you. And I found you. Late. But now I can carry out my father's wishes and protect you. Why is that so bad?"

"Because . . ." She was looking truly distressed now. "Because it's a responsibility to look like you do. You can't *use* it like that on women who aren't pretty and haven't had the attention of men. You smile at them . . . and they're goners. And you get whatever you want."

She made it sound like he wanted to rape them or something.

He raised his hands helplessly. "I can't help it if women are nice to me, Diana."

"I know." She practically spit the words at him. She got up, put her glass down on the coffee table so hard it almost broke, and stomped back to her bedroom.

He sat blinking after her. How had that gone so horribly wrong? He had wanted to help her remember who she was. Didn't she know that? Didn't she want to remember?

His head lolled back against the cushions.

Maybe it was better if she didn't remember.

Diana seethed, and hated herself for it. He was right. It wasn't his fault he was so damned attractive. What did her writer friend Rhonda call it? Sex on a stick. But he traded on it, damn it. He *knew* he was like a honey pot and that they couldn't help but be drawn to him.

Diana kicked off her boots and pulled her sweater over her head.

And that girl in the records office had . . . had been just like Diana—a woman men never noticed. And she had reacted just like Diana had reacted to Mr. I'm Too Handsome for Words. When *he* came into the deli next door to the records hall she bet every woman there just fell all over herself to make room for him at the counter, to offer him a seat at her booth. The little scene played out in her mind as if she had written it. And when he paid attention to the plain girl who worked in the adoption records place, she must have felt like the chosen one. She must have been so grateful that she could do something for him.

The chosen one.

Diana felt her anger drain away. *That* hit too close to home.

Why the hell was it *her* he had to protect? Why had Merlin (*the* Merlin!) sent her forward in time? Why couldn't she remember anything from her former life?

Fool! She'd gotten carried away and hadn't thought about the consequences of getting mad at him. Her gaze fell on her mandolin case, leaning against the wall.

"Do you still play?" he'd asked.

He hadn't just come through time with her. He'd *known* her then. Was that why she felt she knew him so thoroughly sometimes?

That meant she'd just stomped out on the one man who could give her what she'd always wanted—a past, a certain knowledge of who she was. It wasn't that she didn't think of Dad and Mom as her parents. They were her true parents, because they had loved her and raised her and put up with the silence and the nightmares and all of that stuff before she'd settled into being theirs. But it wasn't enough. She wanted to know who she'd been before she was theirs.

And she was going to have to abase herself to get what she wanted.

She jerked her head up from where she'd been standing, frozen like Lot's wife, in the middle of Gawain's spare bedroom in her bra and jeans and stocking feet. She took a deep breath and went to retrieve her sweater from where she'd flung it to the floor.

She pulled it over her head and jerked at the hem to smooth it. Okay. Abasement time.

She stalked back out to the living room. Gawain was still sitting where she'd left him, only now his elbow was up on the arm of the couch and his head was propped in his hand. His Scotch was more than half-full. He sure didn't drink to excess.

At her entrance he looked up, wary. Who wouldn't be, after her tirade? She felt like an abuser, terrorizing all around her because she was liable to go off the handle at any time. *Wow.* That felt awful. Abasement it was, and well deserved.

"I'm *so* sorry," she said. "I have a terrible temper. I know you'd never guess it because mostly I'm shy, but . . . but I do. It . . . it isn't your fault that women find you attractive."

"But *you* don't. In fact, you find me despicable." She caught the hurt in his eyes before he glanced away. And after all he'd tried to do for her.

She cleared her throat. "I . . . I didn't say that. You were trying to find me, and you did what you could to make that happen. Trying to find me was very . . ." *What would resonate with him?* "Very honorable."

He didn't know what to say to that. At last he settled on, "I didn't mean to offend you."

"It's not you who needs to explain yourself." She sat as far away from him as she could get on the other corner of the couch.

"You don't have to explain your temper to me. I've known you forever."

She closed her eyes. It was as she had hoped. He knew her. "Tell me," she breathed. "Please tell me what you know about me."

Gawain filled her glass again, watching her eyes light with each story he told her.

"You were a troublesome child," he said with a smile. "A girl! Can you imagine being stuck guarding a girl? I couldn't believe my father took me away from the raids on Saxon strongholds just to guard a gawky twelve-year-old. But I discovered that you were a bold little thing. If I didn't watch you like a hawk, you'd take my charger out bareback. And if you broke your neck, who'd get blamed?"

"I'm not sure I was ever bold. But I *can* just hear you scolding me." Her eyes crinkled.

"It was mostly the other way round. That temper!"

"Sounds like I was pretty ungrateful. Did I ever get in real trouble?"

He looked away. He didn't want her to see his horror that it had happened on his watch. "Once. I'd taken you fishing. You loved fishing."

Gawain slung his string of brown trout over his shoulder. There must be a score. Four were hers. They'd had a good morning. He looked over at Dilly. He called her Dilly for the circlet of daffodils she wove for her hair each spring. She was standing on some rocks, casting her line in just the way he'd shown her. She looked so purposeful. She was nothing if not competitive, and this was a competition with the fish. But he knew she would shriek with delight when she felt her line bob. His lips wouldn't stay still. He shook his head. These days she could almost always make him smile, no matter how resentful he'd been about his assignment.

He threaded an earthworm onto his hook and slung out his line into the deep green of the pool. The morning was cool, but the promise of summer warmth hung in the air. Best they be getting back soon. . . .

Her delighted shriek made him look up. "I've got one, Gawain. That's five!" She was standing with her feet in the rocks that lined the bank. She heaved her pole to flip the trout. The effort made her lose her balance. She flailed. Her feet! Her feet were caught in the rocks. They both realized her danger at once. He surged forward. She pulled one leg up. The pole dropped to her side. She couldn't get her balance. He lunged through the willows, watching her topple.

"No!" he yelled. "Dilly!"

He could practically hear the bone snap. She collapsed in a heap, shrieking not in delight but in pain. Gods, *he prayed,* let it be a clean break. *All the times he'd seen broken bones flashed through his mind. Gangrene, twisted cripples, long months of pain. Not for his Dilly!*

She was crying and moaning by the time he knelt beside her. There was no question that her leg was broken. "Shush, now. I've got you." *He gripped her hand while he surveyed the situation. Her ankle was trapped between two boulders, each about the size of a big soup cauldron. He scrambled around, glad for the strength that separated him from other young bucks his age.* "Dilly, this might hurt, but I've got to free you."

She nodded tearfully and bit her lip. Her wreath of daffodils lay crushed on the rocks. He got a good grip on the upper stone. Of course it was the larger of the two. He wouldn't think about how he was going to hurt her. He heaved the stone up and off her foot. It clattered over the rocks and splashed into the pool. Dilly moaned.

He had to get her back to the encampment. His father could heal her. But he had departed yesterday to Cerdic's court at Sarum to testify against Raedwald in the matter of a burned village. Who knew when he would return? Dilly would have to do with conventional healing. Would she walk again? He looked around. He couldn't even carry her without bracing the leg somehow. He drew his knife and cut three stout sticks from a young poplar. He ripped off his shirt and tore it into strips. Making shushing sounds, he knelt beside her once again.

"This is going to hurt, child," *he whispered.* "But I have to straighten your leg."

"I know," *she said, and her gray-green eyes were huge. She nodded at him.*

Very well. He could stand it if she could. He laid out the sticks, and before he could think about it he pulled her leg just enough to straighten it. Her scream tore more than the morning air. He couldn't get his breath as he bound her leg into the makeshift splint.

By the time he picked her up she was half-conscious. Just as well. He looked around, fear circling in his belly. They had wandered far that day. It was a long way to help.

He took a breath. "I got you back to the cave we were living in at the time. They set the leg. When my father got back a month later he used his magic salves on you, but it was a little late, and you were still laid up for three months." He managed a smile. "You made it through without killing anybody."

Diana's eyes crinkled in return. "How did you manage that?"

"Vervain kept you drugged for the first week. Then I taught you to play the lute."

Recognition flickered in her eyes. Her face softened. "No wonder I like the mandolin. My parents thought I was a prodigy for a while. But I just already knew how to play." She looked up at him. "I like knowing. Thank you. Thank you for teaching me. I'm sure it saved my sanity. And yours." She took a breath. "I certainly sound like an irritating child."

"Did I give that impression? I was irritated that I was taken from raiding and battles to guard you, but I found you intelligent and curious and courageous. In short, the same things you are today. Unlikely as it seems, we were friends." And what were they now? Now that she wasn't a gawky girl of thirteen but a beautiful woman?

"I'm not courageous. . . ." She ran her finger round the edge of the glass and made it sing. She was thinking. That was dangerous. "So, who were my real parents?"

Oh yeah. Danger plus. "My father raised you."

Her face began to glow. Who wouldn't want to have

Merlin as a father? It wasn't a picnic, but she wouldn't know that. He saw her realize that he might be her brother. A complicated set of expressions raced across her face. Then it fell as she realized he'd said "raised."

"I guess I was a foundling twice then."

"He took you in. Your mother died. Your father . . . too." Nothing more he could say without lying. Another sin of omission. His specialty. He took another tack. "My father loved you just as your adopted parents in this century did. You are a fortunate woman."

"To be abandoned twice . . ."

How he wished he could erase the look on her face. "You weren't abandoned twice. Your parents died. In this time you were lost. I never abandoned you."

She seemed to consider. . . . "Did Merlin send me forward in time to get rid of me, and you just don't want to tell me that?"

"With his son sent along to protect you?" Did his father regret losing him? Probably not. But she didn't have to know that. "He wasn't getting rid of you. You don't know what it cost him to work that magic." It might have killed him. In any case, Gawain would never see his wonderful, difficult, bigger-than-life father again. He would never know what happened. "You were precious to him and important even beyond being someone he cared for."

"But he didn't say *why* I was important?" She looked so puzzled, so frustrated.

How he hated to disappoint her. "No. I asked him. But all he would say was that I would know what to do when the time came."

"Great." She sighed. But she was thinking again. "Why can you remember what happened before you came forward and I have amnesia?"

He heard the pouting note in her voice. He remembered that one, too. But she had a right to pout over something this big. She wanted so much to remember. "My father's magic was a lot more harrowing mode of travel than Leonardo's machine. I was disoriented for days. And I didn't get the head injury you had. You must have landed pretty hard." He saw her look of shock. "Police report and social worker's notes in the adoption file. That's how I knew."

He glanced at the clock on the faux mantel of the gas fireplace. "It's after midnight. You'd better get to bed."

"*We'd* better get to bed," she corrected. Then she blushed.

Oh, she shouldn't have said that. He could feel his reaction even now.

"I mean . . . we have to get started finding Mordred in the morning." She threw up her hands. "Like we know how to do that. And if we do you'll just kill him. And should anybody be killed without a trial?"

She had to understand. "He should. Believe me." But would she believe if she knew the truth? "We'll need to get the morning paper."

"You think . . . ?"

"It won't take him long to make an impact. He's probably working on it even now."

Mordred sat in the dark watching the frenzy as what he wrote on the screen was instantly transmitted and retransmitted, causing comment and excitement each time his words were repeated. He was making quite a splash. He had been quoted on a hundred blogs. Each reader found in his language their own validation. He played on their fears, then showed them they could master the forces that massed around them by following him. He could touch thousands and thousands with this lovely new toy, and each of them could touch thousands of others, more than he had ever imagined. And once he touched them with his thoughts and the force of his personality, they were his.

Now to hook the fishes.

I hear you all. I know your hearts. And yet feelings in your hearts are not enough. In this time when the worst of you lack all conviction while the best are filled with passionate intensity, where are the actions that confirm your commitment? Do you not know that the waters swirl around us? Have you not seen those who despise the very values that support this great nation, the values instilled in us by God, glorified? Why should the despisers prevail? How can you, the brotherhood of the True Believers, allow this, and yet call yourselves righteous? In order to walk in the true path, you must take first the step.

An obstreperous chorus of replies cascaded onto his screen. He waited for the right one.

What would you have us do?

Yes!

Words no longer suffice. Prove yourselves. Take the head of an unbeliever and put it on a pike for all to see, as they did in times when hearts were pure and knights fought for their God and the True Way. Then can you serve the powers that are in you and beyond you and carry you into the new world while others are washed away in the flood. Do this, for my sake, and I will make myself known unto you and lead you into the Promised Land.

And what came back was . . . silence. No messages scrolled across his screen.

They were speechless. He had them. He smiled. The first step was almost too easy. Soon he would have his army. And then this nation, and soon the world, would be his.

Time to order a pizza, and think about how to get to the girl and Merlin's son.

Chapter Eleven

Diana went to the spare bedroom with all sorts of confusing thoughts running around inside her head, and feelings lower down, too.

She'd been an orphan in two worlds. Merlin probably took her in more out of pity than anything else. It was lovely of Gawain to tell her how much his father had loved her. *He* was lovely. And not just physically. But that was just the problem. From what he said, he'd been like an older brother to her, only kinder, she suspected. But she wasn't thinking of him like an older brother now. Not at all. Even now she tingled in remembering the strong column of his neck tonight, the black hair curling out of his open-collared shirt, the forearms . . . she was a sucker for muscled forearms. Who knew they could be so . . . erotic? Yes, he was lovely.

Right. He was Gawain, the parfait knight. What was not lovely, except perhaps that he was too perfect?

That was just it, though. He wasn't. He was entirely human, and that meant flawed. He'd given into lust with the Green Knight's lady. He'd tried to keep the magic girdle. He had scars. He felt he'd failed his father by getting thrown in prison.

That was what was wrong with the hero of her novel.

She'd made the fictional Gawain perfect and then plotted his downfall, when he would discover he was flawed. Boring.

The real Gawain struggled with the fact that he wasn't perfect every day. He struggled with his lusts and weaknesses and failures. He was a human man. Way more interesting.

She glanced to his computer, the one that now held her work in progress. What better way to forget about the unknown parents who had abandoned her all those centuries ago? What better way to exorcise the feeling Gawain engendered in her?

It was only midnight.

He wished he could heal her doubts about herself. He'd tried tonight. But he wasn't sure he'd made much headway. He realized that the resilient Dilly had been damaged by being thrust into a strange and frightening world where no one knew what she was suffering. If she found out the truth, it would only make it worse. He glanced to the light still under her doorway as he closed his own door without switching on the light. What was she doing in there? What was she thinking?

Best he look to his soul around her. Sitting next to her had been a trial tonight. Did she notice that he'd kept his forearm across his lap? Just the sight of her, hanging on his words, her eyes glowing, was enough to raise him. He stripped off his clothes and left them lying in a heap on the floor. How would he get to sleep tonight?

When Diana woke the next morning it was late. She glanced to the clock on Gawain's desk. *Ten!* Well, she hadn't gotten to bed until four. Six hours would do her fine, but she'd resolved to be up at seven. Gawain had wanted to get the morning papers early. She had the noon shift at the Exploratorium today, too. That didn't leave them any time to search for Mordred.

Maybe that was good, because if they found him, Gawain would kill him. She pulled on her work clothes (black skirt, black vest over a white shirt, and comfortable black shoes) and ran a brush through her hair before she hurried to the bathroom to brush her teeth and wash her face.

She came out to find Gawain setting a cup of coffee on the table. He looked . . . wary again, uncertain. There was a newspaper on the table. She approached slowly.

"Grisly display in Union Square," the headline blared. She glanced to Gawain.

"You might not want details."

Nonsense. She watched *CSI,* for goodness' sakes. She cracked open the paper and began scanning the article. "Police found the head stuck on a pike . . . known transvestite . . . may be a hate crime . . . remainder of the body not in evidence . . . no witnesses." "My God," she murmured.

"I think God had nothing to do with it."

"Mordred? But why? You said he wants power? How does this get him power?"

"I'm not sure. But—a head on a pike? They haven't done that for five hundred years, but it was common in the fifth century. It was how you displayed your victory, and showed your strength over your enemies. It's got to be Mordred."

"I thought from what you said, he'd do something subtle and political. That's how you gain power these days. . . ."

"Maybe." He didn't seem convinced. "You want some breakfast?"

She shook her head. How could you eat knowing this?

At least the newspaper didn't have any pictures. "How could this happen in the middle of Union Square? Where were the police?"

"Obviously elsewhere."

"Well, they'll track him down now, for sure."

"What makes you think that?" He turned to the window, gazing out on the gray morning outside. "Even if he left clues, they wouldn't connect to a history or a person in this time."

She blew out a breath. "Do you think this is the end of it?"

He turned. His face was closed. That was her answer. She returned to the article. When she finished, she looked up. He was still standing at the window.

"Still think we can let him live?"

"We don't *know* it's him. Let the police take care of this."

"The police are not going to take care of this."

"Well, neither are we at this rate. I'm going to work."

"No, you're not," he said, turning on her. "How can you even think you'd go to a place where he knows you'll be?"

That struck her. But you couldn't live your life in fear. "And a terrorist attack could occur any minute, but we learned after 9/11 that you can't stop living your life because you're afraid of the worst. I'm not going to let the museum down. I'm going to work."

"I won't let you."

She widened her eyes and set her lips. "Excuse me? Free country and all."

He looked like he might burst a vein. "Free country, my . . ." He took a breath as if to steady himself. "You should . . . take the advice of one who only wants to protect you."

"You were going to say I should 'obey,' weren't you?"

she accused. "Pretty inconvenient that women don't just obey orders anymore. We think for ourselves now, buster." She pushed herself up from the table. "And I think I'm going to work, unless you're going to tie me up."

"Then I'm coming with you," he said through gritted teeth.

"Give me a break," she said, her temper rising. "No way."

"It's a free country," he said. "You said so yourself. And the Exploratorium is a public place. I'm going to spend the day at the museum."

Outrageous. Enraging. But he had her. Hoisted on her own petard. "Okay then. You're going to have a very boring day."

She tried to ignore him. But he joined a tour she was giving because one of the docents hadn't shown up. The cur. Just to rub it in that he was dogging her every step. Worse, he didn't appear to be bored at all. He asked great questions and related well with the kids. No matter how she glared at him, he didn't get the hint to leave. By the time they got to the geyser exhibit, she'd almost gotten used to him. She called the milling children over as the geysers were about to pop. There were three copper tripods holding huge shallow glass bowls overhead. The copper tubing thrust up from the heater into the bowls. Each heater had a temperature gauge and a big sign that said at what temperature the geyser would blow. They had a couple of minutes before the first one went off.

"Okay, kids, do any of you know what makes a geyser?" she asked when they'd clustered around her, with only a little bit of shoving from the boys.

"I personally think it's magic." She glanced up in shock to Gawain.

"Is not!" a little boy called from the back

"Is," Gawain insisted.

"It's geothermal heat." This was from a boy about eleven and he was really proud of it.

"Then what makes geothermal heat?" Gawain asked

She'd better take charge here. "The Earth's core is molten lava. The heat escapes through fissures in the Earth's crust. When it hits an underground water source, the heat turns the water to steam. The pressure of the steam pushes up the geyser, just like the steam on your mother's pressure cooker."

"Yeah," a little boy said. "So there. It's not magic; it's . . . it's science."

"So what made the Earth have a molten core?"

"It's from when the Earth was part of a sun or something and it got hurled out and cooled. We learned that in school." This was a gawky blond girl—maybe ten, twelve?

Good for you, Diana thought.

"So what hurled the Earth out from the sun?" Where was Gawain going with this?

"The big bang!" Several voices at once on that one.

"Excellent! And what created the big bang?"

That had them. Actually, that had her, too.

"God?" A little voice, tentative, from the far right.

"Did not. Science just can't explain that one yet." This was from the older boy.

"Well, who but God could work such major magic?" Gawain asked. "Maybe God himself is magic. Maybe science is magic, too."

The first of the three geysers went off at that point, thank goodness. It shot water up into a fountain high above their heads, complete with steam, that showered into the glass bowl.

"Mom, this man says science is magic." The boy was bringing in reinforcements in the form of a heavy woman in a flowered dress and sagging sweater who was coming up from the rear. Probably from the restrooms.

"Come along, Billy. Really, I'd think that you docents would be thinking about helping children understand the world, not getting them to believe in superstition. You might as well be teaching them astrology."

"I want to see it again. Lady, can you make it do that again?"

"The next one is just about to go. . . ." It shot up into the air.

So half of them believed in magic at the end of the tour and all believed that science and God could coexist in the world. That was a pretty neat trick, she had to admit.

Gawain looked smug. Mr. Grandison, her boss, strode out of his office and over to where her tour was just dispersing. He did not seem happy.

"I've had complaints. Did you or did you not say that science was magic?" He was a small, balding man who always wore a suit. And cuff links. He didn't seem like the kind of guy who ran a children's science museum. But he ran it like clockwork.

"It wasn't me. It . . . it was this guy on my tour." She glanced over to where Gawain was bending over a wave machine and pointing to illustrate something to a little girl and her sister and the children's mother. The mother had eyes only for Gawain's perfect butt inside those tight jeans. She didn't seem to mind that some guy she didn't know was talking to her children. Gawain was engaged with the children, but he also kept an eye on Diana.

"Whose tour was it, Miss Dearborn? His or yours?"

How did you explain that Gawain was a little overpowering as a personality, and that he seemed to just naturally get his way with things? Including her tours.

"It won't happen again, Mr. Grandison. I promise." She set her lips. She'd have to get Gawain out of here, or she wouldn't have a job.

"See that it doesn't." He turned on his heel, a little

too precisely. "Science is magic," he muttered. "Preposterous."

She bore down on Gawain as the children he was talking to waved good-bye and went on to another exhibit. "You are going to get me fired if you keep hijacking my tours and talking about magic," she said in a whisper.

"That man threatened you?" Gawain's brows drew together and his eyes hardened.

Oh, great. Just what she needed. "He's my boss. Threatening me is a perk of supervision."

Gawain started off in the direction of the administrative offices, where Mr. Grandison had disappeared. She jerked him back by the sleeve of his jacket. "Only implied threats," she corrected. Dear Lord but this protective streak was inconvenient. "Can't you wait for me to get off work out . . . out by the cloakroom or something?"

"Mordred could come in at any time," Gawain insisted.

"He'd stick out like a sore thumb in a crowd of families. Just like you do. I half-expected you to get accused of accosting children."

"Me?"

"Yeah. . . ." She narrowed her own eyes. "Why aren't people more afraid of a single man who hangs out in the Exploratorium talking to children?"

He raised his brows. "Because my heart is true?"

"Arrrgh!" She spun on her heel and headed for the point that tours were supposed to rendezvous, to collect her next batch of charges. "Just stay off my next tour."

He didn't of course. But he did keep quiet. Or tried to.

"Hard being a single parent, isn't it?" As Diana sent the children off to line up for a chance to make music in the room with the xylophones she heard the pretty blond woman's question. They were up on the mezzanine floor. She knew exactly to whom the question was directed.

"I'm sure it is," Gawain rumbled.

"Don't I know it? You've been 're-singled' long?"

Re-singled? Diana wanted to spew. She turned from evening out the lines of children and saw that the blonde wasn't as young or as pretty as she first thought. Gawain had no attention for the woman but was watching Diana and her gaggle of youngsters.

"I've always been single," he said.

The woman, of course, was about to assume he had a nephew or a niece on the tour.

"Oh. Then one of the children is a nephew or niece perhaps? How kind of you to bring them here for the afternoon." She looked like she'd just hit the Publishers Clearing House jackpot. A guy who looked like Gawain *and* was good with kids. The woman had no doubt she could interest him. She was the kind who was used to being interesting to men.

"Nope." Gawain turned to the blonde and gave her one of his grins. Diana could see the woman's knees go weak. *Disgusting.* But, she had to admit it was understandable.

"Then . . ."

"I'm here with the tour guide: Miss Dearborn." He gestured to Diana and gave her one of those high-wattage smiles. His face . . . softened. There was no other word for it. Good act.

The blonde sighed, her mouth curling in a moue of disappointment. She got that message all right. She turned her attention to Diana and frowned. "That one?" She looked around as though he might be talking about another tour leader.

Diana blew out a breath. Yeah. It was hard to believe. The woman would believe even less that Gawain had been assigned to protect her by Merlin (yes, *that* Merlin) because she was important somehow. Mousy little Diana Dearborn. Diana turned back to the children, a confusion of feelings ricocheting around in her breast. "Now let's go

over to hear the echo." She couldn't listen to any more
come-ons to Gawain.

At five thirty she and Gawain were finally walking
out, the last of the guests having been collected and ex-
pelled shortly after the 5:00 P.M. closing time. Diana had
never wanted a shift to end more.

"A moment, Miss Dearborn?"

Uh-oh. She turned. She felt Gawain go wary and take
a step in to stand behind her. "Mr. Grandison?" She knew
exactly what he was going to say, of course.

Her boss hurried up, a look of disapproval on his face.
"This man was with you?"

"Uh, yes." Now it would start. *You cannot bring guests.*

"You cannot bring 'guests' to your work environment,
Miss Dearborn. And to have him disrupt the tour, under-
mining the very principles of the museum with our young
visitors . . . highly objectionable."

"I understand, sir." Diana said, holding herself still.
She could handle this if she could just keep Gawain out of
the conversation.

"I'm not a guest, Mr. Grandison. I'm here to protect
Miss Dearborn."

Great. Just great.

"Why does she need protection?" Grandison looked
from one of them to the other, his mouth drawing his
whole face into a pinched expression.

"She hasn't told you?" Gawain asked, his face all in-
nocence as Diana glared at him. "She has a stalker."

"A stalker?" Grandison visibly shrank back. His face
pinched even more.

"It's nothing, Mr. Grandison. Really it's not."

"Don't say that, Diana. You know it's not true." His
deep voice held real concern.

"Miss Dearborn, we cannot have your private issues

endangering our guests. Stalkers are dangerous people. Until this problem with your stalker is resolved, I'm going to place you on an unpaid leave of absence. When the police have cleared the issue up, you can return."

"Mr. Grandison, that isn't fair," she protested.

"Take it up with the City. They have a personnel office downtown." He was looking around, his mind already having moved on. "Now where is my clipboard? I'll have to rearrange the schedule."

"You left it in the men's room," Diana said dispiritedly. "Shelf above the second sink." She grabbed Gawain's arm and dragged him to the front doors.

Behind her she could hear Mr. Grandison muttering, "How could she know that?"

"How did you know that?" Gawain asked as they pushed out into the twilight.

Diana pulled her raincoat around her as defense against the wind, or maybe as defense against the fact that slowly her life as she knew it was being stripped from her. "Never mind that; you just lied to that man and cost me my job." She couldn't help the outrage that was coming up from somewhere deep inside her. "How can you call yourself honorable when you lie so easily?"

"I didn't lie. You do have a stalker."

"We have no proof that Mordred is stalking me."

"Not proof in the legal sense. Still, I didn't lie."

"You just let him think it was a sure thing and it isn't. . . ." She sputtered to a stop. "Did you . . . Did you *want* to get me fired?" She hurried to keep up with him. The parking-lot lights blinked on, but they didn't seem to hold back the growing gloom much.

"You aren't fired. You're on a leave of absence without pay."

"Same thing. He wants a police report that the stalker

has been stopped before I can come back. You said your-self they'll never catch him. Voilà! I can't come back to work. Is that what you wanted?"

He opened the car door for her. "Yes."

As simple as that? "*Yes?* You want me out of a job and unable to put food on my table."

"I'll put food on your table, Diana." Though how he had money enough to do that was something she'd have to explore later.

"That isn't the point. I liked that job. I needed that job. It wasn't for you to meddle and get me fired—all right, all right," she corrected. "Put on a leave of absence I can't get off. And you let me think you were coming with me only to protect me, not to cost me my job. Sins of omission, guy."

A strange, pained look came over his face. "You're right," he said after a moment. "Of course you're right." He took a breath. "The truth is I can't guard you well enough here. Mordred knows you work here. Much as I'd like to lure him out into the open, I refuse to use you as bait. And I would never be able to talk you out of coming to your job. You're too stubborn."

"So you just maneuvered my boss into ensuring that I wouldn't show up for work. The nerve! I can't believe it." She was hopping mad. She took the door and slammed it shut. "I am not going anywhere with you, mister. I've had enough. You walk into my life. You . . . you stalk me. You talk me into staying in your apartment, for God's sake!" She flung her hands in the air. "I can't believe how stupid I was. And now you get me fired?" She stomped back toward the lights of the lobby. "I'll have Clancy call me a cab. I'm going to get my things and go back to my own apartment. Right now."

"I'll take you to your apartment!" Gawain called.

That stopped her in her tracks. How could he always surprise her? She turned. "You will?"

He nodded. His eyes scanned the darkness around her. He glanced to either side. Wary. Even as they had been arguing the parking lot had darkened. He now stood in a cone of light, alone against the blackness. His stance was easy but . . . ready somehow. It was how a warrior must meet his opponent. Was that how he felt about her? No. He was scanning the edges of the parking lot for danger. That scared her more than anything else he could have said or done. "Come on," he said. "Get in."

"You *promise* you'll take me back to my apartment?"

"Cross my heart and hope to die." He made the childish gesture. It seemed so familiar somehow. In spite of the fact that he had at the very least misled Mr. Grandison, she didn't think Gawain would make a clear promise and then go back on it.

She stomped over to the cone of light. "You'd better be telling the whole truth and nothing but the truth, or I'll . . ." But she couldn't finish the threat. At this point in her life, she didn't think she could do much about anything anymore. She found herself scanning the edges of the parking lot for lurking figures as they pulled out into the street.

Chapter Twelve

Gawain slid the Range Rover to a stop around the corner from her apartment on Twenty-fourth Street. "We'll walk down the alley into the parking lot. He might be watching the front door." She fumbled around in that huge bag of hers, looking for her keys. He didn't flip the overhead on to help her. That would attract too much attention.

He was sorry he'd lost her the job. But that was going to happen anyway, sooner or later, if what his father said was true, and she was important. She had another destiny to fill than working at the Exploratorium. He *had* gone with the intention of making her lose her job. In some ways he'd lied to her. He hadn't lied about Mordred. Mordred was after her all right.

"I still think we should have stopped by your place and got my things."

"Plenty of time for that. We'll scope the place out first." If he was right, they'd never get as far as moving her stuff. He opened the driver's side door and slid out quietly. He was armed only with the knife strapped to his body under his jacket. He'd ditched the gun he'd used to shoot at Mordred into the bay, and swords were too hard to conceal. If there were watchers here, they could take her out from a distance anyway and neither gun nor knife would stop them. He'd taken a terrible chance bringing her here. But he had to make her really understand.

He slipped behind the car and stood against her door, covering the window with his body. Inside, she was still looking for her keys in the giant purse. He went still and searched the night. The street still hummed with activity. People were getting off a bus at the corner. Several walkers carried either briefcases or grocery bags. Cars swung into garages. Lights blinked on in apartments here and there as people arrived home from work. *Good.* Harder to kill someone with so many people still about. The night smelled of salt air and the damp of an impending fog, the fumes of the bus that roared off at the corner, and garlic and onion frying somewhere nearby.

He checked the parked cars in each direction. No figures huddled in them. No one loitering. Everybody looked purposeful. Building tops held no silhouettes. Of course they could be in any darkened window with a rifle, even one far away if Mordred had found a marksman already. Gawain stepped out from the car to make himself a better target. Maybe someone would get antsy and take a shot at him instead of her.

Even this was dangerous. If he was killed, she'd be unprotected.

But nothing happened. He jumped when she shouted, "Ah-ha!" He stilled his heart as she held up a key on a ring in triumph. *Good.*

"Let's go." He nodded. *Might as well be now.* They would already know she'd left her apartment, those nameless faces Mordred would have sent. Maybe they'd moved on.

He opened her door.

She slid out, and he tucked her in against his body for protection. "Stay close. I want to present a smaller target."

How strange that she fit so well against him. It still amazed him that the gawky girl had turned into such a wonderful woman. He was only sorry she'd had to endure the uncertainty and pain of amnesia and feeling like she didn't fit in this century. Those experiences had left their mark on her. He hadn't been there to protect her from them. He felt her warmth, even through all the layers of clothing between them. It was almost like an electric shock. She looked up, and shock was in her eyes as well. Did she feel what touching did? Her hip was tucked in against his thigh, her shoulder against his side, his arm around her shoulders. He had the distinct urge to turn her, press her body against his, from chest to thigh . . . push her back against the car door, and lift her chin to kiss her. His body reacted almost violently to the thought. Could she see his lust in his eyes?

What was he *thinking* to frighten her so? When they might be in imminent danger? Answer: he wasn't thinking at all. His body was in charge. Some strength of character *he* had. He looked around while he gathered his wits. But he didn't let her go.

"Are we a target?" She frowned. But she made no further protest as they hurried down the alleyway to the rear door of the apartment building. She had her key out, and she shook only a little as she found the lock. "It won't open," she whispered.

"Let me." Miraculously, she did. The damn thing better work, or he'd have to shock the hell out of her to get her inside. He breathed a sigh of relief as it turned. She was just too shaky. He pressed a hand on her back to scoot her inside ahead of him, let the door close as softly as he could, and peered out. Nothing untoward in the deserted alley. *You never know.* He reached inside his quilted vest and palmed the knife.

Her eyes were wide. "Just in case," he muttered. "Okay. Head for the elevator."

The walk to her apartment was uneventful, but he held her back as he rounded the final corner and only let her move forward when he could see it was clear.

"You're making me nervous," she whispered.

"Shhhh." That probably didn't comfort her.

When they arrived at 406, he again protected her with his body while she fit her key in the lock. The door swung open. Light from the hallway spilled into the room. He heard her gasp.

Instantly he pushed her aside and sprang into the apartment, knife low and pointed slightly upward, his other elbow out to make his forearm a defensive bar across his body.

But no one moved. The dim room was silent. Everything looked just as it had when they'd left two days ago, as far as he could tell. Except for the mirror over the couch opposite the door. That was covered with letters written in bloodred:

I'll find you.

She cupped her hand over her mouth and began to shake. But he couldn't comfort her before he checked the rest of her apartment. The signs of her packing from several days ago were clear in her room, clothes hangers strewn about. Mordred knew she'd taken flight. He just didn't know where. Yet. Time to get out, before they picked up watchers outside.

Gawain came back into the room. She looked at him in question. He shook his head. "All clear." He went to peer at the mirror. If it was blood it hadn't dripped

"It's my lipstick. The only one I have that's red. Mostly

I just wear lip gloss, but I had the red for a . . ." She trailed off. "I can't remember why." She was definitely in shock.

"It's okay." He pulled her into his chest and she let him. He could feel her shake through her jacket. And the swell of her breasts. Dangerous. He was so susceptible to her. Any minute . . . *Yep. Down, boy.* But she needed him right now. He couldn't step away just yet. "You see why you can't stay here, right?"

She nodded, her eyes still big and staring at the lettering. "I . . . I should clean it up."

"Nope. You should come with me." He turned her around gently and guided her to the open door. "Give me your keys."

She didn't protest but handed them over. He locked the door behind them and then pulled her down the hall toward the elevator. He prayed to the gods of leaf and water that Mordred had given up on the apartment entirely when he saw she'd packed up. Uh-oh.

He stopped in the middle of the lobby. "Your iPhone has 3G service."

"Uh, yeah." She nodded. Her eyes were still wide, almost unseeing with fear.

"Then he can find you." He held out his hand for it.

Blinking, she fumbled through that damn big bag with Leonardo da Vinci's book in it until she came up with her iPhone. "Let's hope we aren't too late," he muttered.

He let them out of the lobby to the parking lot and the door clanged shut behind them. They hurried down the alley to Twenty-fourth Street. He looked around. Nobody conspicuous watching them. He spotted a homeless guy sitting under an entry overhang to an empty retail space with a big *For Lease* sign plastered across the window. Not sinister, though.

He put Diana in the passenger's seat and locked her in, then trotted over to the derelict.

"Hey, guy," he said, pushing at a boney knee sticking out from torn jeans with the toe of his boot. The matted head raised and glazed eyes looked up at him. "Your lucky day." He dropped the phone in the guy's lap. "It won't have service as soon as we cut the account. But at least you can sell it."

"Hey, thanks," the guy said from cracked lips. "That's okay of you."

"I'd sell it right away. Enjoy the proceeds."

By the time they got back to Gawain's apartment, Diana had calmed down some. He'd cut the service to her phone. One way of finding her was closed off. He'd opened some white wine for her, and she was seated at the counter, sipping gratefully.

"He . . . he can't find this place, can he?" she finally asked.

"No." He made his answer unequivocal, to reassure her. "I rented it under the name Gawain Trenail. He wouldn't know that last name, since I made it up, even if he knows my real name is Gawain."

"And I definitely can't go back to work."

"No."

"Sorry I lost my temper over that." She clenched her lips together and shrugged apologetically. "You're right. I would have insisted on going to work."

He gave her a grin. "You see? I do know you."

Her shoulders relaxed a little. She even managed a little smile.

"You won't use any credit cards. We got rid of the cell phone. . . ." He went over a mental checklist. "You're using my computer. Don't use your bank account." He saw her look of horror. "And you can't go to the teller machine at the corner and take cash out, either. I'll provide."

She didn't like that. He could tell. She was an independent little thing. Always had been. But there was no choice now. She *had* to depend on him.

"But where does that leave us? He can't find us. We can't find him . . . but my life, well, your life, too, if it comes to that . . . we're just on hold."

"We wait for tomorrow's paper. And hope that Mordred slips up somehow."

That just didn't feel like enough.

Diana could listen to Gawain's deep voice all night long telling stories of Camelot, but she wasn't really hearing the words anymore. It was kind of him to try to distract her. But she couldn't help being worried and her body itched with the nearness of him. He was worried, too, she could tell, but he was trying to cover it up for her sake. It looked like she had no choice but to stay here with him. The image of her red lipstick on the mirror just wouldn't fade. She should be happy to have a protector. But he was doing it because he'd been ordered by Merlin to protect her. Now she was Gawain's obligation. That didn't feel good.

Among other things that didn't feel good. She had no access to her bank account. She couldn't call anyone. (Whom would she call? But that wasn't the point.) She had no job. And, to add insult to injury, she was going to have to change her underwear at this rate. Or keep taking showers. Or both. Just watching him, listening to his voice, was making her wet. Did he have to be so damn virile? Any woman in her right mind would act just like that blonde in the Exploratorium today. And no doubt had. All his life. Which left things where? With her lusting after him with no hope of reciprocation. Not good.

"Life was hard," he was saying. "Fighting the Saxons, living in caves. We were always more or less wounded.

You just kept going." He was actually looking uncomfortable, too, for some reason. He kept readjusting himself in his chair.

"Did . . . did you have women and children with you?"

He shook his head. "Only single knights joined the Resistance. We couldn't provide for families, and if they were left on their own the Saxons would find and torture them to punish us."

"Sounds lonely."

"Worse after my father told me I couldn't go raiding anymore. And better." He smiled. "Then I had you. You were the only family with us. My father wouldn't leave you behind."

"Do you wish you could go back?" He must feel lonely. He was exiled from everything he knew and loved.

But he shook his head. "I want to stay. Whatever changes I brought on by coming here don't seem to have brought the world down."

"I don't actually think we'd know if they did."

"Maybe not. I've been over and over this time travel thing, and I'm still not sure I get it. Would things have been different if I'd never come—if you'd never come, either? I don't know."

They were both thinking of Mordred, she could tell. Could one man change the world? Mordred might well be stuck here. Would it make a difference?

"Maybe if you stay too long then things do change, because you were meant to come here, but you were also meant to go back. Or maybe, if you were never meant to go back, then things don't change at all." She sounded like she'd had one drink too many, even to herself. She shrugged helplessly.

"I finally just quit thinking about it. You get caught in these conundrums that just have no answers." He looked acutely uncomfortable and squirmed in his chair again.

"If you want to go back, you can always use Leonardo's machine." Her voice was small.

"But then you'd lose it back in the fifth century."

She shook her head. "Leonardo's book says it returns to where it started after a while, like a boomerang."

"Well, I don't intend to use it. I never want to go back to that time. I like it here. Dishwashers. Antibiotics. Central heating. Need I say more?"

"Different values. You said that bothered you." Had he really adapted so well?

"I guess things haven't changed all that much," he said, sipping his Scotch. "A good man is still a good man. The strong should still protect the weak. Sometimes they do. A man should still provide for his woman, leave offspring to carry on his name, look for deeds to do that will live after him. . . ." He trailed off.

She grinned. "It's just that now those things apply to women, too."

He smiled with his eyes. "Maybe they always did, at least for some women. Women who were rich enough, or born well enough."

"That's still true, too. If you're born really poor and you don't have access to education, honor probably is a luxury. You're only concerned with putting food on the table."

"I don't believe that. I've known many honorable men . . . many honorable *people* who were very poor."

She thought about that. "You're right. So you really fit right into this century."

"I guess I should lighten up about sex always having to be a sacred bond," he said, shrugging. "I mean the whole point of that was to prevent unwanted children, and birth control made that unnecessary."

She blushed. "Yeah, sometimes a little recreational sex is okay. I . . . I did it myself once." He looked surprised. *Well, let him.* This was the twenty-first century, and being a virgin wasn't a woman's only value. "In college. How can you be a writer if you've never had sex? So I sneaked into a frat party and did it with one of the guys."

Uh-oh. He looked outraged and angry. "You were lucky you didn't end up doing it with all of them, whether you wanted to or not," he growled.

She shook her head. "They were all so drunk, they couldn't see straight. The girls, too. I just left while the guy I was with was . . . in the bathroom." She couldn't believe she was admitting this to him. Was it because she felt she'd always known him? She knew she could depend on him, that was for sure.

Fatigue hit her all at once. Too little sleep and too much excitement. Bad excitement. And she had no desire to continue her personal revelations about her nonsex life. She must seem pathetic to him. "If you'll excuse me, I'm going to bed." She pushed herself out of the wing chair. He stood also.

And she had a revelation. It was very clear why he was uncomfortable. There was a pronounced bulge in his tight jeans. She jerked her gaze to his face. He was saying, "Me, too." But she hardly heard him.

He . . . he wanted sex. His body betrayed him. With her? He wanted sex with *her*?

No. Of course not. All this talk of sex had him excited. That was all. He was a guy. Anyone would do. Even she might do in a pinch, but she sure wasn't the woman he longed for. Guinevere occupied that slot. That was a damping thought. "Well, good night then," she mumbled, and pushed past him.

But once the door closed to her bedroom, she began having second thoughts. She started to undress.

Sure, he didn't really care about her. But . . . so what? She'd had recreational sex before. Now she had no one. She was alone. She might never get another opportunity to have a sexual experience to wipe out the memory of that awful time at Phi Kappa Chi. Or confirm it. If that was really how sex was, she ought to know, shouldn't she? As a writer. And if she did it with Gawain, she'd know what sex was like in the fifth century. It was really research for her book.

Yeah. Who was she kidding?

If he walked in here right now and said, *I want to have sex with you,* would she turn him down?

Like *that* was going to happen.

She knew he could never *love* anyone like her. She . . . she just wanted to . . .

Oh, hell. She wanted to be close to someone. She wanted to feel like she *meant* something to someone. Almost anyone. Even if it was just for a moment. Even if it was false, for God's sake.

Since her father had begun drifting away from her into the sea of Alzheimer's, she'd felt increasingly that she might not be real. She was a phantom, picked up in a suburb of Chicago, connected to no one, with no past and no future. If no one loves you—if no one even notices you—do you exist? She'd been feeling that since her father died. It hadn't improved in the last days. It had just been lost in the rush of events. In fact, it had gotten worse. She'd been an orphan in the fifth century, flung forward in time for God knew what reason, resulting in being an orphan yet again in a Chicago suburb. Her adoptive mother died; her father drifted away and finally died, too. She had no friends, because who would want to be around a person who knew what they would say and could find things in ways other people couldn't? She lived a fantasy life in her books, remote from real life from all indications. Indications like the fact that she couldn't write men who resembled real men in the slightest.

She was pathetic. Gawain was *so* not coming in here.

* * *

Gawain was in physical pain. Sitting there all night, next
to her, wanting her. And when she told him her only sexual experience was with a drunken frat rat at what was
almost an orgy it had made his gut churn with anger. The
guy was in the bathroom puking his guts out and left her
to escape the sordid scene on her own. No wonder her sex
scenes lacked feeling. Not fair that this was what she
knew of men and women coupling. Sex with a woman
should be caring, and gentle. For Diana especially. She
should be cherished, not used and thrown aside. He
wanted to take her to his bed, show her what loving a man
could be like, erase the feeling that made her look like she
had when she'd been talking about her first experience of
sex.

He threw back the spread and stood staring at his bed.
The night ahead stretched long and sterile. He'd either be
awake all night or wake up to semen all over his sheets.
He shook himself. Best get on with it. He unbuttoned his
shirt, stripped it off, and put it in the hamper.

He couldn't have sex with Diana, no matter that he
thought he might be able to heal her. Because she didn't
want it. Because she didn't love him. He *wanted* it to be a
sacred bond when he finally made love to a woman. *How
old-fashioned can you get?* About fifteen centuries old-
fashioned. *I don't want it to be recreational sex between
Dilly and me. I want to wake up beside her in the morning, and roll over, and make love to her because she's a
part of me and we care about each other and we want to
have children together.*

The realization hit him like a load of stones.

He knew he liked the woman she'd become. She had
ideas and needs and a temper and a will of her own. She
was bold and curious, and . . . and he'd known her forever, and he . . . he *loved* her, by the gods. Could it be?

Of course it could. Nothing seemed more natural than that he had fallen in love with the woman Dilly had become.

But how could she feel as he did? She didn't remember him. She'd never felt the closeness they'd formed in those long weeks she'd been bedridden. She'd known him four days. Before that she thought he was stalking her. She couldn't love him. He sighed.

But he could make her feel treasured. He could give her a positive experience with sex.

That would mean that the sex was sacred only on one side. But did she have to pass some test before he could give her what she needed? That was just plain selfish. Of course he wished she would love him. But she couldn't. Not right now.

The honorable thing to do here was to have sex with Diana.

Strange. But there it was. He knew it, deep down inside.

Calmly he unbuckled his belt, pulled off his boots, and unbuttoned his jeans. He didn't carry condoms, but she was a modern woman as she kept telling him. They were all on the pill. When he was buck naked, he went to the door and turned the handle softly. He crept over to the bathroom and turned on the shower. When the steam rose, he stepped in, ducked his head under the water. His erection had eased a little. He was almost loath to touch himself lest he harden again to such a painful degree. He didn't want to frighten her. But he must come to her smelling of soap, so soap himself he did, and tried to think of other things than what he was about to do. He was only partially successful, but that was something. He washed his hair and scrubbed under his arms in haste. He lathered his chest and belly, rubbed soap over his buttocks and thighs. He must be as clean as possible for her.

Stepping out, he toweled himself briskly, skimmed the mirror of steam, and lathered his beard. He could not let her delicate skin be scraped.

And all the time he was thinking. There was every possibility that she would reject him when he presented himself to her. So he had to have a reason she should let him into her bed. Not the real reason, but an acceptable reason, one that spoke to who she was. He stared at his own eyes in the mirror as they changed from gray-green to piercing blue.

And what would that be?

Well, start with who she was. She was a perfectionist. That's why she didn't think she was pretty enough. And why she revised her books so many times.

Books. That was the answer.

He nicked himself in his haste, patted the blood away. He was as ready as he would be. Suddenly he wondered if he was up to this. What if he hurt her? What if . . . ?

"Get hold of yourself, man," he whispered. "She needs you. Gods grant you are enough."

He turned out the bathroom light and pushed into the hall. No light shone out from under the doorway. He tried the knob. She'd locked it. Bad omen, that. But she couldn't keep him out.

The tiny part he had inherited from his father was at least good for that if nothing else. She might see him do it. That meant he would be revealing a part of himself he had never revealed to anyone, even to his father. Well, anyone except the guards who'd seen him get out of the jail cell that first night in Chicago. Then they'd drugged him for being insane. (Saying he had gone berserk on the prisoners he shared the cell with and attacked them when they entered to break up the brawl was easier than telling the truth about how he escaped.) Why couldn't he get a talent that was useful? He couldn't even get himself out of prison with it. He'd been caught four times trying. It took him too long to dissipate at each locked door. And he couldn't hold the dissipation long enough to make it through the ventilation system. They'd had to cut him out of a vent over the cafeteria once. He was a shameful period to his father's hopes for him.

But his small talent could get him into Diana's room.

He put his palms on either side of the doorway to steady himself and stilled his center. His eyes went unfocused and his breathing slowed.

Mist. I am mist and darkness, he sang to himself. *I am fog.*

He felt himself dissipating. His molecules fanned out in infinitesimal thinness. He slid under the door. Inside, he gathered his molecules in a whirling mist that grew heavy and took form. His body warmed. Slowly the darkened room came into view.

She was sitting up in bed, her eyes wide, staring at where the mist had been. Unfortunate.

"How . . . how did you do that?"

"My father passed only a tiny part of his power to me." It hurt him to admit that. But she wouldn't see that in the dim bedroom. Only a little light from the streetlight outside leaked in around the patterned fabric shade. "What you saw was pretty much it." That and the dream-thing. But she wouldn't like knowing he could get into her dreams. Sins of omission.

Her eyes grew big.

"Don't be afraid. It's just parlor trick magic, not real magic."

She nodded. "Looks pretty impressive to me."

"Not compared to my father." But from the light leaking in he saw her expression. *Okay. She might or might not have been talking about the magic.* She'd noticed he was naked. And erect. And his erection was growing. How could he not frighten her?

"What . . . what are you doing here?"

"Well, all that talk about recreational sex being okay in this century. I thought . . ."

She swallowed, her eyes big. Oh, he was just doing a great job here.

He pressed on. He had to make it sound casual. That was the only way she might accept it. "So I was thinking that since you had only that one time, and . . . uh . . . not under ideal circumstances, you'd probably need research for your current book." That was the stroke of genius that had caused him to nick his chin. He'd tie having sex with him to the one thing that must have kept her going through all her travails—her writing.

She looked stunned for a minute. Then . . . interested.

He took a step forward. "So I was thinking . . . how bad can that be in the twenty-first century? A little research, I mean."

Her eyes were like saucers, and they were taking in every inch of him. *Good.* She was at least attracted to him. He could feel it. He had to be ready for the fact that she might be a little nervous. Or even frigid after her disastrous first experience. But he'd be gentle. He might not be a parfait knight, but he was enough of a man to do this for her.

His cock throbbed with a mind of its own.

He *would* be gentle.

Chapter Thirteen

Diana looked up at the body that had haunted her, waking and sleeping, for the last days, and wanted to hide under the covers. He was offering himself to her. Probably a sacrifice. But he obviously needed release, and this was a once-in-a-lifetime opportunity for her.

Funny that he had known she wanted to make love to him as research for her books. It was research. That was all. She wasn't on the pill and he didn't offer a condom, but she'd come off her period just a few days ago. She'd probably be okay this once.

She pulled the covers up to her breasts. All she could do was look at him and wonder what would happen next and what she felt about that and about how big his male parts were.

She didn't have to wonder long. He stepped forward and . . . and knelt at the edge of her bed. How surprising. She couldn't see the color of his eyes right now. They were dark pools, mysterious, unfathomable. Not that they were ever fathomable to her. . . .

He took her one hand and clasped her fingers lightly. He brushed her knuckles against his lips, lightly. His lips were very soft. She'd read that men had soft lips. But to feel how soft they were in contrast to the hard muscle

elsewhere—even now she could see his biceps bulge—
that was an entirely different thing. His breath was hot
and moist against her hand. It made her shiver in unseen
places that shouldn't be able to do those sorts of things.
He was so close she could smell that his hair was wet. She
smelled soap, too, but underneath that he smelled like . . .
Well, she couldn't describe it. Like a man, she guessed. A
very clean man.

"May I come to you, Diana?" he whispered.

He was . . . petitioning her. She swallowed once. This
was it. Now or never. She nodded. He pulled back the
covers and she scooted over so he could slide in beside
her. His arm just somehow found its way around her
back. He smoothed a piece of hair off her forehead with
the other hand as he pulled her in. Her breast seemed to
push itself against his chest of its own accord. *Oh, dear.*
Wet oozed between her legs. He was so big. His shoulders
were massive this close, and his pectorals hard and his
abdomen girded with iron bands. His engorged member
lay across his thigh. She wasn't really looking at it. Not
directly. But she was very aware of it. He was an entirely
different being than she was. Frightening and fascinating.
His very differentness seemed to call to her on some elemental level she'd never really considered. She put her
hands on his chest and ran her hand through the crisp
hair, dark against his pale skin. The air in the room was
cool, and his nipples were pinched. She dared not touch
them.

He didn't try to undress her. He didn't pull up her
nightshirt and just spread her legs. He just turned her chin
up and bent to kiss her. A comma of damp hair flopped
across his forehead. His lips brushed hers. It seemed so
natural to open her lips slightly. He licked her lips. Who
could not have opened further? Then his tongue was exploring her mouth, a gentle quest, not the ravishing she'd

described so often. It stroked her own and she found herself stroking back.

Of course she'd kissed before. She'd kissed that frat rat. But that had been a slobbery penetration, mashed against her tongue. It was not a kiss. *This* was a kiss. She felt his hands rubbing along her back. Stroking her. Somehow one of her hands was holding his biceps and the other was gripping his shoulder.

She could have stayed kissing him forever, but he broke the kiss. His tongue darted over her ear. His breath was warm. He made his way down her neck, sending showers of goose bumps down the length of her body. She shivered and began to laugh, her tension released. Her laugh seemed to inflame him. He held her even closer and kissed his way over to her throat. She found herself leaning back, trusting his arms to hold her. Which he did with one arm only, and distracted her with kisses while he unbuttoned the top buttons of her sleep shirt.

It didn't take him long to ease his way in and cup her breast. He caressed it. That was the only word for it. And that was *very* different from the wild and painful groping on the floor of a frat room. He cupped it, and stroked it, and all the while he was working his kisses down until he found her nipple. She took in a ragged breath.

She'd rubbed her own nipples through her bra, just to see how it felt. It wasn't the same. This moist suckling took every nerve in her nipple and gave it a direct connection to her clitoris. And he didn't stop. He continued on, moving his tongue over her nipple, sucking, rolling the nub of it around. When she thought she couldn't stand any more, he moved to the other nipple. The man really had a very talented tongue.

"Oh, god," she murmured, almost against her will.

He raised his head, smiling at her. His eyes were crinkled at the edges. "Not God. Gawain. Is there anything particular you'd like to research, my lady?"

She shook her head convulsively. "No. Just . . . just anything you'd like to do." She didn't want this to be any more of a trial than necessary for him. And she had no idea what to ask for.

"Well, then, I think I should just cover all the basics." He began unbuttoning the rest of the buttons on her night-shirt.

"Okay. That . . . that sounds good."

He ran his hand down over her belly and palmed her mound. She couldn't help but press against his hand, which allowed his finger to slip inside her folds. Or more than one. She couldn't tell because sensations just seemed to pour over her. He slid his fingers up to her clitoris and down into her vagina, slowly, over and over again, until she was rocking against him. When he withdrew his hand, she wanted to protest. Her body was certainly pro-testing. But he slid down and scooted over between her legs, pressing her knees out. She felt opened to him, vul-nerable, but not in a bad way. It was Gawain. She could trust him.

Oh my God. Was he going to . . . ?

His tongue slid into her, across her, over every centi-meter of screaming flesh. She was having trouble breath-ing and he didn't seem to care. Indeed, he slid his hands under her buttocks and pressed her hips up to have better access to her moist folds. She rocked against him shame-lessly, her fingers twining in his hair.

She could feel it coming. It wasn't like a rolling tidal wave, though she had used that image once. It wasn't a volcano. It wasn't thunder and lightning, or stars spinning out of control. All the neurons in her woman's parts, her brain, up and down her spinal cord, just . . . broke apart.

She keened for something not lost but thrown away, surrendered, and which came back again to her a hundredfold.

It had never been like *that*. The orgasms she'd had at her own hands weren't the same thing at all. Maybe there ought to be categories of orgasms, like they categorized tornadoes. If so, that was a category 5. She gasped for air.

Gawain was up on his elbows. "Ready for the next topic?" His tone was light, but his eyes were dark, dangerously intent. "I'm afraid we have to get to it soon, because it depends a bit more on me."

She nodded, unable still to speak but needing something, wanting something she could not name. She pulled him up, and as she did that, her knees just seemed to come up naturally, rocking her nether parts up toward his cock. It hung between his legs, swollen and questing. It was . . . really big. She looked up at him.

"Don't worry," he whispered. "It will all work out." He took the head in one hand as he held himself up on the other, and guided it to her entrance. She braced for pain. It had been painful last time. But if that was how it always was for her, if it was some lack in herself or her physiology that made actual penetration painful, then she had to know. She had to be able to write that into her stories, if they were to be real.

He pushed at her opening gently. His penis didn't immediately slide in.

"I'm sorry. I'm tight or something."

"You're fine. It's me that's too large. We'll just go slow. Slow can be nice."

It could. He bent to suck her breasts again, until she couldn't be worried about anything but whether he might ever stop, because that would be bad. And he was rocking at her, a little deeper each time, until . . . until he was pressed against her, groin to groin, and she felt so wonderfully . . . *filled*. And it turned out that's what she had wanted, needed, all along.

He groaned and arched above her, pressing himself into her, sliding out and thrusting in again. Just watching him was a revelation. The muscles moving in his arms and shoulders. The way his eyes closed and opened to focus on her. Emboldened, she slipped her hands around to clutch his buttocks as they bunched and relaxed. And then she felt it coming again. Her own breathing was shallow and fast. His motion got faster. She reached now for his nipples and rubbed them with her thumbs.

And then she couldn't think about anything else but the sensation that was about to transform into something entirely, altogether, different.

And it did. It did. It did.

He arched into her just as she was coming down from the mountain and she felt the big cock inside her stiffen and then jerk as he came himself, with a grunt that spiraled up almost into a yell. It was wonderful to watch him, wonderful to feel.

When at last he sank onto his elbows above her, he didn't just roll away. He kissed her, so gently, on the eyelids, and then on the mouth, and then he put his arm around her buttocks and rolled them onto their sides, with his cock still inside her.

"Diana," he whispered into her hair as he cradled her head to his chest. "Diana." The smell of clean man was in her nostrils, and behind it the raw, musky smell of what they'd done.

"Thank you," she whispered.

He cleared his throat. "Good research?" His voice was still husky.

"The best," she said. Oh, she should never have done

this. This felt too right. It made her feel too whole. That was dangerous.

Mordred grinned as he sat in his now-familiar cone of light and tapped away at the computer. He hadn't found the girl today, or Merlin's brat. That was annoying. In fact, Merlin's son had grown up into a very annoying man. Mordred would enjoy making him suffer before he died. The girl he could just kill quickly, or after he had taken her a few times.

He would find them. And if he didn't, he was willing to bet that Merlin's son (was his name Gawain? yes, he thought so) Gawain would find him. Result the same in either case.

He grinned again and sipped his whiskey as he watched the responses scroll down. They spoke in code now on a new site, so the authorities in this time would not yet be alerted to their actions. He kept a running tally with a marker on a paper of the number of heads his followers boasted of taking. Two score so far. Soon the authorities . . . What did they call them now? Police. Soon the police would connect all the deaths and would start searching for him. It would be too late. His army was like a serpent rising from the center of the earth. How wonderful that he could comb the world for the ones he needed, the disaffected ones whose souls had an emptiness at their center that longed to be filled by someone who would transform them. Now they would come from all over, wherever they were, and his army would coalesce like smoke drawn from the air into substance.

"Listen," he typed. "The post arrives at 1113 after dark tomorrow. Wear flowers in your hair. Armageddon is at hand for unbelievers. We are the world. We are the answer."

So, tomorrow night, the loft at 1113 Post Street at Market would begin to fill. They would drop jobs and families if they had them. They would drive and fly and walk to get here, so that he could transform the emptiness inside them into purpose. Some could get here by tomorrow night. Others would stream toward San Francisco as if it were Mecca in the holy month of Ramadan. He'd read about that on a Web site today.

He had to assess their skills, appoint his seconds, find someone who could run supplies and communications. He had to let them look into his eyes and see that he was their answer. He would spout the words they wished to hear, and his followers would give those words the substance they wished the words possessed. And then they were his.

She was a miracle. Making love to her had been a miracle. Gawain couldn't regret it. The way she opened to him, the way she trusted him. He'd worried when she was so hesitant. He'd wondered if she was too damaged by her previous experience. But no, Dilly was ever courageous. Once she'd decided to bed him, she bested her fears.

He hoped he'd been gentle enough with her. It had cost him every ounce of his control to go as slowly has he had, when he had wanted somewhere in his gut to make this coupling an act of claiming. He wanted to claim her as his own, fast and fierce and shouting to the night, with the right to protect and defend her, the right to make love to her, for them to bear children together and stand together against all comers.

He had known her forever. He had loved her first in the only way a man of twenty-three can love a child of thirteen. But now she was a woman. He could love her the way a man was meant to love a woman, and he did. He cradled her as she dozed, but he did not drift off.

He had to find Mordred and dispatch him. To hell with what the villain would do to the twenty-first century if he could. It was what he intended to do to Diana that made him most dangerous.

Gawain felt her stir in his arms. She still had her sleep shirt on, though it was entirely unbuttoned, leaving her soft breasts pressed against his chest. He had captured her thigh between his own. This was how they should sleep together, always.

She wiggled the leg between his. He opened his thighs immediately. "Did your leg go to sleep?"

"No. I just liked the feel of it against your . . . you know."

He raised his brows. "Against my 'you know'? I'll have you know those are my bollocks and my cock you're speaking of."

Her eyes went dark. "Yes."

"I know you know those words. You use them in your books."

"Yes." She cleared her throat. "Well, it's a little different saying them to someone in real life." She cleared her throat again. "I . . . I hope it was okay for you."

"Yelling is a clue. You don't often get yelling."

She tried to suppress a smile and looked down.

He felt his cock springing to new life. Would he ever get enough of her? "I'm not sure your research is yet complete if you have to resort to 'you know' to describe things." He rolled over on his back and scooted her over. A full-size bed was really too small for this. They should be on the king-size in his room. Next time.

"Don't you think you should explore a little yourself? Just in the name of research."

She grinned but looked away.

"You can't possibly be shy after opening to my mouth the way you did."

"Was . . . was I too brazen?" She looked stricken.

"Don't you know that a man likes his woman to be a lady in public and brazen in bed? You were perfect."

"So . . . so I should be brazen now." She slid a glance down to his groin.

"Yes."

She took her lip between her teeth as though she were girding her own loins. "I suppose you know that all those things I wrote in my books—they were pretty much just words to me. I know the words well enough . . . but . . ."

"But you should explore the reality," he said firmly.

She smiled shyly. "If you're sure you wouldn't mind."

"I'll bear up." At least this time he could wait. He'd just had one hell of an orgasm.

"Well, I think I'll start with your nipples. I was very curious earlier, but I didn't like to . . . just . . . well, you know."

"You think you're conveying something with this phrase 'you know.' But you're not. Could you mean 'lick them'?"

She sighed as if relieved. "Yes. Lick them."

She bent over him and touched her tongue to his right nipple. Sensation shot to his groin. He hadn't expected that. Not from just a nipple. Not after having spent himself so forcefully less than an hour before. She ran her tongue over it and then sucked gently. He cleared his throat. Now she raked her teeth across it, not biting, but the mere possibility of biting made him feel open and vulnerable to her. She continued working at it, alternating techniques while her other small hand gravitated toward his other nipple and began to tweak it.

She pulled up. "Now, describe how that feels please."

"Good."

She frowned at him. "I can't just say it feels 'good' in my books."

"Well, I'm a man. Men don't wax flowery over . . . over things like that." He took a breath. "That doesn't mean you have to stop."

She slipped down and slid her tongue into his navel. "I

have other fish to fry right now. I'll try to get back to them later." She pulled his thighs apart and he obliged her. "I've read," she said meditatively, "that the area just behind the testicles is very sensitive." She took two fingers and rubbed the spot in question slowly, deeply. Lord, he was hard as a rock already. Could things get any more intense? "Is that true?" she asked.

"Uh, yes." Where did she *read* these kind of things? In books like hers?

"Pleasurable?"

"That would be yes."

"And balls, do you like them caressed if I promise to be very gentle?"

"I . . . I don't know. No one's ever done . . . that exactly to me."

"You surprise me." She gave a knowing smile. "A man with your experience?"

The women he'd had might have been experienced, but they had not prepared him for . . . for this. The last woman he'd had was the Green Knight's wife, and that was many years ago. At the thought of the Green Knight and his failure of honor, his heart contracted. He had to put that failure away. This was for Diana. He would perform the act of loving with her, for her, as a healing rite. That was the height of honor. And if it wasn't, then honor be damned.

"Is something wrong?"

She must have seen his doubt flicker across his face.

"No, my love. I only hope I have enough experience to keep up with you."

She started, blinked twice, and then turned her attention assiduously back to his genitals. "Can you at least tell me when what I do feels good?" She drew her brows together quickly. "You would tell me if I hurt you, wouldn't you?"

"In the name of research, of course."

A slow smile dawned. How he loved to see her smile. Her eyes crinkled in mischief. "Let me just see if what the books I've read say is correct. Now we rub the testicles together, just softly, inside their sack. We cup the whole and lift, rubbing at the base there, like that. And then, then just stroke across the vein of your cock, like this, and then grasp, firmly, very deep, and stroke up."

He was gasping.

She looked like the cat who'd swallowed the canary. "These books were definitely worth reading, if only for the sex scenes," she remarked, calm as you please while he was barely hanging on. "Now, look, you've secreted a little clear liquid. We can rub that gently across the head like that." He groaned. "Oooh, may I?" She glanced to him, but he was long past saying anything. He was clutching the bedclothes and trying not to writhe. Just the sight of her little hands, grasping him, exploring him, was enough to . . .

She took the head of his cock in her mouth and tried a tentative sucking. Dear God, that was it. He wasn't going to come in her mouth on her first foray into oral sex. He took her shoulders and just lifted her up. He scooted up to the head of the bed and sat her, straddled, across his lap. "We haven't tried this yet. You'll like this." He managed that through gritted teeth. He lifted her and she pulled his cock up. It took some wriggling on her part to find the angle. He thought he might die.

And then she lowered herself. He was sheathed in her, so tight, so hot. He felt her contract around him as she settled him into her. "I may be clumsy at this. Will you help me find the rhythm?"

It didn't take her long. He put his hands around her bottom as she pushed up, which had the added benefit of bringing her breasts to brush against his chest every time she rose and fell.

"I . . . I can't wait for you, love." And he was jerking into her, spurting again and again until he felt stripped inside. He'd failed her.

"Good," she whispered. "Because I had been one ahead of you." And she kissed him lightly on the forehead. That brushing, tender kiss stripped yet more from him, only this time it was from his heart. He drew her mouth down and kissed her as she collapsed against his chest.

"I'm sweating," he apologized as the cool air in the room hit him.

She nuzzled his neck. "Yes. I see that men will do that. Men in romance novels hardly ever sweat when they have sex."

"When they make love," he corrected, running his lips over her throat.

"In most romance novels, I'm afraid they only have sex." She sighed. "And if they achieve a—what did you call it?—a transcendental bond . . . it feels forced. Not real at all."

He'd called it a sacred bond. He didn't correct her. The sentiment was right. He felt himself sheltered inside her and for a moment he wondered who was protecting whom.

She was drowsing on his shoulder now. But he knew he could rouse her for one more climax. He stroked her back gently, then down over her buttocks. She squirmed against him. *That's right,* he thought. *That feels good, doesn't it?* He kissed her neck softly and stroked the side swell of her breast. She shifted against him, her eyes still closed, until the breast was up and available. He rolled her over on her back and began kissing the nipple. He felt her come to full awareness under him. He slid his fingers inside her slick folds and kissed her while he brought her up to orgasm yet again. How he loved to give her pleasure. He loved seeing her gasping and glowing with perspiration under his hands. When she had collapsed again, he gathered her into his chest. "Come lie beside me until the morning," he said, scooting down. He slid her arms out of her sleep shirt finally and drew the blankets up over her shoulders. Only then did he ease out of her. He drank in her sleepy protest and turned her backside into himself, spooning against her with his arms around her. He would protect her tonight, and for all time to come. She might have thought this recreational sex, but for him it was anything but.

He had committed to her tonight in a sacred bond, even if it was one-sided.

Diana woke alone in the morning. But the sheets still smelt of him. Of them. She could hear him moving in the rooms outside the door. Oh, dreadful, dreadful outcome. It had been wonderful. And whatever she had said about her reasons for egging him on to do it with her, she was lost well and truly now. It had seemed so right. He was so kind, so tender, with her. She had enjoyed giving him pleasure so much. And receiving pleasure in return.

Who knew it could be like that? Was that what all those sterile words on sterile pages had been trying to invoke? But you could only know it if you'd felt it. And she'd felt it last night with every nerve she had. She'd lain with a man. No. That was wrong. It was special because she had lain with Gawain. She wanted to rewrite every sex scene she had ever written, but what use? The words still would not express the closeness, the wonder, of last night.

At least on her side, it had been much more than recreational sex. She had lost her heart to the unattainable. That was disaster.

He seemed like someone she knew through and through, trusted through and through. He was a good man. Courageous beyond a doubt—to have survived a mental institution and prison and traveling through time. To have been in the Resistance after Camelot had fallen. All those took incredible courage. And he was smart. He had taught himself about this century and how to get along in it, not because he had some miraculous ability to adapt but because he had courage and intelligence and . . . probably stubbornness. He had called her stubborn as a child, but she knew full well that he must have matched her, will for will.

Then there was the incredibly hot hunk part. Who wouldn't be in love with him?

She was. After five days, she was totally in love with him. But maybe, if what he said was true and they had known each other in the fifth century, even if she had been only thirteen, it wasn't so strange that she could fall in love with him so fast. How she wished she remembered being friends with him. She would never get that back, likely. But she could be his friend now.

That's all he would let her be of course. And that would hurt. He had called her love or my love several times, but that was just the fashion of the time. It didn't mean anything. Gawain the parfait knight was never going to love a little romance writer of the twenty-first century who had to make up a fantasy life in her books.

It occurred to her that he was more even than a parfait knight. The wonderful glow of making love to him had almost erased her memory of what he'd done last night. Before the other things he'd done. He'd come into her room through a locked door. She *had* locked it. There was no question. And right before her eyes, a mist had come in under the door and then he was standing there, telling her that he was his father's son. . . . And she accepted that. Hell, after time machines and meeting the honest-to-god Merlin and Mordred the Adapter, why not?

He could turn into mist and float through doors.

Just one more reason he was totally out of her league. So she would be his friend. If she were to write herself as a character she'd be the steadfast friend who never got the guy.

She threw back the covers. At least she had a friend. That was more than she had five days ago. She retrieved her sleep shirt from the floor and slipped it on, gathered clothes, and slipped out the door to the bathroom. He was humming to himself in the kitchen. The tune sounded terribly . . . familiar.

When she came out of the shower, dressed in black cords and a red suede jacket she'd had forever over a white long-sleeved T-shirt, she felt better than she had in a long time. She pulled a scarf scattered with red and gold leaves on a black background around her neck. Friends might not be all her heart wanted, but being friends was better than nothing.

"What's the word?" she asked as she saw him bustling about scooping out a cantaloupe.

He looked struck. "I . . . I totally forgot to go down and get the paper from the lobby."

She hadn't meant that. She'd forgotten about Mordred, too, in all her thoughts about perfect knights. She blushed. Gawain was not focused on what had happened last night, of course. Men didn't. Especially when it was just recreational sex. "Don't worry. Let's just turn on the tube." She fiddled with his setup and managed to get Channel 4. She thought she'd have to wait for the local segment of the network morning news program to hear anything about Mordred, but she was wrong:

"All across the country, decapitated heads have appeared set on pikes," a pretty woman was saying into a forest of handheld microphones. The label at the bottom of the screen said she was Angela Forten, spokesperson for the FBI. "The only connection between the victims seems to be that they are from a minority group, or activists for various kinds of human rights."

"What are you doing to catch these people?" someone yelled from among the forest. Gawain came up behind Diana. She looked up at him and saw her own horror reflected in his face.

"We have top teams on it in all the affected cities right now. It's early days yet, though," the spokeswoman said, her voice calm. "We have to be patient and let justice work."

"Do you suspect terrorist activity?" another shouted.

"We have no idea who is responsible. It does appear to be an organized effort, though the details of the crimes vary."

"While you investigate, how can the public be safe?"

"We're advising people to observe a personal curfew. It's not mandatory, but I would not go out at night alone. Only in groups of ten or more."

"Why ten?"

"The most . . . bodies . . . we've seen as a result of a single incident has been six."

There was a stunned silence.

"Actually," she continued. "I wouldn't go out at night at all."

"Bars and restaurants are going to love that," Diana murmured.

The station flipped away from Ms. Forten and back to the national desk. "This just in," the black newscaster said. He was normally a jovial personality, but today his expression was grim. "Reports of similar events are coming in from other countries now. Germany and Austria are especially hard-hit."

Gawain reached forward and turned the television off. They stood there, saying nothing, for a long minute.

It was Diana who finally stirred herself. "Is . . . is this what you expected?" She turned to see him swallow convulsively

"Not on this scale."

"The wonders of the Internet. That's got to be how he's doing it. From my computer." The thought of that made her want to vomit. She was involved in this now.

"You aren't to blame for this."

"I am, though. I brought him back here. I changed the course of history, and look what's happened. People are dead, Gawain. Because of what I did. Lots of people."

He pulled her into his arms and just held her, his cheek bent to her head. She was too stunned and appalled even to cry. "If it comes to that," he said softly into her hair, "we have to blame my father for flinging us forward, and causing you to lose the memory of your childhood. You came back because you were looking to return to what you knew, unconsciously. Else why would you pick that time?"

That was true. She must have been unconsciously looking for her childhood with Leonardo's machine. "But I took him back here with me. I should never have interfered."

"You said he was about to be killed. You were kindhearted. There is no crime in that." He took a breath. "It was natural. Now we just have to concentrate on stopping him."

Reluctantly she extricated herself from Gawain's embrace. It *was* her fault. And there seemed to be nothing she could do to stop the awful course of events from unfolding. "The police can track these people through their computer use, can't they?"

"I don't know," he said slowly. "These guys are smart. They change IP addresses all the time. They take down sites and put up others. I think it can be tough to track them. At the very least, it can take a long time."

"Mordred can't be that sophisticated with computers, Adapter or no."

"He's not alone anymore, Diana. He's got an army."

"We've got to go to the police," she practically wailed. There had to be a way to stop the carnage. And whatever Gawain said, that carnage could be laid at her door. She wondered that she hadn't thought of that when the first head appeared on a pike in Union Square.

"And tell them what?" he asked, running his hands through his hair and looking around the apartment with unseeing eyes. "It's the same old problem. Can't tell them he's a guy from the past. We can't tell them where he is because we don't know."

"We'll tell them the guy who was staying with me illegally from Canada is the killer."

"All that does is embroil you in this mess and it doesn't get them any farther toward finding him and stopping him." He stopped. "Uh-oh. We didn't report your computer stolen. If they do find him, and they find it with him, they might think you were aiding and abetting."

She sighed. "Okay. We'll report it. That doesn't seem like enough when people are going to get killed again tonight."

His look said he agreed with her and felt more ashamed than she did that he couldn't make a difference.

The local precinct was a zoo. Everyone was hysterical, it seemed. Gawain had to shield Diana with his body to keep her from getting shoved around. Women were shrieking about needing police protection. Everybody and his brother had seen the killers and wanted to make a full report. Behind the front desk men in shirtsleeves and women in slacks and sweaters mixed in with uniformed police manning phones and all talking at once. When Diana and Gawain at last reached the front, the desk sergeant, the

potbellied and balding man who'd lectured them yesterday before he gave back Diana's car, was back on duty.
He looked like he should have a cigar hanging out of his
mouth and talk with a Brooklyn accent. Right now he'd
lost what patience he was born with.

"You back? What is it?" he growled. His accent was
pure California.

"We'd like to report that Diana's computer was stolen,"
Gawain said calmly as an old woman started berating the
government in general for incompetence in a loud voice
behind him. He kept his eyes down, though in this melee
he wasn't sure anyone would notice them changing.

The sergeant looked up and raised his brows. "You
want to report a computer stolen . . . today."

"Yes, please, sir," Diana said. "Don't say we've waited
in this long line for nothing."

Gawain could see the sergeant melt. Who wouldn't
melt under that soft, earnest stare? He always had. "Yeah.
I see your point, lady," the sergeant said, his tone now
only mock gruff to maintain face. "Let me get you a form
to fill out. Just drop it back by the window when you're
done."

He reached under the counter and fumbled around,
then bent to look. "Where the hell are they? We can't be
out." He turned to the recruit. "Go back in the storeroom
and get me some stolen-property forms, kid. And put a
rush on it."

The recruit made a face. Probably didn't like being
called kid. But he left at a jog.

Gawain and Diana stepped aside to let the woman in a
pillbox hat with a veil and a ratty fur coat demand extra
police patrols on her street. It didn't go over well with the
sergeant.

The recruit finally poked his head back in from a doorway. "We must be out, Sarge."

Diana started to fidget. She seemed torn about something. Gawain was about to ask her what was wrong when she called out, "Have you looked back by the mail room? They could have been delivered and just not put away yet."

The sergeant and the recruit both looked a little stunned. "Sarge?"

The sergeant waved a hand. "It's worth a try." He went back to remonstrating with the old woman. The uniformed kid was back in less than no time hauling a box in his arms.

"Hey, you were right, lady!" he called to Diana. "Mailroom! How'd you know?"

"I lose things a lot, so I'm a good finder. You just think where things would logically be."

The kid pulled open the box and handed her a form. "Here you go."

"Thanks," she said hastily.

She and Gawain pushed their way back to a counter. Diana filled out the form while he watched her. His keys. Her boss' clipboard. There was no way she could have known he left it in the men's room on the shelf above the second sink. And then this. Gawain knew now. He just had to get her to admit it to him.

And if it was true, then there was a way to find Mordred.

Chapter Fourteen

Gawain opened the door for her on his black Range Rover and handed her in like it was some kind of carriage, just like always, and loped around to the driver's side.

"Okay, so we filled out a police report on my silly computer," she said, unaccountably peeved. It felt so bad not to be able to *do* anything about the terrible things that were happening. "Now what?"

Gawain made no move to start the SUV. "I've been thinking," he said slowly. "We have to get Mordred today if we're going to get him. Tomorrow it's all out of our hands."

"Well, that would be nice," she said with a certain amount of sarcasm. "But I don't think that's going to happen." *Wait. What had he said?* "Why is today different than tomorrow?"

He looked at her with gray-green swirling eyes. "Because Mordred will have called his army to him. He's from the fifth century. He doesn't go with the concept of 'virtual army.' They'll be congregating wherever he is, the closer ones first, and then the ones from farther away. They'll bring weapons. Don't know what kind. But after today, he'll have protection. I won't be able to take him out hand to hand."

A series of really horrible scenes flashed before her mind's eye. "So you're thinking this is going to be a pitched-battle kind of war, not a stealthy-acts-of-terrorism kind of war?"

"It's what he knows. He may look to kill the president or the governor to make a point. He might try to take over some kind of military arsenal and threaten a city. I don't know. I know he wants power and he can bend men to his will to get it." Gawain's eyes were gray and hard.

"Maybe he'll just start rallying in public with his fanatic followers and making speeches so he can get elected and secede from the union or something. I mean, he has a right to do that."

"After what he's done so far? I think these murders are an initiation rite of sorts, a proof you're worth a position in his army. Either way, he's generating hatred that will fester and linger in society until it rots from within or is torn apart. If we stop it now, before they can get organized, by taking out the center, it will die out. He's got to be stopped."

It began to drizzle. A really depressing drizzle.

"I . . . I agree with that." Even if he had to be killed. She swallowed. She wondered if she would ever have imagined herself saying something like that when her father was alive. But if Mordred was truly behind inciting people to all these murders . . .

"Then maybe you'll agree to find him for me."

"*Me?* I have no idea where he is." What made him think she would be of any use?

"Use your power."

She had to laugh. "Like I have power. That's the world you come from, guy, not my world. We don't have 'powers.'"

"I think you do." He was so sincere. His eyes went blue even as she looked at him.

Her grin faded. "What makes you think that?"

"You can find things."

She blinked. *Oh. He'd noticed.* "Yeah. I know where things are. That's not a 'power.'"

"Sure it is. Just like I can turn into mist and go through locked doors. I should have realized you weren't what you seemed. I'm an idiot."

"Knowing where things are is *not* a power. It's a stupid little quirk I've always had."

"Are there other quirks?"

She swallowed. Should she tell him? But a longing to tell him came over her. He understood her in ways no one else ever would. He knew who she was. He was the keeper of her childhood. *Truth time.* "Sometimes I know what people will say a few seconds before they say it. Exact words. Strangers even. Everybody except you. And Mordred. I couldn't get anything off him, either."

"That makes sense," he said thoughtfully.

"I can't read thoughts. I only know what people will actually say, even if it's not what they're thinking. It doesn't get me anything except about three or four seconds' head start on reacting. I can finish people's sentences for them, but that's just annoying. And I can always find my keys. Big deal."

"It *is* a big deal. You could find Mordred."

She didn't realize she was holding her breath until a little gasp escaped her. "I don't think it works with people."

"Have you tried?"

"No. It never came up. And this thing I do, it's really a lot . . . smaller than that."

"So no harm in trying, is there?"

She chewed her lip. This *so* couldn't be up to her. She wouldn't be able to do anything about something this big, this important. "I . . . I wouldn't know how to begin. . . ."

"Well, how does it usually happen?"

"I . . . uh . . . It happens so fast it's kind of hard to deconstruct." He nodded his encouragement. "I guess I think about what the thing is, and I ask myself, 'Where would it be?'" She closed her eyes and tried to feel what she felt when those little ideas about where things were just popped into her head. "Actually, I think I really think about *being* that thing, just for a second, and I ask myself, 'Where would I be?'" Her eyes popped open. "And I just know. Maybe . . . maybe the thing tells me where it is." She rolled her eyes. "Now *that* sounds crazy."

"But it isn't crazy because you *do* know where things are. So try it. Try it with Mordred."

Diana looked around as if there were some escape. The drizzle had thickened into a steady rain. The windshield was beginning to fog up. The SUV felt chill and her leather suede jacket was unlined. She shivered. There was no escape. She'd brought Mordred here, and she had to try by whatever means possible to find him and stop him. It was just that . . . failure seemed so inevitable. She was a romance writer, a woman men never noticed. She wasn't up to this.

It didn't matter. She took a deep breath and blew it out slowly. "Okay. You're going to be disappointed. But I'll try."

"Then I won't be disappointed. That's all anyone can ask."

She glanced up to him, and his eyes turned the clearest, softest green you could imagine. Combined with his expression, she thought it might be her favorite. "This is going to be harder than finding a set of keys," she grumbled.

"Aye." He gave a helpless look. "If I had another way I'd take it." He must have seen her look of doubt. "I have faith in you, Diana."

So she closed her eyes and calmed her breathing. She'd try this to atone for her sin in bringing Mordred forward in time, and she'd do it because Gawain believed in her. The fool. She thought about Mordred as she'd seen him last, dark, close-cropped hair, face all hard planes as though he were an unfinished sculpture, the clay not yet smoothed by the creator's hand. Even as she held his image in her mind, the mouth sneered in that volatile way he had. He would still have the wound he'd gotten in the fifth century on his upper arm, though it would be healing. She felt her breath, easing in, easing out. Only her breath in the cold air of the car. That's all she would think about. All she would feel.

Her arm throbbed. Her stomach knotted with anger. Bile rose in her throat. She paced a big, empty space with many windows. It echoed with her steps. *Bastard!* To have taken what was rightfully hers all those years ago. Well, she'd triumphed in the end. She'd have a better kingdom than her father had. Richer, more magical, more wonderful. And it would all be hers. Starting right here, tonight.

"Where am I?" she muttered under her breath. She looked around herself and saw the modern arched glass towers of the Marriott that looked like a jukebox out broad windows, and as she turned she could see the lights of cars in a ribbon across a highway that disappeared over the bay. Square structural towers loomed in the dim mist of afternoon.

Breath in. Breath out.

She opened her eyes, to find Gawain staring at her. Squinching her eyes tight, she felt the buzz of blood in the veins in her head. She shook it violently to get him out of there. The feeling of all that hatred made her skin crawl.

"Diana, are you okay?" Gawain had hold of her shoulder. His grip was strong and warm.

Breath out.

"Yeah. I'm okay." *Right.* She was shaking like a leaf. "He's in an unfinished loft in a warehouse somewhere down by the old Marriott hotel that looks like a jukebox. The building's tall enough to see Highway Eighty just before it goes over the Bay Bridge."

Gawain looked a little stunned. "You . . . did it."

"Don't act so surprised. I thought you had faith in me." It was she who was surprised. And appalled. She'd become Mordred for a moment, and the experience frightened her.

"Doesn't mean it isn't still amazing when you see it happen right before your eyes." His expression was a little abashed.

"Like you coming out of a mist in the dark last night." *Had it only been last night?*

He grinned sheepishly. "Probably pretty much the same."

"By the way, anything else you can do?" *Besides wonderful sex, that is?* "Turnabout is fair play." Just how magic was he?

He swallowed. She could see he was thinking about whether or not he could tell her. This was some kind of a test. If they were ever to be really friends he had to level with her. She saw him decide. She saw his fear. "I . . . I can enter people's dreams."

And she knew. "You . . . you entered my dreams, didn't you?" How could he *do* that? It was like rape. He'd better say something right now to quell the outrage she felt rising in her.

"I . . . I wanted you to trust me. I finally realized you didn't know me because you didn't recognize me in the liquor store. You thought I was a stalker. I wasn't sure how else I could get near enough to protect you."

"They were nightmares, let me tell you."

"I couldn't get past your fear at first." His eyes slid away. "I'm sorry about those."

"And later you could?" How long had this been going on?

He nodded, looking uncertain. "I made you feel better about staying in my apartment."

"Well, stay the hell out of my dreams from now on." She crossed her arms over her chest. Had he been giving her lustful thoughts, too? Her shoulders slumped. He didn't need any psychic help to do that. "Just promise, okay?" He'd been trying to protect her. She had to remember that.

"Word of a knight," he said so solemnly she couldn't laugh. He cleared his throat. "Will you know the loft if we see it? Should we go to a Realtor and shop for a loft?"

Okay, back to business. They had to deal with something more important than her feelings about him entering her dreams. "I'll know it. We might have to drive around a little."

Gawain smiled at her. Yeah. Pretty impressive. He turned the key, and the engine roared to life. "I have to stop back by the apartment before I go after him."

Gawain had Diana by the hand as they ran through the rain for the door to the Oakwood apartments. His grip was strong and sure. But Diana wasn't. He would try to kill Mordred. *But what if that's not how it turns out?* Mordred was hard. He knew how to fight, and he would fight dirty. She had *been* Mordred for a moment and she knew. She never wanted to repeat that experience again. It was if she had disappeared for a moment and all of Mordred's hatred and twisted anger filled her up and became her. *What if he kills Gawain?* Or what if

Mordred's army was already gathering? Gawain was just one man. . . .

Gawain had his keys out and pushed open the door. "You show me where the loft is. Then I'll take you someplace safe to wait for me. Maybe the lobby of the Marriott. You can have a drink at the bar."

"What are you doing?"

He knelt in front of the sofa. Reaching under it, he pulled out a long package wrapped in what looked like oiled cloth. He set it on the couch cushions and unwrapped it carefully. Diana looked over his shoulder, drawn by a glint of red and green. There were two very gigantic swords. They had cruciform hilts with what looked like cabochon jewels set in them, one with ruby, one with a gigantic emerald, but the grips themselves were wrapped in leather. The blades gleamed, even in the rainy afternoon light.

"My God, Gawain, where did you get those?"

He picked up one of the weapons. One palm gripped the pommel in what was almost a caress. His gaze never left the gleaming blade as he spoke. "The police took the sword I brought with me when they arrested me. Real ones in museums aren't in good enough condition to actually fight with. These are the best replicas money can buy."

Where did he get the money for swords like these when he'd been out of prison only six months? But he gave her no time to ask. He wrapped the swords up again briskly.

"Let's go." He was already turning to the door.

She grabbed her slicker. It was gearing up to rain. "Why two?"

"One for Mordred."

"What? Are you trying to make this into some kind of a fair fight? You were willing to shoot him down in the parking lot of the Exploratorium." She pulled on her yellow slicker.

He looked pained. "Not very honorable. But I didn't want you to know it was me, so I had to do it from a distance." He cradled the swords in their oilcloth reverently. "I'm better hand-to-hand with a sword."

"So you brought one for him, too?"

"You can't hack at a man who doesn't have a weapon."

"What if he has a gun? What if he kills you?" The very thought made her heart clench in a preamble of despair.

"He'll fight me with a sword, because it will be more satisfying to hack me to death than shoot me. He is still a man of his times." Gawain must have seen the horrified look in her eyes. He pulled the hood of her slicker up over her head. His gesture was tender. "But he's not better than I am with a sword. No one is."

He was that matter-of-fact about it. She was reminded of those tales of Lancelot's pride. Maybe they'd gotten the idea for those from the real Gawain. She swallowed. Then maybe he *was* that good. Lancelot was that good in all the legends. Gawain grinned at her. There was a kind of tense stillness about him now, a readiness. "Let's go."

They drove around the business district south of Market Street, looking for the angle that seemed right for what Diana had seen out the window of the loft. The rainy afternoon was turning into dusk.

"It must be on the other side of Market."

There were no left turns for miles off Market. Gawain had to make three rights. He took Second Street.

"In this block or the next couple," she said as they crossed Post.

"Jackpot," Gawain said, pointing to a huge real-estate sign plastered to a building obviously undergoing serious renovation just down Post Street. *Lofts,* the sign said.

Give up your commute. Live and work in this modern new environment. All the amenities. Opening January 2011. Various trucks were parked in front, one that belonged to a plumber, one that had great sheets of glass on a rack that made it look like a transparent Boy Scout tent. Workers trooped in and out of the lobby in the rain as Diana and Gawain passed by in the Range Rover.

"Top floor," she whispered, as though Mordred might hear her.

"Is he there now?" Gawain asked.

She hardly had to close her eyes to know. She blinked them open. "Yeah. He's there." That made an icy finger run down her spine.

"Okay. I'll take you to the Marriott. It's only a few blocks." He turned left at the light.

Suddenly that didn't seem right to Diana. "I want to come with you."

He frowned. "I am not letting you put yourself in danger just to watch me in action."

"I have no desire to watch you in action." That was true. She wouldn't be able to bear to witness a fight where he might be hurt. "But I . . . I might be able to help. And I need to be there."

"Not happening." He pulled the Range Rover under the covered drive in front of the Marriott lobby doors.

"It just doesn't feel right to be separated." Maybe that was something he would understand. He was all about destiny.

"Look, Diana. I can't fight if I'm worried about you. You're more important to me than anything. But I have to kill Mordred. When it's done I'll come for you. You'll be free. You can get on with your life." He didn't look happy about that.

She didn't feel happy about that, either. As a matter of fact, this whole thing felt wrong.

"Now, off with you." He didn't look like he was taking no for an answer anytime soon.

So she opened the door and slid out. As she did, Gawain reached over and pulled her scarf from around her neck.

"My lady's token," he said. His smile was small and a little sad. *Tristesse.* That was what *tristesse* looked like. She'd have to remember that for her next book. Like there was going to be a next book. Everything was slipping away from her.

She nodded. "May you have good fortune, Sir Knight. My thoughts will be with you."

She stood there as cars unloaded visitors, bellmen pushed their big carts full of luggage into the lobby, and the doorman tweeted for a taxi. Gawain pulled the car door shut and drove away.

Not right. The feeling churned in her gut until she felt nauseous.

But what could she do?

She *so* didn't want to go anywhere near Mordred.

There was no way she could actually help Gawain.

It didn't matter. She had to be there. She pulled up her hood and trotted out into the rain toward the loft.

Gawain pulled the Range Rover in behind the plumbing truck. Something was niggling at his mind. This whole thing felt wrong. He knew why. He just couldn't remember. He got out and retrieved his oilskin package from the backseat. To an onlooker, the package might seem to be a batch of rolled blueprints. Gawain didn't have time for doubts now. He had to get to his quarry before Mordred's acolytes started arriving. Workers streamed out to their vehicles. Gawain trotted through the open doors behind some workmen. The elevators were hung with that padded cloth. One opened.

"Where to?" a guy with a potbelly and a construction helmet asked. "We're just winding up here for the day."

"Top floor. I won't be a minute. Just want to check something on these schematics."

The man's hand hovered over the button. "Some guy's living up there in a half-finished unit." The construction worker shook his head. "He don't let anyone in."

"I'll convince him."

The guy shrugged and punched in 8. Gawain was glad the building echoed with noise. "Suit yourself. I'm warning you, though. He's a piece of work. Won't even let us finish up so he can have some creature comforts." The guy got off on 2.

The elevator doors slid shut and Gawain took deep breaths as the car ascended. He unwrapped the oilcloth and took a sword in each hand. The leather on the hilts molded to his hands. The blades gleamed wickedly. They were heavy, and the weight felt good. These weapons he knew. He shook off the feeling of wrongness. This was not a time for dithering. By the time the elevator glided to a stop he was ready. The doors opened on a vast, concrete-floored space. It was almost dark except for the cone of light from a lamp next to a couch sitting on a rug in the center of the room. He couldn't see Mordred anywhere. That made his spine tingle. Lights were blinking on all over the city, visible in a panorama through the massive windows. The arched towers of the Marriott gleamed to one side. At least Diana was safe.

"Mordred!" he called. His voice reverberated off the concrete and glass. The place smelled like a basement because of the concrete and drywall dust from a corner partitioned but unfinished, probably for a bathroom. He held up his swords so they were clearly visible.

"Merlin's brat. I remembered you." Mordred walked

out of the shadows to Gawain's right. He had a very large and ugly gun hanging casually in his left hand. "I'm not sure how you found me, but I'm glad you're here. Saves me the trouble of tracking you down."

The familiar face was even harsher than Gawain remembered it. Mordred was like a lean wolf, his face angular with light and shadow from the single lamp. He raised the gun.

Gawain raised one sword and pretended to examine the blade. "I needn't have brought two then. I knew you were afraid of meeting me blade to blade. Still, I had hopes."

"Afraid? Of a child? Hardly."

"I'm not a child anymore. And I'm a better swordsman than you ever were." Actually, he had never seen Mordred fight. He always got others to do it for him.

"But you have no magic. Your father was disappointed in you even then."

"No," Gawain agreed. He wasn't going to tell Mordred about his small gifts. He turned the sword so the light took it. "Fine workmanship." With a slow grin he tossed one sword to Mordred, who caught it easily in his right hand. Gawain saw him heft the weight of it, and saw the satisfaction in his eyes. He had him.

"You are in need of a lesson in swordsmanship. And I am just the man to give it to you." Mordred tossed the gun onto the couch. "Too bad you won't profit by the lesson for very long. Have you ever fought an Adapter?" He sank into his knees a little, balanced on the balls of his feet in his brown suede boots, the leather of his vest hanging open over his blue work shirt. He shifted the sword to his left hand. Gawain was right-handed. Fighting with his left gave Mordred a bit of an advantage. Not enough to signify. What did he mean about fighting an Adapter?

Gawain smiled. This would be a bloody battle before

the end. No shields. Just the swords as both offense and defense. Mordred didn't know him except as a child. He wouldn't be afraid of Gawain's reputed strength, or his prowess.

Mordred lunged. The first clang of metal on metal rang out in the big space. The blades slid along each other in an arc and Mordred stepped in, bringing his blade up and under Gawain's, hoping to get in under his guard. Gawain flipped his hand upside down and swept the blade away with his own. Mordred was bold. But he was also careless.

The clang of blows cascaded over glass and metal and concrete, faster and faster. Gawain used every technique he had. But Mordred fed them back to him just as quickly. Mordred was using Gawain's own style against him. *Adapter.* Gawain had a sinking feeling in his stomach.

"You're better than I thought," Mordred said, trying not to gasp for breath.

"I could say the same." Gawain grimaced as a blow very nearly sliced his sword arm. He parried at the last moment and Mordred pressed forward with renewed intensity. Gawain now tried to pace himself, realizing it had been long since he had wielded the heavy weapon through an entire battle. Sweat rolled into his eyes and he wiped at it with his free hand.

But wait, Mordred had his own weakness. Best to remind him of it. "How is your wound?" Gawain asked through gritted teeth.

Mordred sliced at his sword and spun to the side.

"That scratch? It isn't even on my sword arm." But Mordred was panting now. Back and forth across the floor, first one advantage and then another, the two adversaries danced.

Behind him, Gawain heard the elevator doors open.

He swung to the side to see who it could be. One of Mordred's new allies?

It was Diana. He recognized the big black purse with the book in it slung over her shoulder. "No!" he yelled. "Get out of here." He jerked his attention back to Mordred to parry another blow.

She shook her head. She was looking frightened, almost dazed. "I have to be here."

Mordred bared his teeth in something that might have been a grin. "First you, brat, and then the girl. How convenient."

"Diana, get out. Do you understand?"

Blows rained now, back and forth. Mordred was trying to press the advantage of Diana distracting Gawain. Gawain maneuvered Mordred around so Gawain could glance over Mordred's shoulder to check on her.

So he saw the doorway to the stairs open quietly behind her. He registered her gasp as she turned and swung the big purse with that heavy book in it at the man just coming through the doorway. She caught him full in the face. A gun clattered to the floor, and he reeled backward, lost his balance, and stumbled back into the stairwell.

Damn it! Gawain threw caution to the wind, swept Mordred's sword to the left as he lunged inside and brought the hilt of his own sword up to catch Mordred a blow to the temple. The man dropped like a stone. Gawain stood over Mordred and kicked his sword away.

"Are you all right?" Gawain called to Diana, glancing over his shoulder. She was stumbling over to pick up the gun. Good. Now if only she wasn't afraid to shoot it. He tore his gaze away from her and back to Mordred, who seemed dazed by the blow. "Don't look, Diana." He raised his sword, point down. It hovered over Mordred's throat.

"Gawain?" The voice was so . . . distant, so tentative, he had to turn his head and look.

At first he wasn't sure what he was seeing. It was as if there were a mist in front of her. No. She *was* the mist. She . . . she was transparent, and fading. . . .

"Gawain?" The voice was fainter.

In a flash it all came to him. This was what had been niggling at his brain. He threw the sword away as though it burned his flesh with acid. It clattered to the cement floor and he kicked it away to join its fellow.

Diana wavered into solidity and sank to the floor.

He dashed over to Diana and helped her to the couch. She felt corporeal enough.

He slid her scarf from his neck and, twisting it, went to kneel beside Mordred. He turned him over roughly as the man groaned, and tied his hands securely behind his back. Mordred's temple was bleeding, and his head lolled. Gawain gathered up the swords and laid them by the couch, well out of Mordred's reach, and went to check on their other intruder. The man was heaped on the landing one floor down, limbs at odd angles. His head was balding, with tattoos snaking up his neck. Looked like a pretty hard character. Gawain didn't check to see whether he was alive. He was just relieved that the brute wouldn't be chasing after them anytime soon.

"What happened?" Diana asked, her eyes big, as Gawain came back to the couch. "I felt . . . I felt like everything was fading away."

"I think *you* were fading away." He knelt in front of her and reached to take her head between his hands. His hands were shaking. For the first time he realized how close he'd come to losing her. He'd almost killed her, in a way.

"Why?" she asked, searching his face.

Now. Now he had to tell her in the worst possible way the very thing he'd wanted to keep from her. He couldn't avoid the hurt he'd cause. Not now. She had to know.

"Mordred is your father."

Chapter Fifteen

Diana blinked at Gawain as though he were speaking Swahili or Russian or something. Had he said . . . that Mordred was her *father*?

"When exactly did you bring him here in the time machine?" Gawain asked. "You said that soldiers were about to kill him." Gawain nodded at her, prompting her to think. "What happened/?"

"Uh. We . . . you and your father and I were up on a hill among some standing stones People were fleeing from the town down below." It all came back to her: the smell of smoke, the machine glinting over her head, the man with kaleidoscope eyes. "And Mordred came up to ask your father to support his claim to the kingdom because only he could hold things together and keep the Saxons from overrunning it. We heard soldiers coming up the hill. Your father said Mordred was done for. The soldiers streamed into the clearing, They were going to kill him. So I . . . took him back with me."

Gawain let his head fall back. He sucked in a breath. "Why didn't I realize it before? I thought you met him later." He turned his piercing gaze on her. "Mordred didn't die in the standing stones in the version of history I know. Those were *his* men coming up the hill. They were after my father. My father said Mordred was done for because he knew Mondred would die of the infection in that wound Arthur gave him, though it would take some weeks. And in the meantime, he sired you off a woman in the town." Gawain ran a shaky hand through his hair. "If I had killed him . . ."

"I would never have existed." Her voice wasn't as strong as she would have liked. "But then why didn't I fade when I first brought him here?"

Gawain frowned. "Maybe the possibility still existed that he would get that woman with child as long as he was alive. Only if he was dead would you definitely never exist."

Her gaze gravitated to the man who lay, quiescent, on the floor. She felt her face crumple. "I'm *his* daughter?" Gawain brought her in against his chest and made soft shushing sounds. His arms were strong. He smelled of Gawain, only wet with rain. This felt right. "I don't want to be his daughter," she sniffed.

"You get your 'quirks' from him. He has strong magic in his blood to be an Adapter. He passed that magic to you. That is a gift."

"Maybe I'll go mad and start telling thugs to murder innocent people and put their heads up on pikes." The thought that she, who had wanted all her life to know her parents, now had found that Mordred was her father seemed a cruel joke.

Gawain held her away from him and looked at her seriously. She thought, even in the dim light, that his eyes were blue. "You got who you are from my father who loved you and your parents here who loved you. You aren't like him."

"Why didn't you tell me?" she accused. "How could you keep this from me?" Anger alternated with hurt in closing her throat around her words. Did he not trust her with the knowledge? Did she think she would betray him to her father?

Gawain swallowed. She could practically see him thinking about what he'd done and why and how he could say it. "At first I thought you'd gone back to save him because he was your father. When I discovered you didn't know . . . well, you'd either feel bad that I'd killed your biological father or horrible that he was your father. I . . . I didn't want to hurt you."

"That's not protection. That's lying. Sins of omission."

Hurt flashed through his eyes, and shame. In that moment he wasn't a knight-errant but an incredibly vulnerable man. He swallowed and looked away, toward Mordred. "If we can't kill him, what will we do with him?" His voice was rough.

"We can send him back to fulfill his destiny," she said, a little firmness coming back into her voice. That was the only answer. She should never have fooled with time.

Gawain nodded. "That way he sires you and dies of his wounds as history intended. It's not as sure as killing him, but it will have to do." He made an apologetic face. "It will mean sacrificing the machine."

"Maybe. But if it isn't used to go someplace else, it will bounce back here. Mordred doesn't know the sequence to use it, and we'll keep it that way." She looked up at Gawain. "But if it's lost, it's lost. We can't let him raise an army here. He probably has already changed the future by ordering all these killings. He might tear our entire society apart."

"Very well." Gawain's tone was firm and strong again, just like he was. "Then let's get him out of here before more of his followers show up."

Gawain got up and pulled her to her feet. After checking to see that it was loaded, he handed her the gun that Mordred had tossed on the couch. Then Gawain glanced over to the stairwell. "It'll look like that guy just fell down the stairs," he murmured. Mordred began to stir and groan again. Diana tightened her grip on the handle of the gun. Could she shoot her own father? Gawain strode over to retrieve the gun she'd knocked from the intruder's hand. As he came back toward Mordred his steps slowed.

"How did you know that guy was coming through the door? You hit him with your bag almost before he appeared. Did you hear his footsteps on the stairs? I didn't."

"No. What I heard was that he was about to yell at you to distract you. I got a few seconds' notice." It was her turn to act apologetic.

"Pretty neat trick. And you say your quirks are useless." He gave a rueful smile and rolled Mordred over with the toe of his boot. Mordred's eyes blinked open, but he looked pretty groggy. "Up, Mordred. Time to meet your destiny."

Diana got out as Gawain opened the back of the Range Rover in the Exploratorium parking lot. They had waited behind the trees at the entrance to the lot until they saw Clancy begin his rounds. Gawain untied Mordred. They'd anchored him with some rope to an iron ring in the back section of the SUV meant to secure cargo. Mordred stumbled out, still a little loopy from the blow Gawain had given him on the temple. Probably had a dandy concussion. Gawain eased the hatch shut so as not to alert Clancy and threw the rope over his shoulder.

"You have a flashlight in here?" Diana asked.

Gawain nodded, fumbled in a side pocket in the back, of the Range Rover and came up with a yellow flashlight, which he stuck in his jacket pocket. "Come on," he said as he hustled Mordred across the parking lot, the older man stumbling beside him.

"I don't have a key anymore. I'm persona non grata

here, remember?" she hissed as she hurried behind them.

"Don't worry. I can get us in."

Oh yeah. His "power." She swallowed. This was all pretty tough to get used to.

"What I need from you is to keep that gun on him while I get through." He didn't even look back to see her nod. He apparently just trusted that she was bold enough to hold a gun on her own father and bluff Mordred into thinking she would pull the trigger. Which she couldn't. Not if she didn't want to just blink out of existence. Okay. Maybe she could wound him. Could she actually shoot a man of flesh and blood, who was her father, even if he was Mordred? She didn't think she was the woman Gawain thought she was.

"We've only got twenty minutes or so until Clancy gets back," she reminded Gawain.

"You, stay there," Gawain said to Mordred, leaning him against the wall by the side of the big glass doors. Mordred hung his head, but his bloodshot eyes never left Diana as she pulled up the gun with both hands and tried not to let it shake.

"Just be quick about it."

Gawain put both hands on the glass doors and leaned against them. Diana could feel him go calm. Sureness and a certain . . . serenity poured off of him. Then he began to disintegrate. It looked like he was fading away just like she almost did. Fear fluttered in her belly. What if he was somehow doing something that made him nonexistent? What if he left her alone here, with Mordred? In only a moment Gawain was just a body of mist shaped vaguely like a man. And then the mist was sucked down under the door.

"He's his father's son, all right." Mordred's voice was low and venomous. "I always thought he didn't get his father's powers. Maybe he didn't get much. But he got some."

It was almost reassuring that Mordred didn't think Gawain was dead or disappeared.

And sure enough, the mist formed into human shape inside the Exploratorium, and then the mist coalesced into Gawain. He hit the metal bars and the door opened. "Stand back, Diana. Mordred, you first."

Both Gawain and Diana held guns on Mordred. Diana was glad the responsibility of shooting him wasn't hers alone anymore. "Lead on, Diana. Where's the machine?"

"Behind another locked door," she whispered, hurrying ahead through the dim lobby. Work lights were on back in the maze of exhibits, but otherwise the place was dark.

"Move it," Gawain ordered, and Diana glanced back to see that they were following, Mordred dragging his heels.

"What are you going to do with me?" Mordred asked as if it were a casual question like, *Do you think it will rain?*

"Send you back where you belong," Gawain said. "You are about to fulfill your destiny."

"I rather like it here."

"I'm sure you do. But the fifth century is calling."

Diana stopped in front of the door marked: *Danger. Keep out.* "It's in here."

Gawain took a breath. "Okay. Let's get to it. You." He gestured with his gun at Mordred. "Sit on that bench." Diana raised the gun.

Then Gawain put his palms against the door and the process started all over again. Diana found herself fascinated. He was a miracle in so many ways. The mist fell to the floor and seeped under the door. Out of the corner of her eye she saw movement. Mordred was up and coming for her. Her throat closed. Even though his hands were still tied, he looked murderous.

"Stay where you are," she choked. He kept coming and she backed up. One step. Two.

"Or you'll what? Shoot me? Takes a hard woman to do

that to a man." Mordred lowered his head and butted her. She sprawled on the floor. Mordred turned to run for the front. The door shot open and Gawain came through with a growl. He grabbed Mordred's arm and twisted him back. Gawain hit him in the chin so hard that he went flying across the room and landed with a thud.

Gawain went to her. "Are you okay?"

She nodded. "He . . . his hands were tied. There was nothing he could do. I couldn't just . . . shoot him." Gawain was peering at Mordred. Even Diana could see he was out like a light.

"We'd better get a move on. He won't cause us any problems now." Gawain heaved Mordred over his shoulder and stalked to the now-open door. He held Mordred's limp form with one hand as he fumbled for the flashlight.

They heard a noise from the lobby.

"Clancy," she hissed.

Gawain ducked into the corridor beyond the door and she hurried after him, easing the door shut. They stood still in the dark and listened. The whistled notes of "When Irish Eyes Are Smiling" receded. Diana heard Gawain let out his breath just as she was sighing in relief herself. The flashlight popped on and they hurried down the corridor with its nearsighted cone of light dancing over the dark passageway.

Gawain reached the chamber under the Rotunda of the Palace of Fine Arts first. His beam shot over the jumbled struts that had been used to earthquake proof the Palace and caught the gleam of Leonardo's machine. The brass gears, big and small, were revealed as the flashlight explored them. The glint of the huge jewels shot red and blue and green and clear diamond white from their facets. Gawain let out a low whistle.

"This . . . this is what you used to come back in time?"

"Yeah. Even I can't believe it."

"How does it work?"

"Beats me. The book tells how he made it. I can't say I understand it, even though I've read the translation a hundred times. He says time is a vortex and with enough power you can jump from one place to another in the whirl."

"How do you get where you want to go?" He hauled Mordred through the maze of girders, the beam of light bouncing here and there.

"You just think of it."

"Hmmm," they both said at the same time.

Gawain shot a look over his shoulder. "He can't think anything, and wouldn't even if he was conscious," Gawain muttered.

"So we'll have to do the thinking for him," Diana said. "I'll start the machine." She went to kneel beside the lunch box–sized power module. "Can you shine the light over here?"

Gawain dumped Mordred in a heap and gave her a beam of light over her shoulder. She started the power sequence, flipping switches. "Okay. I'll wait to hit the last switch until you've got him tied to that lever." She watched as Gawain hauled Mordred up and bound his hands to the three-foot-long control stick topped by the huge glittering diamond.

She pressed the final chrome button with her palm. "Let him go. His weight will pull the lever." Then she scrambled up and pulled Gawain away.

Mordred hung by his hands and the lever slowly dipped. Power hummed in the room, stronger and stronger until it felt like a weight on her chest. The gears began to whirl. She threaded her way back through the steel struts like pick-up sticks to the far wall, pulling Gawain with her as beams of colored light began to crisscross over the ceiling.

"Think of that time!" she yelled to Gawain as they pressed their backs against the cool concrete of the wall. "That day that Camelot fell. Think only of that, no matter what happens."

He nodded and they turned their attention to the machine. The gears slowed. Time itself seemed to slow. As hard as she could think she thought of the day she'd seen Camelot fall. Then everything seemed to move all at once. The gears once again whirled madly. Space seemed to be flowing into the machine from everywhere, as though the universe were collapsing in on itself. Even their bodies seemed to have an aura that was being sucked into the machine. What if they were sucked back with Mordred? The pressure was unbearable. Her mind was about to explode.

And then the tension snapped.

She and Gawain fell to their knees, gasping. Diana looked up. The machine was gone.

"Gods of water and leaf," Gawain murmured. "I've never . . . seen . . . anything like that."

And then, quick as it had disappeared, the machine wavered back into sight. But Mordred was nowhere in sight.

"We did it," she breathed.

Gawain reached for her and gathered her into his arms. "And we never have to go back to that time or see Mordred again."

She smiled up at Gawain, relief washing through her. But she could feel her smile go crooked. He had been protecting her against Mordred. Now that Mordred was gone, what reason had Gawain to stay? He might be the next to disappear from her life.

It was over an hour until Clancy made his next rounds and left the building. They heard him whistling. Kind of strange for an Irishman to be whistling "La Cucaracha." They had waited in dark and silence, lest he hear them just behind the door marked: *Danger*. That was a lot of time to think. Gawain was feeling . . . lost. The battle was over. The adrenaline washed from his system, leaving him almost listless. He had done his father's bidding. He had protected Diana from Mordred. He had fulfilled his life's purpose. She would go on to be important to the world somehow. He didn't know quite how. Did it have to do with her ability to find lost things? But what of him? He was thirty-six and suddenly his driving force was gone. Did that mean his useful life was over? There couldn't be much use for a person who could turn into mist and seep through doorways, unless he wanted a career in crime. And Gawain didn't.

A quick run to the car after they heard Clancy pass and they were driving home through the dark of San Francisco. Gawain glanced to Diana. Her face was alternately cast in stark light and shadow from the street lamps they passed. She was abnormally quiet. Her face was pale, her gray-green eyes big. Here he was thinking of himself when she must be feeling . . . what? That she would never have a chance to know her father, rotten as that father was? That she was less because she came from genes that were tainted by something akin to madness?

"You okay?" he asked.

She cracked a broken smile that made his heart clench. "I guess. We did what we had to do. Mordred is now back fulfilling his destiny. And we saved the world from a monster. So . . . why doesn't that feel great?"

"We're just coming down off an adrenaline rush," he said. But he didn't believe that was all it was. Something felt . . . wrong. "We'll be okay when we get some dinner and some sleep."

She looked up into his face, as though she was trying to puzzle something out.

Then her head snapped around. "Hey—wasn't that the corner with the Indian restaurant?"

"I don't know," he said, peering into the rearview mirror. "Was something wrong?"

"I didn't see it there. Oh, never mind," she sighed, turning back and slumping into her seat. "I'm just tired, like you say."

"I'll pick up some dinner from the *taqueria*," he said. "That okay?"

"Sounds great."

Gawain turned in to the little stand with the world-class handmade tortillas and the *carnitas* to die for. "You stay in the car. I'll order."

"I'd like . . ."

"The usual?" She always ordered a *carnitas tostada*. Girls and their salads. They even had to get salads at a *taqueria*. The difference was that this one came with that roasted pork, crisp with basted orange sauce.

"I forgot. You know way too much about me." She gave a tiny smile.

He stood in the cold with a dozen others, mostly Hispanic, some apparently speaking Russian or something, and ordered in Spanish. He was glad for the heat of the bag when they finally handed it out the little sliding window. This place always had a line, but the food was worth waiting for. He handed them a twenty and the guy looked at him like he was crazy.

"Tarjeta decrédito?" *Since when would they rather have a credit card than cash? Whatever.*

He slid into the car and handed Diana the bag. "I got

you a Diet Coke, but we've got some red wine at home if you'd rather." Actually, the Oakwood apartment wasn't home. He had no home, if it came to that. In this time, he'd lived at a mental hospital, two jails, a dirtbag apartment in Chicago, and Oakwood. But if Diana was there, home or not, he was fine.

He glanced across to Diana as the Range Rover sprang to life. It occurred to him that *she* was home, in some ways. She was his destination, his purpose, his past . . . and last night, as he cradled her after their lovemaking, she had felt like the future he longed for. He was in love with her. But could she ever care for him in return? A man from the fifth century, an ex-con, a man who no longer had a purpose? Had he any right to ask it of her?

He turned into the driveway to Oakwood's parking garage. The gate slid jerkily to the right in response to his key card. If only he had the key to his future. What was a knight without a quest? His quest had been finished. He had protected Diana.

Now what?

Diana had the strangest feeling as they rode the elevator up with several Hispanic men and two others she thought were speaking Russian. Oakwood apartments always had a transient population, but Russians were out of the ordinary. The neighbors she'd encountered on her way in and out with Gawain recently had been predominantly Asians. San Francisco, as a center of technology companies and a hub of trade for the Pacific Rim, was always full of Japanese and Chinese and Indian businesspeople. This seemed . . . wrong.

She'd had the same feeling all the way home in the car. She couldn't put her finger on it. Unless it had to do with how distant Gawain seemed.

She had the worst feeling that he was going to tell her he was moving on to some other mission, some other destiny, now that Mordred was vanquished. She could feel that stone-cold loneliness and the dreadful disappointment coming a mile away.

She should be glad she and Gawain had had one night together. He had been such a generous lover, who could ask for more? Not someone like her. Not from someone like Gawain.

She kicked off her clogs as he set out the food from the *taqueria* in its crimped foil tins with clear plastic tops. Besides her tostada he had a wet burrito that looked like it could feed a family of four. He'd gotten a side of guacamole, and the dinners always came with great salsa and loads of big, crisp corn tortillas that were deep-fried. You broke them into your own corn chips. She hated to waste the Diet Coke he'd gotten her, but if she had caffeine this late she'd be up all night, so she opted for wine, and got out some utensils.

They hadn't spoken a word since they got out of the car. It was starting to feel creepy.

"So," she asked, "how do you afford an apartment like Oakwood when you've only been out of prison six months or so? Did you have a purse with coins like Mordred?"

"Jewels, actually. My father sent me with jewels."

"How did you keep them through the whole prison-thing? I would have thought they would have confiscated them. They'd have thought they were stolen or something." She dug into her tostada. All of a sudden she had never been so hungry in her life.

"I hid them under a paving stone I dug up in an alley," he said as he opened the guacamole and put the Styrofoam bowl between them. "That's where I got waylaid by the gang. I went back after I got out. They were still there."

"So, I guess no money problems."

"On the contrary, as an ex-con I couldn't sell diamonds even to a fence right after I got out. I couldn't run the risk of getting caught. So I was broke. I had the hundred bucks they give a prisoner on the way out, but that was it."

"What did you do?" She couldn't imagine having only a hundred dollars, almost no way to get a job, and in an unfamiliar century at that.

He looked sheepish. "Uh . . . we watched a lot of those reality fighting shows in prison. When I got out, I auditioned to fight. I got a hundred and fifty thousand for winning the whole series of fights."

She blinked. She'd seen promos on television for those shows. Those fights were brutal! She hated to think of him selling his body like that and taking those beatings.

"Don't worry," he said hastily. He must have seen the look on her face. "It wasn't bad. I was good at it." Then he looked stricken. "Not exactly a genteel way to earn my bread. But I won't have to do it again. I . . . I figured out how to sell the jewels. And . . . and then I'll find something to do with my life that's a little more . . . normal." The smile that was meant to be reassuring certainly didn't reflect his own assurance.

He was apologetic? The smile that rose to her own lips was more than genuine. Heartfelt if it came to that. "I can't believe how intrepid you are, how smart, and how . . . how brave." There was just no other way to say it. "How will you sell the jewels, by the way? I'd never know how to do something like that."

"I thought I'd have a few set in a necklace every once in a while. Say they were handed down in the family. These days really fine jewels have a number lasered into them so you can tell where they came from. But these won't have that. The cuts are very primitive, too, so that story will ring true. I'll let them be lasered and registered, and . . . voilà, provenance."

"Really clever." She broke off a chip and dipped it into first the salsa and then the guacamole. No one ever made guacamole hot enough, but the combo was perfect.

The silence hung between them. Neither wanted to broach the subject of what was next. On her end, she was pretty sure she knew. She'd find a job. And she'd go on writing. Maybe now her men would be a little more genuine. That would be her gift from Gawain when he was gone. She wanted to ask what Gawain would do with his life . . . what "something more normal" might be. But that would be asking him to tell her that he was going to leave her. Still, she had to say something. "I hope we can still be friends. Do you intend to stay in San Francisco?"

As she had feared, his face closed down. "I like it here," he said noncommittally. How stupid could she be? He was probably afraid she'd become the annoying little girl she once was, tagging along and interfering with his life. She felt the panic rise as she thought that if she seemed too persistent this might be the last night she would ever see him.

The prospect was chilling. She wanted him. Like eating with a coming appetite, the wanting poured over her. Her body responded to his nearness at her elbow with a kind of electrification, though she had been bone tired a moment ago. The very . . . bigness of his body called to hers. He seemed made of a different element, heavier inch for inch than she was, harder, and that appealed to her in some way she'd never felt. Was *this* feeling what she'd written about? How inadequate her words seemed now. Anyone's words actually. This was some kind of alchemy between men and women. Or maybe just between her and Gawain.

The only thing she knew was that she wanted him, this maybe-last night.

He was finishing his burrito, wrapping up the foil around the gooey remains. But she knew he was aware of her. Pheromones. That's what her attraction was. One-sided attraction. His was just male preoccupation with sex wherever they could find it. This wasn't magic.

But that's sure how it seemed.

Gawain looked up at her and knew his eyes were changing color to that dark violet-blue of passion. She was the only person besides his father whom he'd ever let look directly into his eyes. She wanted to be friends when he wanted to worship her and serve her with his strength and his love for the rest of his life. Not fair. He wasn't sure he could be just friends with Diana as he had been with Dilly. Not when he wanted her with every fiber of his disobedient body. His loins were aching, his balls tight, and his cock straining against the zipper of his jeans. He didn't deserve her. He was weak of mind, weaker of flesh, because all he could think about was the soft swell of her breast under his hand and the moist invitation of her mouth. And that felt so right it must be wrong.

"Can a friend—" He cleared his throat and swallowed. He was vile. He knew it. But he seemed to have lost all his vaunted control around Diana. Would she hate him for this? He hated himself. But he couldn't stop. His only hope would be for her to think it was just recreational sex, that it didn't matter to him. Friends had sex sometimes, didn't they? "Can a friend still provide some research occasionally?"

Her eyes went wide as her breath caught. She opened her mouth, but nothing came out. Would she just slap him? Would she shut down and run to her room? Her eyes went from cool gray-green to hot without ever changing color. She wasn't going to slap him. And hateful or not, he was glad, so glad, on an elemental level, that he leaned over the wreckage of their dinner and brushed his lips softly against hers.

He meant to be slow. Like he was the night before. He meant to make it light and friendly sex, nonthreatening—a sex that made no assumptions about how she felt about him. That's what men did. It was women who always wanted commitment. Women were the ones who were supposed to think sex was a sacred bond. Diana wanted only friendship and recreational sex. So he meant to give her some half-measure of intensity she would find acceptable.

But her lips burned his when he brushed his own across them, and when she reached up with both hands and grabbed the collar of his corduroy shirt and drew him in to her he . . . he just lost control. His arms went round her of their own volition and drew her up to standing, and when she opened her lips beneath his, letting his tongue probe the moist promise of her mouth, even as she caressed his tongue with her own, he felt like a huge wave was breaking over him, rolling him over and over in its watery embrace.

He held her to his body like he could never let her go, crushing her breasts to his chest, uncaring that she would feel the hard ridge of his erection against her belly. Let her feel it. Let her know just how much he wanted her, because however much she imagined, he wanted her a hundredfold more.

"Diana," he murmured into her mouth. "Diana. Dilly. Diana." He pressed her back into the semidarkness of the living room. Her tiny hands were combing through his hair, and her kissing had grown frantic. She rubbed against him until he groaned. She shouldn't rub against him like that. Or maybe she shouldn't stop.

Then she pulled away. It was like she pulled part of his

soul with her. She was panting, and her eyes were so intense they burned. She pulled her sweater over her head
in one move. It was his turn to suck in a breath. The white
globes of her breasts swelled in the cups of her lacy bra.
She leaned forward and reached around for the hooks.

"You're getting behind," she rasped.

He came to himself and went to work on the buttons
on his shirt. His fingers were clumsy. In frustration, he
just pulled. Popping buttons leaped in all directions. He
shrugged out of his shirt and pulled it inside out to get it
off his arms. He flung it against the wall and went to work
on his belt.

She had already shed her jeans and underwear in one
move. She stripped off her stockings and she was nude.
He tried to get his breath. Here, in the light from the
kitchen behind them, he could see her as he hadn't seen
her last night. That she had a beautiful body he already
knew, rounded and yet tiny, delicate, something to be
cherished and protected. But now her nipples peaked in
desire for him, her eyes dark with passion. He thought . . .
he didn't know what he thought. He wasn't thinking. His
body reacted as though it had been jolted with electricity.

"Let me," she said, because he wasn't making all that
much progress with his belt. And when she reached for
the buckle she purposely brushed her breasts against his
abdomen. Lord, he was going to come right here and now.
Somehow, he kicked off his boots. And then she was sliding his jeans down over his hips. She made a little "oh" of
pleasure as she realized he wasn't wearing any underwear. He stepped out and gathered her into his arms with
a growl. She turned her head up, hungry for his mouth,
and he obliged, kissing her, probing her. He thought he
was merciless, when he could manage thought, but she
was as merciless as he, sucking his tongue, nipping at his
lips. His erection poked against her belly and . . . and he

just couldn't wait. He lifted her by her bottom. Her legs swung up around his hips. He fell to his knees on the thick beige carpet and he lowered her onto his shaft, all the while they devoured each other's mouths. He lifted her and lowered, and thrust his hips up into her in a fierce staccato. She rocked against him, wriggling to get maximum friction. He grunted, whether in exertion or in some primal demonstration of his lust he didn't know. She was making small mewling noises. But he wasn't sure she could come like this, so he laid her down on the carpet and eased out of her.

"No, no," she protested, groping for his cock. He let her find him, as he pressed two fingers against her clitoris and felt it throbbing and erect. She moaned and leaned into him. He rubbed back and forth. But after only a couple of times, she stilled his hands.

"I want you in me when I come."

He covered her with his body and thrust inside her, jerking his hips into her until she was giving little, gasping "ohs" with every thrust. She cried out first and somehow he held on, knowing that she needed the continuing friction to extend her orgasm. The feeling of her womb contracting around him put him over the top. It felt like she was milking him of his seed as he stilled and spurted inside her. His cry escalated just as hers was fading. It was a spontaneous song that told of lust and love and a million years of men and women together.

"Diana," he whispered. "Diana." He nuzzled her throat, kissing. Then he slid one arm under her shoulders and one arm over her hips to cup her bottom and picked her up. She laid her head on his shoulder. They said nothing. He was afraid anything he said would frighten her away from this moment of caring, this expression of his one-sided sacred bond. He couldn't bear to be light and devil-may-care about it, even if he was only pretending. And if he admitted anything like what he felt, she'd be gone by morning, he was sure. He carried her into the king-size bed and shifted her to one arm while he pulled back the spread. He couldn't bear to let her go even for an instant. When he laid her in the bed, he lay down beside her and drew her once more into his arms. This . . . this felt right.

Diana woke in Gawain's arms. They hadn't bothered to close the draperies last night, so pale early light streamed into the room. Gawain was still asleep, his dark lashes brushing his cheeks. He looked like a boy, with his dark comma of hair and his fair, fine skin. She wanted to reach out and touch it, but she didn't want to wake him. Her eyes moved down to his shoulder. Livid bruises stood out against the pale skin as well as the strange Celtic knot tattoo. Had he been so injured in the fight? She felt a pang of guilt. She'd practically raped him last night, she'd wanted him so badly. Of course he was nothing loath. He was a guy after all. The man had bewitched her. Who said he didn't have his father's magic?

As if he felt her eyes on him, he stirred, and she felt something else stirring as well. It rubbed against her hip. *Dear me! After last night?* Not surprisingly, she felt an answering tingle and its accompanying wetness between her legs. She would make love to him night and morning forever if she could. But she hadn't expected him to want more from her. Maybe it was just a natural morning erection and she should ignore it, because it didn't really mean anything.

"Mmmmmm," he said without opening his eyes, and reached for her. That gave her license to stroke his cheek. And the other tattoo just under his collarbone. He was so warm and sleepy. His lips were soft as he kissed her forehead. He was awake. She knew it. But he didn't open his eyes. He bent to kiss her. So she closed her eyes as well. She was made only of feeling and touch, and smell.

And it was good. They made sleepy morning love, having never said a single coherent word since dinner last night. Well, he'd said her name a couple of times. Did that count?

Afterward, they dozed off again. She should have felt too guilty for that. It was time to get on with the rest of her life after all. She had to call her editor and tell her that the book wasn't going to be in on time, or anywhere near it. She should apply for unemployment insurance and start looking for another job.

But the world could wait. It wouldn't have to wait long. Gawain was bound to go today.

When she woke again, he was already in the shower. He came out fully dressed, his dreadful bruises on shoulder and side covered, his hair wet and slicked back against his head. When he saw her looking at him through the open bedroom door his expression was . . . tentative. When had Gawain, parfait knight, looked tentative?

"I hope I wasn't too . . . uh . . . rough last night."

She shook her head, embarrassed. It had been she who egged him on.

"I . . . I thought maybe we could go out to breakfast this morning. I know a little place that does great dim sum down in Chinatown." He swallowed. "You like dim sum?"

"Love it." Her mouth watered at the thought of the little Chinese tidbits that were brought round on steaming carts through giant dining rooms filled with chattering Chinese. "I'm yours."

That made his face contract somehow before he straightened out his features. *Oh, god. That sounded clingy!* But she couldn't say, *I didn't mean it like that,* without acknowledging the embarrassment, or . . . her thoughts got tangled and she realized she was clutching the covers to her breast just like this guy hadn't seen everything she owned in some detail.

She was nothing short of grateful when he gently closed the door.

They stood at the corner of Grant and Pine, having parked the car in the multilayered parking structure a few blocks down under St. Mary's Square Park. All the way here, Diana had had a terrible feeling of wrongness she couldn't put her finger on. It only grew when they got out of the Mission District. Too many signs in Spanish. Everything looked seedier than she remembered. And now this. She looked up at Gawain, who was staring around in shock, too.

Chinatown was . . . missing.

No crowded streets of milling Chinese and tourists. No storefronts filled with antiques and ivory disappearing into dim interiors. No tacky T-shirt and souvenir shops with little hanging pagodas twirling in the breeze. No markets with boxes of long bean and lotus root on the sidewalk and ducks hanging by their necks in the windows. And no gilded dragons arching over Grant Street as it narrowed to one-way. The Dragon Gate was gone.

They glanced to the street signs simultaneously, as useless as that was. Grant and Pine. Grant thrust up the steep hill to where St. Mary's Church stood. As they watched, a cable car rumbled by on California at the top of the hill. That hadn't changed.

But everything else had.

The simple shops and markets had not a trace of Asia about them. She and Gawain could almost have been standing in the Mission District. Carnecerias. Stores selling brightly colored linens and striped serapes. Signs in Spanish. But . . . what was that? Cyrillic? They hurried up the hill toward California Street. In the restaurant at the corner people were eating what had to be borscht, it was so purple-red. She blinked as she saw onion domes on several of the buildings up on the far corner. St. Mary's comforting brick was still there. But . . . was that an equal-armed cross? St. Mary's was now Eastern Orthodox. The scene was far seedier than the Mission District. People's clothes were ragged. Beggars were everywhere. Some had ulcerated sores on their bodies.

Gawain stopped a man with blond hair wearing a denim jacket that had seen better days. "Excuse me, sir, what . . . what happened to Chinatown?"

"Aprende hablar la lengua, amigo," the guy said, and brushed past. Spanish from a guy who looked like that? And he acted as if everyone should be speaking Spanish

Gawain turned to her, his brows drawn together, blinking rapidly. He turned into the stream of hurrying workers and picked a middle-aged lady, slightly pear shaped, but not Hispanic at all. "Pardoneme, senora. ¿Dónde está Chinatown?"

"Chinatown? Esa es loco. Nosotros hacemos la guerra con esos bastardos." She hurried away, looking back fearfully over her shoulder, as though Diana and Gawain were traitors. They were getting stares from several other people as they hurried by.

"Come on," Gawain said in a low voice as he took her arm and hurried her back to the car. When they were safely inside with the doors locked, he turned and looked at her. She could see in his eyes that he was thinking the same panicked thoughts that were careening around in her head. She didn't want to voice them. But someone had to do it.

"Everything's changed, isn't it?"

"Well. People are speaking Spanish here as the primary language," he said carefully, as if trying not to shout. "And there seems to be a strong Russian component. But no Chinatown. And we might be at war with China."

"Maybe all of Asia. The Indian restaurant near the

apartment was missing last night," she said in a hushed voice.

He took a huge breath. "Could . . . could sending Mordred back change things that much?"

"We sent him back to his death," she protested. "Just like before when he died from that wound he got from Arthur . . ." She trailed off. Their eyes met.

"Except we sent him back all stitched up nicely and loaded with antibiotics."

Diana had a hard time getting her breath. "Library. We need a library."

Chapter Sixteen

Gawain's gut was churning. He'd botched the mission again. He'd only saved Diana's life by a hair, since he was too stupid to figure out that Mordred had been snatched away before he could sire her. But in the process he had changed the flow of history so dramatically. . . .

"Market and Larkin," she said. "At the Civic Center. The City Library is the biggest."

He was about to give the attendant a five when he remembered the *taqueria* last night. They hadn't wanted his money and he had a dreadful feeling he knew why. But credit cards still worked for some reason. He was probably making charges to some account registered to a stranger. He pushed his card into the slot and tapped his fingers on the steering wheel impatiently until the gate arm slowly rose. *Patience,* he told himself, trying to breathe. *You screwed this up the first time by acting rashly. Better stop and think.* "How do we know this isn't exactly the outcome my father wanted?" he asked, more of himself than Diana.

"That's why we're going to the library. Let's see what actually happened."

Gawain turned left on Post and gunned the Range Rover toward a right on Kearny. Now that he knew what to look for, it was as plain as the nose on your face. Lots of Mission architecture that hadn't been there yesterday. Adobe walls would have faired badly in the 1906 earthquake, but if they survived, they would have done better in the fire that followed.

"Look." Diana pointed. Just off Market, where the Moscone Center used to be, there was a huge square populated with buildings that sported beautiful onion domes and bright colors.

Gawain gritted his teeth. All this change occurred just because one guy lived who should have died? They flew down Market until they got to the Civic Center. The library and the City Hall were Spanish-style hacienda buildings. Gone was the gold-leaf dome on the City Hall. And the controversial modern design of the library was a thing of the past, or *a* past that no longer existed. They parked in a garage that charged six bucks every twenty minutes. That hadn't changed. They jumped out, hurried down the street, ran up the shallow steps, and pushed in through the glass door.

Diana whispered to him how the inside had changed. The library still had a beautiful skylight in the central atrium, but now the architecture that had engendered comparisons to a literary mall was gone. Bright murals on white walls seemed to be the theme. The bank of computer indexes was the same. Gawain mustered his Spanish and figured out that the history section was on the fourth floor. He dared not draw attention by asking. On the fourth floor, the titles of the books were all in Spanish and Russian. He didn't even see any books on the history of England.

Diana scanned the shelves and then looked up at him, her gray-green eyes frightened. "Any book should do."

He picked out a book called *Historia del Mundo Moderno* and took it over to a broad, Mission-style oak table

away from the older people reading newspapers and a
woman buried in a book in the corner. Gawain splayed
their history book open as Diana looked over his shoulder.

Okay. It was laid out by year. And it had maps. He
flipped to the atlas part of the book. It fell open naturally
to North America. That was the first shock. There was no
section labeled "United States of America" or "Canada"
or even "Mexico." A huge swath of the center of North
America in a shape a little like a crescent was labeled
"New France." What should have been Mexico, the
Southwest, and California up to just north of San Francisco was called España Nuevo. San Francisco (still labeled with that name) was on the border now of a territory
that included Oregon, Washington, western Canada, and
Alaska. This was the same color as the Russian lands
west of the Bering Strait, as were Japan and the Korean
peninsula. It was all Russia. Only a narrow strip along the
eastern seaboard down to about Virginia—what once had
been called New England—was now called New Trevellyan and looked to have been settled by British people,
though all the place names were Celt.

"My God," Diana whispered, staring at the map.

Gawain was having a hard time getting his breath. He
flipped to another page and found maps of Europe. What
had been Britain was divided into three parts. The east
and north were the same color as something called Scan-
dia that took in all of Denmark, Norway, Finland, and
Sweden, as well as Iceland, Greenland, the Orkneys, and
the north of Scotland and Ireland. The southwest of the
island was called Saxony and was part of a country that
incorporated everything that was German, Austrian, or
Dutch on the Continent. The west of England and the
south of Ireland were called Trevellyan. They were all
crosshatched to indicate that they belonged to "Europa."

France now encompassed all the lands to the south and northern Africa.

"He held the Celtish lands against the Saxons," Gawain said as he scanned the map.

"He said he was the only one who could do it," Diana said in a small voice.

"He was right. And that means there was no united England." He flipped the map to other pages. No India and Pakistan. Along with China and the southeast Asian countries and Australia, the whole thing was just called Asia. Africa was a hotchpotch of microscopic countries with tribal names, except for the North African part of France. The Middle East was comprised of just two countries, called Shiia and Sunni.

"What does this mean?" Diana asked. "What happened?"

Gawain paged back to text. "If Saxons and Celts were separate, then Britain never united under Alfred the Great. I . . . I guess there was no British Empire. They could hold that tiny corner of America but were never a powerhouse to rival the French or the Spanish. Maybe they even lost to the Spanish Armada. . . ."

"I thought the British Empire was bad," Diana whispered as he studied the text.

"Plus/minus. It dominated local cultures. But it also gave the rule of law, the industrial revolution, systems of education, freedom of religion. . . . It kept tribal rivalries under control until institutions of government could prevail and prevented some genocides. . . . It brought countries into the modern world."

Diana went and collected newspapers from the front racks while he confirmed his theory in the history book. No trade of goods or ideas occurred between the powers. New Spain and Russia had been at war for nearly a century with Asia, and it was taking a toll. There was some kind of agreement to keep the conflict contained to several border countries. Everyone had the bomb, and the ever-present threat that one party would use it weighed on people's psyches. Budgets went to defense. No wonder San Francisco looked poor.

"So," Diana was saying slowly. "Is it good or bad that things have changed?"

"Half the world at war with the other half is not good."

"Is it so different from what we had before? Little corners of war all over the place." She pursed her lips in thought as she handed him the newspapers. He scanned them while she thought. "Hard to know what to do." She sighed.

"This doesn't look like a great world to live in." He pointed to an article. "Prisoners of war are tortured routinely. There's a famine going on in big parts of the world."

"Don't get me started on torture. And we had famine before, too."

"Yeah, in small corners of Africa. This is famine over more than half the world. My father couldn't have wanted this." He was starting to be surer of his course.

"As if we can do anything about it now. . . ."

She hadn't thought about it enough. "I could go back and . . ." He looked around at the other patrons in the library and changed his wording. "Carry out my first intent."

"Kill Mordred?" she whispered.

He nodded. "After he sires you."

"I thought you never wanted to go back there."

"I have to put things right, Diana. I've failed miserably. I've changed the world for the worse by sending him back. I *have* to put things right." He could see Diana searching for some way around what had to happen here. Her gaze darted around the room.

Then she stilled, and took a deep breath. "You're right. But I'm coming with you."

He rolled his eyes. Let her endanger herself by coming back a second time to fifth-century England in the middle of a war? "Not happening."

"It's my fault, you know. You can say it's your failure because you always take the blame for everything. But I was the one who brought him here. I took him to the hospital and filled the prescription for antibiotics. And I powered up the machine and sent him back. So I'm going."

How could he make her understand? "If anything happens to you, my whole mission will have been for naught."

Her lips got that determined set to them. "You need me to power the machine up."

True. "You can show me. . . ."

"Nope. Nothing doing. I'm coming with you." She rose from her chair, exuding purpose.

He couldn't let her do that. He'd let her power up the machine. Then he'd take it back alone if he had to tie her up in a corner to do it. He'd be stuck back then and the machine would bounce back just like it had with Mordred.

He'd never see her again.

What would keep her from just using it herself after it returned to now?

So he'd have to damage it to keep it from bouncing back. He couldn't let her endanger herself. She was important. His father said so. And it had been his mission to protect her. He might have botched things by sending Mordred back, but he had at least kept Diana safe. He wasn't going to fail at that, too.

He pushed down the wrenching feeling around his heart. He was a knight. It was his lot to sacrifice. He was going to sacrifice a future with Diana, even if all she would have allowed him to be was her friend.

And then, to serve the greater good, he lied to her. "Okay," he said, standing. "Let's go."

He was *so* lying to her. That was surprising in itself. The parfait knight had stooped to overt lying. Well, not overt. He hadn't told her outright he would take her with him. Maybe having to lie was good for him. He was too hard on himself. He needed to learn to compromise. It didn't mean he was going to get his way. Gawain was *far* too used to getting his way.

Afternoon was waning as they retrieved his sword from the apartment and went to the store specializing in reenactment costumes and weapons where he'd gotten his swords. He bought some hardened leather greaves and a chain mail shirt and a shield. He preferred the small, round shields of the Vikings to the huge medieval ones that covered your whole body. He said carrying a smaller shield conserved strength. That was frightening. He knew he was going to have to fight for his life back there. The grim lines around his mouth said so.

As darkness fell, he took her to the Top of the Mark, which was now a Russian restaurant with snow-white linen and romantic candles at the tables. A few people still had money. Probably weapons makers and arms dealers. Gawain still wore his jeans and boots, though his leather jacket looked like a million bucks on him. She was wearing the short black skirt and green-and-black-striped sweater she'd put on to go to dim sum this morning. Gawain ordered her champagne and caviar. The menu had oysters on the half shell and crab dressed in some kind of yummy cheesy cream sauce that had a zillion calories. They talked of inconsequential things. She watched him arranging his face for her. Did he not want her to see that he was afraid of going back? Or that he still took on the entire guilt for changing everything about the world?

But she also caught him watching her with some expression she couldn't name. She wanted to capture that expression in words. A soft sorrow hidden behind his smiles and small talk? Not quite. A . . . a longing for something . . . The color violet in his eyes meant sadness and longing. She remembered the clear green yesterday afternoon. What did that color mean?

When they finally found themselves staring silently at each other, the check paid, there was no way of dodging the future any longer.

"I have a plan," he said. "I don't have to kill him after he's conceived you. We should go back to the exact same moment you did before and stop you from taking him in the first place."

Liar. He had no intention of making it "we." "Bad idea. We can't meet ourselves in the other time. There was a note with Leonardo's book that said so. That means I can't meet myself coming back there the first time and you can't meet yourself as a ten-year-old boy."

"Why not?"

"The note didn't say. It just said two versions of you couldn't exist at once. All the books on time travel I've read agree."

"And these were scientific books? I thought science didn't acknowledge the possibility of time travel, except in a theoretical kind of way."

"They were science fiction . . . and romances." She refused to blush. "But it just makes sense, you know. And anyway, the note is without doubt from someone who knows." She cleared her throat. "We should arrive sometime later, after we're certain he . . . well, you know."

"After we're sure he's had time to sire you."

She nodded, "And before I would actually be born. We should pick someplace far away from where you lived when you were ten."

"That's tough. We lived in a hut near the hill with the standing stones, so the ten-year-old me is going to be very near Mordred, assuming he's still in Camelot. Everything could have changed when Mordred returned. Maybe we'll even be living inside the castle walls where Mordred could keep an eye on my father or something."

"I bet Merlin didn't kowtow to anyone. He'll live where he wants. And Mordred would never have the courage to challenge him." She looked curiously at Gawain. "You might be able to see him again, if we can separate him from the ten-year-old you. Would you like that?" What she wouldn't give to see her father again, her mother.

"My father wouldn't be glad to see me under the circumstances." He looked away. Was Gawain—confident, brash Gawain—ashamed? Ahhh, but all this parfait-knight stuff—maybe he did it for his father's sake, because his father was the world's most important and powerful wizard and Gawain wasn't, so all he could be was the best knight he could be. That was a revelation.

"Besides," he said, rising from his chair. "This isn't a social visit." He handed her up.

It was time.

Clancy hadn't even noticed that the door marked: *Danger* was still unlocked from the last time she and Gawain had used the machine. Some night watchman he was. But that meant Gawain didn't have to turn into mist again to get them in. Diana watched him carefully—he seemed drained by his effort at the main entrance and stumbled twice in the corridor down to the machine. "Are you all right?"

"Yeah. I'm fine." But she had a feeling he'd never admit that it cost him to use his power.

Deep in the bowels of the earth beneath the Rotunda of the Palace of Fine Arts, Diana powered up the machine; Gawain held the flashlight on the switches. Gawain was dressed now for battle in the fifth century, with a shield on his arm and his sword in a scabbard. He clasped the huge diamond at the end of the lever. The lights flashed on the lunch box.

"Get back," he ordered. It was too dim to see the color of his eyes. She realized she missed watching them change with his moods. "I have to do this alone, Diana. You know I do. If you get stuck back there, or something happens to you, who knows what else might change?"

"Same to you, buddy. You promised me I could go."

He shook his head. "I didn't. You know I'm right. You'll just be a distraction. Don't make me tie you to one of these struts."

She sighed, as though in acquiescence. Two could play the lying game. "Okay. I don't want to be a distraction." She backed up but made sure none of the iron girders were in her way. "Come directly back when you've done it!" she called over the rising hum of power that throbbed in her lungs. His expression was . . . full. Of what she couldn't tell. Perhaps the enormity of what he was about to do.

Beams of colored light stabbed across the ceiling in crazy patterns. Gawain murmured something lost in the whir of many metal gears. Frowning, he slowly turned back to the machine.

"Concentrate on when and where to appear!" she shouted. The gears slowed to a crawl.

This was the moment. She tried to dart forward, but she was moving in slow motion. *No!* Had she misjudged the timing? Her limbs flailed slowly toward Gawain. Half-there. The gears began to grind again. She had only seconds to reach him. But her legs speeded up along with the machine. She was racing toward Gawain. The very fabric of the air begin to stretch. She was too late! She threw herself forward, arms extended, falling. The slingshot snapped. She got an arm around Gawain's waist. Then she was torn apart as they hurtled into blackness.

Chapter Seventeen

Diana raised her head. The world swirled enough to make her stomach churn. About all she could tell was that it was night. She was cold. She laid her head down again, against . . . against something even colder. And rough. Metal. It clinked and moved. Chain mail.

Gawain.

She raised her head again, cautiously. *Better.* It was night. She was sprawled across Gawain, who did not move. Was he dead?

She jerked up and the world went spinning again. She ducked her head to still it. When she could swallow without gagging she stretched a hand to his throat. His pulse beat back at her. She realized she'd been holding her breath. He was alive. She had to get him to someplace safe.

Where were they? She knelt cautiously and looked around. Trees loomed around her, old growth, black sentinels against the shadows behind them. Above them a giant oak spread its canopy, dwarfing even the other trees. She'd never been in a forest at night. The sheer absence of city sounds pounded her senses. There *were* sounds, though, if she listened. Rustlings and wind in the trees, water running over stones. The rustlings were probably animals. Maybe big animals.

Don't have a heart attack for God's sake, she scolded herself. *No time for the vapors.*

Well, *that* was pure romance writer. Apparently being an historical romance writer did *not* prepare you for history. Or forests. She turned around, expecting to see only more trees, or maybe a wolf or something. What she saw was the machine, glinting against the black night and the stars. It was still, just as though it hadn't flung them through time. It looked like something from a Dalí painting, sitting in the forest like this, the contrast between its polished metal and the rough and shadowy nature around it shocking.

As shocking as traveling through time.

She turned to Gawain. There was no place safe to take him in a forest that undoubtedly had wolves in it. At the least. And he was too big for her to drag anywhere anyway. His sword lay a few feet away. His shield was still strapped over his out-flung forearm.

Why wasn't he awake? She took his shoulder and pulled him over as gently as she could. He groaned. *That's a good thing,* she told herself as the sound sent shivers of fear through her. His head lolled to the side. She saw the problem immediately. His head was bleeding above his ear. A trickle of blood trailed down his cheekbone. A flattish rock under him was smeared with some dark substance. Her brain filled with images of crushed skulls and subdural hematomas and all sorts of other things no one could do anything about in the fifth century.

His eyes fluttered open.

"Thank God," she murmured. She took his head in her hands and turned his face toward her. "Can you see me?"

He blinked slowly. "Dilly?" His voice was husky.

"Yeah." She smiled in relief. "It's Dilly."

He put a hand to his head, grimacing.

"You landed on a rock. Probably have a concussion." If not something worse.

He pushed himself up with a grunt, then hung his head. A concussion undoubtedly made the nausea of time travel even worse.

"You need medical attention," she said as he struggled to command his stomach. In the fifth century that probably just meant they'd bleed him with leeches or something.

"No," he said, getting to his hands and knees. "But we do need food and shelter." He looked around, blinking. "The village should be a couple miles to the east." He grabbed his sword and staggered to his feet. She slid an arm around his waist to steady him. He looked at her in sudden consternation. "And what are you doing here?" he growled. "I thought I told you . . ."

"You did tell me. But this is my fault. I wasn't going to let you sacrifice yourself alone."

"I wasn't going to sacrifice myself," he said, looking around to get his bearings. How he would know one section of the forest from another she had no idea. But he seemed to anchor himself on the sound of water gurgling and started off, leaning on her. The forest didn't seem quite so menacing now that she wasn't alone.

"So you weren't going to disable the machine once it was back here, so it couldn't bounce back where I could use it to come after you?" she asked as she stumbled beside him.

He set his lips and wouldn't answer, which was just as good as an admission that she was right. "I thought so." She'd written about heroes all her writing life, and yet this man was the real thing: difficult, stubborn, altogether inconvenient, but a hero nonetheless.

After a few minutes' walking, they came to a large boulder, perhaps twice the height of a man, beside a small stream. Gawain grunted in satisfaction. "The river isn't far now." He knelt and splashed some water on his face. "Do you recognize this place?"

She blinked in shock. She had been here, as a child? "N . . . no." Disappointment stabbed through her. If she'd been here, wouldn't that bring back all her memories? Apparently not. "Should I know it?"

"Not necessarily. This was the stream we fished. You broke your ankle just a little farther down toward the river." His tone was noncommittal, but perhaps he wanted her to remember, too. Why else would he bring it up? He straightened and walked on his own this time.

He was right. The river wasn't far. The Cam was broad and lazy here, with marshy banks.

"We're going to have to get wet to cross it."

Yuck. "Maybe we should wait until morning."

"I don't want to be out in the open. I'm not sure I could protect you in my current state." He seemed disgusted with himself. "We're better off in the village. It's worth a swim."

"In a river with who knows what lurking in it in the middle of the night?" She was *so* not doing that.

"Fish lurk in it. Just fish." He was marching toward the east along the bank. "There's a place up here where you can practically walk across it."

Now that they were out of the forest the crescent moon rose in front of them, clear and cold in the sky. Some things didn't change, even in fifteen hundred years. Were they really back in time? Forests were forests. Rivers were rivers. The moon was the moon.

Diana was bone tired by the time they saw the flickering lights of the village. Gawain pointed. Those warm, flickering lights sure did look inviting. And behind the village were the palisades and the half-finished stone towers of Camelot. This time there were no raging fires, no fleeing families, no knights thundering around on chargers. The scene was quiet and domestic, the castle shielding its village with a protective shoulder against whatever would come.

He came up in front of her and in a single, sudden move threw her over his shoulder as if she were no more than a sack of flour. "What are you doing?" she squeaked.

"Keeping the fish from eating you, my lady," he said, with a chuckle. He was already striding toward the river's edge. "Quit squirming unless you want to risk getting dropped."

She stilled. He waded into the edge of the river. His shoulder was strong against her belly, his arm like iron as it held her. "Will . . . Will they give us shelter?" she asked in a small voice as she stared once more at the village.

"They are a prosperous village. They serve the king and his court, and that is good business. We are visitors to the king and his court. They will give us shelter."

"They'll want payment," she said doubtfully. The water was up to Gawain's thighs.

"I brought enough silver coins to buy most of the village. At least enough to get me a horse as well as our dinner and a bed for the night."

He pushed forward through the rushing water, now almost to his waist. "There's a drop-off here somewhere. . . ."

He didn't even finish his sentence before he stepped awkwardly into a deeper channel and water sloshed up to his chest. Diana gasped in surprise. He stumbled but righted himself. Diana pushed up on his shoulder to avoid the water.

"Sorry," he said, over the current.

Her feet were wet. So what? She was ashamed she'd even worried about it. How could she be such a prima donna when he had a concussion and was carrying her and had gotten totally wet in the bargain? The current was stronger here.

"Can you make it?" she asked. God forbid she drowned him by weighing him down. "I was just being a sissy before. But I can swim."

"I know. You were always a good swimmer. Relax; I'm fine."

It was so humiliating that he knew more about her than she did herself and that he remembered a life she could not. He felt his way forward and leaned against the current. He paused, and then stepped up onto the shallower shelf of river bottom on the other side. Now he could stride out, and he did, until he was out of the water and dripping.

"Okay, put me down," she ordered.

"It's still really marshy here. You're better off where you are."

"I'm not *that* much of a sissy."

"Then let me put it this way: we'll make faster time to the road with me carrying you. I'll put you down when we reach the road."

"All my blood will be in my head by that time," she protested, but not with much intensity. She'd come back to this time against his wishes. She didn't want to be a drag on him. So she swung quietly over his shoulder until he stepped up on a rutted track and eased her down. He was wet from the chest down, his leathers slick with water and his boots squishing still. Her own leather ballet-style shoes were wet, but otherwise she was dry.

"Thanks," she said. "You were brave."

"Yeah. The fish might have eaten me." He turned to the lights of the village. "Come on."

The moon was considerably higher in the sky by the time they reached the first straggling huts of the village. Shutters were closed against the night, though light leaked through them. The place had an unkempt look. Dooryard gardens were untended, plant stalks broken. No one was abroad at all. Gawain peered around, brows furrowed, as they walked.

"What's wrong?" she whispered.

"It's early evening. Yet no one is about. And there are no animals."

"What animals should there be?" The huts were more numerous here. "It's a village."

"Well, the chickens and geese should be in for the night. But that pigsty over there is empty." He pointed. "And that lean-to should have two or three cows in it. Eobert was a careful husbandman." He strode forward with some purpose. "Animals are the lifeblood of a village."

"I thought that was only farms."

"No."

She hurried to keep up with him. He strode toward a larger building in the middle of the village. Light streamed from the doorway as a figure stumbled into the night. Raucous laughter could be heard from inside. Gawain stepped behind a building and dragged her with him. The man stumbled by them, then bent over, hands on his knees. The sound of retching made Diana's gorge rise in sympathy. She turned her head. When he was done, the man staggered on.

"What is that place, a tavern?"

"It used to be the village gathering place, where the Elders met to decide matters, and it served on some days as a church for the new religion. Now, apparently, it is only a drinking hall." His voice was tight, his grip on her tighter. "Something is wrong. Things have definitely changed. You stay here. I'll get the lay of the land."

"I'm not staying here alone." Did he know what he was asking?

"Diana, this is no time . . ."

"Please. Please don't leave me alone here. I'll be safer with you."

He swallowed and gave his head a half shake of disgust. "Stay behind me." He started off through the mud toward the hall. As she got closer she could see that the hall was made of thin poles, set together, probably with pegs. The seams were filled with wattle, and the roof was thatch. Windows had shutters closed over them, but the door gaped open on leather hinges. The sound of male laughter echoed within. Gawain set his shoulders and pushed through the door, Diana in his wake.

The air was thick with smoke from a roaring fire at each end of the huge open room. The place smelled like too many men who hadn't bathed in too long, as well as cooked meat and vegetables, cabbage most prominent among them. Men lounged on wooden stools with tankards and horns of some kind of alcoholic drink, or sat on benches at a long table made of rough planks. Some were eating from bowls with big wooden spoons and hacking slabs of meat off bones with really big knives. There was a game of dice going on in one corner. The men were big and rough looking, dark in coloring, dressed in leather jerkins and breeches. Some had chain mail like Gawain. There seemed to be two camps, one loud and very drunk, the other wary and talking in low voices. The women who were serving them were dressed in layered tunics over what looked like long shifts. One was incredibly pregnant. She could hardly lift the steaming bowl she was carrying.

Everyone turned when Gawain and Diana came in. The room stuttered to silence. Diana was only too glad to stand behind Gawain's broad back. The women in the room went wide-eyed when Gawain walked in, of course. They couldn't take their eyes off him. One smoothed her braids. Another pushed her breasts up into the neckline of her shift. The men had a different reaction. Some were wary, others fierce. One of the largest of the men stood up, his hand on the hilt of a great sword. Diana saw knives being drawn. Gawain didn't seem to notice. He kept his eyes mostly down, though how anyone could see their color change in this smoky light she didn't know. Still he glanced up to the face of the man who stood before him. It was a hard face. This man's brow furrowed in a perpetual scowl and his mouth was used to sneering. His cynicism and hatred of his fellow man shone out of his face. How different Gawain looked, though their experience was undoubtedly much the same. The giant was about to interrogate her and Gawain, and of course he was speaking Proto-Celtic.

"Who are you?" The man's voice was a bass growl.

"A traveler," Gawain answered. Did travelers wear chain mail and really big swords?

The man examined Gawain and his eyes rested on the leather pouch Gawain had tied to his belt. In shock she realized that these men were likely to fall on Gawain and rob him. Then the man cast a glance to Diana. There was something avaricious in his eyes, and it wasn't just for Gawain's purse. Diana glanced around fearfully and saw the same look in the eyes of those immediately surrounding the fierce giant of a man. "And your companion?"

"She is under my protection."

Diana had never heard him sound so . . . definite. He had claimed her, and she had never been so glad of anything in her life.

"So it would seem," the giant man said, but Diana could tell that he was not giving up those avaricious thoughts. "What is your business here?"

"I have come to offer the king my service."

That wasn't what she expected Gawain to say, but really, what else *could* he say? What really surprised her was how easy and relaxed he looked compared to all the tension in the room.

"Perhaps you are fit to serve me, and perhaps not. I am captain of the king's personal bodyguard. I only take the best." The swagger in the set of his shoulders was unbecoming.

"I will let the king determine how I may best serve him."

The man's glower deepened. "You think well of yourself. But you'll not see him unless I think well of you." Two of the men behind him rose and stood at his shoulders.

"Then I hope you will think well of me," Gawain said mildly. "Do any know of a place where I might lodge my lady for the night? She is weary and would rest."

"She can share my bed," one of the louts at the captain's shoulders said. The group around him sniggered.

Gawain ignored him. "I will pay for lodging, food, and suitable garments for my lady."

The silence was thunderous. The avaricious looks increased. They'd seen his purse. But should he have admitted he could pay? That somehow made him seem more vulnerable. Her short skirt and bare legs were unfortunate. She wasn't making their situation any better. If one of these men wanted her, Gawain was even more likely to suffer for protecting her. And she had no doubt he would. She had made his position more precarious by coming back here with him.

The men in the opposite camp looked at their food and drink. Diana turned to the very pregnant little serving woman, surprised that she was about to speak.

"You can lodge with me. I do not have much, but what I have you are welcome to share." Diana really saw her for the first time as all turned to stare at her audacity. She had medium brown hair, not dramatic and dark like the very Celtic-looking men around her. Her skin was fair. One couldn't tell the color of her eyes in the smoky light, but they were not dark.

"Who said you could speak, whore?' the captain barked. He turned to Gawain. "You and your *lady* can sleep in the forest." He made the word "lady" sound like an epithet.

Gawain sighed. "You really want to do this, don't you?" He looked down at his boots, then up, decisively. He glanced around the room. "You there." He pointed to a man from the other camp, with a beard just starting to show gray. "You will see to the safety of my lady while this is settled." He did not ask it as a question. The man stood. He wasn't young, but he didn't look like a pushover, either. He had ropy muscles on a lean frame, and she could tell by the neck coming out of his flaxen shirt that he was strong. More important, as he stood, the men around him rose as well. The man with the grizzled beard nodded, just once, seriously.

"You have my oath on it."

Gawain turned to Diana. "Go with them. Lamorak will protect you. He may be in different circumstances than I left him, but he is an honorable man."

"You know my name . . . ," the one Gawain called Lamorak muttered.

Gawain grinned. "Your fame has spread before you, old man." He motioned to Diana to go to them. "Don't worry. This will be quick. You'll be back under my protection in no time."

When she hesitated, Lamorak held out a hand and gave a roguish grin. "Not that old, young buck. But I do have a shred of honor left." He darted a glance to the captain. "Come, my lady; you are safe with me."

At another encouraging nod from Gawain, she moved into Lamorak's camp.

"My lady," they murmured greetings to her, and studiously avoided looking at her legs.

Gawain settled his weight easily on feet spread about a foot apart. "Here, or outside?"

"Outside," the captain growled, picking up his big, triangular shield from a stack to one side of the great fireplace. He cast a murderous look at Lamorak. "I'll deal with you later." He pushed past Gawain to the door, his buddies in his wake.

Gawain nodded graciously as they passed, then followed them out into the night. At which point the entire room made a dash for the door. Men from any time loved a fight.

"No one can take Gareth," someone murmured.

Gareth, as in Mordred's half brother?

"I don't know. That one looks confident."

"He's a fool."

By the time Diana and her escort got to the door, the captain they called Gareth and Gawain were already facing each other and pulling out their swords. Their shields were at the ready. Gawain nodded to his opponent, who immediately rushed in swinging. Gawain dodged and parried easily. But Diana's stomach flip-flopped. How could Gawain be so certain he would win? And in these times, what did winning mean? The guy left standing with the fewest horrible wounds? The sharp glint of Gareth's sword made her wince.

Gawain waited for his opponent to recover, relaxed. He motioned Gareth to try again with the fingers holding his sword hilt. Gareth's face dissolved in rage. He rushed again, sword swinging. Gawain parried again, but this time, just behind the swing of his sword that brushed Gareth's sword away, he moved to the side and swept a leg out behind Gareth's shield, catching Gareth just behind the knee. Gareth went down on one knee. Now his shield was an unwieldy liability. It canted to the side, and Gareth couldn't get a clear blow with his sword. In desperation he dropped his shield. Gawain brought his own small shield up and caught Gareth a vicious blow under the chin. His head snapped back and he grunted as he collapsed, head lolling.

The whole fight had taken less than two minutes.

Stunned silence gave way to shouts of congratulation from Lamorak and his men. Several left Lamorak's side to go up and clap Gawain on the shoulder.

"I thought you were a dead man, carrying such a small shield."

"He used the shield itself as a weapon," another said, wondering.

"Where did you learn to fight like that?" Lamorak asked as Gawain returned to Diana, surrounded by his new well-wishers.

"I watched a lot of mixed martial arts on something called television." He grinned at Diana. "Besides. Gareth was always a hothead who rushed in before testing his opponents."

Lamorak raised his brows. "I am not sure I understand this . . . mixed martial arts. But Gareth *is* a hothead. Do . . . Do you know him?"

"In a way," Gawain said noncommittally. He came to take Diana's arm protectively.

"What made you choose a shield so small?" Lamorak clapped Gawain on the shoulder.

"The Norse use them."

"The blond men beyond the north sea? Have you been there?"

"No." Gawain smiled at Diana. How she loved that smile. It made her feel right and true. "But I have met some of their fighters in my day."

Or their descendants.

"Then you are a man I would like to know." Lamorak

turned to one of Gareth's men. "Agravain, your brother needs a bucket of water over his head, or he'll lie in the mud all night."

Glowering, the man headed for a watering trough round the far side of the hall. From here Diana could see several huge, heavy-boned horses tethered there. Turning back to the group surrounding Gawain, Diana saw another of Gareth's men peering at Gawain, eyes narrowed.

But then Lamorak swept Diana and Gawain back into the hall, calling for meat and mead for the guests at his expense. Lamorak and Gawain settled into a comfortable relationship, almost as if they had always known each other. Soon Gawain was eating and laughing with them. Gareth's party had decamped. No doubt their leader had a very big headache. And they would not enjoy hearing his defeat relived in so many tellings.

The young pregnant woman came in bearing a great wooden tray loaded down with a haunch of venison. Diana leaped up to help her. "You shouldn't be carrying heavy trays. Let me."

"A lady like you can't be serving drunken men," she said. "It is good for me to be active." She held the plank away from Diana and set it on the table. Something about her seemed familiar. Maybe all pregnant women looked alike. She certainly had a glow about her lovely, translucent skin. She was really quite pretty.

The men stood to carve meat from the great haunch. Gawain sliced some very thinly with his great gleaming knife and put it on a smaller wooden plate for Diana. He scooped her vegetables into a bowl and handed her a wooden spoon. It looked like potatoes and maybe carrots and parsnips, and it smelled wonderful. Excitement rose inside her. She was living and eating in the fifth century! This was how it really was: a little dirty (no restaurant

ratings here) and a hard life, but . . . real. Maybe more
real than the twenty-first century.

She gestured to the little pregnant woman. "What is
your name, so I can thank you?"

"Lambeth, my lady. Mostly I am called Beth."

"Well, join us, Beth. You look hungry."

"Oh no, my lady," she said, bobbing a curtsey. "That's
not allowed. Meat is only for the soldiers, or the castle.
We villagers don't get meat."

Gawain stopped eating in midbite. "What's this?" he
asked, and looked to Lamorak.

"The lass is right," Lamorak said, sobering. "Our king
takes the milk, the animals, the stags in the forest. All
belong to him. The only reason there is meat for supper
tonight is because we're here. Gareth brought venison
with him. He comes down with some of his men to graze
among the local herd." Lamorak gave a glance to the two
pretty young women who were helping Beth.

"What happened to defending the weak? There was
a time when we understood that the health and wel-
fare of those who till the land and make what we need
are our responsibility." Gawain spoke quietly, but he had
the attention of the men around him. Some looked
abashed.

"All that is gone," Lamorak said, his voice husky.
He downed his tankard of mead. "Mordred rules here
now."

"And you serve him?" Gawain's voice was so low it
was almost a baritone whisper.

"He is all that holds the land against the Saxons."

"Surely not all. You are his might. Could not another
lead you?"

"We cannot hold against them divided. We need Mordred's contingent, and they will not fight without him.

Agravain, Gareth, they hold sway with others, and they are Mordred's kin."

"And yet they need you, too. They cannot prevail alone," Gawain pressed. "You could stand against them. . . ." He glanced around to the servants in the hall. "At least in certain things."

Lamorak took a breath. His chest heaved with it. As if it was all he could do to speak, he said, "Merlin has given him new power and tells him where the Saxons will attack. Without Mordred, and Merlin's sight that serves him, we would fall."

"Merlin supports him?" Gawain looked stricken. As well he might. His own father was supporting a man who was capable of any atrocity. Gawain looked away from Lamorak and the other men. "Maybe falling to the Saxons would not be so bad. The alternative seems to be that *we* are our people's worst enemy." Gawain looked defeated. In a way, Merlin was her father, too, at least in nurture, if not in biological fact. She should share Gawain's shame. But she couldn't remember anything of Merlin, and therefore she didn't feel it as Gawain did. She wanted to help him, to comfort him. But what comfort could she give?

"Do you know the Saxons?" Lamorak asked, snorting. "Foreign swine. We may not keep to Arthur's principles, but at least we will save the land from foreign devils."

Things had not changed in fifteen hundred years. People still feared the strange more than they feared what they knew, even if what they knew was evil.

The men drifted back to eating. There was nothing more to be said on their dilemma, and they had made their choice. Lamorak talked of the hunt for the stag they were eating. Gawain roused himself from silence to praise the flavor of its meat. It was the courteous thing to do, no matter what you felt inside. Diana had to admit that eating felt good. The mead was sweet but nonetheless alcoholic. Soon she was nodding at the table. As she jerked her head up, hoping no one had noticed her lapse, she heard Lamorak saying, "Lad, do I know you from somewhere? You look a bit familiar."

Uh-oh.

"I have a common face," Gawain said brusquely, downing his mead.

The laugh went round the table. Lamorak guffawed loudly. "I'll bet the women do not think so. Tell us your name, Sir Knight."

"I am called Gawain," he said briefly.

"Gawain. . . . ," Lamorak mused.

"Well, I think my lady needs her rest," Gawain changed the subject abruptly. "Mistress, does your offer still stand?"

The pregnant server called Beth nodded as she made her way among the men, filling horns and tankards. "Yes, my lord."

"I would not let her rest unguarded," Lamorak said, almost under his breath.

"She shall not." Gawain rose.

"You'll need some rest yourself, if you're going up to the castle tomorrow," Lamorak said flatly. No other explanation was asked for or given. But Diana knew that one of Lamorak's men would spell Gawain so he could get some sleep, too. It was a strange feeling, being protected as though you were a precious object. She shouldn't like it. She was an independent modern woman. But knowing Gareth and Agravain were out there somewhere still probably looking avaricious, she didn't mind having someone outside her door.

"You, urchin!" Gawain called to the boy who had been putting a log on the nearest fire. He was a ragged creature, perhaps ten or twelve, about the age that Gawain was in this time. The boy turned around, casting frightened eyes across the crowd of men to see who called.

Gawain beckoned. The lad hurried forward, pulling his forelock in the age-old gesture of deference. "My lord?" he asked breathlessly.

"Take this home to your family," Gawain said gruffly, pointing to a piece of meat.

The boy looked up, his eyes wide. "My lord?"

Gawain hauled the haunch up by the bone. "Have one of the women wrap it for you."

The boy hesitated, then grabbed the haunch in his arms, careless of the staining juices, and hurried away with his prize.

Gawain looked around at the other men pointedly. "I'm sure there will be other leftovers which will need good homes." A couple of the men looked abashed.

"Aye, Gawain. We can handle that," Lamorak said.

Gawain set another hefty piece of meat on his shield. "Come, my lady. Mistress, will you lead us to your abode?" He handed the woman the shield to carry and lifted Diana from her stool. They followed the little pregnant servant into the night.

"It's just a few steps!" she called back over her shoulder.

"I hope your man will not mind the intrusion," Gawain said graciously.

They saw her hesitate. Then her shoulders straightened. "I have no man," she said, striding forward. "That's why they call me whore."

Diana looked at Gawain and he looked back. Could it be? Gawain pulled her forward and they hurried to catch up with the pregnant serving maid. "I thought she looked familiar," Gawain whispered in Diana's ear. "It was the weight of pregnancy that put me off."

But Beth was pretty—Diana's mind protested. Perfect skin. Big eyes. But it had to be.

This was her mother.

Tears filled her eyes. All those years longing to know where she came from. The mortification of realizing she was Mordred's daughter. The fear that she was tainted somehow . . . but Mordred was only half her answer. She was this woman's daughter, too. And this woman was brave, and kind. She offered them a bed when it took courage to stand against the likes of Gareth and Agravain, who called her whore. And she would die giving birth to Diana. Diana's heart clenched. This was her chance to know her mother. Whether that chance was God given or given by Mordred and Gawain who could know? But Diana would take it.

"But your babe has a father," Gawain said as he caught up with Beth. "I think it was Mordred." Diana held her breath.

Beth stopped in her tracks and turned. "How know you that? I have never told a soul."

What was there to say? *Because we are time travelers and I am your daughter grown*? There was only one thing this woman would believe. "I am a witch," Diana said calmly. "And this is Merlin's son. Will you keep our secret from Mordred?"

"I never see Mordred. He raped me the night our Arthur died, eight months ago and more. He has a dozen swelling with his brats besides me, and no use for any of us. Only a queen will do to bear a child he acknowledges. They say he will bring back Guinevere. So your secret is safe." But all the while she talked her eyes strayed to Gawain.

Diana looked to Gawain as well. Mordred wanted to wed Guinevere, Gawain's true love. Diana expected to see his face contract in rage or pain, but he was covering his emotion well.

Beth spoke again, hesitant. "I . . . I know Merlin's

son. He is but a boy. . . . and yet he has the look of you. . . ."

Gawain looked around, searching the shadows of the muddy street at night. "We should hurry to your house, Mistress Lambeth. . . ."

Beth shook herself out of her contemplation. "Of course." She picked up her skirts to stride across the muck.

Gawain lifted Diana over a muddy section of the road. He didn't ask. He just swept her up and set her down again, as if it were a normal part of walking beside her. They found their way onto a tiny winding path that led to a small hut back off the road in a stand of trees.

Beth pushed open the door. "Let me just poke up the fire. I'll set your meat over here."

"It's not our meat. It's yours," Gawain said. "And I'll take care of the fire."

He knelt and stirred the coals. They sparked up and sent forth a tentative flame. Gawain took a small log from the pile of three set on the little hearth and stripped some bark. He laid the bark across the coals in a crisscross pattern, and when it had caught he laid two of the logs across it. "Where is your woodpile?"

"Around the side." The pregnant woman headed for the door.

"You sit and rest your back," Gawain said, waylaying her and guiding her to a stool.

Beth looked almost frightened by his acts of kindness. Gawain didn't seem to notice but headed for the door. Diana went and sat beside Beth, who glanced occasionally at the slab of meat on the shield she had set on the crude wooden table.

"You should eat," Diana said. "The meat would be good for your babe." *For me,* she thought. *How strange.* And indeed, the woman's skin looked so translucent as to be almost unhealthy in this light. "Don't bother about me; I ate until I can't eat any more." She felt ashamed knowing that Beth was hungry all the time she served the others.

Beth turned big eyes on her. "You are both kind, my lady."

"Nonsense," Diana said brusquely. "Now will you get a plate for yourself or shall I?"

"You're low on wood, Mistress Lambeth," Gawain said as he pushed in through the door with an armload. "But I see you have an axe. I'll cut some for you before we go up to the castle in the morning." He laid his load by the fire. "I'll be right outside the door. Call if you need me."

He turned to go. "It's cold outside," Beth said, leaping up and getting a worn patchwork quilt from the bed.

Gawain looked around, saw how poor the hut was, took in the fact that the bed had only two quilts. "I'll not be sleeping, Mistress Lambeth. I'm on watch. You keep your quilt." Then he softened his rejection with a smile.

In that moment, Diana knew just how much she loved him. She might have thought she loved him before, but seeing his generosity toward the ragged boy, his care for Beth, made her proud and sad, all at once. Here was a man *so* worth loving, and he would never love her back. And Mordred was bringing Guinevere to Camelot. She had a vivid premonition. Gawain would stay here, in this time, after he had killed Mordred. This was where he belonged. This was where his one true love resided. And if Arthur was dead and Mordred was dead and Gawain was a man grown, there was nothing standing between him and his love. Of course, he'd have to take her away from where his self of ten was living. But if she was queen, what was to stop him from being king and sending his boyhood self away to Orkney, where he and Diana would never meet? He would be a great king. Would that change history?

And why was it that when she thought about that, history was the least of her concerns?

It took all her courage, but she smiled at him. His eyes smiled back. Then he pushed out the door into the night.

"He is a fine man," Beth said in a low voice.

"Yes, he is. Sit and eat."

Chapter Eighteen

Gawain marched around the house, looking for vulnerabilities. The trees were too close in the back. They provided cover for intruders. He'd cut down a couple tomorrow for two reasons. He could hear the low voices of the women in the hut but not what they were saying. Diana had found her mother. He hoped that was a solace to her.

Damn her, that she had followed him here. It wasn't safe for a soft girl from the twenty-first century to be here in the fifth. Especially one as pretty as Diana. He had acted as though winning a fight with Gareth was a given. But they could have all fallen on him at once and killed him. What would happen to Diana then? He shuddered to think. He had to protect her. But what if he couldn't? Her very presence made him feel cautious and vulnerable. He wasn't used to that.

He couldn't deny that he found her presence a solace, too, though. The thought of never seeing her again had made his gut churn in that room beneath the Palace of Fine Arts. He had been willing to sacrifice seeing her again, because that was what was required of him. But it would have broken him. He knew that now. So he knew what was in store for him. Tomorrow he would pay Beth with enough silver to keep her from having to serve the likes of Gareth, he'd kill Mordred, and he would get Diana home to the time where she belonged.

He forced his mind into planning. Should he find a horse and arrive at the castle with authority, asking to serve Mordred? At the least he could get an audience with him. But what if that audience was in the presence of thirty of his knights? Gawain would never be able to touch him then. Should he find a way into the palisades surreptitiously and try to find Mordred in his rooms alone or with a woman? What if he was caught before he could find Mordred?

And then Gawain couldn't hold his mind in check any longer. He felt like someone had punched him in the gut more effectively than Gareth ever could. He leaned forward and sagged against the wall of Beth's hut.

Not only was he about to lose Diana, but also his father was supporting Mordred.

Could he have misjudged his father's character so completely? Had he been so overawed by Merlin's power and his own shortcomings that he couldn't see the man beneath? Merlin knew Mordred was a villain. Gawain pushed himself up and completed another circuit of the hut before he sat on the doorstep.

If Merlin was supporting Mordred and got in the way of Gawain's mission, then . . . then Gawain would have to kill his father, too, to save the future. To stop Mordred making his own people suffer. The Saxons hadn't been as bad as this. They took and stole and burned, and then they . . . stayed. And even though he'd fought the ones who transgressed, waging a guerrilla war hundreds of years before that term was coined, still, most Saxons were fair to their people. In the end the country absorbed the Saxons and survived to produce Alfred the Great, who

united at least half the island and held it against the
Vikings. Even the Vikings had been absorbed, and together Saxon and Celt and Viking had held the island
until it fell to the Normans (Vikings or "Northmen"
themselves), and the Normans were absorbed in their
turn. The country became strong and vital with all those
different peoples. It surged toward the Renaissance and
Shakespeare, and a queen who made her island into a na-
val powerhouse that spread culture and law through a
wide swath of the world.

It was the sweep of history he must save. He had to
save the British Empire so it could fall and leave its
seedlings of self-rule and the hatred of despots in its
wake. The British Empire could be cruel, as could the
Saxons. The priggish self-confidence of British majors
everywhere provoked rebellion. But the rebellion was as
necessary as colonization in the first place. It was the
path of history and it had to be restored, the canker of
Mordred removed.

It was only a personal tragedy that Gawain's father
might stand in the way. Gawain would kill Merlin, if he
could. He was setting himself against the most powerful
magician in history. But he would find a way. He must.
He made another circuit, until one of Lamorak's men arrived and took over. He lay down on his cloak and dreaded
the coming of the day.

Diana watched Beth tuck into the beef with a knife
thinned by years of sharpening and a two-pronged fork to
hold it. The wonder of the fact that this woman was her
mother tied her tongue. What should she ask her? What
did she want to know?

"Do . . . do you have family hereabout?" Why was Beth
so alone?

Beth shook her head, a sad smile pausing on her face for a moment between bites. "My mother died long ago. My brothers scattered."

"Your . . . your father?"

"A Saxon," she said sadly. "I never knew him."

"Did . . . did he rape your mother?" Diana wondered if she had been a product of generations of rape. Mordred had raped this girl in celebration of his victory over Arthur. Had anyone ever loved a mate in her family? Was love some kind of aberration?

"Oh no. My mother lived in the land that Cerdic first took for the Saxons, south and east of here. There was a blond Saxon warrior sent to start a colony and bring the families of his men from the mainland to settle their conquered land." Here she smiled, though her look was far away. She was remembering the stories her mother had told her as a child. "They built grand halls in my mother's village. But he had no wife himself. Though many wanted him, he had eyes only for my dark-eyed Celtic mother. And she . . . she told me when I was but girl how blue his eyes were and how blond his hair. By the look on her face I knew she had wanted him, too. He took her to wife and had children by her. Our village thrived." Her face fell.

"What happened?"

"Cerdic wanted to extend his power. He called his warriors to push west, into Arthur's lands. My father fell in battle. They say he died bravely," she added, with a small smile. "It broke my mother's heart, and she no longer had the courage to live among the blue-eyed people. So she returned here, with me."

So, her Saxon father was the reason for Diana's light eyes. She had a history, a genetic heritage. "You have a wonderful family history," she said.

"I belong nowhere," Beth said, pushing her plate away.

"You are the future." Diana reached across the rough plank table and took her mother's hand. Diana swallowed. "I feel I know you. And you are a good woman."

"You don't know me," her mother said. "And yet . . . you look familiar."

Diana's eyes filled. *Now or never.* "You, too. Have you . . . have you seen your reflection in a polished metal mirror or a pond?"

Beth's eyes went round with recognition.

Diana smiled and her tears overflowed. "I look like you. There is a reason for that."

Beth blinked, thought, registered confusion.

"I used the power I have from my father to come back in time and see you," Diana said carefully. Beth watched her face, wary. "I am your unborn daughter, grown."

Beth's hand went, of its own volition, to her belly.

Diana nodded.

Beth searched her face. And then a delicate hand reached out to touch Diana's cheek, exploring what should not be, could not be, but was. "My lady?"

"Not your lady. Your daughter. See?" She pointed to her face. "I have your eyes, your skin, your mouth."

"Do you remember me?" her mother asked. Beth accepted. She accepted that there was magic in the world that could bring a daughter from the future back to visit her mother while the daughter was yet unborn. That simple faith in magic didn't make Diana respect her mother less. It was a time when magic was still possible, when Merlin made kings and protected a kingdom with powers that were accepted, revered. Magic was just a part of everyday life.

Diana shook her head. She would not tell her mother why she didn't remember her. "But I am glad to know you. I didn't want to think that I was made by Mordred alone."

"You have a kind face. You are a good woman," Beth whispered. Then her eyes filled as they scanned the ceiling and the few sticks of furniture in the small hut. "And I . . . I am the one who will bear you." Her eyes came to rest on Diana's face. "And the knight loves you. You will bear his children, and they will bear children. . . ."

Diana didn't disabuse her of that notion. "You are part of the future, Mother."

She hadn't called anyone that since she was sixteen. It felt good.

"You are even kind enough not to tell me that I will die bearing you."

Diana was shocked. She bit her lip, wondering what to say. Her mother touched Diana's lips to quiet her. "Don't deny. Why else would you come back to see me? Because you couldn't know me any other way. Don't mourn. A death is worth bearing you." Beth drew Diana into her breast, across her bulging belly. "I am so proud. So glad."

Diana scooted forward and laid her head against her mother's breasts, swollen with pregnancy. She wouldn't talk about Mordred and what Gawain was here to do. She wouldn't mourn the fact that her mother would die in childbirth. She wouldn't dwell on her misgivings.

"I love you," she said. There was nothing else to say.

Mordred sloshed more wine into his tankard. It was poor wine, compared to the wine he had enjoyed in the twenty-first century, but it was better than no wine. The feast was ended. The trenchers and platters had been taken away by the servant women. Smoke filled the wooden hall. Men lounged and drank. Women, highborn and low-, consorted with the revelers, some more willingly than others. Boisterous laughter bounced back from the tapestries and furs that hung on the walls.

The stone of his future castle grew out of the dirt not two hundred yards from where Mordred sat, but at this rate it would take years to complete. Only the foundations had been finished, and a single tower. There were no more taxes to be gleaned from the peasants. It took resources to supply the men who kept the Saxons at bay. He'd conscripted every able-bodied man between sixteen and fifty to fight Cerdic's Saxon forces. The only way they prevailed was with the advance notice of the enemy's movements provided by the wizard.

This time was forsaken by the gods. Mordred belonged in that shining city by the bay some fifteen hundred years from now. At first when he'd come back, he'd thought about staying here. It was familiar. He easily made himself king, and he'd finally found a way to force Merlin to do his bidding. Things could be worse.

He looked across the room at the great stone that formed part of the fireplace. The hall itself had been built around the stone in Arthur's day, to commemorate his ascension, unlikely as it was since he, too, was a bastard, to the throne. Arthur had pulled his sword from this stone near a lake in Cornwall and proved he was the rightful ruler of the kingdom. During Arthur's lifetime, it was just a stone, rough and irregular, but with no holes or markings. But by the time Mordred came back from the twenty-first century and entered Arthur's hall, the hilt of Arthur's sword once more protruded from the virgin rock as though the rock had been formed around it. There was no cut slot in the stone, no caulking around the blade. Arthur's sword, the one that symbolized his power, just . . . *was* . . . in the stone, waiting for the next knight who was destined to rule.

Mordred had tried to pull it out. Gareth and Agravain, his half brothers, had tried. To no avail. The hilt stared at Mordred now, smugly, as if to say he wasn't fit to rule, or that he'd never be the man his father was. Mordred had ordered Merlin to get him the sword. But Merlin said he couldn't pry the sword out by magic. It must yield itself to a new hand. No threats could move Merlin. Mordred pried the jewels out of the hilt. In a fit of rage, he'd hacked at the steel with his own sword. The grip was roughened a bit but that was all. He wanted nothing more than to escape that sword and that stone. But to dine in his private bedchamber on the second story would be admitting weakness.

So within a fortnight, an insidious longing had poisoned his triumph. Was he truly even king here when that sword stubbornly reminded everyone of Arthur? And though he could enforce his will with the might of easily led men and an aging wizard, in the end what mattered a kingdom in some small corner of an island where a king's lodgings were made of logs and wattle? What was Camelot compared to a kingdom like the one they called America?

So he had decided. He'd go forward into the future once more. But he couldn't make the machine work. For a whole day, he'd tried different sequences of buttons and switches and knobs. He'd enlisted Merlin to cast a spell over the mechanism. Nothing. Mordred had begun to think the machine was broken. But that night the machine disappeared. It wasn't there when he returned in the morning. It hadn't been broken at all. He had been *that* close to having what he wanted and his dreams had run through his hands like sand.

Now he was stuck in this time with no plumbing, no electricity. There would be no computers for fifteen hundred years. And for eight months that damned sword hilt stuck in the stone of the great fireplace stared at him smugly.

He stood and threw his tankard. It splashed wine over

the sword hilt. By the time the tankard clattered to the floor, there was silence in the room. Everyone was staring at him.

Let them stare. I'm the goddamned king.

He stumbled down the long planked table. He was going to bed. He looked around for a serving girl to take with him. Instead, his eyes fell on Agravain, brooding at the far end of the table. *Moody Celts.* Under his eyes, Agravain started up, swearing.

"What is it, man?" Mordred asked irritably.

Agravain looked around wildly, then steadied. "I know who the devil was. Is."

"Who the hell are you talking about?" Mordred didn't have time for drunken maunderings.

"A man came into the village, dressed for battle. He had a woman with him whose legs were bare. Gareth thought to take both his fat purse and the woman." He seemed to see Mordred for the first time. "For your greater glory, of course. But the man fought like a demon and Gareth was vanquished in an instant."

A woman in a short dress? A man who fought like a demon? Mordred had a sinking feeling. "Who?" he barked at Agravain.

"I . . . I think it was a son of Merlin. Not the young one. This one is full grown. But he has the look of him . . . and his eyes. There was something about his eyes. I couldn't quite see. . . ."

Mordred sucked in a breath. They'd come for him.

The possibilities began to click over in his head. They must have come in the machine. That meant it was here in the fifth century somewhere. Gawain had brought the girl. *Excellent. Kill Gawain. Force the girl to tell him how to power up the machine.* And the twenty-first century was his again. Or some other century. All time, all societies, all power, was within his grasp.

"Where is he?" Mordred's voice was soft now, because the possibility of power seemed to hum in the air around him and he could afford not to shout.

"We left him down at the hall, but that was hours ago. He may have moved on." Agravain looked frightened.

Mordred smiled. "Go down to the village. Make inquiries."

"If we find him, should we kill him?"

"You will find out where he is, and report to me. You are no match for him. I am." With the help of Gawain's own father. A scene flashed before Mordred's eyes of Merlin having to make a . . . what did they call it in the future? A "Hobson's choice." He had seen the movie by that name on AMC. Oh yes. That would be delicious. It might even break Merlin. That would be advantageous. It was dangerous to have a vicious dog at the end of your leash. Maybe if he could tame Merlin for good, he would take Merlin with him to the future. Merlin's gifts could help Mordred make short work of any resistance to his path to power.

Agravain nodded and strode from the room, motioning to several men to follow him.

Mordred was suddenly stone-cold sober, with no desire to head for his bed.

"Send Merlin to me," he said.

Diana woke in the bed beside her mother. Light was streaking in around the shutters in dusty golden beams. The sun had been up for a while. Her mother was still asleep. For a while Diana just looked at her. She was pretty. No wonder Mordred had taken her the night he killed Arthur. She was only meant to prove his manhood, but in any group that contained all but the most beautiful of women she would certainly be the chosen one.

Did Diana look like this? There were no mirrors

around. But she recognized the features, the texture and tint of the skin, the fringe of lashes. The chin was small, like her own. She'd always thought that indicated weakness. But her mother was a strong person. And the face was heart shaped, just like her own. Diana always despised that it made her look like a Kewpie doll. But that wasn't how it seemed on her mother. It seemed . . . feminine. What would her life have been like if this was the face that sent her off to sleep at night, that leaned over to wipe her forehead when she was sick? Would she have been a different person? Would she have seen herself reflected in this face and not felt so alone, so different, so . . . lost?

She *was* different and she was lost. Had been lost since her biological mother died and she was passed to Merlin. Lost since he'd thrown her forward in time and her life had broken in the middle, over the spine of the rift between fifth century and twenty-first.

She reached out and pulled a strand of hair from her mother's face. To know her now was an artificial joining of that rift that had rent Diana's life in two. She had proof of where she came from, here in her mother's face. This good and beautiful woman was her past, and lived on through Diana into the present. It was a circle. For the first time, she felt . . . almost whole.

The almost was that she still didn't remember her childhood. She didn't remember Gawain, or Merlin. It struck her that it might hurt Gawain that she couldn't remember him.

Gawain. Where was he? She realized she'd been hearing a rhythmic crack from outside the cabin. That was probably what woke her up. She slid from the bed without waking her mother. The bed was a pallet of straw laid over woven ropes strung between four posts. It had been surprisingly comfortable. She had on an ankle-length

shift with long sleeves that tied at the wrists. Her mother
had given her the shift last night and the long belted tunic
worn over it. She slipped into the tunic now, along with
the knit stockings and soft leather shoes. They were her
mother's best. Diana hated to take them. Her only comfort was that Gawain would give her mother silver enough
to buy a hundred replacements. Diana slipped out the
door quietly. Her mother stirred but didn't wake. As close
to birthing as she was, she needed her rest.

As close to death.

There was nothing to change that. Diana's heart contracted. And if she could change her mother's death, she
wouldn't. It was too dangerous. Diana wouldn't risk
changing history again.

Outside, the morning was a crisp blue that probably
didn't exist in the twenty-first century. The air wasn't
clean enough to let through this translucent light. This
was the way the world was meant to be. Gawain's cloak
lay on the tiny porch as well as his chain mail shirt and
his linen one. His cloak was laid out as though he had
slept there. She headed round the house.

He stood in a green open circle of grass. Several tree
trunks had been dragged from where they fell into the circle. The hewn stumps clustered near the house. Had he
dragged those entire trees away from the house? Now he
was stripped to the waist, swinging the axe like he knew
how to wield one, his hands sliding easily along the handle.
The muscles in his shoulders and back, over his ribs,
bunched, undulating under his skin. Already a sizable
stack of fireplace-sized chunks was growing between two
trees. Their vertical trunks held the woodpile in place.
Even in the crisp air of morning, he was sweating with his
effort. His skin gleamed. A thrill between her legs told
Diana that fifth century or twenty-first, she was vulnerable
to her attraction to him. The axe swung down. Wood

chips made a fountain onto the grass. The log split from the trunk. Gawain's strength never ceased to amaze her.

He must have sensed her there, because he looked up. The smile that lit his face was so tender and sad, her heart swelled open. Her own smile just . . . happened, without her intending it.

She started over the wet grass. "You've been busy."

His eyes were violet again. "I wanted to get an early start, so I can get up to Camelot by the time Mordred is up and about." A preoccupied look came over his face.

"Do . . . do you have a plan?"

He started. "Of course." But he looked quickly over to his woodpile without elaborating, and she wondered if he said that just to reassure her. "This time I don't want any guff from you about coming with me. This is going to get bloody and I can't be worried about protecting you."

"The last thing I want is to endanger you." As she had when she'd appeared during his fight with Mordred.

He shrugged. She realized that he would gladly sacrifice himself to ensure Mordred's death. His eyes went steel blue. "If something happens, you get back to the machine and get out of here." He tossed his axe aside and stalked over to her. "You remember the way?"

She didn't want to face that possibility, but his eyes were so serious she couldn't avoid answering. "I go back down to the main road through the village and turn left. When I come to that flat place by the river, I wade across, then follow it upstream to where that creek comes in. I strike off to the right at the big boulder."

He nodded, and his face softened. "I'm impressed."

"Hey, I'm used to finding my way around San Francisco." As if that was the same.

He had to smile at that. At least it got that serious look off his face that told her he thought he might not come out of this alive. Guilt stabbed her. Her gaze darted around the clearing. "I'm the reason all this has gone so wrong. Why did I have to come back here that first time? Why did I have to rescue someone who should never have been rescued?"

He took her shoulders. "Look at me." His eyes caught her gaze. Her panic stilled. "You came back because, whether you could consciously remember it or not, you were looking for your past. You rescued Mordred because you have a kind heart and a brave one." His gaze softened. "You are much like your mother in that."

She was about to say she wasn't like that at all when Beth herself came round the corner of the little hut. "Oh," she squeaked when she saw the growing woodpile. "Thank you," she said to Gawain. "You are more than kind."

"Nonsense," Gawain returned gruffly. "I'm trying to pay, in some small measure, for the courage and kindness that led you to take us in last night."

"You're more than welcome, Sir Knight. I . . . I was glad to meet your lady."

"Your daughter," Diana corrected. Gawain was frowning. "She knows."

Beth smiled. "I see your knight knows the truth of what you say."

Diana blushed. "He . . . he isn't really my knight." She glanced to Gawain in apology. Gawain's face had gone still. She couldn't read his expression. What kind of a writer was she? But his eyes went a soft, clear green.

"I think he is . . . ," Beth said.

The clop-clop of hooves on the path made them all turn. Horror washed over Diana. She felt Gawain tense, even before they could see the rider, perhaps in sympathy of her own reaction. "Mordred," she whispered. "He's going to . . ."

"Well, well, what have we here?"

". . . . hail us," she finished lamely.

Beth's face had gone white. Gawain glanced from his sword and shield, leaning against the side of the hut ten or twelve yards away, to where he'd tossed the axe, now at least fifty feet from where they stood. Diana could feel him cursing himself.

It wouldn't have mattered, for now there were rustlings all around them as men rode out of the trees. They must have been stationed there for some time, waiting. Otherwise, how could she and Gawain not have heard them approach?

Diana looked for Lamorak and the others from the drinking hall the other night but didn't see them. After hearing that they had acted as Diana's protectors while Gawain fought Gareth, Mordred didn't trust them enough to participate in what was going to happen here. Agravain was there and a glaring Gareth, among a dozen well-armed knights.

Gawain faced Mordred, ignoring the men at his back. The horses snorted and sidled. Steam puffed from their nostrils in the crisp air. How had she and Gawain not heard the danger?

"Because I damped the sound." The weary voice was disembodied until, from behind Mordred, Merlin walked out of the trees. He looked older than he had when she had seen him last. Deep lines cut his face around his mouth and his eyes had dark circles under them. But they still blazed with swirling color. Some of those colors no human eyes should be. His eyes glowed gold and red and orange, mauve and burgundy, as well as blue and gray and brown and green and black. He glanced to her, then fixed his stare on Gawain. Disbelief, wonder, chased across his face as he recognized his son.

Diana shot a glance to Gawain and saw a bleak look there. His mouth was set in a grim line. Here was the first real evidence that his father supported Mordred.

"I have new allies since last we fought," Mordred smirked. "You'd not win now."

Would Merlin stand against his own son? Or stand by and let him be killed?

"Let's try your theory," Gawain growled. He made no move for his sword. He'd never make it. Agravain was swinging a lethal-looking battle-axe casually at his side, waiting for a chance to use it on Gawain. Gawain waited. He didn't even have a shirt, let alone armor or chain mail, or even hardened leather as protection. Diana couldn't help but imagine those sharp swords and axes cleaving his bare flesh. It made her want to vomit.

Mordred laughed. "Why should I exert myself? My men can dispatch you."

"Give me my sword and shield and bring them on. When I've finished with them, I'll take you." Gawain's voice was steady, as if he were talking about taking them on in a game of pickup basketball, instead of in a battle where he would suffer terrible wounds.

"Don't be so eager to die, boy," Merlin said softly. "There's always time for that."

Mordred tore his gaze away from Gawain and glanced to the women. His expression dismissed Beth and came back to Diana. "I want that one, too." Then he blinked and jerked back to Beth. "Oh, ho . . . ," he murmured. The gears churned in his head behind his eyes. "What have we here? Some . . . some anomaly of time?" His horse sidled in impatience. "I must know more of this. Bring all three." He turned his horse in a short circle to steady it. "Bind the man tightly."

Mordred cantered off down the path. The knights bore down on Diana and Gawain. Diana could feel Gawain thinking about lunging for his sword, but before he could act on his intention the sword moved smoothly through the air to Merlin's outstretched hand. The shield followed. There was no incantation, no visible sorcery. Merlin's brow didn't crease in concentration. The sword and shield simply did his bidding. Diana swallowed hard. Magic should have to be harder than that, shouldn't it? Gawain stared at his father, his face tightening into a mask that only just covered the sense of betrayal underneath.

Merlin turned without a word and trudged up the path after Mordred, carrying Gawain's sword and shield, while several of the men encircling Diana, Beth, and Gawain leaped from their horses. They jerked Gawain's hands behind his back and bound them with a length of rope. They tied another rope around his neck, and the end of this one they tossed to their captain.

Apparently no one knew about Gawain's ability to turn into mist. He'd be able to escape any bonds. That gave Diana some comfort. It was little enough. They were outnumbered and weaponless. Even Merlin was ranged against them, in spite of the fact that Gawain was his son.

"Bring the women," Gareth ordered. He spurred his dapple gray into a trot, dragging Gawain into a stumble beside him. The others herded Diana and Beth before them. Diana put her arm around Beth's shoulder as a sword point urged them into a jog. This couldn't be good for Beth so late in her pregnancy. Beth cradled her belly as she ran. Soon they were gasping for breath, but no one allowed them to rest. Now they could see the palisades of Camelot above them on the hill. And just entering the gates was a party on horseback of perhaps a score. The rich colors of their cloaks were like bright jewels in the morning sun.

"Guinevere's party." Gareth turned to shout back to his companions. "She's arrived from the north!" Excitement spread through the men around Diana. Mordred cantered up the hill toward the new arrivals.

"Get a move on," Gareth barked, giving Gawain's rope a jerk. His horse started into a slow canter. Gawain ran beside Gareth's knee to keep up. She wished she could see his eyes, read his expression. Or maybe she didn't. Guinevere was here. Instead of excited to see the legendary queen, Diana felt as though the last nail had been pounded into her coffin.

Chapter Nineteen

The courtyard was filled with milling horses, large men, and scurrying servants when Diana and Beth stumbled through the gates. Beth leaned over to catch her breath.

"Are you all right?" Diana murmured as their guard surged forward to greet the newcomers. Apparently they knew the men of Guinevere's escort well.

Beth nodded, but the face she turned up to Diana alternately flushed and went white. Not a good sign. Mordred was helping a woman down from a heavy-boned white horse. So that was a palfrey. Diana had never been quite sure what they looked like.

She would have known Guinevere anywhere. She must have been much younger than Arthur when they wed, for even though there was a strand or two of gray in her beautiful red-gold hair, she was a woman in the prime of her life. Her pale skin glowed and even from here Diana could tell that her eyes were green. Her dress was hunter green, and flowed like it was wool. Her cape was a rich russet, trimmed in fox fur. Mordred knelt in front of her on one knee.

"Welcome, my queen. I hope your journey was not too tiring."

"Why have my meditations been interrupted?" Guinevere had regal ice in her tone.

"A monastery is no place for a queen," Merlin said, rising. "You belong at Camelot."

"With Arthur gone, I no longer belong here," she said, looking like she belonged here far more than Mordred and his band.

"You must rest from your journey. Take some food and drink," Mordred said, not at all disconcerted by her damping tone. "And then we'll talk."

Gawain's broad back was to Diana. All she could see was the tension in the set of his shoulders. Her own shoulders sagged. Gawain's one true love was back from the nunnery in which she'd been immured. If they somehow won through (however unlikely that was) he would stay here with her. Even if she wouldn't have him as a lover, he would serve her. A parfait knight's honor would demand it.

The issue wouldn't come up. Gawain would never be able to kill Mordred, bound as he was, with all these men around him. And there was Merlin's magic to be reckoned with. Merlin could counter Gawain's power to turn into mist. It looked like Merlin could do about anything.

Merlin was standing to one side, a silent observer to the queen's welcome. His stare shifted from Gawain, to Diana, to Beth, and though he was perhaps thirty feet away, Diana could see his eyes roil with speculative color.

Mordred turned to glance at them. "Take this scum away. I'll deal with them later." He turned his attention back to Guinevere. The queen looked around, apparently to see the "scum," but her eyes registered no recognition. She wouldn't recognize Merlin's son in Gawain. He would have been ten when she last saw him. What boy of that age would even catch a queen's eye?

So the scum was pushed and prodded into a window-

less hut made of unpeeled logs at the far end of the palisade from the great two-storied hall that had been
Arthur's home when he ruled with Guinevere. The smell
of the dirt-floored hut was almost overwhelming: earth,
urine, and body odor and . . . and blood. Old blood. Gawain fell to his knees as they shoved him inside. The door
was heaved shut. A huge squared timber clunked into
place to lock them in.

Dusty rays of light streamed in from tiny gaps between
the logs. Guess they didn't care if the cell got cold in win-
ter. They hadn't bothered with wattle in the crevices. As
Diana's eyes grew used to the dimness she could make
out that Beth was pale and beginning to shake. This was
bad.

Diana glanced back to see Gawain pacing the perime-
ter, hands still tied behind his back, looking for chinks in
the walls big enough that he could peer out. She eased her
mother down into a corner. Diana pulled Beth's hair from
around her face and made soothing sounds. Guards were
talking outside the cell door. Two? No, three.

Apparently Gawain's quest was fruitless, for he turned
into the room, his expression grim. "At least we've bought
some time. Mordred will be busy with Guinevere for a
while."

She heard Beth's cry of pain before Beth made it. *Oh
no!* Diana held Beth's shoulders tight and looked to Gawain. She didn't have to tell him what was happening.
"Relax now. You're close to term and under stress. It
doesn't mean anything."

As the pain passed, Beth looked up at her with serious
eyes. Nothing need be said. They all knew what was happening, no matter what Diana said. Time was running out.

Diana stood and went to Gawain. "How long does she
have?" he whispered in modern English, so Beth couldn't
understand them if she heard.

"I don't know."

"We can't let her baby . . . We can't let you be born in here. It's filthy."

"Then we have to get out before she bears the child."

Gawain's eyes darted around the cell. "I had thought to wait until dark. . . . Even if I get out unnoticed in daylight and kill the guards, how will I get two women, one in labor, out the gates?"

"You won't," Diana answered steadily. "So leave us behind."

Gawain practically rolled his eyes. "I'm not doing that."

"Of course you are. What's the worst that can happen? We can't save Beth. If the baby dies, too, I'm never born, I never come back in the time machine. I don't take Mordred. He dies of his wounds, and history is put right again." What she didn't say was that Gawain wouldn't have to risk being killed by Mordred's guard before he could even reach Mordred. Gawain wouldn't want to do anything just to avoid a fight. That would be against his stupid honor. "You grow up to fight a guerrilla war against the Saxons, which is ultimately unsuccessful."

"Sounds wonderful. I don't think so." He turned and peered out through the cracks between the door and the frame. "My father said you were important."

"You know it's the only way." He had to see it, given time. She would never have existed. What would that be like?

"You're forgetting some things," Gawain said, his back still to her.

"Like what?"

He turned. "What if the baby doesn't die? What if you're here when the child is born?"

He was right. That was bad. "The note in the book says

if you meet your former self, you merge into that self. You can't get out again." She waited for him to say something, but he just stared at her. "Okay, so that's a danger. I would be trapped inside a baby until she grew up. So, after you get out, I'll call for the guard and . . ." Her theory ran out of gas. Why would a guard let her out of the cell? Well, there was one way. . . . "I'll let him think I'll have sex with him if he lets me out for a while." Actually, he'd probably take what he wanted without her consent. But she wouldn't say that. Gawain would never leave them then.

Gawain pressed his lips together. After a moment he managed to say through gritted teeth, "I'm not fond of that one, either."

"Well, I'm not fond of any of it," she snapped. "But we're running out of choices here."

"I'll find a way. I'll get you out and get your mother to somewhere safe to have the baby. You have to survive, Diana." He looked so fierce and so protective it was almost frightening. But she couldn't be frightened of Gawain, not anymore. How long it had been since he was a sinister stalker in her mind? She could be frightened *for* him, of course. That was all too easy.

She moved up to him and put her hand on his bare chest. Even in such horrible circumstances, that stirred the woman in her. It made her feel alive. And that felt good just now. "History is more important than any one of us," she said softly. He knew that. He just had a hard time accepting what it meant.

"Okay," he said grimly. "We wait until dark if we can. In any case, if she gets close to giving birth, I escape. You call the guard and tell him I've gone. Do whatever you must to get out of here when the child is born. You have to survive, Diana."

It always came back to that. Why her? Why Diana Dearborn, romance writer? Or Dilly, the tagalong girl she didn't remember? How the hell could *she* be important?

She sighed. "At least turn to mist and get out of your bonds."

He shook his head. "It costs me some strength, and if I have to do it again, it will come more slowly. I'd better save myself."

That frightened her. "Come here," she said softly. "I'll loosen them."

What Gawain wasn't going to tell Diana was that even if they made it to nightfall, even if he escaped and killed the guards and let them out of the cell, his father would never let them escape. He could see everything. He knew everything. And he served Mordred.

Gawain still couldn't reconcile that with the father he had known. Sure, Gawain was a disappointment to him. Gawain had doomed his father to be forever unable to pass on his great gift. Sure, Diana coming back in time had changed things. But Merlin had always stood for what he believed, and he had enough power to enforce it. He didn't help men like Mordred cause the people of Britain to suffer. Would Merlin help Mordred against his own son? Gawain knew his father had recognized him. If Gawain was killed by Agravain and Gareth and the guard, would Merlin protect Diana and her mother from Mordred's revenge?

He had to. If Merlin stood against them, there was no winning through.

Diana insisted on working at Gawain's ropes until her fingers were raw. She couldn't untie the knots. It was only when her mother began crying out more frequently that Diana's attention was diverted from her task. The afternoon dragged on. After a particularly long labor pain,

Diana sprang up and screamed at the guards to let them out for the sake of the baby.

One laughed, and Diana pounded on the door with her fists in fury. Another called softly, "We dare not let you out, mistress. My lord Medraught has ordered you imprisoned."

Diana sank to the floor. She was feeling utterly ineffectual. Gawain knew that feeling.

But it wouldn't be long now. The light was almost gone. He would turn to mist and try his best for the two women. He daren't fail, and yet he knew in his heart he was not up to the task before him. That feeling was familiar, too.

He sat and waited. He'd lost the feeling in his hands now. Could he even hold a sword if he could take one from a guard?

Diana's mother was sobbing in the corner after the last contraction. It would be touch-and-go to wait for nightfall. The guards outside fell suddenly silent. Very suddenly. Gawain pushed himself up. Something was . . .

A soft sparkling glow started in the corner of the cell, casting a pale light over their squalid surroundings. He heard Diana gasp.

"Don't be afraid," he said. "It's my father." Of course, he couldn't be sure that they shouldn't be afraid. Who knew his father now? He surely didn't.

The silver sparkles resolved themselves into Merlin, except for a glowing ball of sparkles that floated in the air and lit the cell with a cold light. How strange that all the stories of Camelot had him wearing some goofy pointed hat and robes covered with moons and stars. He was never foolish. Merlin was wearing a fine embroidered jerkin over leather breeches and soft, practical boots. He had no scabbard, no sword (what need had he of swords?), but the belt that circled his waist was finely tooled. His beard was less shot with gray than Gawain remembered it when he last saw Merlin, but otherwise the lined face was much the same: more tired perhaps, a little more worn. But his eyes glowed fiercely with their swirling colors. He never hid his eyes. Why should he? He was Merlin.

He went opaque and looked around, frowning. "I apologize for your 'accommodations,'" he said. "Mordred was ever crude."

Beth let out a low moan. She had grown seriously weaker over the long hours of the day. She could barely cry out with her pain. Diana wiped her forehead with a piece of cloth she had torn from Beth's own shift.

"Can you help her?" Diana asked. How Gawain loved the fact that she asked boldly, though she certainly must be frightened by his father's appearance.

Merlin shook his head. "I can help no one except Mordred these days."

"I knew you had a hard heart, but I never thought you'd stand on the side of evil," Gawain accused.

"Sometimes a man has no choice, my son. You *are* my son, aren't you?"

Gawain nodded once. "I'm sorry to say, I am."

"You're from the future." His father nodded to himself. "How else could it be? How did you come?"

"We used my machine," Diana said. "Don't you remember me coming back and taking Mordred with me?"

Merlin shook his head. Gawain didn't remember that, either. What did that mean?

His father had been examining Gawain, and now he smiled. "You've grown into a fine man, Son." Then his smile collapsed. "I hope to keep it that way." He pressed a hand to his forehead, covering his eyes. "I . . . I see so many contrasting images in the pools and the streams these days. I . . . I don't know the true path."

"That's my fault," Diana said ruefully. "I fouled things

up by saving Mordred. I thought he would be killed, you
see, and . . . and now everything is changed."

"I see you in my visions, too, my dear. What is your
name?"

"Diana Dearborn." She turned away to Beth, who
groaned weakly. "I'm her daughter."

"About to be born?"

"I . . . I think so."

Merlin frowned again, thinking. "But wasn't she one
of Mordred's . . . ?"

"Diana is Mordred's daughter, too," Gawain said
roughly. "The only good thing he ever did as far as I can
see." He took a breath and calmed himself. His father
could help them if he would. He might be the only one
who could. "We have to set history right. Mordred was
not supposed to live. He was supposed to die of the wound
Arthur gave him, some time after the battle, from infection. After he fathered Diana. The Saxons were meant to
prevail. When Diana saved Mordred and we sent him
back, he, with *your* help, will hold this area against the
Saxons. It changes everything down the centuries. We're
here to put it right."

"By killing this young woman's own father?"

"Yes," Diana said. Her voice was steady. Gawain was
proud of her. "We must. And it's not as though I have
known him as a father. Gawain can do it. He's strong, and
he has magic powers. If you stop helping Mordred, Gawain will find a way to kill him once we're free."

"Magic powers?" His father's head turned toward
Gawain. "Tell me."

Gawain didn't miss the fact that his father wasn't making any commitments. He colored. His paltry powers
were nothing beside those of his father. He cleared his
throat. "They're nothing."

"They are so *not* nothing," Diana protested. "He can

turn into a mist and get through any door or lock or crevice. He can enter people's dreams. And he uses his gifts only for good. You should be proud of him."

To Gawain's surprise, his father softened. "And did you have these powers even when you were ten and you just didn't tell me?"

Gawain shook his head. "They came on at puberty. I didn't tell you then, either," he added contentiously. Telling half the truth was a sin of omission. It was time to stop that. "They were little enough. You would have been disappointed." *As you must be now.* He couldn't read his father's expression.

"Your wrists must be giving you pain," Merlin said. He held out a hand, and the ropes dropped to the ground.

Blood rushed into Gawain's hands. Pain stabbed through them. His wrists were raw and bleeding from the coarse hemp rope. "Thank you," he said stiffly.

"How is it you and the girl are from the future if you were born in this time, my son?"

"You sent us forward. Well, you sent Diana, and me with her to protect her. She's the important one."

"I did? How interesting. I wonder how I do it?" He considered Diana. "Hmmmm. She *is* important. I feel it. And yet *how*? That I do not see."

"Don't you know how?" Diana almost wailed. "We don't. And *why*?"

"Didn't I tell you when I sent you forward? Or give you instructions on what to do?"

Gawain shook his head. He should be disgusted with his father but felt only his own inadequacy, as always. It seemed his fault he didn't know. "You said I'd know what to do when the time came." He brushed over his failings. He had to get his father to help them. "But however she is important, the fact is, you said she was. You used all your power to send us forward. You can't let Mordred kill her now."

"I doubt he'd kill her," Merlin mused.

"He'd do worse than that." Diana spoke up. "Well, maybe it's not worse than killing, but he's . . . he's sort of indicated that he'd like to . . . bed me."

Merlin rolled that over in his mind. Gawain saw Diana's eyes open wide at the fact that his father didn't appear to be disgusted by that fact. Disgust sure washed over Gawain. How could his father even . . . ?

"No. No, on the whole I don't think that would do. Mordred's powers are considerable, true. Would inbreeding do the trick? Hmmmm. Do you have any powers yourself, my dear?"

"She does," Gawain interjected over Diana's self-deprecating protest. "But you're not going to breed her back to Mordred for the sake of the magic." Like he could stop whatever his father wanted to do.

"What are her powers?"

"She finds lost things, and knows what people will say before they say them."

"Except you," Diana corrected. "Actually except both of you and Mordred."

"That might change things." Merlin got a faraway look in his constantly changing eyes.

"Look, Father, Diana is not going to bed Mordred. Mordred needs to be dead for us to put history right again. You have to help us."

"That's where it gets difficult," Merlin said, coming back from wherever his gaze had gone. "I can't."

"Won't," Gawain said through gritted teeth. "I saw what he's doing to the people. He's broken their spirits. Even Lamorak bends to his will. You can't tell me Mordred isn't evil."

"He is evil," Merlin sighed. "So evil he's taken what's most dear to me and hidden it where I can't find it. He'll destroy it if I don't keep him in power."

"Your scrying bowl?" What was so precious that Merlin would sacrifice his honor?

Merlin looked up and the clouds racing across his eyes went still. "You, boy. He's got you. A younger you, of course."

Gawain stopped breathing for a moment. "Me?" he finally asked, sucking in a huge breath.

"What else would be as dear to me as the only son I ever allowed myself to love? He's got you in a cave somewhere—you know I can't see into caves—with his men guarding you. He'll put you to death if I don't do his bidding. So I can't help you without killing the younger you. The older you would just disappear in a puff of smoke or something if the boy of ten died."

Gawain's mind danced. *He* was his father's most prized possession? Even though he was a constant disappointment? Was his father lying? Not about some things. It was true Merlin couldn't see into caves. "But the nearest caves . . ."

"Are miles from here," Merlin agreed. "By the time I found you Mordred would have sent word and you'd be dead."

"Well, if you don't help us get out of here," Diana interrupted, "Gawain will be dead anyway, just a little later in his life. And my mother will die before she can even give birth."

Beth's breathing was torturous. Her eyelids fluttered. She was sweating and gray.

"She's bleeding internally," Merlin announced. "So let's see. We have to get a live birth here, find my son and free him, and kill Mordred? Even I have my limits. We can't do all three. Perhaps we can ensure that you are born alive, my dear. That must be enough for now."

"She can't be here when the baby is born. Two versions

of a person can't be in the same place at the same time," Gawain said. "It's a trick of time."

"And we have to do all three things sometime, even if we can't kill Mordred today," Diana said. "Because we need all three to make history right. I . . . I can find lost things. I'll find the young Gawain if you can just get us out of here."

"I'll go with you, and do the rescuing part." Gawain was sure at least he could do that.

"You can't be in the same place as the young you, either." Diana looked so frustrated.

"Get her out of this cell and go with her, Father, to protect her and rescue the young me."

"Can you see the babe safely born?" Merlin mused. "Might be cesarean. If the babe dies . . ."

"I'll have to, and hope the babe comes before Mordred calls for me. When they come to get us, I must go. It's my opportunity to kill Mordred." And he was honor bound to do it.

"I won't see you march bravely to your death," Diana protested. "I won't! We'll find another way to kill Mordred, another time. Merlin can help us, if we free your younger self."

But they lost the power to choose. The sound of guards coming across the courtyard was unmistakable. Merlin took a breath and said, "I'm sorry." He faded from view.

Gawain turned to the door. The heavy bar was lifted with a great *chunking* sound. Diana stared in horror at him from her place beside Beth. There was but one choice. They must all go up to the hall. Maybe the women at the hall would take pity on Beth and care for her. Maybe Diana could separate herself from Beth before she gave birth. Maybe he could find a way to kill Mordred before Mordred did whatever he was likely to do to him. Maybe.

The door swung open on a forest of pikes, lit by the torches the guard carried. Was one of the guards Lamorak? But no, Mordred was too smart for that. The flickering torchlight revealed the smirking faces of Gareth and Agravain.

"Come out and bring the girl. The king would see you now." They knew very well that Gawain was unlikely to survive the interview. Diana would survive to be delivered to Mordred's bed.

Gawain stepped out into the circle of pikes. "The pregnant woman is in labor. We must bring her to the women up at the hall. She requires their attendance."

"The king gave no instructions for her. She stays here."

"Oh, ho . . . you've managed to shed your bonds." Agravain snapped his fingers and one of the guards produced some iron shackles. He made his way through the forest of pikes and locked Gawain's hands into the shackles behind his back. At least they didn't cut off circulation. He could fight. And he would have to fight. He was going to have Diana with him. He tried not to think about Beth's chances of producing a live baby on her own.

"Get out here, woman," Gareth barked.

Diana came out into the torchlight behind him, looking small and vulnerable. One of the guards gripped her by the arm and the whole party started toward the lit hall.

He must protect Diana. Somehow he must stay alive long enough to kill Mordred. Then if he died, it was his lot to do so. He only hoped his errant father would take care of Diana once he was dead, if only so she could find his younger self and ensure he lived to fulfill his purpose. He glanced back to the dark maw of the cell where Diana's mother lay, feeling helpless. *Deliver her alive,* he prayed. That seemed unlikely.

Chapter Twenty

The hall was bright with torches after the dark of the courtyard. A feast was in full swing, the smell of food and drink permeating the air. Diana would have bruises on her arm tomorrow, the guard was gripping her arm so tightly. If she lived until tomorrow. Or if she lived, she might just wish herself dead, if Gawain was dead and her father had raped her.

Mordred sat sprawled on an ornately carved chair at the top of the long table. A throne. At the foot of the table an open space had been left in front of the great fireplace. Into this open space the squadron of guards marched their prisoners. Gawain, ahead of her, looked so defiant, so brave. She was incredibly proud of him. And incredibly afraid for him. Women's eyes from around the hall turned toward him.

Speaking of which, where was Guinevere? Surely this feast was in her honor. Maybe she hadn't fallen in with Mordred's plans and he'd imprisoned her. Maybe she just didn't like the dinner show, since it was likely to be bloody. Lamorak and his men were also nowhere in sight.

"Well, well, the traitors!" Mordred called as he took a casual swig of wine. "Shall we start with the girl? An appetizer, so to speak, to whet our appetites for the main

course. You may all have a bite, so to speak." Diana tried
to keep her face from showing her fear. Rape. A lot of it.
Could she bear it? The guard who held her arm took her
tunic and ripped it at the neck. He tossed it away. She was
left in her thin linen shift. Gawain growled and strained
against his shackles. The pikes poked at his bare torso
and several bright drops of blood bloomed at their points.

"She's your own daughter, you tyrant," Gawain bellowed.

"My daughter? Yes, I thought so this afternoon when I
saw her likeness to the whore."

"Would you see your own kin raped?" Gawain asked
from between gritted teeth.

"There are many like her. What is she to me, except
the one who exiled me back to this godforsaken hell-
hole?" His expression darkened as he talked. "She has
betrayed me on so many levels the least she can do is provide some recreation for me and my men."

Diana began to pant. Her own father was going to rape
her. Gareth came up and lifted Diana's chin. "You are
good and great, my king." She reached up to hold his wrist
and bit his finger as hard as she could. Gareth's shout of
pain turned into a hiss. He backhanded her across the
cheek. She fell to the floor. How many times had she written someone getting hit, then just shaking off the effects?
Not true. Not true. Diana couldn't breathe. Her whole
face stung. Her jaw felt like it had been dislocated. Tears
coursed down her cheeks.

"Bastard!" Gawain shouted. They were pulling him
away. He struggled.

Laughter rang around the hall. Serving wenches scur-
ried out the back door, so as not to catch any leftover lust.
It seemed to hang in the air. When she could get her
breath, she looked to Gawain for strength. He had gone
absolutely still.

"Take me," he said. The laughter subsided. "I will serve you and your men in her place."

Diana turned shocked eyes around the hall. Didn't Gawain know what they had in mind? You couldn't just substitute a man for a woman. But she saw the speculation in Gareth's eyes. She glanced around the room and saw it echoed in at least some others. They were willing to rape Gawain. How could that be? She'd seen these lusty men pinching women and nuzzling their breasts. But rape was a matter of dominance and cruelty, not sex. She'd read that many times. They wanted to hurt and humiliate Gawain. Rape was sure one way to do that.

"You can't," she cried.

Mordred raised his brows and shrugged. "Interesting. Do you realize what you offer? Very well. I accept. When you lose the fight, as lose you will, my men will have a go at you. Let's see what we're getting. Strip him."

"I'll take care of that," Gawain said. His face was closed and cold. "You let the girl go."

Mordred gestured with one finger. "Unlock his chains." Agravain stepped forward to do his lord's bidding with a smirk.

Gawain began pulling off his boots. "Send the girl to Merlin."

"Merlin?" Mordred turned his head. Merlin was suddenly standing by his king's shoulder. Diana hadn't seen him come in. Apparently no one had. There were several gasps.

"I'll take her, Your Majesty," Merlin said calmly. But his words had strange force.

"You can't rape him," she cried as her guard dragged her up and hustled her over to Merlin. "And *you* can't stand by and see your own son . . ."

"Quiet, girl," Merlin said softly.

Diana opened her mouth to finish her sentence, but no

sound came out. She tried to shout. Nothing. Laughter rang around the hall from some knights. Others looked repelled. "One of your more useful tricks, Merlin," Mordred observed. "You must teach me how to do that sometime."

"Your wish is my command, liege." Merlin bowed slightly and gestured at Diana's guard to let her go. He gathered her into his side.

"Do you have an interest here?" Mordred's eyes were hooded. If Merlin chose to free his son, Mordred couldn't stop him, and Mordred must know that.

"My son is ten and in your power. That is the son who must interest me now." Merlin's face was expressionless.

"Wise choice. You will live with it for many years." Mordred looked satisfied. "Do you care to watch then?"

Gawain, naked now, looked even more vulnerable against the backdrop of chain mail and hardened leather, sharp swords and pikes. Diana couldn't even scream. She twisted in Merlin's grasp, but he was implacable.

"Violence upsets my ability to conjure for days," Merlin said. "I shall retire."

"Bring the girl to me tomorrow. She shall take me to the machine and give it power."

Merlin nodded. "Call and I will bring her."

Merlin wasn't going to save her. Her reprieve was to be only a day. He wasn't going to save his own son. Mordred would prevail. When she refused to start the machine, he'd torture her. She didn't have an ounce of faith in her ability to withstand torture. He'd range across history, wreaking havoc. Gawain would be raped and killed. Her mother might already be dying without even the comfort of someone at her deathbed. And if the babe died, too, Diana would just . . . cease to exist, she guessed. Merlin put his arm around her shoulders and drew her out. The strangest feeling came over her, as though she was distant from herself. She turned over her shoulder, and her eyes locked with Gawain's. His determined look turned soft violet with sadness and . . . longing. How could he look like that when everything was about to come apart at the seams?

"Give him a sword and your best man as an opponent!" Mordred called out behind her. "And do try not to actually kill him! We want him alive, if bloody, for the festivities to follow!"

Merlin shut the door to the main hall. They were in some kind of storage chamber. Wheels of cheese and stacks of bedding were piled everywhere.

"Quickly, out here." Merlin pushed open the door. "We must get down to the stockade."

"Why?" The spell he had cast on her had worn off. But her voice was faint in her ears.

"Because we have to save the baby. You are . . . you're fading."

She looked down at her hands. It was true. They were almost transparent. Merlin scooped her up in his arms as though she weighed nothing, and the next thing she knew she was inside the cell where she had left her mother. Merlin struck his sparkling light.

Beth's head was turned to the side. Her face was ashen. Her eyes stared at nothing. Merlin knelt beside her.

"Mother? Mother?" Diana's voice was rising. She realized she was wringing her hands.

"You can't help her now." Merlin closed her mother's eyes with his fingers. "We must help you." He placed his hand over Beth's still-full belly. "The babe still lives."

"Then I can't be here." Diana swallowed. Too much, too fast. She had to think. "You save the baby if you can. I'll find your son."

"Go now then," Merlin said. He was taking out a knife from his belt. "I must be quick."

Diana turned and ran for the door still hanging open, as they'd left it. She dashed around the corner and put her back against the wall of the stockade. She felt weak. She dared not look at her hand again. *Think!* She'd wanted to escape with Gawain and Beth, maybe save Beth's life, then come back another day to kill Mordred. Now everything had gone wrong. Gawain must fight, and if he lost . . . Diana pushed that thought aside. If she thought about that room full of knights raping Gawain she'd be paralyzed. And she must find young Gawain and somehow free him so Merlin could help her Gawain. Where would young Gawain be?

And if where he was held was miles away in some cave in the hills as Merlin feared?

But Mordred wouldn't let something so precious as the thing he held over his wizard's head be miles away. *Think!* She forced herself to go still. She thought about the boy as she had seen him last among the standing stones with his father, young Gawain, with his flopping forelock of dark hair and his gray-green eyes that would someday swirl with color like his father's. Reedy ten-year-old body. Freckles from days in the sun. She had him. She felt him.

If I were you, where would I be? The breath sighed in and out of her lungs. She couldn't quite— The cry of a baby interrupted her thoughts, but she felt stronger suddenly. She breathed in and out. *Where would I be?*

She blinked in surprise and took off at a run across the deserted demesne. He was here. Right under Merlin's nose. She ran around the hall, refusing to listen to the shouts from within. *Concentrate. Do your part. Be as brave as he is.* Behind the hall was a huge excavation. Stones climbed out of the hole in several places, unfinished, crude scaffolding hugging incipient towers like spidery lovers. One tower thrust, almost complete, into the air.

Diana stood at the edge of the pit. He was here. In a cave. She could feel the damp from the night collecting on the stones. She looked down.

Part of the excavation was already floored with stone. But that wasn't the lowest level. She spotted the stairs to her left and scrambled down them. There was a second flight down from the first. She peered down into the dark. But there was no choice. She felt her way down the stone walls into the darkness. At the bottom she waited, hoping her eyes would adjust. She felt along the wall to a gap in the stone. Her hand hit steel. A cell bar. She was in a dungeon.

The dungeon of Mordred's new castle. He'd built the dungeon first. Young Gawain was being kept in the dungeon, and no one had thought to look there because it wasn't a cave and it wasn't finished and it wasn't yet supposed to house prisoners. But it was being used, and it acted like a cave as far as Merlin's powers were concerned.

There! A faint glow flickered ahead. She made her way as quietly as she could toward the light. She couldn't hear anything. Maybe there wouldn't be guards.

Then a shadow crossed the light. There was at least one guard. As far as Diana was concerned it might as well be a dozen. She'd never be able to get young Gawain out now.

Gawain leaned on the sword they'd given him, getting his breath. The biggest man of the guard squadron lay sprawled on the floor, his lifeblood leaking into the wood. Gawain had a shallow cut across his left pectoral, nothing more, in spite of the fact that he was naked and they had given him no shield.

"Well done." Mordred clapped. "Such ingenious fighting. You learned well from the twenty-first century. But that just means we'll have to up the odds."

Gawain stood, sword held lightly in his hand. He could take some out before they could subdue him. Just go berserker and start killing. It was tempting.

"Uh-uhhhh," Mordred scolded. "You have to play by the rules. I get to say who you'll face next, and you have to keep fighting or we'll go get the girl and go back to the original plan."

Gawain swallowed. There was no getting round this. When there were few enough that he could be sure to take them all, then he could start wholesale carnage. After that he could kill Mordred. God willing that his strength lasted. In the meantime, his job was to keep them busy and away from Diana. He took a breath and nodded.

"I doubt you'll do as well against three. Gareth? You choose the opponents. And remember, don't kill him. Wounds to weaken him only."

God give me strength, Gawain prayed. *I can do this. I can do this for Diana.*

Merlin dared not translocate with a newborn babe in his arms, and one who was a bit premature and stressed from long labor at that, no matter how much of a hurry he was in. The child might not survive it. So he took the outside staircase to the great hall two steps at a time, the babe carefully covered in the linen he had torn from her dead mother's shift. He was glad the upstairs sleeping chambers had an entrance to the outside, as well as a staircase up from the hall.

It had taken some time to perform an operation that felt more like butchery than surgery, but he had to be sure not to damage the child. The poor little thing was tiny, but she had a fierce spirit. Her first cry had been mewling and weak but determined. Now he could but hope she could last until he could find a wet nurse to tend her. She would have to wait until he could save her future self, and his son. Actually, he had to save both versions of his son. And judging by the raucous cries from inside the hall, he didn't have much time.

He wouldn't think of what he had left Gawain to suffer at the hands of those bastards. There was but one way to thread this needle. Gawain was strong. And he was a good man. He would survive until Merlin could get to him. Could Diana really find his ten-year-old son? He prayed to the gods who had given him his powers that she could.

There was but one knight standing at the landing. "I would see the queen," he said in his most commanding voice. A raucous cheer rose from the hall below. Merlin steeled his heart.

The guard recognized the king's wizard and stood aside. Merlin pushed into the room.

Guinevere was surrounded by four women in nuns' garb. The golden light from the sconces bathed her red-gold hair in radiance. Her nose was aquiline, her lips full. He had never seen a more beautiful woman, even though she had been crying.

"Your Majesty." He inclined his head as she jerked around.

"Don't call me that, Merlin. I am no longer queen here. My liege is dead." Her lovely brows drew together. "And I will not be Mordred's queen, though I die refusing. So you, who serve him so willingly, will not find a companion in the demise of your honor."

"That is just what I wanted to hear."

She examined him. "You were ever loyal, not only to my husband, but to the kingdom. To see it suffering so . . . My companions say he is torturing that poor knight down there. . . . How can you keep him in power?"

"Despite appearances, I serve him most unwillingly and would now shed my yoke. You can help me. Care for this child." He lifted the linen reveal the wrinkled and red visage too weak to cry. "She is important, but I have work before I can see that Mordred gets his just desserts."

Guinevere rose at once. The nuns hovered, making cooing noises. One gathered the tiny bundle from Merlin's arms. Guinevere frowned. "A nunnery is no place to raise a child and it is the last place to find a wet nurse. A nunnery must be my destination, if I can leave here alive."

"It is my job to raise her, my lady. Just take care of her tonight."

Guinevere softened. She nodded.

Merlin straightened. "If my intrepid friend prevails you will have another charge on your hospitality tonight. I would stay to give you solace, my lady, but I must hasten to help her."

"Go," she said. "And give my worst to Mordred."

Merlin shut the door behind him. He could only hope that with a pool of water for scrying he could find Diana before she entered the cave and was lost to his sight. She would need his help this night. Now where to find a pool of water? The compound was muddy, but there were no pools. No time to get to the river . . . Barrels! The ones they used to collect rainwater in case Camelot was besieged. There was one near his quarters. He took off at a run.

Diana slipped up to the turn in the corridor and pressed her back against the cold stone wall. The guard paced. The sound of his boots on the stone echoed in the passageway. She felt naked in her shift. What could she do against a big man like that? How was she going to get young Gawain out? Her heart fluttered in panic as she thought of

Gawain the man fighting for his life in the hall. They would weaken him, and then . . . She wouldn't think of that.

She couldn't get Merlin to help her unless she wanted to confront the baby and lose herself and all she fought for. She must do this on her own.

Okay. How would she write this? What would her heroine (name TBD) do to get the boy out of the dungeon? Get the key. The guard must have keys. Distraction. That's what she needed. But then what? The guard wouldn't just stand by while she unlocked the cell. He'd overpower her, grab back the keys, and toss her in the cell, too. In a book she would have had the heroine bring him a drugged batch of mead. Not happening here.

Well, if she had to distract him, there was only one way. Would any man look at her that way? She was her mother's daughter. Her mother had been both pretty and courageous. A thrill of grief made Diana's eyelids flutter. *Not now.* She blinked back the emotion. And after that, she'd have to try to wound him at the least. No other choice. She wished she were one of her favorite characters, Anita or Sookie, who were hard as nails and could beat most guys in a fight just by playing dirty. She wasn't like that at all. What could a five-foot-nothing girl do against a guy with a sword and a knife when she didn't even know how to fight dirty?

She slipped around the corner and waited for the guard to see her. He was young. His beard was straggly. The remnant of pimples dusted his cheeks. But he was big nonetheless. He started when he saw her and drew his sword. "Who goes there?"

She smiled, hoping it wasn't a grimace. "Mordred sent me to summon you to the feast." She slid her gaze to the cell and saw the pinched and worried face of the young Gawain peering out from behind the bars set into the arch of the stones. She sent him a look that she hoped said, *Be silent*. She might have just looked terrified.

"I can't go. I must guard the boy." The young guard resumed his pacing.

She glanced to his belt. Keys. Lots of them. And a knife. A very, very big knife in a kind of scabbard on the hip opposite his sword.

She put what she hoped was heat into her eyes and thought, *Coy*. "I must tell Mordred of your dedication." She sidled up to him, acutely conscious that her shift was thin and the cold had made her nipples peak. The young guard was aware of it, too. His eyes drifted downward. "Did you know I'm a bastard? You know what they say of women born out of wedlock. . . ."

"No," he breathed.

She was inside the range of his sword now. "That we are cursed with the lust that created us."

"Is this true?" The young guard's Adam's apple bobbed.

Diana blinked. Behind the young guard's shoulder, hands came out and gripped the bars in the cell next to Gawain's. There was another prisoner here. Well, lucky him. He might get free as well. Or he might just get to watch her die. She shifted her eyes back to the pimply-faced guard. "Yes." She let a slow smile cross her face.

She was close enough now to run her left hand up around his neck. His breath reeked of wine and garlic. He grinned and showed a missing tooth, knocked out in a fight no doubt. He reached out to encircle her waist and draw her to him. "I can scratch your itch, mistress."

Now was the time if there was one. She let her right hand go to his waist. He began to nuzzle her. She fumbled for the knife and grabbed the hilt, pulling. She meant to stab him, there and then, but she found herself backing away instead. He clutched at her, realizing his mistake, but she crouched, knife held low and pointed up. She'd read about how to hold a knife.

He backed up, raising his hands, then broke into a grin. "What now, my feisty maid?"

What now, indeed? She'd blown the whole thing. She'd never be able to get inside his guard again. She was no fighter.

But she didn't need to really fight. She needed the keys. Then she'd hold the knife on him while young Gawain unlocked his cell door. She'd force the guard into the cell and lock it. It could work. All she had to do was make sure he believed she *would* stab him. And of course, she had to keep him from overpowering her and getting the knife back. "Keys. Toss them here."

"Or you'll what?" He was still grinning.

"You're right. I may not be able to kill you. So I'll just go for the groin. Cut those pretty balls," she hissed. "Or maybe mark your face. Then how will you fare with the ladies?"

That made his eyes widen. Just what she wanted. "Now give me the keys."

She could see thoughts skimming through his eyes. It didn't take being telepathic. He thought he'd give her the keys. Then while she was unlocking the door, he'd take the knife and she was his to do what he wanted with. "Very well." He unhooked the keys and tossed them to her. She snatched them out of the air with her left hand.

Speculation passed through his eyes. "I don't think you have the nerve to use that knife on me, little bird." He swirled his cloak off and wrapped it around his arm to protect it.

Uh-oh.

"I will . . . ," she began. But she wouldn't. She couldn't kill a man just because he'd been unlucky enough to draw guard duty tonight. Could she wound him? The last thing she wanted to do was stick a knife into human flesh. He looked like he knew how to prevent her from getting to any vital parts. Why wasn't it as easy as books made it sound?

But there was another way. She backed around to her left, circling the approaching guard. And then, without warning, she tossed the keys into the cell next door to Gawain with the two hands on the bars and the shadowy figure within. Whoever it was, he'd want his freedom. And she needed an ally who would do what she wasn't certain she could.

The guard glanced over, surprised. The hands at the bars caught the keys. The guard must have realized they would soon have company. Diana didn't wait but launched herself at the guard, catching him off balance before he could draw his sword. They tumbled to the stone floor. Diana sent the knife sliding up to the bars of the unknown man's cell where it would do the most good, before the guard could take it from her. He had her by the hair. She kicked and raked her nails across his face, wishing she had kept them longer. Her knee found his groin. She couldn't really get a good swing at his balls, but she did what she could. He bellowed in rage. Diana heard the keys clicking in the lock behind her, clicking again. He couldn't find the right key. The young guard struggled to his feet and jerked her around by her hair.

"Look out, my lady," the boy cried from his cell.

The cell door snicked open. She threw herself as far to the right as she could. The man coming out of the dark cell was Lamorak. He swung the cell door so the outer bar caught the young guard directly in his face. Lamorak followed it with a kick to the guard's belly and bent for the knife. The guard was trying to rise and pulling at his sword hilt at the same time, but he was clearly dazed.

Lamorak grabbed his hair, pulled his head up, and buried the knife in his throat. Blood spurted everywhere, including over Diana. She shrieked and shrieked. The guard's hand relaxed around Diana's hair. She watched his eyes glaze as she gasped for breath. Lamorak pushed him away. He fell backward, dead as a doornail.

Lamorak pulled her to her feet. "You did well, my lady."

"You were great," the boy said, from inside his cell.

"I couldn't kill him," she babbled. "I wasn't strong enough. Or maybe I just didn't have the will to do it. He would have taken the knife away from me. Then where would I be?"

"Look at me." Lamorak turned her face away from the body and made her look into his lined warrior's face. "So you freed me. I was your weapon, and you used me well. You did what you had to do. I wouldn't mourn him. He was one of Mordred's favorites."

"No one deserves that." Her eyes slid back to the body and the growing pool of blood on the floor. He wasn't the only one who didn't deserve what had happened to him. Gawain certainly didn't deserve what was happening to him. She swallowed and tried to get hold of herself, looking around for the keys. "I have to free the boy so Merlin can help us kill Mordred." The keys were still in the door to Lamorak's cell. He retrieved them and handed them to her.

"Kill Mordred? That would be unwise, my lady. He alone keeps back the Saxons."

She fumbled with the lock. When the boy was free, she motioned to them both to get up the stairs. They stumbled up and into the excavated maze above. As they made their way to the second stairway, a sparkling light appeared. Merlin. He solidified into flesh and blood.

"Father," the boy called. "I knew you'd come."

Merlin surveyed his son, Diana in her shift, and

Lamorak, who had brought the guard's sword. "I see I am not only too late but unnecessary. It couldn't see your image in the water until you came up from underground." Young Gawain threw himself into his father's arms. "I'm so sorry you had to go through this," the wizard said. "It was all my fault."

"You couldn't see me," the boy said. "This cell is too much like a cave."

Diana realized that Gawain had always been bright. And forgiving.

"You are a brave boy. You will make a brave and honorable man," Merlin said, his voice husky as he held his son and ran his fingers through his tousled hair.

The boy looked up with total adoration in his eyes, surprised and pleased at the praise.

"Let's get a move on. Now *my* Gawain needs help." She pushed them all forward.

"I must take the boy to Guinevere."

"Well, for God's sake, hurry!" Diana urged. The little party broke into a run.

Gawain had killed four men. A single the first time and three at once the last time. They were laid out by the fireplace. Mordred was furious.

Gawain wouldn't survive, of course. A deep cut on his thigh bled freely. Blood leaked from his shoulder. At least it wasn't his sword arm. He wasn't done yet. But he had to get to Mordred while he still had the strength. After he'd killed Mordred, those who were left would fall upon him. That would be the end of his ordeal. He picked up his sword, panting, and propped his fists on his knees.

"Who's next?" Mordred called, his brow dark with anger. Maybe Gawain could turn Mordred's fury to advantage.

"Perhaps you'd better take a turn yourself," Gawain

growled. "Just weaken me with more wounds, so you can get straight to the finale."

"You're not worth a king's sword," Mordred sneered. "My men can finish you and then we'll see you bleed from your back passage as they take you."

"You're afraid I'd best you." He waited a beat. "Like I did before."

Mordred's eyes narrowed in rage before he arranged his face into boredom. He glanced around to his men. Several were shifting uneasily, even the ones in Gareth's camp. Courage was essential in a king after all. Justice was apparently optional. Honor? Not valued by at least half the room. But courage? "It would hardly be a fair fight. Merlin has given me the true strength of ten. What would it prove for me to kill you?"

"That you are a leader of men."

"I'm the only thing holding the Saxons at bay."

"Only with Merlin's help. He could help someone else." Gawain caught a shift in Mordred's expression that might have been fear. Then the king's eyes narrowed.

"I don't think you can take six men. Gareth," he barked, "you and your best."

Gareth pointed to Agravain and several others.

Six. And Gawain was already weakened. This was most probably it. He'd never get to Mordred now. He'd failed the final time.

Chapter Twenty-one

Diana hurried behind Merlin through the storeroom. They'd sent Lamorak with young Gawain up to Guinevere. It was Lamorak's job to take out the guard on the landing, who probably wouldn't be so eager to let Lamorak and the boy who was supposed to be incarcerated in to see the queen. The sound of clanging swords and grunting men from beyond the storeroom door was frightening. Diana could only take comfort in the fact that it meant Gawain was alive.

"Stay here, Diana," Merlin whispered as they came to the door.

"No way," she hissed back. "I've come across time with him; I'm not chickening out now. I don't care what happens to me."

Merlin frowned. His only choice was to put some kind of spell on her. He apparently decided against that. "Tell me one thing before we go in."

Was the man mad? His son was in there and might be killed at any moment.

"No, he won't," Merlin said, and whether he could read minds or just knew by her expression what she was thinking she couldn't say. "Not yet. I saw it in the scrying pool. Things are sorting themselves out now that the baby is saved and young Gawain is freed. I see that you have been given a book. It is the tool that makes everything else happen. I see that you must come back with the machine or I will never know to send you forward. I just need to know one thing."

"What?" She couldn't keep the impatience from her voice.

"Why didn't he tell me about his powers? You love him. You know him. Why?"

She didn't have time to protest that she didn't love him. That was a lie anyway. There was no time to ask how Merlin knew. So she tried to answer the question. Anything so Merlin would help Gawain. "Because he's always felt he wasn't good enough. You're famous through the ages for your powers. He thought you would despise him because he could never be what you are. That's why he tried so hard to be a perfect knight. It was the best he could do with what he had. He's devastated when he fails at anything. But who can be perfect? Who can be you?"

"I'm far from perfect." Merlin frowned. "I saw the look in his eyes today when I said he was my most precious possession. That was a surprise to him."

"So go help him now, or you'll have failed him twice," Diana said, pressing the older man's hands as if she could press her urgency into him.

Merlin nodded once and pushed through the door into the smoky hall, Diana in his wake.

What met her eyes was a fearful scene. At the far end of the room, beyond the feasting table, Gawain, naked and bleeding, was whirling like those scenes in Bruce Lee movies where he takes on all the members of the rival kung fu school at once. Gawain's sword flashed, parrying madly. Even as she watched, a sword found his hip and sliced the flesh before he could sweep it away. She gasped in horror. Mordred watched from his throne chair,

his back to the newcomers. Some knights cheered wildly.
She heard shouts of, "Well done, Sir Knight!" They cheered
Gawain's prowess and his courage? But they made no
move to help him!

"Enough," Merlin's voice thundered through the hall
like an echoing voice of God.

All turned to Merlin, stunned. Gawain crouched ready,
chest heaving.

"Merlin, I thought you retired." Mordred was wary. He
could sense the change in Merlin.

"Only to fight on another front. Now I return to see to
my son."

"Then you know what will happen." Mordred went
hard.

Merlin looked deeply satisfied. "You no longer possess
that which is dearest to me." He smiled, and Diana had
never seen anything so terrible. He glanced to where Gareth and Agravain had begun to attack Gawain again. "I
said, enough," Merlin said quietly. He held out a palm.

Diana was expecting incantations or something, maybe
a lightning bolt. Instead the men around Gawain just . . .
froze. Gawain was standing in a circle of statues, frozen
in some position of aggression. The thirty or so knights
still cheering from the sidelines were frozen, too. Several
serving maids stood poised with flagon or platter. Only
Gawain, Merlin, Diana, and Mordred seemed to be mo-
bile. Gawain turned, dazed, to survey those around him.
He blinked and shook his head. Diana wanted to run to
him, but Merlin held out a hand to stop her. "It isn't over
yet." That sounded ominous. "Now this is more fair,"
Merlin continued reasonably. "Gawain, you want to dispatch Mordred, I believe."

Gawain nodded, gasping for breath, his eyes big and
blue even from here.

"Mordred, your only chance to kill this troublesome intruder is to do it yourself."

Mordred smirked. "Not a problem."

Merlin held up both hands and parted them. The men surrounding Gawain stalked like puppets backward to the walls, clearing the space in front of the great fireplace. Mordred stood and unsheathed his sword. He came around the long feasting table, his smile broadening.

"Lest you miscalculate!" Merlin called. "Know that I withdraw the special powers you insisted on having." He made a small circular motion with his hand, just at the level of his waist. Mordred looked shocked for a moment. He must be feeling his power ebb away. "You are just a man now, with whatever strength you had before my gift."

Mordred chuckled. He glanced to Gawain, whose hair was plastered to his head with sweat, blood seeping over his body. "I'm fresh and he's not. The outcome is foregone." Mordred turned back to Merlin, frowning. "Unless you intervene."

"I will not intervene," Merlin said. Diana couldn't believe her ears.

But Gawain nodded once to his father. "Let's do it," Gawain said, straightening.

Mordred stalked forward.

"You've *got* to intervene." Diana tugged Merlin's arm. "Gawain doesn't have a chance."

"Yes, he does, my child," Merlin murmured, staring at his naked son about to face a very fresh adversary. "And from what you've said, he needs this victory to be his."

That stopped Diana. Gawain's father was letting him face this terrible danger, for his own *good*? But she could tell from Merlin's clenched jaw that she wasn't going to move him. The first clang of sword on sword riveted her attention. Merlin put his arm around her, effectively anchoring her to the spot.

Mordred was on the attack. He swung the heavy sword with a fresh arm. Again and again it clanged against Gawain's. Gawain was able to defend, but he was backing across the floor in the face of Mordred's onslaught. Diana found herself clutching Merlin's jerkin as she watched Gawain barely parrying each blow. How could he survive this?

Then the unthinkable happened. Mordred's sword clanged against Gawain's, and Gawain's sword broke. The point clattered to the ground. Diana gasped. She felt Merlin tense. Mordred swung his sword for an overhand blow and it came down across Gawain's stump of a weapon. Gawain didn't have the strength to push Mordred off. He was slowly driven to his knees. This would be the end; it must!

Gawain reached down into himself for strength. He shoved Mordred away with his little stump of a sword. Mordred staggered back. But without a sword, the end was inevitable. No other sword was in reach. Gawain's back was almost against the fireplace. Wait—a sword was sticking out of the fireplace itself, out of a great rock that formed the side.

"Gawain!" she yelled. "There's a sword right behind you!"

Gawain turned even as Mordred surged in for the kill. With no hesitation at all, Gawain pulled the sword from the stone. It slid out like butter.

"By the gods," Merlin muttered beside her.

Mordred stopped in his tracks, giving Gawain time to stagger into position. Gawain seemed to take strength from the sword. He looked at it with mild curiosity. Diana's heart stuttered. He might just be holding Excalibur, the sword that could only be wielded by the one true ruler of England.

Mordred went red with rage. "You are *not* the rightful king!" he shouted. "I am! *I* am the rightful king!" He came in swinging once again. But this time, Excalibur seemed to know where Mordred's weapon would be and just . . . just be there first. The sword was doing Gawain's work for him, or they had become one, man and sword, and Gawain's will imbued the weapon.

Gawain went from defense to offense, now beating Mordred back. Mordred was talking, half to himself, half to Gawain: "You won't prevail. You should be dead already. You don't deserve the kingdom. You don't deserve Guinevere. She'll marry me. I am the rightful king."

And then his guard slipped. Excalibur found the opening and drove for his heart. It pierced the rich, embroidered wool over Mordred's chest. A darker stain spread on the purple cloth. Mordred's eyes went big, blinked twice. He fell to his knees.

Gawain pulled the wonderful sword from Mordred's body and stood holding it as Mordred toppled. Gawain stared at his dead adversary as though he couldn't believe it. Diana broke from Merlin's arms and ran forward. Yet as she approached, she hesitated. Gawain seemed lost in some other world. And why should he not be? He was probably relishing the strength the sword conferred on him, the prospect that he was the rightful king and his one true love, Guinevere, might well be his at last.

Gawain broke his stare and looked up at Diana. His eyes were filled with pain, but they softened as he recognized her. He stretched out his arm. She threw herself against him, blood and sweat and all, tears coursing down her cheeks. Even if he was lost to her . . . he was alive.

"Diana, are you all right?" he asked.

"Am *I* all right? You were almost killed, and . . . and God knows what else."

His eyes darkened at that. He looked away. "Yeah. I'm glad it didn't come to that. I'm okay." But she had to half-support him as he staggered over to his father.

"You did it, my son," Merlin said, a look of love on his face. "I'm very proud of you."

Gawain looked away. "You don't know all my failures. You sent me to protect Dilly . . . Diana, and we were separated. It took me twelve years to find her. I sent Mordred back in time where he caused all this suffering . . . and brought Diana back into terrible danger. . . ."

"Hey, buddy, you can't claim all the blame. We agreed on sending Mordred back together," Diana protested. "I came back here all on my own and had to trick you to do it. And how could you help that we were separated and those thugs attacked you and they put you in prison? I think you did a great job."

"I do, too, Son," Merlin said. He glanced to Excalibur. "Only the most worthy could have pulled the sword from the stone."

Diana's heart sank. That meant she'd be heading back to the twenty-first century alone. But she couldn't let Gawain see how that made her feel. She wouldn't spoil his moment of triumph with selfish thoughts. "He's the true king of England now, isn't he?"

"He can't stay here," Merlin said, his voice sure. "My ten-year-old son is upstairs with Guinevere and the baby. You can't stay, either, Diana."

"You could take the children somewhere else. Gawain could rule here," Diana said stubbornly. He'd be a great king. Maybe better than Arthur. Gawain deserved the chance.

"Yes. And he could join the knights together and face off against the Saxons. They might win. But I thought that was what you were trying to prevent." Merlin raised his brows.

Diana and Gawain looked at each other. "Once you start messing around with time it's . . . it's all so confusing," Diana said. "What is supposed to be, and what is not?"

"You have to go," Merlin said again firmly. "I have seen it in the waters of a rain barrel. Take Excalibur with you. You might well be a king in some other time, some other land. We have no way of knowing. I only know there is one true path, one future I see now."

Gawain's knees started to buckle and Diana dragged him to a bench. The frozen knights still sat with glasses raised or mouths open in a cheer.

"I'm not sure Gawain is strong enough," Diana said. "Time travel is hard on you." She shot Merlin a glance. If he let Gawain die, after all his travails . . .

"What am I thinking?" Merlin muttered. "Come, Son. We must care for your wounds. Can you make it to one of the outbuildings?"

"Of course," Gawain growled. But his eyes were swimming. Merlin got him up off the bench and dragged one of Gawain's arms over his shoulder. Diana ducked in under his other one. Together they pulled him out the main door of the hall into the night. Behind her, Diana heard the room break into confused sound as the knights and servants came to life again. Outside, people had been frozen, too. They shook themselves and looked around, then started instinctively for the shouting in the hall. One of the women was carrying a baby.

"You there!" Merlin called.

The woman's eyes opened wide in fear.

"Don't be afraid. Come here. Ranwith, is it not?"

She nodded, obviously wondering how the great Merlin knew her name, and crept near.

"There is a newborn girl child with the queen upstairs

who needs what you can give her. Her mother is dead this night." Lamorak came stumbling down the stairs from the queen's chamber. "This knight will escort you, if you will agree to help?" He made this last a question.

The woman bobbed a curtsey. "I've milk enough, my lord. I can suckle another."

"Thank you," Diana and Merlin said in unison. Lamorak bowed to the baby Diana's new wet nurse and turned to escort her back the way he had come.

Diana and Merlin took Gawain to a building set at the edge of the palisades. Inside, Merlin waved a hand and the lamps lit. The place was a comfortable jumble of scrolls and little jars and pots. It had a bed in one corner with a trundle half-out beneath it. With a start Diana realized that these were Merlin's rooms. His son probably occupied the trundle bed.

Gawain seemed to swoon. "Young Gawain won't come here, will he?" Diana whispered.

"No. We won't be long." That was good news. Merlin seemed confident he could heal Gawain. Diana surveyed Gawain's injuries as they laid him down. To her the wounds were horrifying.

"He's lost so much blood," she said in a small voice.

Merlin straightened. "That's why we must start with a plain old needle and some dried catgut," he said briskly, and began moving about the cabin.

"What can I do?"

Merlin cast a glance at her. He gave a quick smile. "I might have known you'd rally. Go out and get me some water from the barrel to the left of the door. You can wash his wounds while I make preparations."

It took her a long time and it was grisly work. But a woman could do what a woman must when someone she loved was in need. Diana used a clean cloth Merlin gave her to tie a tourniquet around Gawain's thigh and cleaned that wound first. Merlin poured and mixed and set various bowls over tiny candle flames. His whole workbench looked like some kind of primitive scientific laboratory. Then, when his pots were bubbling, he sewed up the wounds she'd finished cleaning with quick, precise movements. He would have been talented at needlepoint or tapestries. At least he'd stopped Gawain's bleeding. She loosed the tourniquet.

When Merlin had finished stitching, he gathered up his pots and began smoothing Gawain's wounds with the various salves.

"Uh, no magic or anything?" she asked as Merlin was wiping his hands and standing up.

"Oh, there's plenty of magic here." He gave her one of his quick glances that seemed to take in everything. "You mean you'd like more of the sparkles—that kind of thing?" He chuckled at her embarrassed shrug. "You need sparkles for illumination. Other than that, effects like that are just showing off. Real magic is just . . . part of you." He looked over at his workbench. "And understanding that you are part of the world and can channel the power that exists all around you. It's both more marvelous and more mundane than people expect." He turned to Gawain and pulled a blanket up over his naked body. The stitches that wound over his flesh made him look so . . . mortal. "But I expect you know that. How do you find lost things like my boy?"

"I try to just be . . . peaceful in my mind," Diana said. "And I sort of think like whatever is lost, and then ask it where it is. That's not magic."

"Of course it is." Merlin chuckled. "It's just like my magic and probably just like his." He nodded at his son.

"I don't feel very magic," Diana said somewhat forlornly.

Her life stretched ahead. Gawain couldn't stay here. His father said so. But that didn't mean Gawain wouldn't mourn Guinevere all his days. Diana looked up to find Merlin's magical swirling eyes fixed on her.

"Has he offered for you, child?"

She half-snorted. It was very unladylike. "A man who looks like Gawain doesn't offer for an ordinary woman like me. He can have his pick." The stunning Guinevere, for instance. "I just hope he'll let me be his friend." Merlin looked puzzled. Maybe. Wizards were hard to read. "I've always been an outsider. I'm not pretty. I write stories for a living about *other* people finding love. A parfait knight, even without the shining-armor part, isn't meant for me."

Merlin looked at her thoughtfully. "You are what, child, twenty-five?" She nodded. "I would have thought you older." He put away his pots and tiny bottles of irregular colored glass. "I'd better check on the children and see that your mother is prepared suitably for burial. He needs to 'cook' awhile."

"May I go with you? I'd like to pay my last respects to my mother."

Merlin's eyes turned a sad, swirling gray. "She is not a sight for you now. Remember her as she was."

Diana's eyes filled, but she nodded. Her mother was gone. But Diana had been given the gift of meeting her, and even of saying good-bye last night. It was more than she ever expected.

"I could use some help with Gawain," Merlin said, as though apologizing.

"Anything," she said promptly.

"I would be grateful if you would keep him company. Maybe sing to him?"

"Sing to him?"

"The presence of those who care for you is very important magic in the healing process. Since I must leave, it would be good for him to know you're here."

"Oh, okay." She could do that.

"I'll be back." Merlin glanced to Gawain. "I'd better retrieve his clothes, too. He's bigger than I am, broader across the shoulders." With that Merlin ducked out of the little hut.

Diana glanced around self-consciously. *Sing to him. Right.* Her eyes were drawn to a lute that hung on the wall. She gave a little gasp. Gawain had said he taught her how to play the lute when she broke her leg. Was . . . was *this* the lute she'd used when she was twelve or thirteen? She took the lute from its hook. It was well worn but finely made. She sat on the end of the bed and gave it a tentative strum, fiddled with the pegs a little, and strummed again. Pretty close. She started with "Greensleeves," singing softly. That was medieval music, but she didn't know any Dark Age songs. The notes tumbled from the lute in mellow waves, much nicer than a mandolin's twang. Before the last chord was ended, she started another song. . . .

A song she didn't know, in chord progressions that were very different from anything she'd ever played. She blinked and tried to get her breath. After a moment, she recognized it. It was a tune Gawain had been humming in the apartment after they'd made love, but now she knew the chords to the song intimately, as if she'd played it a thousand times.

Memories cascaded over her as she played song after song from those lost days. A cave, a big one. Merlin, seen from afar, as he wove his spells and looked into a limpid underground pool. The crazy crush she'd always had on Gawain. Doing anything to get his attention, including stealing his horse. Going fishing with Gawain. How happy that made her. Gawain carrying her all the way back to the cave after she broke her leg. The pain. Merlin away at the Saxon court. Gawain splinted her leg, made vervain decoctions, showed her the chords to take her mind off the pain. Merlin coming back, helping her to heal as he'd helped Gawain today . . .

She blinked her eyes open. Gawain was staring at her. How long had she been in that trance of memory? His eyes were filled with heat. She could feel the energy, the *life,* pouring off him. He pushed himself up. The blanket fell to his waist. The terrible wounds on his body so recent had . . . disappeared. He still had the scars and the tattoos she'd come to known, but it was as though he had not been wounded recently.

"You remember." There was apparently no doubt in his mind. Maybe it was the songs she'd been singing. "I'm glad. It's good to know where you came from."

She nodded. It was as though she'd been half and now she was whole. She knew her mother. She remembered growing up. Even knowing Mordred was her father was part of the puzzle. She *knew* who she was. That made her feel alive, too. The pull toward Gawain was suddenly virulent, almost like she was sick. He sure wasn't. He was pulsing with vitality. More than that. Even under the blanket she could see his erection. "That salve sure . . . works."

He glanced down. "Sorry about that. Part of the cure, I think. Too bad he was away when you broke your leg that time. He could have saved you a lot of pain. He . . . he was pretty busy back then, trying to make a difference. He . . . he sometimes couldn't make room for us." Gawain cleared his throat. "Not that I needed him. My training took up a lot of time."

But Gawain still made time to see to her. She really *had* known him forever. No wonder she could fall so deeply in love with him in such short order. And he had known her. As a pesky and troublesome girl. She sighed. Yet another reason he would never be madly in love with her.

Merlin pushed through the door with an armload of clothes at that moment. "Dress, Son. We'd better get down to that machine before you change something else."

He meant before anything else could go wrong. Diana stepped outside. Gawain would want a private leave-taking with his father.

Chapter Twenty-two

Gawain dressed briskly, wondering what he could say to his father. He finally settled on, "Thanks for saving the day."

"Diana found young Gawain in the dungeon and fought a guard to get him free. You staved off Mordred and his minions, regardless of the cost, to allow me time to perform a cesarean on her mother. I just evened the odds. I didn't save you. We all did our bit."

Gawain wished his smile wasn't so rueful. "Some bits were bigger than others." He couldn't change that he was not the magician his father was. Gawain felt his smile turn soft as he thought of Diana. "She sure is something, isn't she?"

"Yes," his father said. "She is a remarkable woman." He pressed his lips together. Gawain pulled the shirt his father had brought over his head. "Will . . . will you be glad to get back to the time from which you have come?" his father asked almost cautiously.

"Absolutely. Don't get me wrong. This time is where I grew up. It always will be. But it's no place for Diana. She's used to the comforts and ways of the future now." He reached for the breeches. "And I can protect her better there."

"She hopes you will let her be your friend when you return."

Gawain looked up. He could never read his father's expressions. Merlin sometimes seemed like a different species altogether. Now, if Gawain had to guess, his father almost looked . . . anxious. That was ridiculous. Merlin, the greatest practitioner of magic the world had ever known, couldn't be anxious. "I'll protect her until the day I die," Gawain said simply. "Since friendship is what she wants, I'll be her friend."

"Ah," his father said as Gawain pulled on his boots. He looked up to find his father biting his lip.

"What?" Since when had he gotten courage enough to question his father?

"She . . . she thinks she isn't pretty enough for you."

Gawain drew his brows together. That was nonsense. "When did she say that?"

His father looked really anxious now. "I shouldn't have said anything. Forget it."

Gawain didn't want his father to know how raw his heart was, or how much he wanted Diana. What would he do if she wanted "recreational sex" with her friend again? Could his heart bear it? Could he refuse her? He dragged his mind away from those thoughts. But what he landed on was no better. "Do you see your own future?" He'd never had the courage to ask.

"Yes." The response from his father was flat, and all the more emotional for that.

"Your own death?"

Merlin nodded. And Gawain had to know. When he and Dilly had been cast forward in time by his father's magic, the last image, burned on Gawain's brain, was of Merlin gasping for breath, weak because he'd sacrificed all his power to thrust them forward fifteen hundred years.

Merlin must have seen it in his son's eyes: the doubt, the guilt. He smiled softly. "It was worth it. Like Diana's mother, I continue through you."

Not good enough! Gawain's mourning turned to anger, anger that had only one target: himself. He was only a fraction of his father, a poor copy with the text blurred and faint, like a document from the twenty-first century that had been Xeroxed once too often. Gawain closed his face down. It was the last failure, that in saving him and Dilly his father had died.

Gawain stood at the edge of the river ford with Diana and his father. They had not run into the children who were themselves. Gareth and Agravain had watched them go but dared not cross Merlin to intervene. It had been easy. Not that the journey had been fun. Merlin seemed to be brooding. Gawain trudged the muddy road carrying a metaphorical load, if not a real one. What was he supposed to do when he got back to the twenty-first century? His father had only said he'd know what it was. But he didn't.

"This is as far as I go," his father said. "The rest of the journey is up to you two." He smiled fondly at Diana, kissing her cheek, then clasped Gawain in the only real embrace he could ever remember receiving from his father. "Thank you so much, both of you."

Gawain saw his amazement echoed on Diana's face. "You're thanking *us*? It's we who are in your debt." Gawain and Diana would take Merlin's life before the tale was through.

Merlin shook his head. "No. I have been granted the rare privilege of seeing my mistakes in time to change them." He took Diana's hand and held it to his lips. "I will name the baby Diana and tell her, tell *you* how beautiful you are and how good and true, every day, so you will never doubt it." Gawain saw Diana's eyes fill. His father turned to him. "And you . . . you I must show that being a good man does not mean having magic or being perfect. We all make mistakes. We have all failed. But we can still be valued and valuable." He looked down, as if gathering his courage. "I never told you. I have other children."

"What?" Gawain had . . . half brothers or sisters?

"When I was young," Merlin continued, gazing off across the river, "I worshiped the magic. I would mate with those who had some shred of power themselves, thinking to create progeny with more magic even than I had. I sought out sorceresses, priestesses of the old gods. But I was not interested in the children themselves, or their mothers. I kept track of them only to see whether they had my powers. None did, at least to any degree that I could see. So I abandoned them. They never knew me as their father. I was not so different from Mordred, to my shame."

Gawain had always thought his father distant but not so . . . heartless. He . . . he didn't know what to say. He would have liked to know those children.

"Most were hundreds of years ago." Merlin looked down at his hands. Gawain saw Diana's eyes widen. He'd never known his father was so old, either. "I took you in only because your mother died. Her name was Nimue, the last of my liaisons. At first I didn't care about you, only about the magic that might be yours. But you won me over. You became more important to me than whatever magic you might have, more important than Camelot, or even Arthur. And yet I must never have made time to tell you how much I valued you just as you were, without even a shred of magic apparent to me. I never helped you cope with having a wizard as a father. You have given me a chance to change that . . . both of you. And for that I'm grateful."

Gawain felt his eyes fill in a very unmanly way.

"Can you forgive me, boy?" His father's voice was almost a whisper.

Gawain wanted to say there was nothing to forgive, but that wasn't true. He wanted to tell his father that he felt as though he had been set free by those words. He wanted to grieve for the death he would cause. But he had no words for any of that, so he just took his father in his arms and held him fiercely to his chest.

It was his father who finally held Gawain away and turned to Diana. "I am afraid to interfere in the flow of time and destiny," Merlin said, glancing back and forth between the two of them. "We have learned how dangerous that is. You both must do what you must do on your own to achieve what I have seen in my rain barrel of the future. But perhaps I can tell you this. Magic does call to magic. And somewhere in the future, the bits of magic left in the world will gather together like rivulets to make a mighty river that will change everything. You are important. You are *both* important, not just you, Diana. You are both strong. And you already know what to do. Now go. More delay jeopardizes all."

He turned and walked away. A sparkling halo grew about his form. He was consumed by it. He had disappeared before he had taken five steps.

Gawain turned to Diana. "Does he mean the machine will go back without us?"

"My God." Diana looked horrified.

He swept her up in his arms and headed into the river.

When they got to where they had left the machine, Diana knew Merlin had been right. Even in the dim light of the crescent moon, high above the trees, she could see the machine was fading. She raced to it, knelt, and turned it on, flipping switches frantically. It solidified under her hands. It wasn't too late. "Get over here," she called to Gawain. "Take me by the waist." If she was separated from Gawain by fifteen hundred years and couldn't get back to him, she might just commit suicide.

The machine began to fade again. His arms snaked around her. *Thank God.* "Think of March in San Francisco," she said. "I'll pull the lever." She reached for it, grabbing the great diamond. But before she could pull, the machine faded out. She felt them being sucked along with it. The feeling of being torn through space and time ripped through her body before she lost consciousness.

Diana woke to a familiar smell of concrete and metal and . . . dirt. She was on the earthen floor of the basement under the Rotunda of the Palace of Fine Arts. And she could not breathe a sigh of relief because she was under a heavy weight.

The heavy weight gave a groan.

Gawain pushed himself off her. "Are you okay?"

He was speaking modern English. She began to laugh with relief until she could hardly control herself and then the tears started pouring down her cheeks and she couldn't properly tell whether she was laughing or crying.

He held her to his chest and made soothing sounds: "You're okay. You're okay."

When she had gotten her breath she looked up and he smoothed her hair back and ran his thumbs over her cheeks in the dark to wipe away her tears. "Shall we go see what's out there?"

The world. Had the world changed back? Or had it turned into some dreadful third option based on some unknown action they'd taken? She nodded. "Let's go."

They worked their way out to the door marked: *Danger.* Gawain's scabbard clanked against the metal girders. The sword in that scabbard was Excalibur. What did that mean? As they passed the wave exhibits and the gift store, she heard Clancy whistling from somewhere in the back, probably by the optical exhibits. He was whistling "When Irish Eyes Are Smiling." She looked up to Gawain. He nodded and moved silently toward the glass entry doors, taking her hand. Their car was still at the very farthest end of the parking lot. They ran together to the Range Rover.

"Where to?" Gawain slung his scabbard into the back and slid into the driver's seat beside her.

"Chinatown," she said.

Gawain parked the car illegally in a red zone on Post, and they ran up the street toward the Dragon Gate. People were everywhere even this late at night and the crowd was a cultural mélange. There was an Asian family. Diana began to grin.

The Dragon Gate loomed above them. The green ceramic tile of the little roof, the gold of the shiny dragons rampant facing each other, the two stone Chinese-style lions—it had all never seemed more beautiful. On each side the stores selling Asian antiques and carved ivory, both called Michael's, were back where they should be. And the lit red lanterns swung gaily across the crowded one-way street. Not an onion tower in sight.

Diana giggled and Gawain grinned for all he was worth. He gathered her into his arms.

"Let's go home," he said.

All the way down to the Mission District they pointed out new evidence that things were back to the way they had been. The public buildings at the Civic Center stood stoically in their original varied styles of architecture. The Hispanic character of the Mission District was familiar rather than ominous. A crowd celebrating something gathered outside the Indian restaurant.

They tooled over to Dolores Heights and around to the Oakwood Apartments. Diana made a beeline for the shower and felt better when she was clean. She skimmed the condensation from the mirror. Not a bad reflection. She had her mother's heart-shaped face and eyes. What she needed was a new haircut—something short and sassy. She changed her fifth-century linen shift for her chenille bathrobe. When she opened the closet to put the shift in the little hamper there, she noticed that the clothes hanging there were really *vin ordinaire*. They didn't really fit with her self-image. She'd have to save for a shopping spree. Shoes. What she really needed was a great pair of "fuck me" shoes.

Gawain had opened a bottle of white wine and poured her a glass. He handed it to her and disappeared to take a shower. Excalibur's scabbard was propped on the corner of the couch. The sword seemed to exude vitality. When Gawain came out of the bathroom he was barefoot, wearing only jeans, and his hair was wet. Lord. He outdid the best of the firefighters on calendars. Even March 2008. And she once had thought no one could outdo that guy. They sat on the couch and clinked glasses.

"I think we pretty much did it," Gawain said.

"We might have changed some things. I guess we'll find out. But it doesn't look like it was anything earth-shattering." She sipped her wine.

There was just one thing left to resolve.

She loved this man, damn it. And she might not be Guinevere, but Guinevere was fifteen hundred years dead. She wasn't chopped liver, either, and she'd seen the heat with which Gawain looked at her. Had he made love to her just because he was desperate for a lay? Now that she remembered everything, she couldn't imagine him just taking casual advantage of her. He *knew* her. She was his friend, someone he'd cared for, even if it was in a platonic way, as though he were her older brother. But he wasn't her brother. And she'd never been so glad of anything in her life. No. He'd *wanted* to make love to her.

So why couldn't he love her? They shared everything. Didn't they both have mothers they'd never known? Weren't they both afflicted or blessed or something with a little magic? They had things in common few other people had. They'd traveled through time, for instance. Twice or, in her case, three times. Maybe she couldn't make him forget Guinevere. But she was never going to know if she didn't try. If it didn't work, she'd lose him even as a friend. Big risk. Big stakes. But strangely enough, she realized she was a risk taker and she wanted what she wanted. First step was to see if he was mourning Guinevere.

Gawain glanced down to his glass. He didn't want to show Diana what he knew were hungry eyes. If she really thought of him only as a friend, why were her eyes heating up like that? Oh yeah. Recreational sex. Was that all she wanted—a release after the excitement of their adventures?

Nope. He was not doing recreational sex with Diana. He wanted more. He might not be perfect, but who was? Certainly not his father. You made your mistakes because that was inevitable, and you corrected them as best you could and you learned from them and went on. He wasn't saying sex with Diana had been a mistake. He hadn't held to his pure ideals, true, but if he wanted to make her his wife and share his life with her forever (which he absolutely did), if she needed at the time to be shown that she was special and loved, if it had been a spiritual bonding for him, then it was a step on the way to their true relationship. He wanted her to feel that same spiritual bonding. He might not be perfect, but . . . but she wasn't immune to him entirely. He'd felt that when they'd been making love. And holding her in his arms, bloody and sweaty as he was, after he'd killed Mordred, had made the ordeal almost worthwhile. If he'd gone through an ordeal to win her love, he couldn't stop now.

"Are you sorry you couldn't bring Guinevere forward with you?" she asked, her eyes serious. That was a shocker.

He snorted. "She was old enough to be my mother."

Diana looked skeptical. "Not the last time around. Probably not even ten years older."

"She was the right woman for Arthur, not for me."

"You had a crush on her when you were ten."

"And who was your first crush? Probably some Beastie Boy or something."

"When I was twelve I had a crush on you."

Just a crush. That hurt. "Well, we both grew out of it." He took too big a swig of wine. Maybe this wasn't going to work out after all.

"I was sure glad you weren't my brother back then." Her eyes were doing that molten-lava thing. "Still am."

Was that a sign? By god he was going to take it as one. He wanted to sweep her up in his arms and take her into the bedroom and pull off that robe and bury himself in her. He wanted to claim her as his own and dare her to deny they belonged together. They had always belonged together. But he didn't want her to mistake what he wanted for recreational sex.

He slid off the couch and went down on one knee. He sucked in a breath. It was as if his lungs were independent of him, like sucking in air when you surged up after swimming underwater. "Will you marry me?"

She looked dumbfounded. That was bad. "You . . . you want to *marry* me?"

"I wanted to marry you before you said, 'Excuse me,' in the liquor store."

She smiled at him, a sly and knowing smile. "It took

me a few days longer. But only because I thought you were stalking me and I didn't remember knowing you at all." She ran a hand around his neck and bent to kiss him softly. She was the one who deepened the kiss. Surprising. Diana was getting bolder. He responded in kind, feeling his loins tighten further in response to her. She could rouse a dead man.

Suddenly she pulled back, stricken. "What if this is just that 'magic to magic' thing your father was talking about? What if it's just kind of a sexual need, not love?"

She had a point. Gawain looked inside himself.

And he was sure. "My father said I'd know what to do when the time came. And I do. I love you, Diana. The 'for all time' kind of love." To his horror, big tears rolled down her cheeks.

"You don't believe me?" How would he prove himself to her?

"I do," she said simply. "Your eyes are blue. That's the color they go when you're serious about what you're saying." He felt his eyes change. "Now they're green. And *that* means . . ."

His eyes told that much about him? And she had bothered to notice? But she hadn't said she loved him in return. He closed his eyes and took two breaths. If she wanted him as a friend, he'd do it, though it cost his soul.

"What?" Concern drenched her voice.

"Why are you crying?"

"Because I love you and part of me couldn't quite believe you could love me. I'm glad that part was wrong. That's worth some tears."

He blinked at her. She'd never looked so lovely. She was even looking . . . a little bit sure of herself. Diana? Who never thought she was pretty, according to his father? " Diana," he said slowly, "do you feel different since we got back?"

She looked uncertain. "Maybe." Her eyes darted around the room. "Yeah. I feel . . . I feel like I know who I am. You?"

"Yeah. I . . . I guess I don't feel like quite such a . . . failure."

"My God," she whispered. "What we changed by going back was . . . *us*. Remember your father saying that he was going to tell us he valued us every day? Well, he did. And we're . . . we're not as . . . damaged as we were."

"You remember him telling us those things every day?" He did. But he also remembered going back and hearing his father promise him to do it as though it were the future.

"Yeah. I do. And I remember how lost I felt before, how invisible. . . . But . . ."

"But it's getting harder to remember how it felt to be who we were before." He could feel that awful, bleak guilt he'd once carried like a weight on his soul fading even now.

They looked at each other, tense.

"So, did those other people even exist?" he asked slowly. "I mean if we aren't now who we were before, would you have gone back and tried to find Camelot and started this whole thing? Would my father have flung us forward in time, if we hadn't gone back and told him he had to do it?"

They stared at each other while they thought about that. "Weird, huh?" Diana finally said. "It's no use trying to explain it. It's one of those time travel things."

Gawain felt himself relax. You couldn't know. So all you could do was live life the best you could. And he felt stronger, happier, more whole than he ever thought he could. Except for one thing. He cleared his throat. "So . . . what's your answer?" He felt stronger now. Strong enough to tell her he wouldn't be just a friend. "And I won't take a marriage of convenience. I don't want you to marry me because you want recreational sex. I want a sacred bond, Diana, and I won't settle for anything else."

She put her arms around his neck and slithered onto his knee. Diana? "Well, can't we have both? I mean sacred-bond love and spectacular sex? I won't settle for anything else."

"You're saying you love me." He knew he was being stubborn, but he wanted to hear it.

"Yeah. I love you. I thought it was hopeless once, but now it seems almost inevitable."

"Good," he said. He drew her up and picked her up in his arms. "Then it's settled. Love and great sex it is." He bent to kiss her, his attention beginning to narrow to one thing. Diana.

"The book!" she said suddenly, pulling away to look around. He blinked, a little dazed. Sure enough, the book by Leonardo da Vinci was still there on the end table.

"We should destroy it, so no one can go back and change time like we almost did." He nuzzled her neck. Did she have to be thinking about the book now?

"No," she said thoughtfully. "The red-haired woman said I would use it to make myself happy. Your father told me it started the whole thing. In a way, it's responsible for me going back, and therefore your father knowing that we should be sent forward. . . . It had a purpose, Gawain. To save the magic. And I *am* happy, so that worked out, too. Maybe I'll find someone else who needs it someday. Maybe its work isn't done yet. I'll keep it just in case."

"*We'll* keep it," he growled. "Because I'm not letting you go, ever."

"And we're going to keep Excalibur, too. I have a feeling it's not done with you yet."

"Let it do its worst." He swept her into the bedroom and laid her carefully on the big bed. She untied the belt of her robe and let it fall open. He was having a hard time breathing. His jeans were positively painful. He knew an answer to that. He unbuttoned them and just pushed them down. His erection sprang free. He let Diana look her fill. She wasn't shy about it.

She smiled. "Well?" Challenging him. He liked the change.

He lay down beside her and draped one knee over her thigh. He kissed her thoroughly even as he ran his hands over her body until he had her moaning and her hips moving involuntarily to make the most of his caresses. He moved from her mouth to her breast and watched her arch her back to give him better access to her nipples. He would make her scream tonight with pleasure. Several times.

She reached for him. Her hand might be small, but it was just the right size for that. He wanted to hold out, to make this special for her, but she was making that awfully difficult.

"I want you in me," she breathed into his hair.

"Your wish is my command, my lady." She guided him into her. He thrust home. He wanted to shout that she was his and he would protect her until the end of days. He moved in and out. She writhed beneath him. He had never felt so complete.

Diana stirred. The room was dark. Gawain was awake. She could feel him looking at her. She felt sleepy and sated and a little sore and entirely . . . wonderful. He was a generous lover. She'd known that about him before they went back in time. The first time tonight had been fierce and needy. The second had been slow and almost . . . worshipful, a mutual thanksgiving that they were who they were and they had found each other. No less explosive at the finale, of course.

She reached out and smoothed a hand over his shoulder.

She could feel the scar there, slick and tight. A wound he got in prison, when Merlin couldn't heal him. He reached and took her hand and raised it to his lips.

"What will we do with our power?" Life ahead with Gawain rolled out like a red carpet before her.

"Make magical babies," he whispered. She could feel his smile against her palm. "You heard my father. Magic calls to magic, and our rivulets need to flow together. Our children will find others like them, and my father's magic will live and change the world."

Babies. Gawain's babies. That sounded . . . good. It was not something some part of her had ever thought she'd have. She admitted for the first time that she'd always wanted them. "Well, besides that. We have to do something else." *Hmmm.* "We could be jewel thieves."

"Steal from the rich and give to the poor? Maybe. Been done, though."

"We could find stolen things for insurance companies. Bet they'd pay well for that."

"Aren't *you* entrepreneurial? A little bureaucratic for me, I'm afraid." He paused. "We'd be really good on search and rescue in disasters. You find trapped people, and I'll get into wherever they are and save them."

"That's a thought. Or maybe I find lost children and you vanquish the bad guys who have them? Every milk carton holds a new job."

"You'll still write books of course," he said firmly. "That's in your soul."

It was. And she was so glad he knew her that well. "Maybe I'll finish my work in progress. I'm going to make the hero a *lot* more difficult." A new thought occurred. "Maybe the fact that you pulled Excalibur from the stone means you should be a politician."

"Ugh. I hate all that raising money and lying to get elected."

"Well, there are other kinds of leaders," she said, snuggling into him.

"We'll find something," he said. His voice was confident in the darkness. "Might take a little trial and error."

How good it was to hear him say that. He was more courageous, more honorable, more openhearted than any other man she'd ever known. She remembered how he was before, even if he was forgetting. He would remember how she was before, too. They would be the keeper of each other's history, so who they'd been would not be lost in the mists of time, so they could rejoice in who they had become.

"That's what life's like. Trial and error," she whispered, tracing his lips with a finger. "I think that's what relationships are like."

He kissed her. "I'm going to like figuring out how to make a life together. Might take me fifty years or so."

"I'll like trying to figure out a real-life, difficult man."

"If at first we don't succeed," he murmured, his lips finding hers. "Try, try again."

And they did.

Don't miss these other novels in the Da Vinci Time
Travel series from *New York Times* bestselling author

SUSAN SQUIRES

TIME FOR ETERNITY
ISBN: 978-0-312-94354-7

A TWIST IN TIME
ISBN: 978-0-312-94354-7

Available from St. Martin's Paperbacks